Praise for Sonny's Vendetta

"Having known Mike since childhood and his understanding of the city, its people and the passions they possess, I can't wait to see this story unfold."
— *John Kincade, 97.5 The Fanatic Sports Talk Show Host*

"Mike is witty, fast thinking and eloquent with his words. All characteristics that our Catholic high school teachers found sinful."
— *Shawn Lynch, attorney and Philadelphia native*

"As someone who has traveled widely and is an avid reader, nothing compares to the wit, grit, and humor of my hometown, Philly. Mike captures it all!"
— *Alicia McDonald, teacher and Philadelphia native*

"Growing up in Philly, it helps to have to a great sense of humor and wild imagination. Think about it ... Next to Ben Franklin, our most admired son is a fictional club fighter from the poor part of town. Michael Attiani has the wit and wisdom to tell a good story. His hysterical, thought-provoking social media posts have always left me wanting more. With *Sonny's Vendetta*, my prayers have been answered."
— *Tom Stiglich, syndicated cartoonist and Philadelphia native*

"Mike's irreverent and self-deprecating sense of humor has whipped me into a frenzy for years. As a writer myself, I will always choose to read whatever he has to say because I know it will grab me and pull me right in. He is the master of the set-up....so if 'writing is the food of life, write on, maestro!' Speaking of food (well, yes, of course) ... he leaves me hungry for more!"
— *Rhoda Rogers, Producer, Writer, Poet*

"Great slice of South Philly life with captivating characters, complicated relationships, and just the right amounts of intrigue and revenge to make everything boil over. Don't be surprised if this story leaves South Philly accents chirping away in your head and your body craving biscotti or meatballs on a nice sesame bun."
— *Margaret McConnell, publishing professional and avid reader*

"Having ~~suffered through~~ enjoyed Mike's friendship for years, I can vouch for his ability to be funny. And if the subject at hand is food, he's probably unstoppable."
—*Todd Clark, syndicated cartoonist and author*

"Mike is hysterical, writes incredibly well, and God knows he can eat …so all evidence indicates this is a binge read!"
— *Jeff Hall, Master Gardener, attorney and entrepreneur*

"Are you from Philly? Are you Italian? Do you like 'spag and balls'? If so, and even if not, you'll love this character-driven, laugh-out-loud romp about a multi-generation Italian family and their cursed restaurant, Sonny's. It's like having Rocky Balboa and the Corleones over for dinner."
— *David Aretha, award-winning (Italian) author*

"Mike Attiani's debut novel has captured the flavor and texture of South Philadelphia. When I read his book, I'm transported to my nonna's plastic-covered couch, where I'm shoveling Christmas manicotti and sausage into my mouth. Attiani folds in bittersweet nostalgia and pungent wit. All in all, *Sonny's Vendetta* tastes best when followed by cannoli, torroni and coffee. Great stuff."
—*Tim Ireland, former Philadelphia newspaper reporter and Philadelphia native*

Sonny's VENDETTA

Sonny's VENDETTA

SUSPENSE AND SPAGHETTI IN SOUTH PHILLY

MICHAEL ATTIANI

Sonny's Vendetta is a work of fiction. Other than the actual historical events, people, and places referred to, all names, characters, and incidents are from the author's imagination. Any resemblances to persons, living or dead, are coincidental, and no reference to any real person is intended.

For more information, visit www.sonnysvendetta.com

Edited by David Aretha
Book design by Christy Collins, Constellation Book Design

ISBN (paperback): 978-1-7372794-0-2
ISBN (ebook): 978-1-7372794-1-9

Printed in the United States of America

Dedicated to my beloved Pop, Sonny—the sweetest, most wonderful man to ever grace this planet, and whose childlike optimism, joy and kindness set the bar too high for the rest of us. Of course, in real life, the man couldn't cook toast.

What a Day!

This past week was horrible.

On a scale from zero on the left to a guy with a fresh vasectomy getting punched in the nuts on the right, my week is a little further to the right from there. And that was just this week.

Today was even worse!

Today was *so* cartoonishly bad, it included a physical beating (mine), a kidnapping (not mine), and a murder (also not mine, but still someone I really liked), and it was all the product of a mistaken vendetta against my father's side of the family.

Finally, by the end of today, I'd had enough of fate's shenanigans, so a couple hours ago I threw my arms up in surrender, got in my car and drove off in the middle of the night, heading west for absolutely no other reason than my car was already pointed that way. I arrived outside of Pittsburgh, five hours and three hundred miles later, parked in front of a generic hotel.

My name is John Valmonti. I'm a second-generation Italian from South Philly, my city's version of "Little Italy."

Imagine a guy from a mobster movie, but not one of the powerful, flashy main character types. Look behind them, and you'll see guys like me. I'm one of those prototypical "extras" wandering around in the background of some neighborhood scene, like homogenized filler.

My entire life has been like that—a kid playing in the water blasting out of an open fire hydrant; a teenager tryin' to pick up innocent, skinny Catholic school girls; a regular guy getting drunk with his buddies; or today, a fifty-year-old man playing the role of "paesan."

Paesan, pronounced PIE-ZAHN, is an Americanized version of the Italian *paesano*, which translates to *peasant* which—believe it or not—is a term of fraternal endearment between Italian people. A paesan is an "everyman" and being one doesn't mean you're poor, even though most of us are. It means you're a small part of something larger, and that's what being from South Philly is all about. Alone we're of little consequence, but together, we are strong.

That word defines me: *paesan*, a guy from the neighborhood, a face in the crowd.

I should mention, even though this particular paesan is middle-aged, I wouldn't play the role of one of those fat old bald guys sittin' in front of a meat store peeling a pepperoni with a pocketknife. I also wouldn't be some round-shouldered "mook" walking along with a wife and five kids in tow. I'd be one of the unencumbered characters, with his head up and shoulders back, strolling briskly down the street, alone or with friends, like an "extra" with a purpose.

That's me, always with a purpose. I walk fast everywhere I go. My diminutive Indian friend Raj (sounds like *garage* without the first "ga"), has to run to keep up. In this regard, I take after my mother. My father is about my height, but he and his size 14 feet saunter like he has all day to get wherever he's going. Not my mother. She could've been an Olympic fast-walker, except she'd have competed in heels, holding her purse in one hand, and dragging me by the hair with the other—click click click. I *still* hear the tacks on her heels in my nightmares.

I'm a little taller than my dad, an inch or two over six feet, in decent shape for a guy my age, and have a full head of dark hair. My facial hair grows in gray, which is why I keep it shaved. I'm not vain or anything. I'm just not ready to be old.

Unlike the mugs in those Mafia flicks, I don't go out in public in wife-beater T-shirts (the kind with the deep-cut neck and no sleeves) either, and I don't wear patent-leather shoes with the toes narrowing to a pencil-sharp point. I wear collared shirts and jeans and sneakers, and underwear, like normal people do.

If you saw me, you'd think I look like any other tallish, run-of-the-mill American with a light tan, except I also have a full, lush head of dark hair. Did I already mention my hair? It's very lush, not a wispy comb-over like the balding blond country-club set. The biggest difference between me and them, though, is I have a South Philly swagger, making me irresistible to women everywhere … or so I'd like to believe.

That swagger's a common trait for guys from this part of town. It's not arrogance, although it probably comes across like that. I think it comes from our heritage.

Italian guys will waste no time before telling you about the Roman Empire, and how our hearts beat with the blood of that dynasty. Never mind the empire collapsed in dramatic fashion fifteen hundred or so years ago, and few of us have ever been east of New Jersey, let alone nestled somewhere in the "old country." Regardless, however tenuously we're connected to greatness, that legacy provides us with a sense of pride, misguided as it may be, and we take it with us wherever we go, probably because we don't have a whole lot else goin' for us, except our hair.

This past year, I ventured more than 50 miles from Philly for the first time in my life, and people everywhere asked me where I'm from, probably because of my distinctive accent (even though I'm a college graduate, I sound more like Philadelphia's favorite punch-drunk Italian boxer than an Ivy Leaguer), and I'd tell them "Philly." They'd always lean back in deference and say "oh." It's the same sort of reaction I'd get if I said "I'm a cancer survivor," or "I used to be an alcoholic," or "No, really. I *like* liver and lima beans," all of which would be a lie, by the way, especially the part about lima beans and liver. They're both disgusting.

Even if we can't really claim much of a connection to the former greatness of Rome, those of us from this neighborhood earned our swagger. There's a certain toughness one develops growing up in this part of town. Blue-collar sections of big East Coast cities are gritty, not because of street violence, but because the residents don't have it easy. We're grinders, struggling to maintain employment, to pay for shelter, to put food on the table, or to just live long enough to see the next generation move out and struggle on their own.

We *are* tough. We've been fighting all of our lives, and we've learned to keep getting up, no matter how many times we get knocked down. That toughness, that resiliency instills within us an indomitable spirit, and that spirit comes with a swagger.

And I guarantee, my family had it as tough as any other. We didn't work in a mill, or on the dock, or installing wire or pipe in someone's house. We *fed* those people, and if you think it's tough earning a laborer's wage, imagine how tough it is separating those laborers from their hard-earned cash!

My grandfather opened our family restaurant back in the '40s, and named it after my dad who was a little kid at the time: Sonny's. It wasn't fancy, and we only ever had one location, but it was enough to keep a roof over our heads, and our stomachs full for more than 75 years until my parents recently sold it. That sale is what triggered all this weirdness this past week.

Sonny's was a community within a community. It's where our neighbors came to be together, to listen to music, to dance and eat and drink and laugh. It's where first dates occurred and weddings were celebrated.

The food was delicious, but not unique. There was a bar staffed by one bartender (often my dad or me). At the end of the bar, there was a small platform where a four-piece band could barely fit, and a ten-by-ten dance floor of glued-down parquet where no more than twenty people could dance comfortably, but where more than 100 jammed together on special occasions. The rest of the floor was a sea of one-inch squares of white and navy blue mosaic tiles, and the ceiling was pressed tin panels.

I don't think the place had been renovated since it opened. There was never any money.

There were a half dozen booths along the wall opposite the bar, and on the other side of the wall from the booths was the florist next door. We shared walls on both sides with next-door neighbors. A florist on one side, and a kids clothing store on the other. They specialized in Holy Communion and Confirmation outfits.

In between the bar and the booths were freestanding two-tops and four-tops (tables for two or four diners). When the need arose, we shoved the tables together in a single row to seat parties of forty. The main kitchen was behind the bar, but the walk-in freezer and the bread oven were both in the basement. The bathrooms were on the main floor at the back, behind the bandstand, and my mother (and grandmother before her) would perch at the hostess podium at the front end of the dining room, a few feet from the front door. The only windows on the first floor were along the front wall facing the street.

Ever since the place was built, around 1900, the heat came from a coal-fired furnace in the basement. That furnace also heated the bread and pizza oven. Between the furnace and the kitchen, the place was never cold in the winter, but in the summer, the only cool air came from a single mammoth, noisy air conditioner wedged in the opening above the front door where the transom window should have been. I swear, when that thing turned on, the lights in the neighborhood dimmed.

My mother always hated that eyesore. It was loud, and it pumped so much cold air down on the hostess station, she'd routinely wear a parka when she worked the hostess desk in the summer. The air in the back of the joint near the bandstand would be hot enough to boil water, but the front reception area was like the tundra. My Pop would open the door at the end of the hall beyond the bathrooms that led into the alley, figuring that would create a draw and pull the cooler air through the dining room, but it didn't. That plan only made the back section hotter and noisier since the gigantic kitchen fan that was louder than an army helicopter vented into the alley to the left of that door.

The hideous window air conditioner may have been the size of a 1960s Buick, but it really wasn't that visible from the street. Our front door was set back in an alcove, even though the building and its storefront windows came right up to the sidewalk. Patrons would step from the sidewalk, through the alcove and into our restaurant, as if we were welcoming them into our home.

And it *was* our home, because the second floor of the restaurant was the apartment my grandparents occupied with my father when they first opened Sonny's. My mother moved in after my parents married in the mid-'50s, and the two couples lived there together until I came along and my parents decided it was time to get their own place. My grandparents stayed there the rest of their lives. After they were gone, my dad rented the apartment to our bartender. After we fired that lying, thieving son of a bitch, my sister Angela and I moved in while we went to college. Ange ultimately moved out, and moved on with her life with her husband and kids. I stayed in the upstairs apartment until Sonny's was sold, and I consequently became homeless.

There are literally dozens, if not hundreds of restaurants in Philadelphia arranged exactly like Sonny's, and at least a couple dozen of them have nearly identical menus to ours. Some of them survived as long as ours or even longer, but most failed within the first two or three years. A portion of any restaurant's success should be attributed to good luck, but most successful restaurants also have a combination of good food, good value, ambience, friendly service and a solid, efficient operation. Sonny's had all of that, but we had something else as well. We had our sign.

Over the years, outsiders would identify our entire neighborhood by our iconic sign. It ran the length of the front of our building, blocking the view of the sidewalk and street from the second floor apartment's front windows. It was twenty feet long, four feet high and two feet deep. It was like a big, shallow steel bathtub, turned on its side with dozens of high-wattage lightbulbs encircling its interior perimeter, sequentially blinking clockwise nonstop for decades. On the flat section of the sign (what would be the upward facing part of the bathtub), in the middle of those flashing lights, was scrawled the word "Sonny's" in bright red paint, on a black background, in a cool 1940's script.

If you looked up the word "pizzazz" in Webster's dictionary, you'd see a picture of this sign.

Everyone from passersby to neighbors to competitors always wondered how in the world we got the city's approval to install such a ridiculously garish, oversized monstrosity on our façade. They'd joke the airport could use our sign as a beacon in a dense fog, or ships would run aground trying to dock in the nearby port, mistaking us for a lighthouse. The fact is, that sucker burned almost as much electricity as a tower of stadium flood lights and was twice as bright. The heat generated by all those big bulbs probably raised the neighborhood's ambient temperature by five degrees. The only way we got it approved is the only way *anyone* got *anything* approved in South Philly. My grandfather knew a guy who knew a guy.

As much electricity as that thing used, and as much of an albatross as it was to maintain as it got older and older, it was never turned off, not once between the moment it was first turned on until the moment my family sold Sonny's. That fateful day was the first time the sign was extinguished, and as it turns out, our family was almost extinguished with it.

Like the sign above Sonny's, our family has been resilient and stood the test of time, but that run nearly ended this week, and that's no exaggeration. It was one hell of a lousy week—and I'm going to tell you all about it—but first, I have to settle in for the night, because I've been telling you all this from behind the wheel of my parked car in a hotel lot a few miles outside Pittsburgh. If I don't go inside, I'm going to fall asleep right here in the driver's seat.

I'm John. Close friends and family call me Johnny, and I'm a 50-year-old man running away from home.

The Runaway Paesan

I just spent the last several minutes trying to muster enough energy to open the car door, step out and make my way to the front desk.

In retrospect, after all I've been through, a long haul along the Pennsylvania Turnpike was not a great choice. The western half of the road is surprisingly twisty, desolate and hilly and it's so dark, the light from the high-beams gets swallowed up by the pitch black night only a few feet in front of the bumper. Between all that and being so nearly comatose I don't remember the last two hours of the trip, I knew I had to pull over and get some sleep before I nodded off behind the wheel, misjudged a bend in the road and sailed off into a ravine.

Once I finally made it inside the hotel, I felt I'd been magically transported back in time to a 1980s soap opera, and believe it or not, that was okay. I was actually thankful for the horrible swirling mauve, hunter green and khaki designs on the wall covering and carpet because their visual assault on my eyes was keeping me awake. I reached the front desk, drunk with fatigue, struggling to make any sense of my surroundings, and tapped the bell on the counter waiting for a hotel employee to appear.

This place was hideous. Clean, but wow, so much ugly. If I was an interior decorator, standing in this room, I would have shot myself.

I shuddered to imagine what the rooms looked like, and was pretty happy none of it would be visible once the lights were out and my eyes were shut.

The desk clerk appeared and I instinctively handed him my driver's license, because nothing happens at a hotel without a picture ID. I looked across the counter and grumbled at the kid on the other side, "Room. King-size bed, and hurry, before I collapse on your ugly carpet."

"Welcome to the Grand Pittsburgher," he said *much* too enthusiastically. "Let's see what we can do for ya t'nite, Mr. Val … mont … ee" he recited as he read my driver's license.

"Yes. Valmonti. First name John. Now, how about that room?" "No problem at all, sir. We can *absolutely* put you in a single room with a big king bed tonight. With tax, that'll be $115.89. What type of credit card will you be using this evening?"

"Can I just pay cash?"

The kid continued to talk and smile at the same time. "Well, you *can* pay with cash, but we'll still need a credit card on file in case there's any damage, or sundry charges incurred between now and checkout."

This is the point where Chad, the teenaged night desk clerk from Breezewood (assuming the hotel badge on his chest was correct) and I stared at one another for what seemed like three years. He was probably barely out of high school, was wearing a double-knit grey uniform with red piping and a high collar, and had a gigantic, angry red zit glowing in the middle of his forehead.

Between my colossally shitty week, the long drive out here, and the fact I was about to pull a Rip Van Winkle right there in the lobby, I was in the mood for neither the late-evening smiling face of Chad, nor a recitation of his off-brand hotel's check-in policies.

"Chad? As you can probably tell by the fresh, multicolored bruises on my face, I have had one hell of a day. I have been awake for nearly

20 hours, capped off by a nonstop drive to Pittsburgh from America's vacation paradise, Philadelphia, Pennsylvania."

Chad chuckled at the obvious sarcasm.

I held up a single index finger to shush the boy and continued in a very deadpan manner. "Don't giggle, Chad. This is not a time for giggling. It is a time for a hot shower, and many hours of uninterrupted sleep in that king-size bed I requested a moment ago. Where, exactly, in that chain of events do you see me damaging anything, or incurring any sundry expenses?"

Chad's giggle immediately changed to the look of a young man about to have his first adult confrontation. He was not prepared. He stammered …

"Chad, is there a night manager who can help me?"

"I'm the night manager," he said almost apologetically.

No doubt, at that moment he was regretting the "night manager" title he so cherished when his shift began.

"Well, buddy, here's the thing. I don't *have* a credit card. I have good old-fashioned United States currency, and unless your hotel is filled to capacity right now, I'll bet you could really use some of that currency to run this fine operation. Turning away a paying customer is not really great for business. Am I right?"

"But our policy clearly states I can't run your room through our system without a credit card."

I held up my index digit again in a shushing manner. "Chad, are you working the front of the house by yourself tonight?"

"Yes."

"So there's no one else here to help you, is there?"

Chad stammered for a second. He had no idea what direction this was headed, but he was probably sniffing the faint aroma of a possible threat.

Before he panicked, I dove right in to put his mind at ease. "I think I have a solution, Chad. Would you like to hear it?"

Chad nodded reluctantly.

"Chad, there are a lot of expenses built into the cost of a hotel room—mortgage, all sorts of taxes, insurance, labor, utilities, amortized décor expenses, office equipment, advertising, corporate overhead, and the list goes on and on. Everything you see around you costs money, and those costs are all wrapped up in the price of each room rental. Once all that stuff is figured into the equation, the profit margin that's left is skinny as a blade of grass, probably no more than a couple dollars per room per night, at best. What would you say if I showed you a way to increase those profits to one hundred dollars per room per night? Would that interest you, Chad?"

Chad's nod became much more enthusiastic.

I pulled a hundred-dollar bill from my wallet and slapped it on the counter in front of him.

"Don't ring my room through the system, Chad. Give me a key and keep the cash. The room didn't cost *you* anything, so the hundred dollar bill is all profit. *Your* profit."

Chad stopped nodding his head. He looked down at the hundred dollar bill on the counter. Ben Franklin stared back at him. Chad kept his head tilted down and peered up at me from the top of his eyes. He looked left. He looked right. He grabbed the room key, handed it to me, swiped the C-note off the counter before anyone saw anything and said "Enjoy your stay with us, Mr. Valmonti, and *please* come again soon."

"Which way to my room, Chad?"

He looked at me, pointed down the hall to the left, and then retreated quickly from the front desk to the office behind it, presumably to complete his nap, or ponder ways to spend his new windfall.

I adjourned to my room to ponder my life, which has been pretty overwhelming of late.

This week, a mysterious vendetta against my family took shape, and that included me getting beaten up (more than once), and being deceived by someone I've trusted since I was a little kid, but on the positive side of the ledger, I had sex with four different women—one of them twice—so when you think of it that way, maybe this week wasn't so bad after all.

All of this—Sonny's, my family, my neighborhood, who I am, where I'm from, why I'm here, whom I've pissed off and how—started scrolling through my mind a few hours ago as I sat in a restaurant chair, enjoying a celebratory meal with family and friends. We thought everything was finally over and done, and we could go on with our lives, but then, from out of nowhere, an old guy in a fancy suit approached our table and disrupted a perfectly lovely evening by dropping one *hell* of a surprise on us.

There I sat, elbow on the table, head propped up on my fist, watching the most important people in my life lose their minds and scream at me because apparently, this whole thing was my fault. Not five minutes earlier, they were toasting me, and telling me how proud they all were of me. All of the sudden, their tune changed, and I sucked, and you know what? They were right, because if it wasn't for me, a wonderfully fascinating and accomplished man wouldn't be dead.

I gotta be honest with you. I'm having difficulty wrapping my head around the whole thing, partially because I'm almost definitely concussed from all the beatings I took, but also because this week has been seriously surreal.

I swear, after what I've been through, nothing else could possibly surprise me, *nothing*. I could walk outside right now and the sky could be full of flying monkeys, and the only thought I'd have is "Damn! I hope they're wearing diapers!"

I've come to discover my entire life has been a charade. I feel like a colossal idiot for not seeing through it years ago, but I see it all pretty clearly now, even with the brain injuries I suffered this week. I'm doing what any sane person in my situation would do. I'm running away.

Pants on Fire

Until a few months ago, my life had been pretty unremarkable, at least compared to 99% of everyone else living in one of the most-densely populated, ethnocentric neighborhoods in the US. If you compared my life to that of someone growing up in the village my grandfather came from in Italy, it would seem *incredible*, but growing up here, in this urban outpost for Italian immigrants, it was not. It was very routine and I blended into the scenery.

I grew up playing basketball on the courts in the urban park across the street from our world-famous cheesesteak joints. I played stickball on narrow streets between long rows of parked cars, and I played tackle football on the street, or in vacant lots. Of course, we'd check for broken glass first. We were tough, not stupid.

As it turned out, tackle football on broken glass would have been a welcome departure from the other injuries I sustained from the vendetta, which all stemmed from a very big mistake that occurred more than a hundred years ago, when a teenaged Romani girl (people used to call them gypsies) desperately plucked a little lie from thin air to cover her ass. That started the gears turning. That's really it. All the craziness that happened to my little family this week started with a single, stupid lie.

The girl hadn't planned to lie. In fact, ordinarily, she was very honest, but this situation was anything but ordinary. It was a moment when her enraged father was screaming in her face, and her lizard-brain could think of nothing but survival.

Well, to be honest, that last little bit there wasn't entirely honest. Survival *wasn't* the only thing on her mind, because as horrifying as the whole situation was for her, it too was surreal. Even in the midst of her father's conniption, as if she was watching the scene play out as an impartial third party from somewhere else in the room, the girl kept thinking how shockingly out of character this behavior was for him.

Her doting father was infamously calm and level-headed. His neighbors often sought him out as *the* sober voice of reason to settle disputes whenever everyone else around him was losing their minds. He was so grounded and stable, people twice his age called him Papa.

Can you imagine calling some guy half your age "Papa?" Well that term of respect and affection was natural for someone with a resting heartbeat hovering only slightly above comatose. Papa calmly sauntered through life like a man well beyond his years, nodding his head with a peaceful half-smile, and calm, half-shut eyes shrouded by bushy black eyebrows. If you saw him strolling past you today, you'd swear he was stoned, just out lookin' for a cheeseburger and a bag of Doritos, but you'd be mistaken.

He was just that mellow, and why not? His life was perfect—comfortable little home, loving wife, betrothed daughter, a couple of virile sons, a few acres to call his own and a blazingly bright future ahead of him.

It should be of little surprise, therefore, in her entire life the girl had never heard Papa raise his voice to *anyone*, let alone *her*. She wasn't even sure he *could* raise his voice. It would be like hearing a fish bark.

Well, now she could check that box off her list of life's unanswered questions. This fish barks, and the bark is very loud, and very wet.

Regardless of whether or not anyone could have imagined it, Papa was, in fact, screaming like a rabid grizzly bear in his precious baby girl's face, and why wouldn't he? His perfect life just turned to shit in less time than it takes say it.

His daughter had detonated the volcano within him, and his eruption was so intense, she couldn't even process what he was saying. To everyone in the room, it sounded like thunder and gibberish went out one night, got really drunk and then got into a fistfight in Papa's mouth. He was so out of control, even *he* probably lost track of what he was saying. His mouth was on autopilot, and words kept blowing past his lips into his daughter's face.

All they both knew for sure was he was out of control, and she caused it.

What had she done that was so terrible? One word: pregnant. Two more words: not married.

Even under normal circumstances, in early 1900s rural Italy, this wasn't taken lightly. In fact, back then, it simply did not happen. Period.

Back then, there was no "third date rule." No decent person had sex until they were married. Marriages tended to be arranged, but if courtship happened at all, it was formal and always chaperoned. Rarely would the couple be left alone, and even if they did somehow elude their watchdogs, a stolen kiss was about all they'd have time to muster. Even that was considered scandalous.

If just a kiss was bad, imagine what intercourse meant.

No civil person would accuse someone else of such behavior without solid proof, but in this case, a baby was going to be pretty good proof. Reputations would be destroyed.

Today, having a child out of wedlock is commonplace, but back then, it was more than enough to ruin a family. That is not an exaggeration. It was a disgrace of the highest order, and would be a yoke of shame worn by the entire clan. In this small town, word of this abomination would spread like wildfire, and anyone within earshot of that kitchen was probably already churning the rumor mill.

There would be shunning.

For Papa, shunning was the least of his concerns, however, because this pregnancy would undo his life's work. His plans were unraveling before his eyes. That may sound a little over-the-top, but it's 100 percent true. For Papa, his daughter's pregnancy was the one thing which *could not happen*, but it did. He knew exactly what it all meant for his family—hence the conniption.

Once he started screaming, the young girl recoiled and immediately realized she had grossly underestimated his capacity for anger. That became more apparent when his reaction escalated from anger to fury to nuclear mushroom cloud in the snap of a finger.

She was instantly frozen with panic.

Caught off guard, and incapable of rational thought, her flight instinct was triggered. Her subconscious convinced her legs to try slipping away, slowly and nonchalantly sliding her bare feet backward across the kitchen floor away from him without ever breaking eye contact. He'd have none of it. Without slowing his verbal bile expulsion, his hands lunged out and grappled onto her arms, pulling her back in toward him, like a monster reeling in its terrified prey.

There was no way to engage him in logical discourse. She had already stopped thinking of words, and instead focused on not peeing down her leg in fear.

This was bad.

Of course, with the specter of confrontation monopolizing her thoughts every waking moment for weeks, she had seriously considered avoiding this day of reckoning entirely and simply running away with her lover, never telling her parents about the baby at all.

Mind you, running away with her lover wasn't actually an option. Unbeknownst to her, that cowardly piece of garbage who knocked her up feared his comeuppance so badly, he joined the army to escape. Just imagine the depth of this guy's fear of commitment. He would rather join the army at the brink of war and risk standing in front of a hail of bullets than man up and stand by this girl when she needed him most.

He was shot in the war, by the way—took one right in the ass as he ran away. Just thought you'd want to know that.

It was too late for *her* to run away, but she still desperately needed some peace of mind, if for no other reason than to finally get some decent sleep once this argument ended. Not only had her incessant worrying kept her awake for the last few weeks, but nightmares of her plight consumed what little sleep she *did* find. Entire days passed without her sleeping at all.

Naturally, without sleep, she was chronically frightened, fatigued and confused. Her personality was eroding. She became increasingly irritable, and she wasn't concealing it well.

She was failing.

Her mother noticed the change, as a mother naturally would. Her ordinarily sweet, carefree daughter's recent metamorphosis into a paranoid, bedraggled recluse wasn't difficult to detect. Fearing the worst, she asked what was going on. The girl mistook her mother's concern for an opportunity to seek counsel. Instead of receiving the comfort and solace she sought, though, she was greeted with her mother's own panic and rage.

Deep down, at her core, her mother was concerned for her daughter's well-being, but the thoughts occupying the forefront of her mother's mind were of her life's work crumbling before her eyes, and how her husband was going to react.

Soon after her birth, the girl's parents had arranged her marriage to the only, and much older, son of a prosperous local landowner. Her future husband was already forty years old when she was born, and had no designs on ever marrying a woman. His ailing parents were nearing the end of their own mortality, and were desperate to perpetuate the bloodline. Their final wish was for their son to marry, and for their name and legacy to continue. Marriage with this baby girl could ultimately bear multiple male grandchildren, even if they themselves were long gone by then.

Papa negotiated the perfect deal, and the contract was signed. Once his daughter turned 15, she and her husband would wed, and that union would increase the family's holdings ten-fold.

With that carrot dangling in front of them, Papa nurtured that arrangement for 15 years, and finally, with the nuptials nearly upon them, his family was ready to reap their rewards. Everyone in the family knew what was at stake, and everyone marched in unison to ensure the perfect result.

And then this happened.

She had ruined everything.

As Papa ranted in their kitchen, her mother stood by, arms crossed, face contorted in a scowl, staring into her daughter's puddling eyes. Without an ally in the room, it's no wonder the girl's intent turned immediately to preservation for herself, and for her lover, with whom she unwittingly still planned to run away.

Then the devil's inspiration was delivered to her mind in that instant.

In her moment of weakness and cowardice, instead of telling the truth, she had an epiphany from out of the blue and laid all blame for her pregnancy at the feet of her best friend, an innocent scapegoat of a boy named Fredo who had left town for America just days earlier, never to be seen by anyone locally again.

She was acting at her most basic, instinctual level, which is exactly how lies like this come to be.

To her credit, the girl was very quick-witted. Hers was an especially well-crafted impromptu lie—almost perfect. A hundred years earlier, it *would* have been perfect, simultaneously deflecting her father's fury, and protecting everyone, even Fredo because he'd be unreachable. In that precise instant, that lie *seemed* perfect. Then again, don't they all?

She certainly never intended to hurt anyone, especially not her best friend. To the contrary, she was trying to diffuse the situation, stifle *all* potential harm, and protect *everyone*. This particular lie could have accomplished everything, except it didn't. It worked only briefly, and then it ruined *everything*.

She failed.

It seemed perfect and harmless, but no lie is really perfect or harmless, is it? She thought her dearest friend Fredo was gone forever—safe and untouchable, so she spun a tale of him forcing himself on her. She described how she resisted his overtures in vain, and how he overpowered her. Then, she told her parents how, when she discovered her pregnancy, she confronted Fredo in hopes he would do the right thing by her, but instead he abandoned her and ran away to America.

Of course, the lie could not have been farther from the truth. Fredo was the shyest, meekest, most naive boy in the world, and about as physically imposing as a candlewick. There's no way he'd ever concoct such a plan, let alone actually follow through with what she said he did. He had no idea she was pregnant, and if he did, and she asked him to stand by her, he probably would have, even though the child she carried wasn't his and would subject him to scorn for the rest of his life. He'd make that sacrifice for her, because he was precisely that kind of selfless friend.

Aside from holding her hand as friends, he'd never touched her, but that's not what she now led her parents to believe. They had always been suspicious of her relationship with the boy, and she exploited their suspicions with a lie.

This tidy lie encapsulated everything. She assumed the role of the victim, concealed the existence of her actual lover, and gave her parents the villain they so desperately desired and suspected all along.

She had no way of knowing her lover was already gone, so she protected that louse for no reason, and placed a curse on her dearest friend instead. That decision would haunt her and Fredo both for the balance of their lives.

Fredo, the hapless sap wearing this misplaced yoke, was an oblivious teenage boy whom she'd known since birth, and with whom she had spent countless hours of countless days discussing the future, and birds, and trees, and flowers. One day recently, he had conjured every ounce of intestinal fortitude he could muster and left their village to sail to America and begin his new life as a self-sufficient man. In his mind, all those in his wake would miss him and wish him well. What he didn't know was a lie was following him—a dirty little lie that existed only out of convenience once he was gone.

As cataclysmic as this debacle seemed in the moment, rational, sober minds would prevail and everyone would adapt, wouldn't they? Seriously, this conversation in Papa's kitchen should be little more than a flashpoint. And like most flashes, the family would figure out a way to get past the pregnancy. Although the future wouldn't go as originally planned, they'd figure things out and move forward. They'd hate Fredo forever, but they'd never do anything about it. Right?

Well, in simple terms, no.

The entire incident, but specifically the story she told, had a profound, indelible impact on Papa. He believed his entire future had become unhinged, and all because some cowardly local boy had raped his daughter. If all that wasn't bad enough, he could not exact revenge on a ghost. The local rogue had skipped town and vanished, never to be seen again. Papa's need for revenge would never be satisfied, and that lack of satisfaction drove him mad.

Ultimately, the young girl's lie took on a life of its own, far beyond her momentary, clumsy attempt to dodge repercussions. It became the nucleus of her father's consciousness for the remainder of his life. For the rest of his days, he bit down on and swallowed this betrayal, and it festered like an open wound. He had no way of knowing at the time, but his only source of solace would have been knowing his torment would be brief. He would barely live four more years to see the war end, and he would never live long enough to see his grandson, or the repercussions of Bella's actions.

The news of her pregnancy never became public (more on that later), so he couldn't risk this secret getting out. He couldn't seek consult from friends or confidants. He could only replay the incident in his mind nonstop and fantasize about exacting his vengeance. The lie changed him. He was no longer the calm, kind, sage diplomat everyone adored and respected. He became the bitter man with a constant scowl and faraway eyes who grumbled to himself, and whom everyone avoided. He appeared to age ten years in that kitchen, and the more he obsessed, the more the lie's impact grew until his deep-seated hatred for Fredo became the framework for his family's raging vendetta.

That little lie and the vendetta it spawned became the toxic fuel that sustained her family for decades. It was the driving force behind their success. It was the single cell that spread like a cancer through generations. Ultimately, the chip on her family's shoulder, which she created, evolved into her tribe's battle cry.

So what of it? There are angry people all over the world all the time who aren't gaining satisfaction. Why should this family's collective angst be any different? It lifted them up, collectively. They found strength and purpose in it. Good for them.

But none of that mattered because Fredo was long gone. This little clan didn't have the means to find him, let alone hold him accountable.

Well, that all would have been true, if this had occurred in the early 1800s, but this happened in the early *1900s*. Although we look back on those days now like they're the dark ages, the fact is, the turn of the last century was the cusp of vast, global change. As the ensuing century progressed, the world became more connected. Little towns like theirs were quickly and seamlessly linked to everyone, everywhere. It started with telephones, and progressed with every other technological advance that followed. In a handful of years, Fredo could ultimately be found and held accountable for his actions—or at least for the actions blamed on him.

With no way of knowing what she would unleash, the innocent, cover-her-ass, century-old lie she plucked from thin air under duress—coupled with the changes looming ahead of the early 1900s—would doom Fredo and his family. He and his family would be found, and they would suffer consequences for something that never actually happened.

As it turns out, Fredo—that pitiful, naive kid—was my father's father. Pop to him, and Pop-Pop to me. Everyone else in America who knew him, knew him as Al.

BELLA

Her name was Isabella, and she was beautiful and lithe, just as you might envision a teenaged girl in Italy in the early 1900s to be. Her skin was neither white, nor brown, except during the summer when the sun baked her to a dark golden hue—typical for her part of the world. It was also smooth and marred only by a single imperfection: a hole in the upper cartilage of her right ear—a family trait, nearly all of them had it. Her long, wavy brown hair was so dark, it was nearly black, and always tousled. She always wore light, airy sundresses, and rarely wore shoes. She would run and jump as fast and high as every local boy, and was as strong as any of them too, even though she was barely five feet tall and weighed less than 90 pounds.

She wasn't Sophia Loren beautiful—voluptuous and aloof. She was more like Audrey Hepburn—just as much of a firecracker, but far more exotic.

Even in the dim, early-evening light of that kitchen, disheveled and vulnerable, within inches of her father's tirade, she was beautiful. She wasn't remotely radiant at that moment, however.

You might want to romantically attribute a glow to her because of her pregnancy, but that would have been entirely inaccurate. First of all, she wasn't really that far along yet, but beyond that, she hadn't slept in days and was throwing up constantly. She was kind of a mess.

Regardless, although she was dehydrated, sleep-deprived and ravenous, she stood before her father, rigid like a soldier being berated by a drill sergeant: exhibiting an almost regal posture, projecting an image of strength and fortitude. That was all a façade of course, because on the inside, she was terrified and knew she was on the verge of collapse. Her only hope was for her impromptu lie to quickly diffuse everything and grant her peace.

She was being naive. Papa was too deep into his rage to be redirected with logic or compassion. Instead, the air was split with a *"crack"* when his open hand hit her face. This wasn't merely a quick, reactive swat. It was an open-handed punch. He had consciously drawn his hand back in anger to a full extension, stretching his shoulder as if he was reaching for something behind him, then uncoiling with all of his might. It was only at the last possible moment he opened his fist and hit her with his palm.

She stumbled a couple steps to her right from the impact. Her knees buckled, but her fingers never touched the ground. She was knocked off balance, but not down. Regardless of whether she hit the floor or not, though, the combination of the physical impact, and the shock of being struck at all, had her head reeling.

She had never been hit by anyone, let alone her doting father, yet here she stood, the skin on her cheek enflamed from his slap and the taste of blood on her tongue.

Instinctively, she quickly took inventory of her teeth with her tongue to be sure none were knocked out or loosened. She wouldn't have been surprised to feel a couple wiggle against her tongue's pressure, but they were all fine and accounted for. Her cheek didn't fare quite as well, however. Caught between her teeth and her father's hand, the inside of her cheek had been cut, which was why she was tasting blood. Her lip had also been split and was bleeding, as had the skin below her left eye, which boasted an inch-long gash.

Facial wounds bleed quite a bit and the one beneath her eye was no exception. Ultimately, it would scar, providing her skin with its second imperfection and serving as a life-long reminder of this incident.

Immediately, the left side of her face began swelling.

Her entire being quivered, and she called upon every shred of character she could muster to resist the urge to crumble to the ground and sob. She wanted her father to be proud of her for being tough and not collapsing, hoping he would see his own strength of will in her. So instead of falling to the floor in a blubbering heap, she returned to standing bolt upright, staring at an imaginary point in the distance directly in front of her—lip quivering, nose sniffling, and eyes on the verge of pouring tears, but she refused to break.

He had hit her, *hard*! This powerful man, who became strong over the course of many years working the fields for the benefit of his family, had hit his precious daughter—the small, delicate, pregnant girl who, until only moments ago, had been his greatest source of pride and his means to elevate his family's status and fortune.

He had hit her with every ounce of his fury, yet she still stood before him, defiantly. In that moment, he didn't see a reflection of his own will. He saw a petulant child figuratively spitting on all he had done for her. He misconstrued her unwillingness to fall as an insult. He grabbed her arm and flung her across the room like she weighed nothing. When she collided with the doorframe, physics took over, stopping her moving progress and dropping her to the floor. She curled up in a protective ball, ultimately surrendering to the impulses of hysteria and sobbing.

Her mother had finally seen enough and broke her silence.

Typically, Papa was the calm, methodical voice of reason, and she was the quintessential, incendiary Italian woman, but tonight, her husband was beyond cognitive thinking, so she needed to suppress her rage—at least temporarily—and consider the bigger picture. While her husband exploded and acted out physically, she listened and began devising a plan to get past this volcanic crater in the road and protect their lives' work.

Her feelings could remain suppressed and seethe long enough for her to be sure the wheels of a solution were in motion. Once she was sure the future was secure, she could—and would—purge those festering emotions. She and Papa would spend their remaining days regurgitating this nightmare in rants, discussions and *spectacular* arguments. They would never get past this, not ever.

"*We* need to get *you* out of here," she calmly told Bella as she helped the child from the floor, brushed away some of the dirt from her hands and dress, and wiped some of her tear stains from her cheeks. "There's still hope for your marriage to work, but you need to leave, now. We'll send you away, far away. My sister in Triana, in Spain, will take you. I'll make sure of it. Go collect your things and come back here immediately. Your father will take you to the train, and I'll get a message to my sister to let her know the situation and what we'll need from her. Now, go!"

Papa wasn't finished yet, though. He held up his hand for Isabella to stop, and yelled at his wife "What are you doing?!"

For a single moment, when her mother intervened, the light of salvation glimmered for Isabella, but just as quickly as it appeared, it vanished when her father raised his hand. The girl shut her eyes and bristled, preparing herself for the beating to continue. Frozen, she awaited direction from the recognized authority in the room—her father.

Her mother turned to Papa and continued in a calm, quiet, metered tone. "No one else but we three know she's pregnant. If anyone asks where she's gone, we'll say she's going to Spain to help an ailing relative. It will illustrate her kindness and usefulness. She'll have the baby in Spain and leave it there. Then she'll return home as if nothing happened. When she returns, she can marry her betrothed as a virgin and our plans will still work out. They will merely be delayed."

"What if they check to ensure she's pure?" he asked.

His wife shrugged. "We'll pay off a doctor to confirm it. It certainly won't be the first time," and she raised her eyebrow only to him so her daughter couldn't see the gesture. "Once the marriage is confirmed, Bella can have many legitimate babies and consummate our families' union."

Papa had calmed down at least enough to hear the plan, and when he realized it could salvage his life's work, he barked his command at Bella without looking at her. "Get outside and into my car!"

"But, my clothes, my things ... my *shoes*. Mama said ..."

He stood up and roared, "You're lucky I'm letting you live! Get outside!" and he smacked her face for the *second* time in her life and shoved her tiny frame *through* the door this time and onto the loose gravel beyond. She slid to rest with a thud against the side of her father's car.

He followed closely behind. "Get in and sit on the floor so no one can see you're in here. I'll tell you when to get up," he bellowed as he turned the crank below the radiator, pressed the button inside the car and got the anemic motor of the little blue coupe to sputter, buck and start.

He channeled his anger into speed, driving off as quickly as the car could muster. The FIAT bounced and pitched over the rough, loose roadway all the way to the train station. Isabella banged around inside the passenger footwell where she was balled up out of sight, constantly losing her balance and sliding across the filthy floor, but she dared not complain or otherwise make a sound for fear of rekindling the flames of her father's rage.

Papa sat stoically, hunched over the wheel and looked forward, focused on the road ahead, both literally and figuratively, fearing the union they've counted on for years could be slipping through his fingers.

They reached the modest Valmontone train station. He dragged his daughter from the car like a brute, pressed her against the wall next to the ticket window and held her there with his palm pressed firmly into her upper chest. He used his free hand to buy the train tickets—first to Rome and then to Spain. He threw them in her face and pointed to a bench beside the tracks, ordering her to wait there for the train to arrive, and then get on and not come back until she was summoned.

He turned and stomped away, unable to even look at the girl whom he loved more than any*thing* or any*one* in the world. He knew, if he faltered a little now, he would falter completely. He needed to remain strong.

She couldn't fathom the idea of him leaving her there. She believed with all her heart he would have changed his mind somewhere between the house and the station, that he would rescue and protect her, the way he always did, but that didn't happen. Instead of going home with him, she sat on the bench and didn't move because he told her not to. She still cried and called for him not to do this, though, pleading with him to take her home.

Her father never broke stride, though. He returned to the car, where the engine had been left running. He climbed inside, engaged the gears and departed undeterred, never looking back.

Stones were kicked up by the wheels of the car as it rumbled back up the road toward their home. Isabella intently watched the car mirrors until the car was out of sight, praying her father would glance back at her. She craved a simple acknowledgement, a tilt of his head, *something* to prove he still cared for, or even loved her, but the glance never came.

Her father was a proud man. He refused to look back. Just as he'd done during the first leg of the trip, he only stared forward, steadfast, seemingly with no regrets of leaving his fifteen-year-old daughter behind, alone on the dusty, wooden planks of the train depot.

Until this afternoon, he'd never understood why anyone would physically lash out against someone else. He considered such a physical outburst a display of mental weakness, an inability to negotiate verbally.

Under the weight of today's grave disappointment and perceived disrespect, he understood the urge. He succumbed to it and attacked the most precious person in his life.

Less than an hour later, he was driving home alone. The events of the incident in his kitchen replayed over and over in his mind as he sped away from her, leaving her to fend for herself at the train station, peering back at her through the rearview mirror but only from the corners of his eyes. He couldn't dare move his head for fear she would see him do so and perceive weakness or a lack of resolve in his actions. He had too much pride to let her see him waiver.

Of course, in his heart, he didn't *want* to leave her there. If he had been rational, he would have rushed back and enveloped her in his arms, holding her face deep in his chest, protecting her from the world as he had done every other day of her life before this one, but she had left him no choice. She had to go away. If she stayed and grew visibly pregnant and had her child, their plans would die.

He consoled himself with the thought, when she finally returned home, he'd welcome her and cry tears of joy, but today, he believed his job was to teach her a lesson and protect his family's future. She had betrayed them all and jeopardized the future he and his wife had been planning and managing for years. He could not condone her selfishness. She needed to be taught a lesson.

At last, once he could no longer see the station, he broke down and wept. The gravel under the car stung the wheel wells as the tires spun more and more quickly. Dust from the dirt road swelled and swirled around the little blue coupe. Its engine whined and its body seemed on the verge of collapse. The nuts and bolts were barely holding it together, straining through the violent vibration of tires banging over the uneven corduroy of dirt and stone. He was oblivious to the bone-jarring ride, the blinding cloud and the cacophony of his car rattling itself to bits. All of his senses were dulled. All he felt was shame.

As the fog of blind fury cleared in his mind, he should have turned back and retrieved her, but he had not yet reached the point in his contrition to swallow his pride. Sadly, that hurdle would be crossed too late. By then, Isabella would already be gone.

His shame would live with him to the grave. The tears of joy he dreamt of crying when he saw her again would never come. When she finally returned, he would be dead and gone.

That was the last time Isabella saw her parents, or her siblings. After all the affection she and her father had shared every moment of her first 15 years, it was those final moments together that lingered forever. He hit her, yelled at her, treated her like garbage and disposed of her without remorse. That would be her final and lasting impression of him, and she blamed herself for all of it.

Her baby was born months later in Triana, Spain, as her mother had arranged. She couldn't return home as planned, at least not right away, because only a few months after she left, Italy was fully engaged with its allies against Austria and Germany in World War I, and there was no practical way for her to re-enter Italy. Spain remained neutral throughout the war, so that's where she stayed for the next three years.

When she finally returned home, she did so alone and found everything had changed, except her marital arrangement and her family's sworn vendetta against Fredo's family, the Mantellis. Those had both survived.

She had left her son behind to be raised by her mother's sister. As long as she had been in Spain, she raised the child as her own, but when she left, the child was taught to believe Isabella was her aunt.

Neither Bella's mother nor father would ever know their only grandchild, and Bella came to realize when she returned, as traumatic as that fateful day had been three years earlier, being sent away from home may have been what saved the lives of her and her baby. If her parents had been more accepting and made a home for her and her child, instead of sending her to Spain to have the baby under the close care of Mama's sister, Bella and her baby may have perished after the war along with her parents. Ironically, her parents survived the war, but succumbed to the pandemic that followed and killed nearly five percent of the rest of the world's population. Had Bella shared their home, she'd have been exposed and shared the virus as well.

Aside from her Romani connections in Spain, she was the only member of her immediate family left. At the age of eighteen, with neither financial means nor physical support from others, she assumed control of what was left of her family's enterprises.

She was a child when she'd left, but she returned a woman, forced to take control of her life and everything around her. In her disheveled, entropic post-war world, she had to bring order and reason and rebuild what her family and others around her had lost. There was no longer time to sit and dream beneath a giant fig tree with anyone, anymore.

She was determined to enforce the contract her parents had executed when she was born, marry the man to whom she had been promised, and fulfill the destiny her father had charted for their family years earlier. She considered this her duty, and a means to honor the parents she believed she had betrayed.

The local community always assumed her betrothed remained a bachelor for all those years because he was shy or was physically impaired or sickly. The simple fact was he was not interested in women, but at that time, in that place, such a truth would have destroyed his family, so he dutifully suppressed his sexuality to preserve his family's reputation. He had hoped to remain a bachelor—albeit a lonely one—indefinitely, but when Bella returned from Spain, she convinced him reneging on their contract would also shame his parents. By marrying, his other secret would remain intact. He did not desire her, of course, and she certainly didn't desire him. Theirs was a business arrangement and they were married for twenty years, until he died. They dutifully produced four sons, heirs to the family land and business.

Together, they combined their families' land, but land alone would not pay their bills. Her husband had never been motivated to do much more than sit home and live a life of leisure as a pseudo aristocrat. Once his parents died, he spent recklessly on a lavish lifestyle, even though there was no revenue being generated to support it. By the time Bella arrived, the estate was depleted and bordering on collapse. His servants were gone. The residence was exhibiting signs of rampant decay, and their once lush and valuable fields had turned to seed from neglect. The investment required to restore the farm operation exceeded their means.

Although he was ill-suited for life when his family's fortunes changed, Bella was extremely intelligent, resilient and resourceful. With limited means, and virtually no other options, she assumed control of the family business and pursued her Romani family, first as financial investors, but ultimately as partners. The farm was just the beginning. Ultimately, she diversified their interests, and in the years between the two world wars, the partnership's collective influence expanded throughout the region. After the second war, their enterprises expanded into other countries, including the US.

Bella and her family became opportunists, identifying those susceptible to suggestion, and grifting them out of money and other assets through carefully designed and orchestrated confidence schemes. They opened legitimate businesses, but operated them illegitimately, and then disappeared before any consequences could find them. They exploited the restoration of western Europe after the war, and then tapped into a stream of ready cash in the naive optimism of the post-war United States.

Although she had hoped her lie had died with her parents, her mother had shared the secret with her sister in Spain, to convince her to take Isabella in. Isabella's mother had worked her entire life to distance herself from her Romani roots and live a quiet, legitimate life with her husband, but by requesting this favor of her family, Mama was pulled back into their nefarious business, expanding the family's influence in Italy.

Even though Bella's parents were gone, the vendetta against Al's family didn't die with them. The Romani members of her family nurtured the seed of the vendetta, mostly because they recognized a good motivating tool when they saw it. They also resented anyone betraying any member of their family, and because Mama wasn't aware Bella's story was a lie, she shared it with her sister as a horrible truth. Once the story gained a foothold, Bella was never able to dispel it. Over the years, in hushed tones, and with Isabella's children's promise to conceal the truth from their father, the Romani shared her story of Fredo and his betrayal. They knew how such a story would bind the family together, and they craved restitution. The flames of the vendetta against Fredo's family were fanned for decades, and it became the reason Bella's family strove so hard to expand their international empire. All to administer justice. Her children vowed to search every corner of America, find Fredo and hold him accountable for the wrong he committed against Bella. They would defend their mother's honor, even though there was no offense against which they needed to defend it.

A century later, worlds would collide, and the vendetta would reach its crescendo.

It all started with one little lie.

PRELUDE—
THE FIRST STEP OF MANY

Welcome back to the 21st Century.

Unemployment is pretty unfamiliar territory for me. I've always had a job. When I was little, I did odd jobs and collected a couple bucks here and there from my grandparents for being such a big helper, but by the time I was eight years old, I was working steady hours every week for pay. From that moment until just a few weeks ago, I worked for the same employer. Then my job of more than four decades, the one I thought I'd have until I died, came to a sudden end.

Maybe I lived too long?

That week started like any other, with me working on Sunday, but then things changed and I *didn't* work on Monday. That was that.

Unemployment is an inadequate term too. It needs context. For example, let's assume it's Christmas dinner and there are two unemployed family members in the house. One starts crying over his turkey and cranberries when he shares the news of losing his job before the holidays, and how his kids didn't have a visit from Santa this year. Pretty shitty, right?

Then that guy's obtuse father-in-law chuckles and sanctimoniously says "I've been unemployed for years, and I love it," because he's retired and financially comfortable. I mean, sure, he's an insensitive dickhead too, but that's not my point, nor unemployment's fault.

In the end, if you *choose* unemployment, it can be great. *Involuntary* unemployment is what really sucks. See? Context.

I suspect most people have dealt with involuntary unemployment during their careers, but no matter how common an occurrence it may be, when it happens to you, it's personal, and it sucks. It's sort of like a relationship. If you're the one doing the breaking up, it's far less painful than when the breakup is thrust on you. Then it hurts like a mother. Sometimes, when both parties are on the same page, it's just a footrace to see who breaks up first, but often one party is blindsiding the other.

In our fantasies, we may dream of storming into our boss's office, emphatically slamming down that imaginary, glowing, red "fuck you" button on his desk, and then storming out triumphantly, leaving him slack-jawed in your wake. Sadly, that sort of satisfying departure is pretty rare. Quite often, the decision is made for us by others.

And let's be candid. No matter the term—fired, laid off, furloughed, downsized … goddamn there are a lot of euphemisms for getting shitcanned—the result is the same. You're out and you're scrambling.

Scrambling for replacement employment can be scary too, especially the older you get, and the farther up the ladder you are. The higher you rise up the corporate pyramid, the fewer spots there are to be had. Ironically, the older, more experienced and more competent you become, the less valued you are too, which is completely counterintuitive, but 100% true.

Fortunately, finding work is easy for me. I'll tell you why in a minute, and although my financial reserves are pretty meager, so are my needs, so I'm okay for money, at least for a few months while I bounce around. And even though I don't desperately *need* money, I desperately need to work to maintain my sanity.

I can't be idle. I go nuts if I have a free hour on a Sunday afternoon, so I have to keep myself occupied, and if I have to do something, I might as well get paid to do it, right? The fact is, I like my work. It's creative. It requires excellent organizational skills, the ability to work with others, the ability to lead and, most importantly, the ability to remain calm when everything and everyone around you are in a state of high-speed entropy.

I possess all those skills. Am I a fireman? A Wall Street trader? A right-handed "closer" in the Phillies' bullpen? Nope. I'm a cook.

Before you say it, yes. I realize cooks move from kitchen to kitchen all the time, but I'm not a typical, transient commercial cook, and I'm not looking for a job at Applebees. My entire life has been spent in my family's Italian restaurant, Sonny's, and I'm only interested in working for another family-owned operation. I have no desire to be a cog in a corporate machine. That would be soul-crushing.

Seventy-five years ago, my grandfather opened Sonny's with my grandmother. When his health started failing and the rigors of being a restaurateur became too much for him, he handed the reins to my Pop, and my parents have run the place ever since.

I always believed I'd assume the mantle of ownership myself one day, just as my Pop had done after his Pop before him, but that obviously didn't happen. Part of me is heartbroken over that, and it has nothing to do with money, or control or security.

What it has everything to do with is my family's legacy. Sonny's was more than a restaurant for us. It was the common element holding my family together. It was the center of our universe. Everything we did was because of Sonny's, and it was the reason for everything we *didn't* do too. We didn't take vacations. We didn't move out of the neighborhood. We didn't live normal lives.

Most people go to a restaurant because they're hungry. They select the joint based upon their palate and their budget and the time it will take to get a table. They order what they want, eat what they want, leave a tip when they're done (hopefully), and then decide what to do next that evening. Not us.

For us, going to a restaurant was like going to school. What did they do better than us? What did they do worse? Were there any ideas we could glean from their menu, or décor, or operation? Was there a waiter, or bartender or cook we should poach? And we didn't just tip and leave. We tipped generously out of empathy and then went somewhere else and discussed the experience.

In some ways, Sonny's provided us with everything, and in other ways it was an anvil chained to our ankles.

If it sounds terrible, I've done a lousy job of describing it, because it was more magical than Disneyland. I worked with my entire family every night for decades. My friends and I always had a place to go and hang out when we were kids. As soon as we'd arrive, we'd get fed, and when we were older, we'd sit at the bar and a drink would magically appear in front of us. There's nowhere else in the world I'd rather be right now, and I miss the place every single day. It's as though the last time I turned the key in the lock, the resultant click broke the chain tethering that anvil to us. What I didn't realize until that moment was that chain also bound us all to one another, and once the sale and closure of Sonny's severed it, we all spun away from one another, in opposite directions, never to be linked the same way again.

Sonny's was so important in my life, it's actually the reason I *have* life.

It's the reason my parents met, and after they married, they lived with my grandparents in the apartment above the restaurant and raised me and my sister in the same room where my Pop had been raised a generation earlier. My parents moved into their own place a block away when I was a kid to raise me and my sis, and my grandparents stayed in that apartment for the rest of their lives.

Sonny's wasn't just a restaurant. It wasn't even just our *restaurant*. It was our *home*.

Then one day last year, out of the clear blue sky, a stranger walked in our door, and our lives changed completely, and forever. My mother sat him in a booth, just as she had done with tens of thousands of other guests over the course of more than sixty years. He had an ordinary meal of Spag-n-balls (Spaghetti and meatballs), a glass of "house red," some homemade tiramisu for dessert, paid his tab and asked to speak to my father. Before he left, he'd offered my Pop more money for Sonny's than it would have been worth to anyone else, including us!

Of course, there's a perfectly legitimate reason for him to offer us so much money, and it's because his intent was *ill*egitimate. Sound familiar? It was a "confidence scheme," but more on that in due time.

Not knowing he was being conned, Pop should've accepted the offer on the spot, but that would have been selfish, and that's not his style. He asked for time to discuss the offer with his family, and the man agreed and walked away.

We'd owned the place since my grandfather opened it, but he and my grandmother were long gone, and my mother and father were both old. The operation had become too much for them to manage. I did my part, and then some, but they were still both exhausted all the time, and the place was falling apart.

My folks came to me for advice, which was really more like permission. They wanted to take the offer, but not if I wanted to take Sonny's over from them. How could I possibly justify depriving my parents of the reward for their lives' work? I loved the *idea* of Sonny's—the family business, the meeting place, my family's legacy, the hallowed halls of my life's greatest memories—but I wasn't passionate about the business.

Somewhere along the line, Sonny's transitioned from a dynamic entrepreneurial adventure for my grandfather, to my Pop's precious chance to honor his father's legacy, to me taking over a place with a rundown kitchen, bar, dining room and apartment. The roof leaked, the plumbing and electric pre-dated the Eisenhower presidency, and with all the restaurant competition invading the neighborhood, the margins here were too small to earn much of a living, let alone pay for all the desperately needed upgrades and repairs.

This offer was manna from heaven. That stranger was an angel sent by god, and his offer would be enough for my parents to retire with the means to sustain them for the rest of their lives, which goodness knows, they deserved. My sister and her husband both supported themselves with careers outside Sonny's, and I was being offered the opportunity of a lifetime, whether I realized it or not.

So there. I practically pleaded with my parents to take the offer. The sale went through. My parents got their check, they insisted on giving a portion of the proceeds to me and my sister, and I was faced with reinventing myself, now that I'm completely unattached and unencumbered.

So? Now what do I do?

Since the pot of money my parents staked me from the sale of Sonny's wouldn't be enough to sustain me in a luxurious fashion for too long, I needed to keep working.

That's the practical end of all of this. The real opportunity, though, isn't the "what," but the "where." My entire life has been spent in one city, and my residence has never extended beyond one single city block, so my plan has been to combine my job with something I've always dreamt of doing: traveling! All I needed to do was decide what sort of work to pursue.

This may defy your preconception of a restaurant cook, but I earned a bachelor's degree in business from a private university (my parents insisted on it) *many* years ago, so I guess I could always try to get a job in an office somewhere, but that would be like training a dog to quack—could be possible, I suppose, but for the love of all that's holy, *why*?

Banker's hours? Sitting behind a desk for eight hours a day? Eating PB&J sandwiches in the office kitchenette? Getting two whole weeks of vacation every year? None of that is really "me."

Oh, sure, I could really go off the reservation and try something totally new and exciting, like being a secret agent or a male model. I'd starve or get murdered at one or both of those careers, though, so that wasn't really in the cards for me, either.

Although I realized long ago, preparing other people's food would never be personally fulfilling, it's what I know, so I decided to continue cooking in family-owned restaurants, just not *my* family's-owned restaurant. Cooking jobs are reasonably plentiful, and that sort of work lends itself perfectly to my real goal: picking up and leaving for the next destination at a moment's notice—untethered and open to anything.

Practically speaking, I'll be more like a retiree than an involuntary victim of unemployment, because I'm choosing my own path, and I don't need much money to do it. Honestly, I don't care about money— never have. I own my car. The sum total of my personal belongings fit in a single, black trash bag, and my housing expectations are limited to "someplace where I can stay dry and hopefully not get murdered."

It may not sound like much, but my life of low expectations is pretty freaking awesome. It doesn't take much to cover my monthly financial "nut," because I don't have one—no house, no spouse, no kids, no pets, not even a goldfish. I can come and go on a whim, and that's exactly what I've done since we handed over the keys from Sonny's.

This is a remarkably liberating way to live. It's the path I've chosen, instead of the path that's been chosen for me, and that's been the best parting gift I could have received from Sonny's.

This past winter, I left Philly—I thought forever—and headed south to get warm. I spent a week or so learning to make she-crab soup in Baltimore, then worked a couple more weeks in a "Hot Chicken" joint in Nashville on my way to selling shave-ice for a few days from a stand on a beach in Florida. I then did the short-order thing in a couple places—a week here, and few days there—as I headed from the east to the west side of the state, until I arrived where I am now, in Louisiana.

This latest stop has been the longest one yet. I've been here a couple months already. Everything is great—except the humidity—but having grown up in Philly, where humidity is as oppressive as it is anywhere, I felt like I was prepared. I was wrong. Louisiana is worse, but I can actually see myself staying here for a while.

I have a job running a boutique kitchen, and a free place to live, complete with a woman who works the same hours as me (evenings) and likes to parade around in front of me bare-assed naked in an apartment *she* pays for. It may not exactly resemble a typical retirement dream, but if I knew a gig like this existed before, I'd have run away from home years ago!

And So It Begins ...

It was the beginning of another shift at the Louisiana restaurant, standing on the line in a shiny stainless steel commercial kitchen with a gigantic exhaust fan sucking out heat and drowning out any hopes for conversation.

The rest of the cooks were all quietly performing their assigned duties.

Waitstaff was milling around, assembling setups—utensils wrapped inside a napkin for quick table setting when the place gets busy later—and making sure salt and pepper shakers were full.

The dishwashing crew was outside grabbing their final smokes before all hell broke loose. Bartenders were running from the pantry through the kitchen en route to the bar with buckets full of ice to be emptied into their sinks so they can stash their mixers and juices there for quick pours. There's no time to make Bloody Mary mix when the orders are stacking up.

The hostess was joyfully humming a tune and placing little vases with fresh-cut flowers at the center of each table. Busboys were polishing utensils and straightening plates and glasses on white-linen-covered tables.

As I had been doing for years, I was preparing my kitchen for dinner with military precision, like I was anticipating a major offensive assault by the enemy. I surveyed the troops and checked all the food prep to be sure we had everything we'd need for the night. I made sure everyone knew their duties so when we got "in the weeds"—the inevitable, crazy-busy rush, for you non-restaurant types—in the heat of the dinner rush, no one would be walking around aimlessly, panicking, looking lost and not pitching in.

Through all of this I could feel my phone vibrating in my pocket. Without looking, I almost knew it was my Uncle Guido calling. I hadn't heard from him since I'd left home months earlier, and certainly didn't expect to hear from him now, but that's where my mind went with the first buzz.

Getting a call from my uncle Guido is like getting a call from the cops at 3AM. The hair on your neck stands straight up and your entire body tightens. I expected him to report one of my elderly parents was sick or dying or dead, so I stepped outside, away from the din of the fan and the bustling kitchen crew and answered the call.

"S'up, Unc?"

"Where you at, kid? We needa talk."

"Isn't that sorta what we're doin' right *now*, G?"

"Not on the phone, smart guy. You need to come home, kid. How quick can you get here?"

"Seriously??? Day or two probably … Why? What's going on? Are Mom and Pop okay? Are Ange and the kids okay?"

"Not on the phone, kid. Come home. Call me when you get here and I'll come to you."

And then he clicked off the line. I tried calling back right away, just in case I'd accidentally dropped the call, but there was no answer, so I stopped calling. A sane person may label that "quitting," but that's not the case when you call my uncle. I was facing facts. G had said all he was going to say over the phone, and no amount of callbacks was going to change that. He'd learned to be cautious over the years, especially as technology improved and surveillance became less of an art and more of a "given."

Because of Uncle Guido's paranoia, no one in my family had a cell phone like a normal person.

Normal people go to a phone store, select a carrier and a contractual plan for calls, texts and data and then pick out the latest cool device and feel like the hottest person in the world until the next newest techno-gee-whiz phone hits the market.

My family uses "burners"—the sort of cheap-assed, flimsy, no-name phones that don't come with a plan, but rather a specific amount of data assigned to them. Once the data are used, the phone gets tossed in the trash and you go get another one. They're the phones you buy off a spinning rack at the gas station, right next to the beef jerky and fried pig skins. Burners are the single-ply, recycled toilet paper of cell phones. Technically, they're phones, but they're only barely functional.

It's not so bad though. I've never had a "smart" phone, so I guess I have no idea what I'm missing, and for that reason, I don't care. I can still call or text the people I want to, but instead of going into a file on my phone to find the names and numbers and addresses of the people in my life, I refer to a little book I carry everywhere, where names are written in pen, but addresses and phone numbers are written in pencil. It's old school, but you know what? It works, and I don't sit in restaurants or in the living room, or walk through town, or stand in line at Wawa staring at my phone like all the rest of you chumps.

There's not enough time here to explain what a "Wawa" is, so suffice to say, it's a Philly-based string of convenience stores and I don't stare at my phone when I'm there buying soda and a hoagie. I'm not about to explain what a hoagie is, either.

I learned at a very young age, when someone like Uncle G is being serious and tells you to do something in no uncertain terms, you get up and you do it—sometimes because you're being summoned, and sometimes because someone is coming for you and you have about eight seconds to get out. So without a second thought, I went back inside, quietly untied my apron, set it down on the stainless steel prep table next to the kitchen door, walked past the gawking waitstaff, dishwashers, hostess and owner. Without making eye contact with anyone, I walked to the parking lot, fired up my car and left. I knew I wouldn't be coming back, and with the exception of some toiletries and a couple pairs of pants I'd pick up on my way out of town, there was nothing in my rearview mirror that mattered to me anyway. It was a nice stopover, but there will be others.

As I've come to learn, quitting without notice wasn't going to scar my resume, either, because I don't have one, and even if I did, these temporary jobs wouldn't be listed on there.

One of the many great things about working for privately owned restaurants is nobody ever fact-checks employment histories—or personal histories, for that matter. The universal assumption is every employee leaves every other restaurant because they ended up getting in a fight with management or a coworker, so whom would anyone call for a reference anyway? Restaurants are high-pressure, emotional powder kegs. Screaming outbursts and fistfights are par for the course. What matters in restaurant interviews is proof you can do the job, and hold up your end when it's busy—possibly even picking up a little more than that when you're in the throes of battle. No one cares about anyone else's past work history, least of all how much notice was given when you left.

As for personal background checks, the pasts of most kitchen workers would scare the shit out of you anyway. Better not to ask.

It took me all of three minutes to collect my belongings from the apartment and throw them into a trash bag. I travel pretty light and learned long ago the key to independence is living lean, owning as few possessions as possible and keeping the list of people in your life to a minimum. That means not putting down roots.

I'd been living with a blond nurse for about two months. Her name's Hannah, but introductions aren't really in order now because I'm leaving. She's a nurse I'd met at the hospital after I cut myself at the restaurant—a more common occurrence than I'd like to admit. She's beautiful—way out of my league. Probably the only reason I had a shot with her was because she's lonely. It turns out, dating a middle-aged cook was better than being alone.

At the hospital we shared a friendly conversation. I mentioned being a cook. She mentioned she was ravenous and couldn't wait for her shift to get done so she could go home and eat. I asked if she had to take care of her family when she got there. She replied she lived alone and, well, one thing led to another and we went back to her place. I made her dinner and have been living with her ever since. She also insists on paying the bills, and who am I to argue?

Don't get me wrong. I can afford my own place. I earn a paycheck, albeit a meager one. I also have a few bucks left over from the sale of Sonny's. I'm just really frugal. Restaurant people tend to be like that. I also don't really feel like committing to a lease term. It impedes my ability to grab my shit and run when the spirit moves me.

Come to think of it, I've never actually paid for a place to live in my life. I lived for free with my parents as a kid, of course, and then I lived for free in the apartment above Sonny's ever since. Once Sonny's sold, I lived in my car, or on the sofa of some kind soul, or I spent the night with someone I met at the restaurant or someplace after hours—sometimes a coworker, sometimes a customer, and sometimes a stranger. I've been pretty nomadic, like I've been paroled from house arrest in South Philly.

In this case, Hannah insists on paying the bills because it's her place and she doesn't want to blur any lines. In return, I pay whenever we go anywhere, or order takeout. I'd like to believe it all evens out.

She's been wonderful, and I hate to leave without saying goodbye, but like I said, when Guido calls and says get out, there's a reason, so I'm gone. Besides, it's not like she and I were destined to be soul mates or anything. Still, I owe her an explanation. I'll call her on my way to Philly, and hopefully keep the door cracked open so I can come by if I'm ever in town again. For now, though, I left a note on the kitchen table. It just said "sorry" with my name signed below it.

A Time to Think

Although most of what I own can be stored in a Hefty bag, that bag has to go somewhere, and for me, that's into my lone prized possession: my car. After my parents cashed out the family restaurant, they gave some of the proceeds to my sister and me. She's practical and paid down the mortgage on her house in the 'burbs. I'm not practical. I bought a '70 Dodge Challenger and put the rest in the bank.

I could have afforded something new and eye-popping, but that's not what I wanted. I wanted this, a burnt-orange coupe with tinted windows, nice rims and aggressive rubber. For what it is, it's understated—not full of stripes or ridiculous wings or body scoops, or anything. It almost looks stock, but it sits a little lower and it sounds like the apocalypse—in a good way.

This was my ticket to anywhere in the continental US, and I wanted to travel in style. The paint's clean. The interior is pristine and comfortable. The original engine was swapped out for something much bigger and louder than stock. The exhaust is loud. The transmission is manual, and although it has a radio, it's rarely on because the melody coming from under the hood and through the pipes is all I want to hear. It's fast, handles okay and basically makes me feel like something special when I'm behind the wheel.

Most guys my age will show you photos of their kids or their dog when you meet them. I'll show you a picture of my car.

Most people probably dread driving twelve hundred miles, especially on the spur of the moment, but honestly, the call from Unc gave me an excuse to go for a drive instead of working the line. I was getting stale there, anyway.

Except for getting gas, drinks and food—and occasionally draining my bladder—I intended to drive straight through to Philly. When I got there, I'd probably be a little sorry because the trip would be over. Sometimes, in my heart, I wonder if I'm part gypsy.

Like I said, it wasn't always this way.

Not so long ago, I barely left my old neighborhood. The extent of my travels back then was back and forth from home to work—and I lived upstairs from the restaurant, in my grandparents' old apartment.

I'd get up, go down to Sonny's, work in the kitchen or behind the bar and then go home, upstairs. My commute was a flight of stairs, and I'd repeat that routine for weeks at a time. On my free time, I'd hang out with friends at a club in town, or at another restaurant, or at someone's house, but wherever we went, it was always either within walking distance, or accessible by train or bus.

None of us ever had a car. Very few of us even had driver's licenses. Who needed them? If it was too cold to walk, we'd take a bus. If the weather was too bad for the bus, why the hell were we going out anyways? I lived on top of a bar, for Christ's sake!

Back then, I'd dream of traveling, seeing the country and maybe the world, settling into a town for a week or a month or six and then getting up and going to the next place. As a cook, I knew I could find work wherever I ended up, so I never worried about earning a living. Traveling was just a dream, though, because Sonny's held me in place.

As long as we owned the restaurant, I stayed in the neighborhood, which may sound like torture to someone with an overgrown ambition, but I liked it. It was uncomplicated. I knew my path and I enjoyed it.

The key to life since I was a kid has been simplicity, and to this day, the "KISS method" (Keep It Simple Stupid) is my motto.

Growing up how and where I did, I learned a few things, and some of it was practical. There was no room in our little South Philly row house for trinkets, so we placed little value on extraneous stuff. In my travels, I've met people with big homes full of possessions, garages full of cars and closets full of outfits for every occasion, even if there's no chance that occasion will ever happen. It's all wasteful, and waste was a cardinal sin to a family who owned a restaurant, where margins were small. The goal was to sell inventory and never throw anything out.

Managing inventory is an art form that serves me in all aspects of my life—in a restaurant, in my home and with people. I don't keep fringe people or acquaintances in my life any more than I store keepsakes on my shelves. If they're not family, they'd better be damned close to it. I have a finite amount of time to share, so I focus on those who are important to me and don't waste my time engaging with others just so they can like me. I don't give a shit what strangers, or quasi strangers, think of me. What they think is their problem, not mine, but I care deeply what my family or close friends think. They matter, and I treat them accordingly. Again, probably something Uncle G taught me.

You've probably heard the phrase "Keep your friends close and your enemies closer." Well, forget you ever heard that, because it's crap. We keep our friends and family close, in a manageable cluster so we can protect them and be protected *by* them. Enemies? Fuck those guys. Life's too short for guile. If your enemies won't go away on their own, then you and yours need to give them however big a push they need to change their minds. Address things head-on.

I learned all that growing up in South Philly, not just from Uncle G, although he certainly reinforced it every time he saw me.

Where I grew up, nearly everyone was Italian, which means nearly everyone had a temper. Nearly everyone was passionate. Nearly everyone spoke loudly, and virtually no one was subtle. There was very little guile where I grew up. If someone was pissing you off, you didn't tippy-toe around and conspire and create subterfuge to deal with it. You stood up and addressed it directly, often by screaming, hollering, pushing and sometimes punching.

The same goes the other way around. If you planned to piss someone off, you did it to their face, and you wasted no time doing so.

Sometimes the fight was just a flash event, and after the fireworks, everyone got over it—but not usually. Italians, at least the ones I know, aren't famous for their forgiveness. We have memories like elephants, and we exact revenge. Fuck with me? You'd better kill me, because if you don't, the fight's not over, and given the chance *I* will end it. And it's not "an eye for an eye" either. You take an eye, I take your whole face. You punch me, I'll stab you. You stab me, I'll shoot you. You shoot me, I'll blow your ass up.

That's how it was where I grew up, and you know what? It worked. It kept the fighting down because we all knew consequences were often worse than the joy of a little victory. You might lose your temper, but before you step over that line you'd better use your head, because you can't take certain things back. Long, drawn out battles are exhausting and sometimes fatal.

This all played in my head as I drove into the night, heading north, heading home. If I stayed on the gas and didn't sleep, I'd get back in town in about a day—less if I was able to push my speed a little, more if the weather didn't cooperate.

The Long Drive Home

After about seventeen hours of hard driving, I caught my first glimpse of my city's skyline, heading east on the Schuylkill Expressway.

For those of you who aren't from around here, that word is pronounced "school-kill," but the highway is so twisty and treacherous, over the years it's earned the nickname "sure-kill." Everyone and everything around here gets a nickname.

Anyway, Schuylkill's a Dutch word and is the name of the river that runs east into the city. The expressway follows alongside the river. You'll hear more about the river later too.

As I drove along my own personal memory lane, I knew I was about twenty minutes out. I grabbed my phone off the passenger seat and dialed Uncle G.

He didn't say hello. He wasn't much of one for chitchat.

"You here?"

"Yup. Where'm I meeting you?"

"Same place everyone else goes when they know." G was always afraid someone else was listening on a phone line, so he kept things cryptic.

"Got it. See you there in a few. And thanks. That place's old jingle is going to be in my head for the rest of the day."

"You're welcome" he responded sarcastically, and then of course hung up.

Back when dinosaurs roamed the earth and compact cars were the size of today's SUVs, the Melrose Ponderosa Diner had a radio jingle. "Everybody who knows goes to Melrose" was the tag line.

I guess you had to be there.

Uncle Guido wanted me to meet him there, a diner near the old neighborhood. I remember sitting there many nights after "last call," inebriated enough to eat a couple slices of their famous cheesecake, but not shit-faced enough to fall asleep facedown in it. We'd all crowd into its booths, ordering coffee and cheesecake and club sandwiches and gravy-fries. We were boisterous, but never rude. After all, Melrose was family-owned, too (by Germans, of all things), and the people who worked there had worked there for decades and were our neighbors and friends. There would be consequences if we got out of line, and not by the cops, but by our community.

Invariably, at some point during the sobering-up process, before we called it a night, someone would say something profound, like "If the Melrose is 24/7 and it's been open for decades, why do they have locks on their doors?" and we'd think about that for a second, then bust out laughing and start settling the tab because we'd realize our brains were exhausted and needed sleep.

I pulled the Challenger into a spot at the front of the diner, next to Guido's black Cadillac sedan and went in. He was already seated at a booth along the window when I walked in. I sat across from him, reached for a menu and he started right in on me.

It's Never Just Coffee with This Guy

"Listen, kid."

He always called me "kid." Even though I'm in my 50s and he's only a couple decades ahead of me, I'm still "kid," and that's fine. I call him Uncle Guido, and he's not really my uncle, so I guess that makes us even, calling each other the wrong name.

"Have you spoken to your parents lately?"

Like thousands of fellow Philadelphians, as I mentioned, I spent a lot of late nights in this diner in my 20s and 30s. I could almost feel the ghosts of my youth lingering around every un-changed corner of the place as I sat across from Uncle G, nursing our bottomless cups of coffee. I was playing with the sugar dispenser, gently swirling it around on its glass base in slow circles with one finger on its top, trying to keep it from tipping over and consequently dumping sugar everywhere.

"KID!" Guido said abruptly, as he grabbed the sugar jar from under my finger and set it down loudly away from me. "Stop playing already. Are you listening to me? Have you spoken to your parents lately?!"

"Unc, I been drivin' for the past day-and-a-half, and I'm a little tired. During that span of time, I have consumed nothing but caffeinated beverages, not even food. My attention span isn't so great on a good day. Forgive me if it sucks even worse when I'm sleep-deprived, hungry and hopped-up on caffeine. And yeah, I've talked to my parents. What sort of son would I be?!"

"What have they told you?"

"Nothin' out of the ordinary. They're watching game shows on TV. They had dinner with Ange and the kids. You know, the usual."

"Did you speak to your mom, or your dad?"

"Both. You know how they are. Every time I call it's a big frickin' event I guess, so they put me on speaker. There's no talkin' to one w'out the other."

"So you haven't spoken to your mom alone?"

"Why would I wanna do that?!" I guess I said it a little too derogatorily, because G, who was leaning forward, slumped over his coffee cup, raised his eyes, but not his head, to glare at me with his patented "you watch your ass" expression in his eyes.

Uncle G and I always looked at my mom a little differently. I always figured he had a crush on her since before she married my dad, and he'd stuck around ever since to remain close to her. And it wasn't some weird "waiting in the wings" sort of thing. He liked and respected my dad. Everyone did.

I guess he figured, even if he couldn't have mom for himself, he'd still be around her and watch out for her and her interests. For sixty-five years, he occupied the same booth every night in Sonny's, the one right next to the hostess podium where Mom stood a couple feet away. No one else ever sat there, even if it was empty and the rest of the place was packed. Even when there was a wait for tables, that one stayed empty.

Mom worked the front of the house, meaning she was the hostess and supervised the waiters and waitresses. They didn't need much supervision since most of them were with us since Jesus walked with the dinosaurs. Her job was really to be the pretty face greeting the patrons, welcoming them into our restaurant with her infectious personality, and then seating them. She'd check on them while they ate to let them know if they needed anything, she was the owner and she'd make it happen, and then when they left, she'd urge them to return soon. Most people did. Customers fell in love with my mom, when she was young and pretty, when she was a middle-aged mom, and when she was a cute, sweet little old lady. To everyone who walked through the front door, there were three reasons to come to Sonny's: the food was consistently delicious, you got a lot for your money, and Toni (my mom) welcomed you home.

She was born and raised a couple blocks from Sonny's—the oldest of three. Her younger sister and brother were a couple years each younger than her. It was a normal Depression-era family until the War came along. Her father, not to be confused with Al, went to fight. He lost, leaving my grandmother with three young kids, no husband, and no money. In typical Italian fashion, she was too proud to accept monetary charity, but she'd accept gifts. When my mom would go to the grocer, for example, there would always be an extra bag for her to take home with "essentials."

"This is for your mom, Toni." The grocer would say matter-of-factly. No one made a big fuss, everyone looked after one another. This was even more the case if someone's husband was lost while in the service of the U.S. Italians considered defending our adopted country to be a great honor. When someone falls doing so, everyone else rallies around his family—forever.

There was a lot of that going on back then in that part of town because a lot of local boys didn't come home.

My dad's family helped too. Every week, my dad would go to my mom's apartment and formally invite her mom and family to dinner that night, as my grandparents' guests. Every week—every single week—for *years* he did that. It started when Dad was 10.

For the first few weeks or months, my mom would just answer the door, see my dad and walk away, yelling to her mom that "that boy" was there for her. Mom was only a year older than Dad, so she didn't see him as anything more than the boy down the street who comes by every week to talk to her mom.

After a while, they'd linger and pass time at the door talking to one another until my grandmother made it to the door. It wasn't any sort of "Hey, baby, you look gooood," kinda thing, either. It was two neighborhood kids passing the time, talking about a kid at school, or just grunting questions and answers back and forth.

It went from there to a couple years down the road when they'd hold one another's gaze a little longer than necessary when Dad would bring water or bread to the dinner table at his dad's restaurant. When they were in their mid-teens, they'd start to sneak off together on innocent dates.

My grandmother sternly forbade my mother from dating my father. In an exhibition of laughable elitism, she could not tolerate her daughter dating anyone who worked in a bar, even though his family owned the place. My father and his saint parents were good enough to provide my grandmother with hundreds, if not thousands of meals as gifts, but they weren't good enough for her daughter. Even as I got older, I recall my mom's mother asking my mother why she didn't hold out for some millionaire instead of settling for my father.

As you might imagine, blue-collar South Philly was absolutely *littered* with eligible millionaires back in the early 1950s, so she had a point. (By the way, for those of you not familiar with South Philly's local art form, that last sentence was an example of sarcasm.) Every time my grandmother would ask that question, I'd come to my dad's defense with some quip like "Knew a lot of millionaires back then, did you Mom-Mom?" or "What, my dad's not good enough for you?" My dad would say something like, "Watch your tone with your grandmother," and then wink and smile at me.

I guess my grandmother had high expectations for my mom, as delusional as they may have been, because of how my mom looked. Imagine a five-foot-tall version of Anne Bancroft. At the risk of sounding like Oedipus, my mom was smokin' hot. She was *way* out of my dad's league, and if he didn't already have a casual friendship established with her since she was a young kid, he'd have probably never gotten a second look from her.

Don't get me wrong, my dad's not a bad lookin' guy. Mom always said he reminded her of Gregory Peck, but she was probably wearing her version of rose-colored glasses when she said it. He was perfectly okay, but she was downright blessed.

Uncle G always knew it too. He came along after dad got drafted into the army. Even if no one else would have given him any shit for it—and trust me, they would have, Unc could never have brought himself to steal a girl out from under a soldier who was on duty overseas. No way.

Unfortunately for him, that was his only chance, because between the letter-writing campaign and the photos they sent to one another while Pop was in the service, Mom was locked-in. She just waited for him to return home so she could marry his ass, and that's pretty much exactly what happened.

After honeymooning in Williamsburg where they spent the sum total of $100 for a week's vacation (one of my mom's favorite stories)—did I mention my family's cheap?—my mom immediately moved in with her new in-laws in the apartment above Sonny's and took a job at the hostess podium. This would be the first and last work location she ever had.

When Dad left the army, he started tending bar at Sonny's while *his* dad ran the kitchen and his mom ran the business. In time, Mom's conversation with patrons would go from showing off her shiny wedding ring and talking about being newly married, to being pregnant a couple times and people asking her to sit down when she'd visit their table to "take a load off her feet," to carrying us as infants while she seated people, to excusing our behavior as we ran through the aisles of the dining room, to calling us out from the kitchen when we were working to show everyone how much we'd grown, to bragging over pictures of her grandkids.

Mom had a natural ability to make everyone who came through the doors feel like family, and Uncle G lived vicariously through every act of the play.

And that's just what it was—a play.

Mom was not the same person behind the scenes that she was in front of the customers. She was acting for their benefit.

Away from customers, she was a strict taskmaster. There's no arguing the fact that she was passionate about her family. She loved her husband and kids and protected us all like a lioness would her cubs. She was tough. She'd go toe-to-toe with anyone who messed with her, but she'd go *after* anyone who messed with her family. I always respected her for that.

Unfortunately, with all her passion came a hot temper that occasionally resulted in me getting my ass beaten. She was proud of her methods for achieving conformity, to the point she would display a broken wooden spoon to visitors, happily regaling them with the story of how she broke it on my rear end. Much like a deer mounted over the fireplace, I was far less enthusiastic about my hunter's methods.

She didn't rely exclusively on corporal punishment to keep us kids grounded, either. Her words got the job done quite well on their own.

I knew Jewish kids whose moms had freaking blinders on. Those kids would strike out ten times in a row in little league and their moms would say how nice their swings were, or how good they looked in their batting helmets. Always building them up.

Not Toni. She was like a human wrecking ball, smashing egos in her path. Any time we did something good and felt the slightest sense of self-confidence, she'd say her famous line: "They can replace a President in an hour and a Pope in a week. Get over yourself. You're not that big a deal!"

She could be brutal, but the public would never see that side of her. She was effervescent when she was on display. Total strangers would laugh and call her "Bubbles." That's how Uncle G saw her. I think that's how Dad saw her too.

"Sorry, Unc. No. I never speak with her privately."

"Probably wouldn't do any good, anyway. She wouldn't tell you what's going on."

"What *is* going on, G? What the hell is going on?!"

"Those motherfuckers robbed them blind. That's what's wrong. Your parents are broke. They got nothin'. They lost their business. They lost the building and everything in it. They lost their identities. They lost their purpose. They lost everything. They have the clothes on their backs, and their little row home and that's it."

I was shocked. It was like he threw a cup of hot coffee in my face.

"How's that even possible?" I asked dumbfounded. "A couple months ago, they had millions!"

"No. They *never* had millions. They had the *promise* of millions—big difference."

"What's that supposed to mean? They had the business and the building, and they sold both for millions. What am I missing here? Did they get crushed with taxes or something?"

"No. The sale was a scam."

"Come again?" I said, this time leaning my ear toward Uncle G with my eyebrows raised like someone just said something and you know you heard it wrong.

"You heard me. A scam. The deal was structured to pay three hundred grand up front and the balance over a year in equal payments of one hundred and fifty grand per month."

"Right. I know all that. They gave me and Ange most of the three hundred they received up-front."

"Yeah. Turns out that's all they received."

"What? … Okay. Slow this down for me. Tell me what happened?"

"Absolutely nothing."

"Well, correct me if I'm wrong, but that just turns into a collections deal then, right? Isn't that kinda your bailiwick?"

"Not sure I like how you said that, kid."

"No disrespect, Unc, but this doesn't sound like that big a deal. You've been getting people to live up to the terms of agreements for … forever. What am I missing here?"

"There's no one to collect from."

"'scuse me?!"

"You heard me. There's no one to collect from. The buyer was a corporation and we can't find anyone behind it."

"And by 'we' you mean???"

"Me and Joe Acchione."

"Oh Christ. That geezer lawyer? No wonder you're running in quicksand. Finding the owners of the corporation probably requires using things like the internet … or a telephone, and Mr. Acchione? He's a sweet guy and all, but he's probably chiseling messages on clay tablets somewhere. Christ. Dude's in his 90s!"

"Hey! Show a little respect."

"I'm just sayin', call Ange or Tom, especially Tom. He can use his big center city firm's well-oiled research machine to find it. I'm sure he'll get answers."

"You're sure, huh? Well, it's a good thing I brought you up here to provide such tremendous insight. Where would we be without your strategic genius? Do you seriously think we didn't call Angela and her husband right outta the gate? I'm telling you, kid. There's nothing there."

"So that just means there's no one to stop us from taking it back. We walk in, take back the keys, kick their people out and take the thing back over. Let them come after us in court. Then they'll show themselves and we'll be able to sue them for the balance of what they owe."

"You've been locked in a kitchen too long."

"What?! They haven't paid what's due, so we should get the place back, right?"

"Theoretically, yes, but there's a little difference between theory and practice, or didn't they teach you that in business school? We signed over the deed, numbnuts. Fair or not, we have no legal claim to the premises or its contents."

"Fine. There's a legal process. I get it. Then let's go that route. We sue them and attach their income. We serve a subpoena to someone at the restaurant and they give it to whoever in their organization should deal with it. Put the onus on them. Then we sue for breach of contract, get the restaurant back and, in the meantime, garnish their revenue. There. See? Business school at work, motherfucker."

"Gee, again, I wish our *lawyers* and I had thought of that. Oh yeah. We had, and it won't work."

"Why not? You go in when they're open for business and either leave a subpoena with the hostess or the acting manager. What's so difficult about that?"

"There's another ripple."

"… ripple?"

"Yeah. That plan of yours only works if they're open for business. They're not."

"What do you mean? They bought the business, a *thriving* business. That's where all the value was. I'm confused."

"A condition you're no doubt very comfortable with. The last day your parents operated Sonny's was the last day Sonny's operated.

Immediately after the sale, the big neon sign out front was turned off. The door was locked and that was it. It's been sitting there, dark and rotting ever since."

The shock of this wasn't sinking in. The magnitude of that restaurant closing was impossible for me to fathom. Every single day of my life … *every single day* … the 20-foot-long, neon "Sonny's" sign out front blazed as a beacon for our business. The place was named after my Pop. Shutting down that light is like turning off the light on my family, on my Pop.

Uncle G broke the silence.

"I'm sorry, kid. I get it. That's why I brought you up here. Your parents are crushed too. We all are. It's not the money, although they could certainly use it. It's the fact your family business has been scuttled. Everything of value to your family—the intangibles of their business, all the photos and fixtures, all the memories. It's all been shut down as if it never existed."

"We need to get that place back, G. We need to get it back now. This isn't right. They stiff us on the sale and then they shut down the business? What the hell are they trying to do? I mean, even though they're not paying us the two mill' they owe us, they're still three hundred grand deep into it. I mean, if they were going to scam us, why would they throw away that much cash? There must be a plan, right? The longer that place stays closed, the harder it'll be for us to resurrect it."

"You're askin' the right questions, kid, but that doesn't mean we have answers. There's an old saying: To find the answers, you have to peel the onion—meaning you keep going down layer after layer until you hit the truth. Well, every time we try to peel this onion, the onion gets bigger."

He stopped for that to sink in, and then he continued.

"If you think like a typical operator, they should be rushing to get the place reopened, but instead it's just sitting, decaying. The by-product of that is the neighbors are starting to get upset with your parents for letting the place fall into disrepair. Nobody knows the circumstances—just that your parents shut down one day and never reopened. We tell people there's a new owner, but they don't care. They all see the tenuous nature of the neighborhood tipping the wrong way with one more business shut down and becoming an eyesore. Right or wrong, they're blaming your parents to the point your mother and father rarely leave their house."

I sat there and shook my head in frustration, gasping "what the fuck" over and over again. "Is it a real estate play where someone's trying to blight the place before buying up the neighboring buildings at a deep discount?"

"Down here? There's no money to be made from a redevelopment down here, John. Good people are *fleeing* this area, not coming in. It's old-timers like your parents hanging on by their fingernails who are holding the place together, and now your parents are out of the picture. This place is decades away from urban renewal kid. *Decades.*"

"So what, then? They threw three hundred grand into a big hole and walked away?"

"That's what's happened. That's why we need to start peeling that onion."

... AND???

He finished his story and then abruptly stopped. He didn't say another word. There really wasn't anything *to* say.

I sat there, numb. I blinked hard and opened my eyes as wide as they could get, as if I thought somehow more light would enter my mind and I'd see things more clearly. It didn't, and I didn't.

This was the sort of news that scorched your mind like napalm. How could we have all been this collectively stupid? How did we not see this coming? How? WHY?! What the fuck?!

After sitting in silence for what seemed like an hour—but was probably only a minute—I started in with "I shoulda ..."

But G interrupted me right away: "—no way you could've done anything, kid. Don't blame yourself. The worst thing any of us can do is blame ourselves, so stop that right now. We didn't do this. Those fuckers did this. The blame's all on them. Let's keep it there. The most important thing right now is to control ourselves, remain a united front, and not react. They're not goin' nowhere, and neither are we. Let's catch our breath. Putting our heads together is how we're going to hit back."

"How can you be so sure they're not gone already?"

"Trust me, okay? I've been around the block once or twice. Besides, they've been removing stuff from the restaurant."

"Stuff? What stuff?"

"From what I can see? Everything—valuable or otherwise."

"We need to stop them. Otherwise, the place'll be empty by the time we get it back. We need to get in there now and stop them. They didn't pay us for it, so we should get it back!"

"There's nothing *to* get back. Anything of value has been stripped, removed and destroyed already. It's dispersed all over the place. You'll never find it. All that's left is the shit that wasn't worth nothin', and they've been bustin' that up for fun."

"Then we kick their asses! They might get us, but we'll get more of them!"

"You won't get the right guy. Oh, you'll get *a* guy, but not the right guy. You don't get revenge by hitting the wrong people. You want to hit them? Find out who the right guy is and hit *him*."

"Who's the right guy?"

"Damned if I know. Have you heard nothing during our conversation? We're checkin', but nothin's turned up yet. It's not just one guy. I can tell you that. These fucks are organized—structured. Strings are being pulled from somewhere else, but we don't know from where yet."

"FUCK! … then I want what they promised us, what they owe us. I want the money … and *then* some. "

A smile slowly crept across his old face, and a lightbulb grew brighter behind his eyes. "Now you're thinkin', kid. Hit 'em where it hurts. That's how we'll get to the architects of this nightmare. We'll flush 'em out, but for now, we don't know shit, so we all need to stay cool and be patient. It doesn't seem like money is their trigger anyway, so we need to find out what is."

"You summoned me up here in a rush so you could tell me to be patient?" I'd hit a nerve. Until this moment, he'd been classic Guido—quiet, measured voice, as if his blood pressure never got above 65. Now, his voice escalated and he started talking more and more quickly. "I *summoned* you, as you said, to get you in the loop as soon as possible, out of *respect*. I *summoned* you up here hoping you can look after your parents and maybe help them maintain their sanity, which—as you might guess—is under tremendous strain right now. I *summoned* you here to be an *adult*—to be a man and help me hold *your* family together—including your sister, who is also an absolute mess. I *summoned* you here to give you a chance to partner with me to get a little justice and maybe, along the way, get your parents a little bit of what they were promised and what they've earned. Is that *okay* with you?!"

It was time for me to backpedal.

" … sorry. I'm pissed and I spoke out of turn, Uncle G. Thank you for reaching out to me and getting me involved, sincerely."

I suspected his reaction was more theater than anything else, but we needed each other. I had a role to play, so I got back in line.

I'd pissed off the most powerful ally we had. I had to suck it up quickly or I was going to be excluded from what he had planned, and I did *not* want to miss out on this. I owed these motherfuckers some sort of beating, and Guido was my best hope to deliver it.

"S'all right, kid. I'm fucking pissed too. I don't like it when my family and friends are targeted, especially in my neighborhood, right under my fucking nose."

And then a little nugget of truth popped out when his defenses came down. "I have my own reasons for getting to the bottom of this, and quickly. Where are you stayin' while you're in town?"

… oops.

"I hadn't really thought about it. I guess with my folks, although I haven't even checked in with them yet. You got any room at your place?"

"No, and *HELL* no. 'No,' don't go see your parents, and 'hell no,' you're sure as shit not stayin' with me. I need you to stay at your sister's place, out of plain sight. She's fully aware of what's going on, and she's expecting you. Everyone's pride's hurt right now, Johnny. Be patient. We'll all get together tomorrow to start figuring things out. For now, don't make trouble. Stay away from Sonny's. Capisce?!"

"—capisce." He probably knew more than he was letting on, or possibly less. Guys like G? They're always working some angle, and he's been doing it forever. I didn't doubt his sincerity about wanting to help me and my family. I never questioned his affection for us, but at the same time, I never once believed he'd shared the whole story with me—at least not yet. He was keeping parts to himself for some reason. I just didn't know what those other parts were … yet.

So, I changed topics. "You paying for coffee?"

I knew he'd just get up and leave at that point and stick me with the tab. That's one of his quirky things. He never pays for anything. I don't think he paid for a meal at my parents' place ever—not directly, at least. He always tipped his waiter or waitress, and then he'd slip money to my mom on the sly on the way out the door (always more than the cost of his meal), but he never got a dinner check, and he never paid face value for the meal.

Uncle G was closing in on eighty, but if you didn't know him, you'd swear he was sixty. He was tall—easily my height, but he seemed bigger. He was built like an athlete, but not one of those guys who spent half their life in a gym bulking up. He was one of those broad-shouldered guys who was naturally strong. He couldn't be bothered sculpting six-pack abs, but he didn't have any fat around his middle either. He was also a roll-up-the-sleeves guy whose collar was never buttoned, whose tie was never pushed all the way up, whose sport jacket always looked a little tilted to one side, and whose shoes were always scuffed. Why? Because he was a doer. He walked everywhere—several miles every day—and always in a sport jacket and dress shoes. He probably wore out a pair of dress shoes every week. He was always moving at a near-trot, and he never relaxed.

He was like a human version of a bull—even to the point he'd lean over whenever he sat down like he was about to launch himself across the room—and he breathed in and out loudly, closed mouthed, like he was chronically angry.

People would ask us why he was angry, and we'd tell them he's not. He's just intense. We let them know: when he's angry, they'll notice the difference.

Imagine a pissed off grizzly bear, and that's Uncle G when he's on the warpath. He's always surrounded by bodyguards who all look like the Incredible Hulk with a more natural skin tone, and they are all, to a man, *terrified* of G. Even at eighty, if you saw this man suddenly spring up out of his chair, you'd curl up in a ball and shit yourself.

Some guys put on airs to try to be intimidating. Guido's mere existence is intimidating.

The shit I say to him? It would get other guys killed. Literally. I get away with it because we're about as close to family as two people can be without having a genetic connection. When I give him a hard time, his cadre of gorillas look at me wide-eyed. They'd *never* risk saying such things.

Guido also never had a problem attracting women. He's never been shy about enjoying their company, but he never married and he never had children of his own. Our family was all the family he seemed to desire, and in his world, I doubt there'd have been enough room for his business and a family. I also don't think he'd give his enemies that ammunition to hurt him. For guys like Guido, families are a liability. They're a weakness to be exploited, and he was shrewd enough to limit such exposure. My family made him vulnerable enough, and he knew it. He always assumed someone would come at him through us. He was probably thinking that's what's going on now.

Oh, and although he was *clearly* from southern Italy, with the thick head of black hair and the dark olive skin. His eyes were so blue, you'd think Sinatra's were brown. When he glared at a man, that man would turn to stone, but when he'd gaze upon a woman, she'd melt into a puddle. He was a man's man, and not in some pathetic, misogynistic way. He stood up and attacked life head-on, and when it punched him in the face, he kicked it in the balls.

He wasn't a boss, by the popular definition. The newspapers never knew he existed, but everyone knew him. He was like a corporate vice president who everyone wanted working for them. Because they clung to the idea of him possibly joining them someday. Each captain in town gave him the authority to run his own game, unimpeded. He outlasted family after family and always maintained the loyalty of his crew. He rarely got involved in plotting schemes and never went for power grabs—or aligned with ladder-climbers—because he always had his eyes on the long play. The lower profile he kept, the longer he could linger.

He just maintained order in his little corner of the world, and everyone respected him—stay in line and the world can spin in peaceful little grooves; step out of line and you're escorted out of the game. It was really that simple.

And don't think of him as some bully mobster who smeared the blood of his enemies all over town and would one day meet a similar fate. He ran in some pretty tough circles, of course, so he surrounded himself with muscle accordingly, but he was a diplomat, a businessman, and a chess player. He was smart and strategic and avoided wrestling in the mud with pigs, but if he had to do it, he would—and the next day, there would be bacon for breakfast.

He had a pocketful of loyal confederates who worked *with* him more than *for* him but make no mistake: if his authority ever came into question, he'd clarify the situation quickly. Quiet, powerful confidence would define his entire life—rarely raising his voice because he rarely had to.

None of us ever really knew how far his authority stretched, or who was under his umbrella, but we could all attest that it was rare when anything bad happened in our neighborhood—and when it did, it didn't happen twice.

20 Hours of Driving? Why Stop Now?

My sister Angela didn't live too far, but she wasn't exactly close either. She was out in the dreaded suburbs, where men spend weekends cutting grass and pruning trees, and you have to drive a car to get anywhere. No one walks in the 'burbs.

It took about a half hour, door-to-door, to get there at this time of night. Once I got there, I coasted, trying not to give the big HEMI under the hood too much gas. This motor was loud enough to shake windows and wake the neighbors, especially out here in the silent suburbs. If my sister didn't live here, I'd revel in being that sort of "shit disturber"; since she'll be here long after I leave, though, I didn't want to create any lingering issues for her.

It was getting late, and all the homes along the tree-lined streets were dark—all except my sister's. Hers was lit up like an airport runway so I could find her, which was very helpful. The houses out here were huge compared to where we grew up, but they were all "cookie cutter." The only way to tell one from the next was the color of the vinyl siding, or by a particular tree or shrub in the front lawn. It's tough to discern house color or landscape nuances in the dark, so I relied on Ange to turn her house into the equivalent of a lighthouse beacon so I could find my way.

The architectural sameness didn't seem to matter to Ange. She loved it out here. She always raved about how good the schools were, how close shopping was, and how peaceful it was to sit on her back patio and have a cup of coffee—even though, knowing my sister, she probably spent fifty grand putting the patio and landscaping in but only sat out there twice since she moved in. Like me and my mom, Ange lived her life like a shark—never stopping or she might drown. She never sat down and she never relaxed. She was a loud, frenetic, fast-talking, dark-haired knockout who took command of every room she ever walked into, no matter if she knew everyone or no one in it.

You can take the girl out of South Philly, but …

She met me at the front door, still wearing office attire except for the tea towel over her shoulder and fuzzy slippers on her feet. She jumped up on me, wrapped her arms around my neck and her legs around my waist. She slammed a huge loud kiss on my lips, but I playfully ignored the attack and kept walking into the house, one hundred pounds heavier than I'd been two steps earlier and nonchalantly acting like I didn't have a five-foot-tall Italian stuck to my torso.

That's the game we'd been playing since we were toddlers, and it never got old.

She just kept playfully kissing my cheeks and my forehead until we got inside. Then, all hell really broke loose. When I crossed the threshold, her two little urchins grabbed onto my legs like humping poodles. Now I had my sister up top, and her two monkeys dragging me down from below as I kept going through the foyer, trying not to lose my balance along the way to the kitchen. My brother-in-law was seated at the kitchen table, tapping away on his computer and nursing a beer. He barely looked up.

"You wanna get in on this, Tom? I think there's an open spot on my back for you," I said to him.

"I think I'll pass for now, Johnny. Beer?"

"Sounds like a plan." And with that, Ange hopped off and I bent over to bear-hug the tykes.

"I'll make you a sandwich to go with that beer. Meatballs on Sarcone's?"

"I'd fucking kill for one of those right about now." Sarcone's is an Italian bakery in town with the best bread in the universe. No shit. French bakers would commit suicide if they tasted this vastly superior product.

"JOHN! Little ears!"

"Oh, shit. Sorry."

"JOHNNY!"

"… ugh. Sorry?"

The kids were laughing like hearing those words was the funniest things they'd ever heard. Between the utterances of their uncouth uncle and getting tickled mercilessly by hands as big as their chests, they both flopped around on their backs on the kitchen floor like spastic turtles on laughing gas.

Their infectious hysterics and squealing were intoxicating, and in what seemed like an instant, Ange had placed a sandwich-laden plate on the table with a heavy thud, along with a very cold bottle of Yuengling. As is often the case with little kids, especially when it's so close to bedtime, my momentarily taking my eyes off them to spot my snack resulted in the oldest, Joey, bonking his head on the tile floor and immediately reverting from hysterical laughter to equally hysterical tears.

Ange helped Joey up and guided him and the baby toward bed (we called him the baby, even though he was three), and instructed them to say good night to Uncle Johnny and Daddy as she never broke stride taking them upstairs to their room. In this five-bedroom monster of a house, the two boys still shared a bedroom.

You can take the girl outta South Philly …

FOOD!

In many cases, even if the first taste of something is so delicious it defies description, each subsequent taste pales slightly to the last, diminishing the euphoric sensation a little more and a little more until some point on that tasting continuum where the next bite will actually be revolting. That point may be a billion bites after the first, but that point on the continuum exists nonetheless and there's a gradual decline to it. I raise this point so you can appreciate the spectacle of eating my sister's meatballs and gravy.

My sister's meatballs and homemade gravy (and yes, we call it *gravy*)—especially when they're nestled in a sesame seed encrusted Sarcone's roll—don't merely fly in the face of this theory of diminishing returns, they spit ragu in its face. Every bite of that sandwich is a "Holy shit, this is the best thing I've ever eaten in my life" moment. Each subsequent bite is as euphoria-inducing as the last, possibly even more so because now you're anticipating that wonderfulness and you're salivating like Pavlov's dog at the promise of a meat pellet.

I'm not the suicidal type, but when I finished that sandwich, I understood the urge driving other human beings to end it. It's like all meaning and purpose have evaporated and you're left with a hole in your soul and an empty plate. Of course, I don't need to kill myself. I can just go and make myself another sandwich, which is exactly what I did.

Her recipes aren't secret, nor are they her own. They're the same ones my family refined for generations. There are multiple reasons our restaurant stayed in business for 75 years. The prices were good—and the service was attentive and friendly—but it was the food. The food was absolutely amazing.

By this point, I'd also given my brother-in-law my beer because I actually don't drink. It's not a moral or compulsive thing. I simply prefer soda or iced tea, a fresh batch of which was chilling in the fridge, so I helped myself there too.

One of the great things about Italians is when they say "my house is your house," they actually mean it. It's standard operating procedure for the hostess in an Italian household to serve you your first round of everything—food, drink, etc.—usually the moment you walk in the door. After that, though, you're not only entitled to get yourself whatever you want, you're expected to do so. If I said to my sister "I could go for another sandwich," she'd look at me dumbfounded and ask if my legs were broken or if my hands stopped working. Conversely, if I just got up and got myself refills, she wouldn't assume I was being rude. She'd think I felt at home enough to help myself, and that would make her warm all over ... unless I put an empty iced tea container back in the fridge or neglected to clean up my plates and utensils. Then she'd become a cold-hearted bitch.

The entire time I was scarfing down her food, my sister was interrogating me about where I've been and what I've been doing, asking if I met anyone interesting, or if I saw anything out of the ordinary, or if I learned any new culinary tricks. I mumbled or grunted in response as I chewed and gulped. She was like a little kid who hadn't had a new playmate ... ever. She was practically bouncing, sitting at the kitchen table with me and her husband. Her legs were crossed and her airborne foot never stopped bobbing up and down the entire time we sat there.

Her husband, on the other hand, never broke stride. He kept reading the newspaper from front page to last and looked up only to comment aloud to no one in particular about an approaching weather front or some crazy event in a place none of the rest of us ever heard of.

Ange had dated her share of guys growing up. Like my mom, she was exceptionally pretty, the kind of pretty that stopped traffic and evoked catcalls. On the continuum of physical beauty, there were the ugly girls on one end, the average girls in the middle, pretty girls beyond those and then jaw-dropping girls like my sister—who inspired infatuation and fantasy—at the other end. People in the neighborhood would always tell her she could have been a model if she was a half-a-foot taller, but I always told her they were wrong, not because I was being mean, but because she wasn't an anorexic stick like most fashion models. She was curvy, without an ounce of fat on her, and her skin was flawless—no wrinkles. Even after having two kids and being in her 40s, she could pass for being in her 20s.

Regardless, as if to answer my father's prayers, Ange was a good girl growing up. She got good grades in school, and never gave up much to the local boys when the lights went down. She was smart enough to know we all talked. She didn't want to be the topic of tales of exploits, and she never was. Some guys called her frigid because they couldn't get what they wanted out of her, but I always just thought she was smart and selective.

Once she got out of the cloistered environment of South Philly and she was coming in contact with people who didn't know everyone else she knew, she blossomed. She dated in college—sometimes seriously—but she found her husband at her law firm. A couple years after that, she started squeezing out puppies and decided to stay home and raise them. Her law degree didn't go to waste, though; she started her own business taking in legal, transactional work she could do from home and now makes more than most practicing attorneys. She is smart, beautiful, bubbly, and a great cook. I am halfway jealous of my brother-in-law, except when my sister is in one of her moods. Then I pity him—a lot.

The best thing was, her patience was rewarded and she found a guy just like my dad who adored her more than life itself and who failed to see any of her shortcomings—and yes, she certainly had her share of those, too. The trick for me, in the midst of this new situation with Sonny's, would be to deal with the extraneous family shit going on and avoid causing unrest in *their* household.

After I finally finished gorging myself, Ange and I retreated to the family room for a little privacy. Tom didn't mind, either. He worked in an office all day, dealing with people. The more time he could spend alone in peace and quiet at night, the happier he would be.

Ange and I sat down. She turned off the TV the kids had left on and leaned toward me like she was about to discuss secret missile plans. She stared into my eyes and started in on me.

"Uncle G briefed you on what's going on, right?"

"Yeah. I'm up to speed. How're Mom and Pop doing? I mean, they're probably a little straighter with you than they'll be with me."

"They're disasters. They blame themselves for being stupid, no matter how hard we protest otherwise, but they're also not fighting back. It's like they've given up. They're fish outta water with this sort of business hostility, and they're too old to take these guys on. They're in their eighties for god's sake, Johnny."

"I know they are. But with the exception of being about 35 years younger than them, I'm not much better equipped to handle this than they are. Obviously, whatever money they gave me, they can have back. I'll sell the car too, but I'm not sure how much that'll get 'em."

"Selling your car would absolutely kill them. The fact they were able to give you that, or at least the money for it, is one of their proudest accomplishments these days. If they knew this was taking money out of their kids' pockets, it would destroy what little pride they have left."

"So how are they surviving? The proceeds from the restaurant were everything for them."

"Tom and I are subsidizing them."

"So explain to me how *you* giving them money is somehow more permissible than *me* giving them money."

"Because they have no idea we're doing it. We made an arrangement with their lawyer."

"—not Mr. Acchione!" I blurted.

Ange closed her eyes and slowly nodded her head in the sort of resigned way you do when you're embarrassed to admit something, "The very same."

"Mr. Acchione? I can't believe he's still alive?"

She kept her eyes closed and continued to nod. "Don't get me started, and yes. He's convinced Mom and Pop there's an investment from Pop-Pop they forgot about. He found it, it's matured, and it's paying them an annuity. The money's coming from us, of course, but at least it's floating them and no one besides the five of us know."

"Well, count me in."

"For what?"

"For financial support. Whattaya think?!"

"You don't have any money."

"I have what's left of what Mom and Dad gave me, and a few bucks I've been able to set aside along the way. I realize you two make shit-tons more than me, but your 'nut's' a lot bigger than mine too. I don't have a mortgage, or a pair of car payments, or two kids, or all the other shit you have around here. I do all right for myself, thank you very much."

She sat up and started backpedaling. She hadn't actually offended me, but I wasn't about to stop her from being embarrassed, either.

"Whoa! Whoa! Whoa! Sorry, Okay? I didn't mean to offend you. I just don't want you to feel obligated. We can cover this, at least for a while."

"Bullshit. I'm in. How old is Acchione now, anyway? 130? 140?"

"I know, right? He was Mom-mom and Pop-pop's lawyer before he started working with Mom and Dad. Mom and Pop are mid-eighties, so he *has* to be mid-90s, right? He was completely useless in the sale, by the way. We tried to get them to let Tom and his firm review the paperwork and vet the buyer, but they refused, saying he'd been their lawyer forever and they didn't want to hurt his feelings. Pretty sure a top-tier Philadelphia firm would have done a *little* more thorough vetting job than 'Geezer McFumbleturds, attorney at yawn,' but whatever... What's done is done."

"Shit. He was old when we were Mike and Joey's ages."

"Yeah. He was around the same age then that we are now. ... ancient." And she started getting a little melancholy.

She had a tendency to get a little sensitive about her age. She actually had a panic attack when she turned 40. We rushed her to the hospital thinking she was having a heart attack. Sometimes I forget these things.

"Ummm ... so, that was a good meatball sandwich."

"Nice try, geezer. I may be old, but I'm younger than you and at least I have a family. What have you accomplished so far?"

"Wow. Nice. Feel free to attack me for trying to be nice, bitch. I'll have you know my greatest accomplishment is I've successfully *avoided* having a family. So there."

She smiled and stared at me, and then the momentary levity ended. She just spat out "this whole thing is fucked!"

"No shit. Do Mom and Pop know the whole story otherwise? "

"They're up to speed with it, but they're not engaged in figuring out what to do next. Like I said. They've just quit."

"How'd ..."

"When the checks didn't show up, Acchione went to Uncle Guido instead of to Mom and Dad. Why? I have no idea, but he did. Turns out, it's the only thing I think Acchione did right so far. He did it by accident, and he *shouldn't* have! I mean, shit. Law School 101—client privilege. He has a fiduciary obligation to Mom and Pop, and he outright violated that by going to Guido. I could have him disbarred!"

"Pretty sure, at 95, losing his license to practice law isn't going to exactly devastate him."

She angrily snorted through her nostrils like a bull who's about to charge and said "I know. I'm just *super* fucking angry! Anyway, Uncle G told him to call the buyer's attorney and bank to find out what was going on, and he found out the two entities don't exist … and never did. Uncle G figured out what's up pretty fast. He came up with the story to tell Mom and Dad and he came to me to find out about funding them. So, what are we going to do now? How are we going to make those fuckers pay?!"

"Angela, you're going to do nothing. You and Tom have too much to lose. And as you so gracelessly pointed out, I have accumulated nothing in my many years on this Earth, which means I have *nothing* to lose, making me the perfect antagonist. Uncle G and I will come up with something. I promise to keep you in the loop, but for this to work, you need to stay clear—all of you. If they get to you, we're hobbled, so I need you out of the way. Got it?"

"I can't just sit on the sidelines waiting for a call."

"You're not on the sidelines. You just won't be on the front line. I'll come to you for legal guidance, info gathering and as a sounding board. You'll also continue to keep Mom and Dad sane, and keep feeding them our money. It's like Mom and Mom-mom always said: The restaurant wouldn't exist as a kitchen alone. The business part is at least as important, and that's where you shine. I need your help behind the scenes. Having both of us on the front line would be redundant and stupid."

"You're not just saying that to protect me, right? 'cause I can handle myself."

"And I have the scars to prove it. No. I'm doing this because for us to succeed, we need to be clear about who does what. Not only are you the best person to do all the things behind the scenes, it makes the most sense for you to be doing them. *You* need to protect your family, especially Mike and Joey. They need a mom, not a ninja, and we need to keep these crooks away from your boys. The less you seem to be involved, the less likely they'll be to use your boys as leverage. According to Guido, these guys aren't just run-of-the-mill thieves. They're bad-assed and organized."

She paused for a second, like she was in deep thought, and without breaking her distant stare into the carpet in front of her, she said "Michael."

"What?!"

"My son's name. It's Michael, not Mike. You keep calling him Mike, but his *name* is Michael."

"Jesus Christ. You're worse than mom."

"His name isn't 'Jesus Christ' either. It's Michael." Then she looked me in the eye and smirked. "Say Mike again, and I'll kick your ass."

There was an extended pause. We just sat there staring at each other in the silence, and then I started to move my lips "… Miiii …" She leaped from the ottoman, landed on my lap, and started slapping me on either side of my head, laughing hysterically while she did it.

Bitch still hits hard too.

MR. ACCHIONE

Being raised in restaurants and then spending my adult life running them has probably contributed to a number of personal quirks and neuroses, foremost among them is my inability to function in the morning. Restaurant kitchens typically close every night at 10. That's when cleanup is really in full gear—scraping and scrubbing the grille, wiping down all the stainless steel prep area, washing the pots and pans, cleaning and sorting all the utensils and plates, refilling all the preparation containers, scrubbing the floor, hosing down the floor mats—the list goes on forever. The logic is that every day when you come into work, the kitchen should be spotless, practically new condition, ready for battle. The only way for that to happen is for the night crew to kick ass.

It's a daily ritual and it doesn't get done by gnomes. It gets done by the kitchen crew and waitstaff and it takes at least an hour of coordinated effort every night. The last of the cleanup is rarely completed any time before midnight. Then the crew assembles at the bar, which stays open until 2AM. When the bar closes, there's an hour of cleanup there too—restocking, cleaning, draining, etc., but that was always fine. No one on the staff was in a hurry to leave. We were all friends or family, so hanging out all night at the bar—and then working together to cleanup—was actually a pleasure.

It was rare to ever get home before 3:00 a.m., and no one just falls asleep when they walk in the door. Some nights, we'd clean ourselves up and go right back out to after-hours clubs, but regardless when the night finally ends, it takes time to unwind—maybe a shower, or changing into comfortable clothes and watching reruns or infomercials—so maybe an hour later, as the sun starts to come up, you actually climb into bed in an attempt to sleep. As your lights go off, early risers working the first shift at the plant are turning theirs on to start their day. The idea is we'll be up and running by the time their work day ends.

Rarely do I ever wake up before noon, and most days I'm not rousing until around 2:00 p.m. Today, since I didn't close a restaurant and a bar the night before, I'm strolling into the kitchen—albeit groggily—a little after 10:00 a.m., which to me feels like 4:00 a.m.

"Still keeping restaurant hours, eh?" Angela smiled as she said it and pantomimed checking her wrist like she was checking the time, except she wasn't wearing a watch.

I couldn't even muster a grunt. I just flipped her a half-assed bird and uttered a single word: "Coffee."

She gestured for me to sit down, grabbed a mug, filled it with coffee and set it down on the kitchen table in front of me. I cupped the mug in both hands and brought it to my lips, closed my eyes, inhaled the steam and sighed like I had just smelled the essence of Jesus himself. I sipped the scalding hot beverage and set the mug back on the table. I opened my hands for the first time to see the mug's graphics: "World's Best Mommy."

I looked out of the corner of my eyes at my sister, who smiled and shrugged, "Oh, like it's the first time someone called you a 'mother,'" and laughed. She cracked herself up. "What's the plan for today, hotshot?"

"I'll probably go find Raj and say howdy, then catch up with Indi and see what she's up to. Walk the neighborhood. Maybe stop by Federal and grab some pretzels."

"So, no plan to go confront the guys at Sonny's?"

"What, am I an idiot? What am I going to do there? March in and kick some ass? Get the keys to the restaurant back? Beat a few hundred grand out of them?"

"I know you. You have the strategic grace of a caveman."

"Oh, thanks so much for the vote of confidence, sis. You're far too kind. Do you treat all your houseguests like this?"

"Only the morons."

Her cell phone rang. It was Uncle Guido.

She grunted a couple times, hung up and said "Change of plans. We're meeting Guido at Mr. Acchione's at noon. Finish your coffee and get a shower. You stink." Then she nurtured her OCD by straightening a coaster on the kitchen island so the picture on it was perfectly lined up with the edge of the stone countertop, checked her reflection in the microwave, ran a hand through her hair, then dropped her shoulders, and sighed: "Fuck."

"You're gorgeous," I told her.

"Clearly," she sarcastically replied, "but all this radiance will be wasted on you today, which seems almost criminal."

"Even when I compliment you, you have to bust my balls," I said as I gulped down the remaining coffee.

"That's because you're so goddamned sarcastic, I never believe you when you compliment me."

"Smart woman. Wait. Did I mean 'smart woman,' or was I just being sarcastic? Life can be so cruel for you sometimes."

There are few things I enjoy more than going back and forth with my little sister. Nothing is off-limits or out of bounds, and we're ruthless. Of course, if anyone else said these things to either of us, the other one would kill the outsider—no questions asked—but between us, it's all good fun.

"I really do *hate* you, you know? Now, go get your damned shower, so just when I know your head is full of shampoo, I can flush every toilet in the house and give you a goddamned heart attack! We need to *leave* here by 11:00, so we have about 45 minutes and you're not the only one who needs to get ready. Hurry up."

"Okay, but you're driving."

At 11 o'clock on the button, OCD girl's garage door went up. She pulled out and headed down the driveway. It was an off-hour commute to the city, but that didn't mean traffic didn't exist, and we still had to spend a few minutes dropping the kids off at a neighbor's.

There was still a ton of volume on the roads, but at least at this time of day it's moving.

We were heading to South Philly, the first part of town you'd encounter on the way to center city from the airport. The sports arenas are all down there. It's where all the concerts are held and where all the docks and distribution centers are. In the summer, if the wind is just right, we residents of South Philly could smell the sewage and oil refineries in our homes. Well, that's if you could get past the smell of the decaying fruit and fish in the dumpsters at the Italian Market, and all the wet grime in the street gutters.

In Singapore, you'll get beaten for spitting gum on the street. In South Philly, you'll get a pat on the back because that used gum practically serves as a temporary air freshener.

Not all of the area is disgusting, though. It's actually a pretty amazing city with incredible culture, architecture and history. The restaurant scene is one of the best anywhere, and between sports, theater, museums and clubs, if you're ever bored here, you're just not trying.

After being away, even if only for a few months, I was able to look at my city more objectively. To be honest, I like what I see even more now than I did growing up here—the attitude, the accent, the toughness—it's all a part of me, and I wear it all like a badge of honor. I actually found myself smiling at the thought of that while Ange was maneuvering her minivan through traffic at 90MPH as we headed north past the airport on I-95. Trust me, smiling on that stretch of highway *rarely* happens.

A few minutes off "95," we'd turned down some streets and cut through a couple alleys to avoid gridlock, and ultimately pulled up to Mr. Acchione's. I'd never been here before. In fact, I'd rarely even been in this part of town before now. The first thing I said when we parked was, "Your car might actually be safe here," which is a huge statement about how nice this neighborhood was. Mr. Acchione was apparently a pretty big deal in his day!

His house was a big, stone place built in the early part of the 20th century. The best word to describe it would be "substantial." The Big Bad Wolf would've stepped on the sidewalk, taken one gander at this solid stone behemoth and said "Nope. This ain't happenin'," walked to the supermarket, bought a pork roast and gone home.

The front doors were two-inch-thick, solid wood affairs that stood at least 8 feet tall and weighed a couple hundred pounds apiece. They were hand-carved and perfectly weighted. Someone as frail as Mr. Acchione could swing them open and closed with just a finger. The door hinges were brass, the size of my head, and were intricately detailed with Beaux Arts engraving.

Every detail was attended here. The mere fact the door hinges were ornately carved should offer some insight into how elegant and impressive this man's home was, which was shocking, because the man himself was anything but. He was just an old man whose time had come and gone at least thirty years ago, and who'd made his career as little more than a neighborhood lawyer.

Never imagined getting kids out of jail and writing wills paid this well. I guess Ange and Tom must make *BANK* working for their downtown firm! Maybe I *should* let them keep subsidizing mom and pop without me.

"Welcome, young Valmontis. Come in. Come in," he said as he opened the door before us.

He stepped aside to make room for us in the doorway and half-bowed as he swung his left arm aside, gesturing for us to cross the threshold. It was like the old man was his own butler. I half-expected him to be wearing white tie and tails.

Inside, the house was more gorgeous than the front doors and hardware. I was instantly overwhelmed.

We had stepped into a vestibule with another set of double doors directly in front of us, only these were wood-framed with full-height leaded glass inserts. The pair probably weighed as much if not more than the wooden pair we'd just passed through. The interior of the entry hall was covered from floor to ceiling in custom wood paneling with sconces providing dim ambient light that danced off the huge nine-foot-tall mirror mounted to the top of a bench that matched the wood used on the walls. It all looked like a dark wood—maybe mahogany—with 100 years of patina, and was immaculate. As we stepped in on a white marble floor, giant pocket doors were to our right and reached almost to the ceiling, which was at least a dozen feet above the floor, and through the pocket doors was a parlor—at least I think that was what that room would be called. Maybe it was a receiving room or a drawing room. Either way, it was also richly covered in wood panels that surrounded a massive limestone fireplace whose mantle and surround were intricately carved and darkened by a century's residue from bygone fires. The morning sun streamed in through the enormous front window that was almost the size of the entire front wall and was trimmed at the top by a row of brightly colored stained-glass, which glowed as sunlight stream through.

This house was downright magical. It looked like something the Rockefellers or DuPonts or Biddles would have owned back in the heyday of the robber barons. Maybe they did own it back then. Who knows? Either way, it's Mr. Acchione's now, and he seemed absolutely minuscule within this cavernous space.

How the hell did this guy own this house?

Of course, the room was tastefully furnished in dark reds and purple velvet. Leather-covered sofas and chairs and a full-sized grand piano sat in the far corner between the fireplace and the front window. As nice and immaculate as everything was, it was very old. It may not have all been originally purchased as antiques, but it all qualified now.

Mr. Acchione moved very slowly as he shuffled into the room behind us. He clutched a cane, but didn't rely on it. He may have carried it as little more than security—there if he needed it to help himself up, or stabilize himself if the world suddenly tipped to one side or the other.

His body tremored noticeably, but not violently as he once again gestured with his extended hand, only this time—instead of encouraging us to enter a room—he offered an invitation to have a seat.

Even though the house was immaculate and exhibited little if any use, it smelled like an old house. Perhaps it was the wood panels and their old varnish, the dust that had permeated the velvet furniture covers and clung to the cushions within, the old thread in the oriental rugs, or the years and years of human oils mingling with the armrests and wood table tops—or maybe it was just the old, lingering stale air of a structure whose doors and windows rarely open anymore. Again, who knows? It may have been a combination of all these things, but regardless of the cause, it felt like Mr. Acchione, although standing in front of us breathing, had actually been dead for quite a while and we were merely visiting his mausoleum.

This time, gesturing with the rubber knob at the bottom of his cane, drawing our attention to the middle-aged woman standing in the archway leading into the next room, he asked "Could my nurse get you anything? Soda? Wine? Coffee? Tea? Something stronger, perhaps?"

We all declined as Uncle Guido and Angela both sat down and

Mr. Acchione dismissed his nurse who, as a matter of course, closed a different set of pocket doors to ensure privacy as she left. I stayed on my feet. I'm not much of one for sitting—probably all those years standing in a kitchen.

I started to casually walk around the room, looking at the various keepsakes displayed on tabletops and shelves. G sat in a chair and leaned forward, his feet set apart from one another, his elbows resting on his knees, and his hands clasped together in front of his lap, as if he was about to say grace. This was his standard position. He was never the type to collapse into an upholstered chair and lean back with his arms draped across the armrests. He always looked like he was about to lunge forward.

Ange sat in a dark, velvet arm chair that swallowed her up like a giant purple monster. She looked at me and gestured with her eyes for me to sit down.

Mr. Acchione pointed to an oxidized metal trophy of a running guy in football pads on the shelf in front of me. His pointing was that of an old man—a wrinkled, bent index finger and a hand too old to form a tight fist behind it, wavering in the air as if it was trying to hover like a hummingbird.

"That's from 1941. I was 16 years old. I realize it's hard to imagine this, looking at me today, but I lettered in three sports in high school—football, track and rowing. Being a good student got me into the University of Pennsylvania, but being an athlete paid for it. Without scholarships, I'd have spent my late teens and early twenties standing in bread lines with every other adult male during the Depression, and then I'd have gone to war and probably gotten killed like your mother's father. In the unlikely case I actually made it home after that, I'd have spent the remainder of my adult life standing on an assembly line instead of in a courtroom. Sometimes you have to be lucky to get old, and usually you have to make your own luck.

"Did you know I used to row out of the same boathouse on the Schuylkill as Jack Kelly? Imagine that—one of the greatest Olympians of the modern era, and he and I rowed out of the same house. His daughter Grace—*Princess* Grace, that is—was just a little kid back then, and sometimes she'd come by the river to watch her father—so sad what happened to her, a car accident. She was a beautiful girl." And his voice trailed off as he seemed to get caught in his own mind, watching a movie of his past.

"I rowed at Princeton too when I attended law school. I was competitive about everything then. Sports definitely affected the way I conducted my business. I kept rowing on the Schuylkill until I was in my sixties. I wish I was still doing it today. Thinking back, I should have never quit. I would love to get back out there on the water, at least once more."

He leaned forward a bit and crossed his arms in front of him as he stared forward intently, like he was watching it all play out in front of him. "It was a great source of exercise, and also peace. Being on the river early in the morning, crisp air, fog lifting off the tranquil water, the sound of the oars dipping below the surface, the sound of water rushing past my scull as the oars dragged forward. Then the sound of them erupting out of the water entirely with water dripping off them, only to be plunged back in the river behind me to repeat that same series of events again and again and again for miles in one direction and then back. It was intoxicating, mesmerizing. Everything else in life—obligations, conflicts, concerns of every form—disappeared while I was on the river. People think rowing is all about upper-body strength (he patted both of his biceps for effect while his arms remained crossed), but it was really all about the legs (he lightly pounded his loose fists against his thighs). I sincerely believe it was the rowing—not the football or track—that strengthened my legs enough for me to still walk today. Rowing is why I have always loved getting up so early in the morning."

Clearly, we had so much in common. Again with the sarcasm.

I interrupted. "I wonder what it was about rowing. My dad's pop was a big fan. He used to take me down to the Schuylkill and watch the races, or sometimes we'd just sit there on the bleachers, eat lunch and watch individual rowers going up and down the river. He told me he had been going there since my dad was a little boy in the mid-30s to watch their favorite rower, but I don't remember who that was."

Mr. Acchione perked up. "Really? He went down there with your dad in the 30s?"

"Yup. He was funny about it too. Even when he and I would go years later, he'd stare at the rowers like he was looking for somebody. He also had this odd tendency where he'd get so involved watching a race, he'd actually start rocking back and forth like he was rowing in it himself. Did the same thing watching Westerns on TV. He'd rock back and forth during fist fight scenes because he'd get so wrapped up in the action. He was a great guy."

Mr. Acchione just sort of let me go on and smiled like he just ate something savory, then he continued on his trip down memory lane, making sure to draw my attention to a black and white photo on the next shelf of two virile men in tank tops and shorts, proudly standing on a dock, holding long oars at their sides.

"That's a shot of me and Jack, there. He was a big strong guy—a bricklayer. I guess carrying all those bricks gave *him* pretty strong legs. I was only 14 in that shot. Just look at how young I was, and how strong—best shape of my life. I had the entire world ahead of me, and no idea what it had in store. Part of my fitness routine then was running from my home in South Philly to the boathouse near the art museum at the crack of dawn, and then I'd run to school after I finished on the river. My mother swore if rowing took me away from my studies—or got in the way of working—I'd have to stop, so I was out of the house by 5 every morning and back home right after football or track practice to go and do odd jobs to help support the family.

"I'd never really thought of myself as college material, but after spending all that time rowing with college boys, I realized the only thing they had that I didn't was money. Some of those college guys were idiots, even the ones from Penn."

He chuckled a little and continued, " Jack pulled himself up by the bootstraps, and he told me I could, too. His wife used to work at Penn. Did you know that? She made some inquiries on my behalf, helped me get enrolled, and made some connections for me for a scholarship. He was a good man, and she was a nice lady. That Grace was adorable. Jack was a bricklayer. Did I mention that?"

And he caught himself as his mind started to drift and his voice trailed off. He waved his hand in front of his face, like he was waving gnats away, and found his way to the sofa.

"Listen, I'm embarrassed, kids. I want to believe I'm better than this, but I fell into their tiger-trap like a feeble-minded old coot. Maybe when I was younger I wouldn't have fallen for it, but I did this time, boy—hook, line and sinker."

He continued, "The men who did this were good, and well-informed. One doesn't assemble 'the long con,' without careful preparation. They didn't just wake up one day and decide to decimate your family. They've probably been at this for years. Do you have any idea who they are or why they're targeting you?"

"Targeting me?!" I said.

"No. No. Not you *specifically*, but you collectively. Your family."

"I have no idea. Ange? Uncle Guido?"

They both looked at me and Mr. Acchione and shook their heads.

"Well, it must've been a Duesy (pronounced "doozy," for those unfamiliar with Duesenbergs), because they came loaded for bear."

He waited a moment and licked his lips. He pressed a button on his desk and the nurse reappeared at the pocket doors. "Can you get me some water please? Would anyone else care for anything?" We all shook our heads and held up our hands in front of us in what, I assume, is the international symbol for "nope."

"Just me then, if you'd please."

He sat quietly, patiently looking at us with a content look on his face until the nurse returned. She poured him a glass of water and left the crystal pitcher behind so he could refill his glass at his leisure. Then she exited as silently as she had entered and slid the doors closed behind her.

He drank half a glass and smacked his lips together—followed by the obligatory "ahhh"—and then continued. "Where was I? Oh, yes. 'loaded for bear.' They know us all. They probably have several-inch-thick dossiers on each of us. They knew Guido was the protector, so they distracted him and played on his insecurities. Guido, you were so busy worrying someone was coming after you and your business that you never suspected the subterfuge of them going after Toni and John."

"And me. I was the biggest fool of all. Angela dear, as I'm sure you'll agree, I don't come across as the most savvy attorney—just some doddering old fool who probably defecates in his pants and can't remember his own name, let alone know how to practice the law. The fact is, I've forgotten more about the law than the best attorney in your husband's firm probably ever knew."

He gestured again in a long, slow sweeping motion with both his hands toward the walls behind him. "Just look at the certificates and photographs on these walls: letters of commendation from Supreme Court justices, mayors, governors, even presidents—that's presidents with an 's.' I helped write bills and tried cases in front of grand juries in federal courts, setting precedents you probably learned in law school. That was all many, many years ago, of course. Once I hit my 70s, I semi-retired and took on the role of the old country lawyer."

Again, gesturing to Angela—who was now completely enthralled and hanging on Mr. Acchione's every word—"As you are aware, my dear, knowing the law is only part of the game. One must also be a skilled actor, playing whatever part is necessary to gain the upper hand on the opposition. For me, my stock in trade was playing the part of the absent-minded old fool who stumbles over his words and appears to be struggling to keep up. On occasion, I've gotten so into my character, I've actually misbuttoned my sweater to appear even more oafish and disheveled."

He wryly grinned over at her from the corners of his eyes as if to say, "Gotcha."

"Which firm did you work for, Mr. Acchione?" she asked.

"I never worked for anyone but myself, dear. Back then, only blue bloods from the Main Line were recruited by the big firms. If you were Italian, even if you were graduated from Penn or Princeton, you were expected to *make* the attorney desks, not sit at one. Jack Kelly introduced me to his friends, and they introduced me to other friends, etc. In time, I had some of the most influential people in Philadelphia as clients. I was never short of work. Those clients are all long gone now, though. Their families still call occasionally, as do their companies, but these days, mostly just to see if I'm still alive and if I recall a particular incident or case from a thousand years ago."

"Once I drifted toward retirement, I played the fool so others would underestimate me. Then I'd swoop in without them realizing it and do an end-around on them, slipping language into a contract, or leveraging details and facts they never realized they'd divulged."

"So what happened this time?" I asked.

He hung is head down a little bit, and for the first time in the past half hour, fully appeared to wear every one of his many years. "They were onto me before they got here. They treated me exactly the way I'd expected them to treat me, and I responded in kind. They played on my arrogance. Instead of me doing an end-around on them, they turned the tables and did it to me. I never saw it coming. I've gone up against some of the best legal and business minds in the nation and bested them, but these guys played me like a child."

"Thanks for falling on your sword, Mr. Acchione," I said with a respectful nod toward Guido, "but as someone much wiser than me mentioned recently, let's place blame where it belongs—on those who perpetrated the con, not on those who were conned. They knew us and they knew what they were doing. There was no reason to suspect them, so why would you? Let's move forward. What do we know about them?"

Uncle Guido spoke up for the first time. He was like that. It's as though he hated to hear his own voice. He was prone to sitting quietly for hours, just listening to others. When he finally spoke, everyone tended to listen.

"We know very little. They're biding their time in Sonny's, but there's nothing coming in or going out.There's been no sign of a capo, just soldiers. The only thing I've observed so far is one of their weaknesses."

"They have a weakness?" I asked?

"Yes. Remember when I was telling you how important it was for you to stay objective, to not get emotional because emotions blind you? Well, that's their weakness. They're emotional. They're not thinking objectively."

"How can you possibly know that, Uncle G?! We don't even know what they want. You said that yourself, and now you're saying they're emotional? About what?!"

Mr. Acchione interrupted "We know a little bit about what they want. They came after someone in your family. We're not sure who, but someone. We're not sure why, and we're not sure specifically who the target is, but it has something to do with your family."

"Mr. Acchione, with all due respect, they're thieves. They stole our business and are making money from it. Aside from us having something they wanted, I don't see it being personal."

"What money?" he asked.

"The money for our business. It was worth millions."

"And exactly how much of that have they put in their pockets? There were two things worth money there: the physical building, which may be worth a few hundred grand, and the business itself—the profit stream. They shut the business down—so that 'goodwill' value has completely evaporated—and they aren't selling the building, so that money is completely illiquid. We tried to buy it back through a third party. They're not selling, so there that money sits. They made money selling everything from inside the restaurant, right? Wrong. That *all* went to a landfill—all the pictures and the nicknacks and the tables and chairs—everything. The kitchen equipment was so old, Mary probably cooked dinner for Jesus on it. It's worth little or nothing.

"If anything, they've actually *paid* for the privilege of dismantling your family's legacy. They gave your parents three hundred thousand dollars up-front, and they have a dozen guys whom we've seen—who knows how many others are around, lingering, doing nothing. Why? If this was about money, they'd have cut their losses. They'd have sold the business and the real estate to someone else and they'd have gotten their personnel—their 'earners'—out of town and onto the next job. The mere fact they're still here tells me they're not done yet. The goal of their game is still out there. No, son. If this was about money, they'd be long gone. This is personal to them. They're emotional about *something*."

"So if they want to hurt us so bad, why don't they just come at us and get it over with?"

Uncle G asked, "Why do you think?" and then he let that question hang for a moment. I didn't know if he was asking rhetorically or if he actually wanted me to respond. We just sat there for about ten seconds, in silence.

He continued "Because a quick hit doesn't inflict enough pain. Ever hear that phrase 'death by a thousand paper cuts'? It's one of my favorites. It illustrates how you can drag out the pain for a long time before ending someone. Two bullets to the back of the head is quick and is usually reserved for someone who is cooperating or who provided valuable information in exchange for a quick death. When it's personal, you want your prey to suffer—for as long as possible. These guys are having fun at your expense, and they're willing to pay the monetary price for the show. They didn't clear out your parents' restaurant because they were bored and wanted to remove debris from their hangout.

"They did it so your parents could watch the stuff leaving, one item at a time—paper cuts. Your parents would see the entirety of their lives disappear methodically, and every item that was disrespectfully disposed of would hurt them. That brought joy to the sadistic bastards who are orchestrating this folly. They don't sell the restaurant because they want your family to see that structure gradually decay—the 'Sonny's' sign above the door rusting, never to be lit again, breaking as juvenile vandals hit it with rocks. The storefront paint gradually cracking and peeling. The windows get scratched while a film of filth collects on them. The apartment upstairs—where your father was raised by your grandparents, where your parents lived the first five years of their married lives, where you and Angela did homework every night after school—is sitting dark and lifeless. In time, the roof will leak. Rainwater will rot the walls and roof trusses and floor boards. Ultimately, the apartment floor will collapse down into the restaurant below and that floor will cave into the basement. The entire structure will gradually collapse into itself, and it will become an ever-increasing blight on the neighborhood. Your parents' long-time neighbors and friends will ultimately resent them and hold them responsible for this neighborhood decay, and those who perpetrated this all will be smiling. Your parents will have lost their business, their money, their home, their friends, and even their memories. These guys are good. They're systematically tearing your family apart at the core, and right now we're all along for the ride."

It hurt to hear all of this, but for the first time since Uncle G called me, a small light of understanding was starting to glow in my mind. With that glow came clarity, and with that clarity came purpose. I knew what I was hearing was going to help us strategize and counter their assault.

We all sat there in the quiet, sun-lit, wood-paneled room. It smelled old—musty, but not dirty or unattended—just old. After a few minutes replaying what Mr. Acchione had said in my mind, trying to make sense of it, I had a thought.

"You can't have a play without an audience," I said calmly, almost in a metered tone.

"Say that again," Uncle G responded.

I stood up, now appreciating what I had said and recognizing it as the first step it was. G and Mr. Acchione were watching me intently.

"You can't have a play without an audience," I repeated. "I mean, they're going to *all* this trouble to hurt us, to have us witness the decay of everything. That only works if we're here to see it. If we're gone, the joke's on them. It would be like going to all the trouble to set the table and prepare the meal, only for all the guests to ignore the invitation. We just need to leave, for good."

Acchione turned to Guido. "I hadn't thought of that approach. Sometimes the best tactic is to run away and pick your own battlefield. We've been so busy reacting, we failed to consider leaving. It flips control to us, at least to some degree. I like it. Good thinking, son. Now what are the cons?"

"No clue. It's easy for me to disappear. I was already gone before Uncle Guido brought me back. We'll have to figure out how to get my parents to leave. The real problem as I see it is Angela."

We all looked at Ange and she shrugged back like she didn't understand the problem.

"You're our weak link, sis. With the rest of us gone, they can focus on you. If they come at you hard enough, we'll come back. You're their leverage. Ideally, you'd leave right along with us, but you're too entrenched here—house, job, family, etc."

"I guess saying, 'I can take care of myself' is not going to carry any weight here, right?"

"Not one bit," Guido said, as Mr. Acchione and I both shook our heads emphatically. "But I think I can help here. I can keep an eye on her and her family. No one would get to them without going through me or one of my guys, but Ange is not your real problem."

Uncle Guido continued "Your real problem is getting your parents to leave. Remember, they've lived here all their lives. Do you really think two people in their eighties are going to just up and leave their church parish? Their familiar streets and buildings? Their familiar shops, shopkeepers, and familiar faces? Kid, this may not resonate with you yet because you're still chasing life, but your parents are coasting. They find comfort in familiarity. Picking them up and moving them will quite possibly, *literally* kill them. This plan won't work, guys. John and Toni aren't going anywhere. As long as your parents are alive, we're going to need another plan."

Mr. Acchione's shoulders slumped. His optimism quickly turned to melancholy. He knew Guido was right. He knew he'd never leave either, if presented with the option.

"Well, shit," I said. "Then if we can't leave, we need to take what they're doing in stride and act like we don't care. Let's upset their apple-cart. We won't go anywhere near Sonny's or them. Let them think up a new plan. We have their money. As far as we need to be concerned, the jig is up."

"That's not the way you deal with bullies, kid." Uncle G continued.

"You can't ignore them. They'll just find you and push you and push you until they have you against a wall. You either have to run from them or punch them squarely in their nose. They may hit you back harder and better, but no matter what they do to you, you bloodied them, and they'll remember that. Next time, they'll be a little more cautious around you. Even though they can win the fight, it'll be painful and they'll want to avoid that. We need to punch them in the nose."

"How do you propose we do that? Blow up a car, pull one of their men off the street and beat the shit out of him? Leave a bag of flaming dog shit on their front step and ring the doorbell? What?!"

"No, smart ass. You don't respond to manipulation with violence. Unless you can completely wipe them out, incidental violence is a weak response that tells them you're no match for them. We need to figure out their game, figure out what's important to them and then flip their world upside down. Make them give up their game against us, fold up their tents and cut their losses."

"So how do you propose we find this information?"

"Old-fashioned investigation, my boy. Pound the pavement. Talk to people. Follow leads. Build a story and then write an ending."

"When do we start?"

"Yesterday. You're already a day late. Get out there and start turning over rocks, kid. I'll work my contacts with the cops and the local operators. Mr. Acchione, if you're willing, please contact your legal network and see if anyone knows anything. Angela, go home, be available and keep up with your parents. You all have your phones. *Call* one another. Don't text, and don't hold information back. As soon as you learn anything, let someone know. You never know if your piece of the puzzle will bring things together for others. But we're not accomplishing anything sitting here in Mr. Acchione's lovely home. I have things to do and so do you, so let's break up this coffee clutch and go to work."

Everyone adjourned. We thanked Mr. Acchione for his hospitality and headed to the door.

"Johnny, can I speak with you before you go?" Mr. Acchione asked.

"Certainly. What can I do for you, Mr. Acchione?"

"Where are you staying while you're in town?"

"With Angela and Tom."

"All the way out in the suburbs? Seems like a lot of wasted travel time. Why don't you stay here with me? Obviously, there's ample room and I'm here alone. I'd enjoy some company and you'd have much better access to your neighborhood."

"Mr. Acchione, that's very generous, but I'd be putting you out. I get up late, stay out late. I've been living alone for a long time and am really not much of a housemate."

"I'd consider it a favor. With all that's going on, it wouldn't hurt to have a young man around to keep an eye out for me."

I didn't buy that excuse for a second because I'm not that young, but I wasn't going to make him ask twice. This was an amazing house, and it would be a rare privilege indeed to call it home, even if only for a few days.

"Well, since you put it that way, I'm in!"

He turned and doddered back to his desk, opened his center drawer and produced a house key. "This will get you in the front door. Come and go as you please, and help yourself to whatever is in the kitchen."

He extended his hand to me. I shook it, and he smiled broadly.

"Not sure how many more days I have on this Earth, young man. I'd rather not spend what little time I have alone in this big old house. It would be great fun to share more old stories with someone who never heard any of my stories before," he said with a laugh and patted me on the arm. "Now, go and begin your investigation, and I'll do the same."

OFF TO THE RACES

When I got outside, everyone had already gone their own way, including my sister, who decided to ditch me and head into town solo to grab lunch with her husband. I can't say I necessarily blame her (who wouldn't prefer good food and pleasant company to lingering with one's sibling?), but if I had known she was going to do this, we could have taken two cars this morning. Now I had to make my way back to her place to retrieve my car without her.

One of the best things about living in a big city is commuting options. No car? No problem. Even though my car was quietly sleeping fifteen miles away in suburbia, I could get back to it with a couple transfers on public transportation.

My first ride was on the bus. I could have taken the bus all the way to Ange's town, but that wasn't my plan. Now, no offense to the Ralph Kramdens of the world, but buses are god-awful. Every surface within the passenger compartment is hard-plastic, and there's a very good reason for that: it's much easier to powerwash the three Ps (Puke, Poop and Pee) off hard plastic than it is off upholstery.

You see, many riders mistake these buses for rolling toilets, and as punishment for the bad habits of the few, the rest of us must suffer through a harsh battering from the hard surfaces surrounding us.

By the time I exited the bus, between the many turns it made, and the many more pot-holes into which it plunged and rebounded, my entire body was covered in fresh, new bruises. The entire ride, brief as it was in actual miles, would have looked like a 1960s Batman TV episode with word bubbles above the heads of the passengers, all displaying onomatopoeia like "OOF!" "UNGH," "BANG," "SLAM," and—well, you get the idea.

It didn't take too long before we reached city hall, but it felt like the ride had taken years off my life. Fortunately, the next ride would be far more civilized.

There's an underground network of walkways and shopping beneath center city, and it's all accessible from city hall, among other places. If you need to reach any suburb outside the city, the regional train or subway to get there is accessible two levels below the street. Oh, sure, the corridors leading to these trains and subways reek of urine and are lined with homeless people, wig stores, and one-dollar-slices of pizza—but there are also train platforms to get you the hell out of there, and that makes it all worthwhile.

On the train platforms the sub-sub-terranean air (for the sake of simplicity, let's call it air, even though a chemical test may prove otherwise) was polluted and acrid, and every surface—ground, walls, columns, ceilings, benches, fellow daytime commuters—was covered in a layer of grime. One could actually scrape off the outer grime coating to find out the original color of what lies below, but the price for that little piece of knowledge would be forfeiture of at least one's fingernail, and possibly the entire finger from infection.

I couldn't help but smile. I was home.

The ride to the 'burbs was a fairly brief one—45 minutes and painless. Everyone aboard minded their own business, almost ignoring the fact they're seated in a metal box with other sticky, oft-noisy humans. Thanks to technology, the risk of making personal contact with someone else was almost completely eliminated, as passengers stared at their cell phones, shunned everyone in every possible direction by listening to head phones, or simply fell asleep.

I also discovered a new wrinkle in the rail system since I last rode SEPTA (that's the name of Philly's public transportation—South Eastern Pennsylvania Transit Authority)—the advent of the "Quiet Car." As if riding the train wasn't insular enough already, now the front car of a multi-car train was dedicated to silence—no speaking on cell phones, no conversations amongst one another at anything above a hush, and no publicly audible music of any kind. "Dude it's Rude" signs were plastered here and there reminding riders not to eat while riding, and every other vertical surface within the car was covered by advertisements for local attractions, universities, shops and—oddly enough—a suicide hotline.

For those of you who don't know it, trains are inherently noisy—metal wheels clanging over the seams of metal rails, loud air handlers in the ceiling banging away, and train motors grinding overhead. The whole thing is a cacophony of unwanted, disruptive noises. The idea that cutting conversation would somehow create tranquility was laughable, at best.

Imagine sitting track-side at the INDY 500 on Memorial Day Weekend—with massively loud race cars roaring past you—and someone a few seats away asks you to stop popping your gum because the sound was annoying them. That's how stupid the practical application of the Quiet Car is, but SEPTA was not to be deterred.

To add to the quest for ambient silence, the conductor's voice came across the public address system. It was completely indecipherable—and would be considered close to a scream in terms of decibels—if someone could actually scream that loud. She (the conductor) was either announcing the next stop, informing everyone she needed to see their tickets and passes, or that she was stuck on her crossword puzzle and needed a 5 letter word that starts with "t" and means a rolling metal box that transports passengers from one station to another.

We had absolutely no idea what she was saying.

She emerged through the Quiet Car's single front door moments later, and as the train jostled back and forth and up and down across the uneven tracks—ensuring no one could possibly fall asleep—she called out more clearly and demonstratively "TICKETS AND PASSES!"

She also yelled "THIS TRAIN IS THE QUIET CAR!!!" and "NO ONE SHOULD MAKE ANY NOISE!!!" The irony of her yelling in the quiet car was not lost on many of us even though, to be fair, if she hadn't yelled, none of us would have heard her over the train's mechanical noises. Riders were informed we could use the text features of our phones, but everyone needed to silence the "ringers." She notified everyone, if she heard a phone ring, she would confiscate it.

"This car is for quiet contemplation and not for disruption." At least I think that's what she said. I could barely make her words out over the spinning, grinding, screeching noise of the out-of-balance ventilation fan in the car's ceiling.

We approached the University City station. Once the silver metal tube stopped, she stepped off to bid farewell to departing travelers and to welcome new riders. She announced, loudly, to the dozens of would-be passengers on the platform awaiting their opportunity to hop on board, they were to stand back and clear a path for anyone who was leaving the train.

She was very clear about that, and did *not* mince words.

A flow of riders disembarked, and then there was a slight lull in the exiting traffic. One young man on the platform thought no one else was getting off, so he stepped onto the ladder leading into the cab. Just then, more people appeared from inside, trying to exit. He had unwittingly caused a log jam and was momentarily caught in the midst of a crippling brain-cramp—"Keep going and get on? Back up and get off? Uhhhhh …"

When confronted with option (a) or (b), he chose (c) "stand still, paralyzed and become an obstruction." Let the record reflect that was not the correct choice.

The diminutive conductor erupted. "BOY! I TOLD you to stay on the platform until I TOLD you you could get on. Now STEP BACK and get off my train."

Her eyes were as big as dessert plates. "DO IT NOW!"

The young man, probably a college student at Ivy League Penn—and standing at least a foot taller than the conductor—sheepishly looked at her and slinked off the train. He stood on the platform, head down, waiting for the remainder of those exiting to leave—and for future instruction from his new personal drill sergeant.

Once the exiting flow finally ended, he started toward the steps to get on the train again, but the conductor yelled "Oh, no you DON'T. You just wait there. You wanna be impatient? You gonna wait until everyone else gets on and THEN you can climb on board MY train!"

And the kid did as he was told.

This conductor was the personification of my home town. She didn't spew expletives. She didn't physically accost the interloper, but she also didn't let his error in judgment go un-punished. She should not and *did* not tolerate his actions, no matter how unintentional his insurrection may have been. She was assertive and direct. She was an unofficial ambassador for Philadelphia, spreading the word of its people: Stay in line and we'll get along just fine. Step out of line and I WILL SHUT YOU THE FUCK DOWN!

God, I loved my city.

A few stops later, I hopped off the train, and as I did, I passed this conductor. I tapped her shoulder lightly (knowing full well she might punch me in the face for doing so). She turned quickly and glared at me as if her eyes were sternly asking "What. Do. You. Want?" and I complimented her. "Ma'am, it has been my distinct pleasure to watch you work. You handled that impatient young man at Penn beautifully, and as one service person to another, you are my hero."

Instantly, her façade melted. She shyly looked down and giggled, quietly said, "thanks" and patted me on the side of the arm. Then, just as quickly, she stood up straight and yelled, "BOARD!" She climbed up the steps and was gone.

Philly is a tough, in-your-face town, and if you turn your back on it, it might just eat you. It may not have always been this way, but as it emerged as an industrial powerhouse in the mid-to-late 1800s and early 1900s, it became a hardened, blue collar melting pot where the two things everyone had in common were toughness and a strong work ethic.

The city's name, which translates to "City of Brotherly Love," always reminded me of Greenland. I know that sounds odd, but follow me here.

The Vikings lived in Iceland. They went exploring and found a new land. It was much worse than Iceland. It was cold, windy, and covered with ice. *Iceland*, ironically and by contrast, was *green* most of the time.

The new land was virtually uninhabitable, but in order for the Vikings to expand their tribe's footprint, they needed to colonize this glacier. So the geniuses who ran the tribe became the world's first real estate marketers. Instead of calling it "The worst fucking place on the planet," which would have been the truth—but would have attracted absolutely no one—they put a spin on the message and called it "Greenland."

Doesn't that sound like nirvana? "Greenland." That beats the SHIT out of "Iceland," right? Everyone who heard the name and the explorers' bullshit accounts of this heaven on earth could hardly wait to move there. Of course, once they got there, the Vikings burned their boats so they couldn't leave. It was at that very moment they realized they had been sold a bill of goods, but it was too late. They had to stay and make it work. That's how Greenland became Greenland.

That's how I always suspected Philly got its name too: Philadelphia. "Brotherly love" may have been a goal of the city's Quaker founder back in the 1600s, but in modern day, that name is grossly inaccurate. Of course, if they renamed it something more honest today, like "place-where-at-least-one-person-gets-murdered-every-day-town," everyone would run away. So, we continue to call it the City of Brotherly Love and talk about the great food, historic attractions, theater, shopping, and professional sports franchises (which more often than not completely suck ass) so people come and visit and spend their money and hopefully don't become one of those one-person-per-day statistics.

Ironically, those of us from here wear the city's edginess with pride. "Oh. Your town is tough? Ours threw snowballs at Santa during an Eagles game. Speaking of the Eagles, we threw bottles at the Dallas Cowboys from the stands *after* the Eagles had just dismantled them during the game. GLASS BOTTLES! By the way, they only permit plastic bottles in the stadiums now for some reason … Our city is so tough, we had a judge *and a jail cell* in the *basement* of our stadium to convict and contain rowdy fans. Top *THAT!*"

After I reached Ange's town, I would have hailed one of those mobile-phone-app car services at the station to go the last few miles back to Angela's, but as you may recall, I have a burner phone—no apps. I called a cab instead and one arrived soon thereafter.

Once I was in her driveway, I didn't bother going into her house. I just climbed into the Challenger, turned the key, awoke the beast lurking under its hood, and wheeled out onto Angela's street—or lane or whatever-the-hell they called this little sliver of family-ville.

Two hours after leaving Mr. Acchione's on foot, I had finally returned, parking in Mr. Acchione's garage. Not the most productive first day of information gathering thus far, but I had high hopes things would improve from here.

All That for Five Minutes of Surveillance?

My plan all along for today was to go to the old neighborhood and poke around and probably hook up with Raj, a buddy of mine from childhood. I stepped outside Mr. Acchione's garage, ready to begin this phase of the plan. The air was warming up and the sun was shining. Sonny's was about ten blocks away, so I closed the garage door behind me and started walking. "No time better than the present to start figuring shit out," I said out loud to no one, and God knew, I couldn't possibly spend another moment on public transportation that morning, especially not a bus!

Ten blocks later, I was standing in front of Sonny's.

Now what?

I was supposed to investigate someone—or something—somewhere, but I really had no idea what I was doing. I'm a cook, for Christ's sake. Give me some eggs, ricotta and pasta and I'll make you lasagna. This surveillance business? I'm a fish outta water.

Logically, I figured, investigating started with looking and listening, so I subconsciously found myself across the street from the source of this mess—Sonny's. Staring at the dark storefront, there was nothing visibly going on. I could only assume the place was full of douchebags, but it was equally likely the place was empty and all the douchebags were out doing horrible things to other people. I imagined a voicemail: "We can't come to the phone right now because we're fucking up someone's life. If you leave a message, we'll fuck yours up when we return."

The look of the place made me physically ill. What had been a thriving enterprise for nearly eighty years, now sat derelict and decaying. The big sign up front was dark—light bulbs were broken, paint was peeling, and if I didn't know better, I'd have sworn it was a little off kilter too. The marble steps leading up to the front door—the very ones my sister, my mother and my grandmother scrubbed to a gleam with toothbrushes all those years—were covered in city grime and gum. The sidewalk had met the same fate. In a matter of only a few months, Sonny's had gone from a shining beacon of hope on the street, to the poster child for urban blight. It was painful to see it, let alone *watch* it get worse and worse!

I was looking at Sonny's but I wasn't really *seeing* anything. A lack of honed surveillance specific skills was one thing, but staring at something for more than ten seconds is a problem for ADHD poster children like me. Our minds wander all over the damned place, so fixation wasn't exactly my strong-suit.

My ADHD and I stood out there, just staring, for about five minutes. Then I started bouncing from one foot to the other out of boredom. Then I realized I hadn't peed since breakfast. The more I thought about that, the more urgent peeing became. I had to find some relief—and fast! Obviously, my old home base, Sonny's—though convenient—was unavailable at the moment. I needed to figure out an alternative … quickly. I'd lived here forever, so I should be able to knock on someone's door, right? But whose?

I Now Pronounce You Unemployed and Nearly Dead

While I was seeking an appropriate place to relieve my bladder in South Philly, someone was getting belittled in his own office, uptown at city hall.

There, a trim, dapper man in his sixties with olive skin and an expensive suit sat across the desk from one of the most powerful political figures in the city. Not a hair was out of place on the visitor's head, and not a wrinkle was visible on his tailored suit.

The same could not be said for the man whose office this was. His armpits had immediately sprung a leak when the visitor sat down, and he began nervously running his hands through what was left of the hair on top of his head.

The visitor's laser blue eyes bored imaginary holes through his host's soul. His was the glance of legend, the one which could strike fear in the most steadfast foe, without the need to utter a single word.

If *we* were to use a single word to describe *him*, it would be *intimidating*.

Imagine the devil sitting down in *your* office.

The balance of power in the room clearly favored the visitor.

What the government official had in local political clout was not only temporary, but also inconsequential compared to that of his guest, whose virtual reach extended around the world, who came and went as he pleased, did as he wished anywhere on the planet, and never feared repercussions. The commissioner knew this man by name, rumor and reputation, but he feared not mention any of them, because the visitor was not to be tested—nor disregarded. Any visit by this man's agents struck fear in a sensible man. If the man himself visited, there was a very strong chance you're already dead. The commissioner was abundantly aware of this.

The visitor casually glanced at his watch, which cost more than the commissioner's annual salary, and began to speak slowly and deliberately, as if his script was being cued-in by an off-screen director. He seemed bored, almost put out by being there, as he nonchalantly crossed his right leg over his left knee, placed his hands in his lap, leaned back and surveilled his prey, who fidgeted uncomfortably in his desk chair *in his own office.*

The commissioner was like a character out of central casting. He was average height, but about two croutons shy of three hundred pounds. He was doughy everywhere, and his clothes seemed chronically rumpled. He had a St. Francis of Assisi hairstyle, except in his case, the bald crown of his cranium was covered with sweat and adorned with six lonely strands of hair lunging from just above his left ear and landing just above his right one. If he ever went into a swimming pool—and god help any of us unfortunate to witness that eye-cancer—these hairs would trail behind his head like party streamers.

Overall, his hair was salt and pepper, which for his age was fine. There was so little of it, though, that you could easily see his pink skin through his ever-thinning hair—back, sides—it didn't matter.

Any self-respecting man who gave two shits about his appearance would have shaved that head, but this guy was clinging desperately to his high school days when he had something to comb.

Because he was bloated and sweaty and balding, it would be tough to pinpoint his age, if not for his elevated professional position. It was not something a young man achieved, and he was definitely not a young man. He may have been the same age as his guest, but to any outsider, their appearances were on two entirely different poles of the same continuum.

"Would you agree I have had a long, productive relationship with your office, Commissioner?"

The panicked commissioner nodded over-enthusiastically.

"Good. You and your predecessors for decades have enjoyed success and prosperity by my benevolence, and those perks have *always* far-exceeded the paltry requests I or my people have made of you. Is *that* a fair assessment?"

The commissioner silently—almost spastically—nodded his agreement, never moving his hands from their clenched grips on the wooden arms of his desk chair, for fear any gesture would be misinterpreted and result in his own termination.

The man calmly continued: "I need you to take care of something. There is a law firm in this city. It's very large—even prominent—and is quite respectable. It has handled some of my business—yours as well. Perhaps you recall that federal matter in which you had become unfortunately entangled not so many years ago? They assisted with the dissolution of that matter. Do you recall that? Are you familiar with the firm to which I am referring?"

The spastic nodding continued.

"Very good. There's an associate there. He works in the tax department, I believe—Tom Klingsley. You've never heard of him. He's on track to be a partner, but he's entirely irrelevant otherwise. You need to have him disbarred. All of the information necessary to warrant that disbarment is contained in the files your assistant placed on your desk at my request."

A thin pair of files he hadn't noticed until this very moment were, in fact, resting on his desk. The visitor gave them a gentle nudge with the back of his hand for effect, and then sat back again, folding his hands across his lap, waiting patiently for the commissioner to frantically reach across his own desk, retrieve the files and read them.

A few moments passed and the commissioner looked up from the file. "Is this for real?" he asked incredulously.

"Does that matter? Are you somehow under the impression that I am *asking* you to do this?"

"I don't know why I even asked that question. Ha ha—force of habit, I suppose. My office is happy to assist you in any way possible."

"Not your office. *You*. No one else is to know anything about this, and my visit is not to be discussed."

"No, sir. Of course not. By 'my office' I simply meant 'me.' I under-stand completely. Please rest assured I have your best interests at heart and will do everything in my power t…"

The visitor continued in his same hushed tone. "Relax, and for god's sake, stop talking. Get this done quickly, or the next time I visit will be the last time I visit. It's really quite simple. There is a long line of toads I can install behind your desk. You will never be missed, so do as I instruct, and you will be fine." With that, he stood up from his chair, buttoned his suit jacket, tugged on the bottom of the jacket to ensure it was straight and crisp and then "shot his cuffs" to straighten his sleeves.

The commissioner sprung to his feet and extended his right hand to shake that of his guest, but the visitor ignored the gesture and turned to leave with an eye roll. The commissioner ran from behind his desk to reach the door before the man, so he could open it and bid his guest safe travels. The visitor simply walked past him, ignoring the commissioner and his gesture.

Arrogant men like the commissioner do not gracefully accept being disrespected. Once his guest left his offices, the commissioner puffed his chest and exerted his authority over his minions like a jilted peacock. "Get me the chancellor of the Philadelphia Bar Association!" He bellowed in the direction of his administrative assistant as he turned and stormed back into his office, closing his door most of the way, but not fully. It needed to remain open slightly because the commissioner planned to yell during this phone call, and he wanted his staff to be an audience to his show, an exhibition of his authority.

His assistant jumped, recognizing the bully tactics of one of the most powerful men in the city and began calling the chancellor, whose number she knew off the top of her head. After all, the Bar and the commissioner worked together often, exchanging favors and assistance. In this case, the assistant feared relations were going to be strained by this call, but her job was not to infer. It was to do the bidding of her powerful boss, and she was not about to be deterred.

"Chancellor on one," she announced over the commissioner's intercom. She watched the light on her phone change from a flash to a solid green glow and she sighed relief. The commissioner's request had been satisfied and—at least for the moment—he wouldn't have cause to scream at her when his door reopened. Of course, he didn't always need a reason. He'd proven that often enough in the past, but at least the odds of him not yelling were improved when he got what he wanted.

The commissioner picked up the receiver. The chancellor, who had no reason to believe anything unusual was afoot, began the call with typical pleasantries, asking the commissioner how he was doing and inquiring about his family. He was quickly interrupted—much as the visitor had interrupted the commissioner only a few minutes earlier.

The commissioner began yelling, asking how such an outrage could occur under the chancellor's watch and by a mere *associate* at one of the most prestigious firms in the city. He ranted, undeterred, for a full five minutes, reciting chapter and verse of the bogus file he had received from his distinguished visitor.

Of course, the chancellor had no knowledge of the offenses the commissioner was citing, (primarily because they didn't exist), but he backpedaled quickly and diligently in deference to the commissioner's station on the political food chain and the impediment he could become if he wasn't sated. The chancellor begged for time to rectify things and hung up.

So began the cascade of calls down the ladder, from chancellor to managing partner, to Angela's husband sitting in front of his boss, the tax partner, and being suspended without pay pending an investigation by his employer, the bar, and the commissioner himself.

He sat there in shock, being accused of—and berated for—an offense he'd never heard of by a man who had recently assured him he was on a direct path to partnership. Tom began to sweat—nearly burst into tears—not from sadness, but from panic and anger. What would happen to his family? Would they lose their home? Would he emerge from this as an attorney, or unemployable? He had kept his distance from the attacks on his wife's family, hoping that distance would insulate him from those shenanigans. Instead, he assumed the only logical reason for any of this was he was being used as a pawn to hurt his in-laws, and short of committing a crime—a real one, not the one for which he was being falsely accused—he had no way to mount a defense.

His boss handed him a file, more like hurled it at him, and Tom's trembling hands fumbled to open it. It cited chapter and verse of a variety of legal atrocities he was accused of committing as an agent for the firm that just fired him—fraud, outright misappropriation, extortion, racketeering, and all with signed, notarized affidavits from witnesses, accomplices and victims. The evidence was staggering, insurmountable and utterly fabricated. He had no evidence to disprove any of it. How could he? None of the facts existed, but the evidence contained in the file told otherwise. There's a presumption of innocence until proven guilty in court, but in situations such as this, the onus was on Tom to disprove the allegations to his employer. The bar and court would have the burden to prove the case if it came to a suit being filed against him, but defending himself would cost a fortune—a fortune he didn't possess, even with the recurring wages he no longer had, and besides, this evidence was beyond damning!

Because the only defenses at his disposal in that moment were "nu-uh," or "I know you are, but what am I?" he stood up and exited his former friend's office. He returned to his desk only long enough to collect his immediate personal effects—keys, wallet, briefcase—and walked quickly to the elevator lobby to leave. He avoided all human contact in hopes of not explaining what was going on, or being humiliated because he was unceremoniously dismissed. He reached the ground floor, exited to the street, and walked so quickly he almost jogged to the train to get out of town.

Angela reached his office floor moments after he had gone. His assistant informed her he wasn't there and she didn't know where he was or when he'd be back. Angela returned to the elevator lobby and called Tom's cell phone, but he didn't answer. She had no way of knowing he was outside at that very moment, not more than a half block away, but he either couldn't hear his phone above the din of the city, didn't have reception where he was, or simply couldn't answer her call because he had no idea what to tell her.

She left him a cheery voicemail, informing him of his missed opportunity to treat the most beautiful woman in his life to a "romantic" lunch at a downtown street cart and then concluded with a sincere "I love you and will see you at home tonight." Then she returned to the parking garage, got in her car, drove down the ramp, paid her fee and headed back to the suburbs. She had no way of knowing her world was coming down around her ears, not just as it related to her parents, but within her own home as well.

She'd find out soon enough.

Angela drove the route along the requisite surface streets to enter the flow of the expressway. She balanced between driving aggressively and defensively as she merged onto the highway heading west. Traffic volume was heavy as she entered at highway speed and navigated her way into traffic safely, aware that the slightest misstep would cause a giant cataclysm.

She hadn't noticed the black Chevy Suburban that began following her on the way out of the garage. To be fair, those rolling barges are omnipresent these days, so why would she notice this one in particular? It stayed close behind her on the surface roads and trailed her down the on-ramp into traffic. Just as she merged, the Suburban accelerated to pull beside her, and within the first hundred feet of entering the highway, abruptly and intentionally turned to the right, came into contact with her minivan and pushed it sideways into the barricade where the shoulder should have been. She slammed on her breaks upon impact, was almost immediately rear-ended violently, slid and spun through the crowd of nearby vehicles all traveling at highway speeds. She ultimately came to rest facing the wrong direction after being hit twice more by a pair of delivery trucks. The fact she wasn't hit head-on by someone going 70 MPH once she came to rest is an absolute miracle.

In all, fifteen different vehicles—cars, trucks, vans—were involved in the pileup, stopping traffic for two hours as the collectively crumpled mass of steel took that long to be disentangled. It blocked the highway's lanes from left to right and pissed off hundreds of westbound commuters. The culprit sped off undetected in all the hullaballoo.

No drivers nor passengers were killed in the incident, but airbags were deployed throughout the mess, and injuries were sustained. Angela escaped death by the narrowest of margins. Aside from being shaken badly and bruised by her seatbelt—and the air bag explosions—she was okay. She isn't the praying type, but she thanked god profusely for not having the kids in the car when that disaster happened.

The balance of the afternoon was spent answering questions from the police and other drivers, exchanging identification and insurance data, being poked and prodded and examined by EMTs on site and later by physicians in the emergency room. Ultimately, she was collected by Tom, who listened to her lighthearted voicemail only after the police called him with the news of her accident.

Whoever was attacking the Valmontis had stepped up their game and was sending the message that the family's lack of participation would not discourage fate. It would only reinforce the resolve of their foes.

An Indian in an Italian Neighborhood

My old buddy Raj's folks lived around the corner from Sonny's. His mom would be home watching her grandkids, so I decided to try there first in my quest for a bathroom.

Mom opened the door.

I'd called her mom since I was in the fourth grade. The instant she saw me, she gave me a huge, enthusiastic hug, the pressure from which put immense strain on my full bladder. I almost peed my pants. Although we had some catching up to do, I explained my immediate purpose for the visit and she told me to "Go! Run!" and I did, like a 4th grader who just made it home from school before his bladder burst.

A couple minutes later, fully relieved and breathing easier, I sat at the kitchen table with Mom and we caught up.

It had only been a few months since I'd seen everyone, so it wasn't like monumental changes had occurred in my absence. That didn't stop us from talking about absolutely nothing important for about an hour.

Her son Raj has been my best friend for more than 40 years. Her daughter, Swati (whom I affectionately call "Indi") had been my on-again/off-again sexual partner and one-time girlfriend. Although Indi is a year younger than me and Raj, she's smarter than both of us combined and tested ahead a grade when her family moved to our school district. The three of us were in the same grade from fourth grade on, and Raj and I cheated off Indi's tests during our entire tenure together.

Anyone who didn't know them figured they were twins, but they weren't. They couldn't have been more different. There was more than merely a single year on the calendar separating them. Indi was beautiful, smart, and self-confident. Raj wasn't.

If anything, Indi's transition into our school was more difficult than Raj's. Not only did he have me to watch his back (more on that later), but girls, especially cliquey Italian girls, are ruthless to outsiders. Indi was physically and verbally abused by classmates, but she always kept her head up and she always acted like she didn't care. She probably didn't.

One day, months after we became friends, I held Indi's hand in the hallway. I had a young boy's crush on her, and although I don't know if her feelings were ever quite as strong as mine, she wasn't totally against the idea of me holding her hand, either. And that was it. Classmates saw us holding hands, and the bullying ended. Back then I thought it was because of me, but in reality, I think it was because of Uncle Guido. I didn't realize it then, but every adult in the neighborhood knew G, and they told their kids to give me and my friends space because they didn't want to have to answer to him.

The hand-holding was short-lived, but the deference to Indi by the South Philly girls was not. Once she was included in my circle of friends, she was under G's umbrella. I wouldn't go as far as to say the other girls were friendly to her, but they certainly weren't abusive anymore.

On-and-off for the rest of our school days together, Indi and I would get close and then drift apart, then get close again, then drift apart again. We even dated briefly. More on that later too.

When I returned to the living room, Mom told me all about her grandkids—what they were doing, what grades they were in, how tall they'd gotten, and on and on and on. If you ever need to pass time, find a grandmother and ask her about her grandkids. Holy shit, they can go on for*ever*.

It was early afternoon by then and the school-aged kids would be reappearing in a couple hours. Since I had accomplished exactly nothing during my first day as a super-sleuth, I stood up, kissed mom, made my apologies for having to leave, and did precisely that.

All this time with her, though, gave me an idea for what to do next. I needed to visit with Raj.

Like Indi, Raj and I had met in the fourth grade. It was the first day of school and he was the new kid. When I was young, I was physically incapable of not talking. This made me very out-going, so my teacher approached me before class one day, introduced me to Raj and asked me to show him around school.

Of course, with a name like Raj, you could probably assume he stuck out like a sore thumb—an Indian kid with a strong accent in a sea of South Philly Italian kids with equally—yet completely differ- ent—strong accents. He was also tiny—about the size of a first-grader and about 12 pounds soaking wet (he's not much bigger now!). His mom could have sent him to school wearing a big red circle on the middle of his shirt and he wouldn't have been more of target than he was just standing there.

He was quiet, polite and nervous as he looked at his shoes and said hello. I was a gregarious kid—completely in my element among kids I'd known practically since birth—so I didn't know from shy. I greeted his meekness with an arm around the shoulder and a bellowing "How YOU doin'?" I walked back into class, arm still around Raj, and announced to everyone "Hey! This is my new friend Raj!" And that was that.

Anytime anyone else in the school gave Raj shit—and believe me, as much as he stuck out, and as easy a target as he was, everyone from kindergartners to sixth-graders took their shots—my buddies and I had his back. As was always the case with us, fuck with one of us, and you fucked with all of us. Raj's life was secure from day one.

Looking back, I always felt a sense of satisfaction, as if I did something good that day for Raj, but in time I realized it wasn't me. My teacher, whom I never really liked, was the one who saw a way to help the kid out. She picked the class catalyst to get the ball rolling, and that was that. Pretty smart of her, even though she was really sort of an asshole. In addition to my out-going nature—as I mentioned earlier—she was also probably familiar with my connection to Guido, and she figured adding Raj under his protective hand wouldn't be so bad, either.

That was all about a thousand years ago, though. Now I was aimlessly walking around our old neighborhood and my boy Raj was sitting somewhere in a cubicle, under a fluorescent lamp typing computer code on a keyboard. Ah, the glamour of adulthood.

I may not have had the internet on my burner phone, but I could call or text. I decided to type out a message to Raj. The fortunate masses of the world would simply open up a screen and type on a virtual QWERTY keyboard, but to type on my phone required pushing the "7" button three times for "R" and the "2" button once for "A," etc.

I'll receive texts now and then that are witty and wordy and poignant. Mine are the epitome of efficiency. My message to Raj was "call Johnny."

I'd have called him, but since I didn't know office etiquette, I didn't want to get him in trouble taking a call from me at work. I figured he could call me when he was free.

My phone rang instantly.

"Raj? Sorry to interrupt you, buddy."

"Dude! You're not interrupting. I'm just working. The keyboard and screen are remarkably patient and don't give a shit if I type now or ten years from now. They'll just wait."

"Must be nice to work somewhere where your efforts are so valued."

"—said the guy who tosses salads for a living."

"Speaking of which, what sort of food am I spitting into for you tonight?"

"The way you cook, that couldn't do anything but improve the flavor."

"You realize you'll still be eating my spit then, right?"

"…crap."

"Yeah, you really suck at trash talking."

"So, where are you right now? Still in Louisiana banging that naked nurse?"

"No. I'm standing in front of your mom's house."

"That's not funny. Don't make naked sexy jokes about my mom, man."

"No. Raj, I'm actually in front of your mom's house. I just stopped by and went pee."

"So where am I meeting you after I get off work?"

"Well, I'd suggest Sonny's, but …"

"Yeah, no kidding. Let's think of something else."

"Name it."

GEEZ

I had about two hours before I was supposed to meet Raj, which left me plenty of time to linger right where I keep ending up—across the street again from Sonny's.

It was fall in Philadelphia. Halls & Oates didn't want to spend another one here, but I really enjoyed it. It was my favorite time of year in this town, a time when leaves are changing colors and dropping on sidewalks, when people put away their Phillies T-shirts and are wearing Eagles or Flyers sweatshirts, and when the weather can go from sunny and warm to grey, damp and chilly in a matter of minutes. Today was nice, though—certainly warm enough to stroll the streets surrounding my parents' restaurant, or what *used* to be my parents' restaurant.

There was an abundance of places to go for a leisurely walk in town to pass two hours, but I chose Mom and Pop's neighborhood partially for the sake of nostalgia, and partially out of purpose. I'd only been gone a few months, so everything looked similar, but not exactly the same. Little things were different.

Our restaurant was mid-block on a street named after a tree. Philly's full of one-way streets. Numbers run north and south, and names like Chestnut or Walnut or Reed or Miflin run east and west. The vast majority of them are one way. In this part of town in particular, nearly all of them are loaded with parallel-parked cars along both curbs, with a narrow lane to be navigated in between. Far too frequently, that one lane is blocked by a delivery van, or some jackass who couldn't find a parking space, so he left his car parked, blocking traffic because "he only had to run inside for a minute." In the meantime, cars collected in the queue behind him, while horns and expletives filled the South Philly air.

Our block only had structures on one side. There was a park across the street, occupying one city block. Kids played there, dogs walked there, homeless people slept there, and drug dealers tried to conduct business there—but if a neighbor saw it, they'd contact someone. Word would get back to Guido, and he'd dispatch one of his crew. The drug dealer would summarily disappear (presumably peacefully to a different part of town), but no one knew that for sure—nor even cared.

No one here called the cops for such things. No one wanted the drug dealer to get arrested or cited. They wanted the perpetrator to disappear, and that's what Guido's guys did—quickly and quietly. That's how a community operates, at least around here.

Old cities in this country are interesting. Like most cities, the big ones on the East Coast—Boston, New York, Philly—were carefully planned, Philadelphia in particular. William Penn had a very specific, gridded-out design for his city, as illustrated by the numbered and named street convention I mentioned above. However, given enough time, old cities evolve from their original development stage and adapt to needs as times change.

In South Philly, rows (and rows and rows) of brick row homes were built over the course of a couple centuries. Each block shared a single façade from one end to the other, even though behind that façade were separately deeded homes. Imagine a pound cake sliced into ten equal-width slices. It's all one cake, but each slice is separate. That's what row homes are like. Now imagine hundreds of pound cakes with streets running between them north to south and east to west. That's South Philly.

Except instead of the golden-glazed deliciousness of pound cake, these row homes were clad in brick and stucco and taste terrible.

Most of these rows were built during the first portion of the last century, and since then, many of those structures were converted from residences into businesses—and in many cases, restaurants. That wasn't the case with Sonny's or our neighbors, though.

We all shared walls where we abutted one another, but our block was built with storefronts on the first floor and apartments on the floors above. Some places had two apartments stacked one on top of the other, but Sonny's was pretty simple. One restaurant downstairs, and one apartment above.

Our block was pretty typical for a retail street. Every store but ours had an awning with a business name and street address painted on the front flap. Ours, of course, eschewed the awning for the garish Sonny's sign. One thing all the buildings had in common, though, was they were brick, and if the brick wasn't exposed, someone had stuccoed over it at some point—usually in the seventies. A lot of architectural character was lost during the last quarter of the century. Stucco was slathered to excess, and walls of windows were replaced with small windows separated by broad expanses of stucco. Some of that was done to address structural flaws or deferred maintenance, but some of it was done for security purposes. This neighborhood went through some seedy stretches, and those living in apartments—even on upper floors—preferred solid walls to windows for the additional security. Not Sonny's, though.

Most storefronts featured large plate glass panels, two or three across to provide maximum visibility into the store, so passersby could clearly see a merchant's wares from the street or sidewalk. Sonny's had those too, but the two feet above those big window panels were filled with stained glass. There was no fancy design. They were just randomly colored, solid panes of blue, green, and amber. In the afternoon, the sun would hit those westerly facing windows and Sonny's waiting area would be lit by the glow from those stained-glass panes. In my mind, that room was never white. It will always be blue and green and amber like the inside of a kaleidoscope.

Over the years, our neighbors on the block changed (butchers, delis, sandwich shops, pastry shops, etc.), but our next-door neighbors were the same all my life. Looking from the street, there was a florist to the right, and a kids clothing store specializing in outfits for Catholic occasions to the left.

The city was gritty, no doubt about it—especially down here—but there was also warmth and beauty, especially when we'd step inside the warm glow of Sonny's where the aroma of fresh-baked bread and homemade gravy mingled with the din of conversation and laughter.

The more I thought about it, the more I longed for the days inside Sonny's, and the more disappointed I became looking at the dark, dingy hulk it had become in such a brief period of time.

Of the many changes I noticed, one stuck out the most: Sonny's sign was dark. Today was the first time I'd ever seen that light out in my entire life, and now it was extinguished for good. That was a hard pill to swallow, and it made me sad to my core.

Back in the day, whether Sonny's was open or closed, that sign stayed lit. It was our way of announcing to the world we were still in business—perhaps closed for the moment, but most certainly reopening later, just as it had done every day for the past 75 years.

Now the sign was out, and what had been a vibrant, festive, illu-minated, meticulously maintained beacon of bright paint and flashing incandescent bulbs was now dead and quickly decaying. Dents appeared on various surfaces from delinquents pelting the sign with rocks or bottles or whatever was handy. It looked like the rusting hulk of a '59 Cadillac whose long-ago bigger-than-life presence and spectacle had been reduced to a dim, dented mess. It was a sorry excuse for its former glory.

I stood across the street in a trance for what seemed like only a moment. It must've actually been several minutes, because I didn't notice Gina Giannetti ("GG"—again with the nicknames) tugging on my sleeve, talking to me. Slowly, my mental fog started to lift and I could hear her voice. I blinked once or twice to reboot my brain and focus on Gina.

Gina and I grew up together, literally from birth. She was two days older than me. We had gone through school together, taken Holy Communion together, been Confirmed in the Church together, hung out with the same friends, gotten drunk together on the same beach, and thrown up under the same boardwalk. She's one of those people who's so close to you, you don't wipe the top of the bottle when passing it back and forth. Her family lived in the row house next door to us one block from Sonny's on the numbered street running perpendicular to this one. As far as I knew, her mother was still there.

Although our lives seemed to parallel one another forever, by high school we started to move in our own directions. By the time the rest of us were getting our high school diplomas, GG was pregnant, and then she had four kids—boom, boom, boom, boom—by the time any of our classmates got their college diplomas (and for our high school class, those college diplomas were few and far between, let me just tell you).

Girls being pregnant in high school aren't that uncommon these days, or even back then, but what was rare was when those girls were married two years before having that first baby. For whatever reason, GG got married when we were sophomores in high school and she became Gina Giordano. Her nickname changed from "GG" to "Gs" (which sounded like "Geez"), probably because GGG sounded like a stutter. She finished 10th grade, moved in with her new in-laws and never returned to the classroom, which was just as well because she never took school very seriously in the first place. She always told me her job was to be pretty, get married and have babies—in that order.

We've hardly seen each other in thirty-five years.

"Johnny! What the fuck?! You don't acknowledge me when you see me?! S'up wi 'dat?"

"GEEZ!" And I gave her a huge hug. It was like hugging a piece of my own self.

"You are a sight. Look at you!"

And she was a sight too. She was a hot little thing when we were growing up, and she hadn't lost a step since then, four kids or no.

"It's not Geez no more. It's GG again."

"Uh oh … What happened to the other G? I leave for a few months and you dump your old man?"

"It's a long story with an unhappy ending. Let's just say I won't be hearin' from *that* asshole anytime too soon."

"Well, his loss. You look great. Single life clearly agrees with you—not bad for a mother of 4."

"… and a grandmother of 10."

"What the f …?"

"- not hard to do when you figure my youngest is in her early 30s. Besides, my family likes to have babies early. You forget my *grandmother* and your *dad* were the same age."

"Well, I feel like I'm late to the party, me with no kids at all at my advanced age—the fuck I been doin'?!" I said jokingly.

"You just never found the right girl—always waiting for that Indian girl. You know, you coulda had any number of girls from the neighborhood if you wanted. The one next door to you for one …"

"Mary Constantine would have had me? Damn! And she was HOT!"

"Next door the other way, jackass, and Mary Constantine was not hot. Her nose was like a friggin' hood ornament and her body was … lumpy."

"Oh yeah. The *other* side. Right. You mean your sister? She was a pretty nice piece too."

"I'm going to have to hurt you now."

"How 'bout I buy you lunch instead. It's past noon and I could use something with broccoli rabe in it. Five miles outside Philadelphia, no one knows what broccoli rabe is anymore, let alone how to cook and use it. It's a lot like you, a bitter bitch, but I miss it." And I squeezed her.

"Aww … you flatterer, since when do you buy me lunch? You're comin' to my place and I'm *makin'* you lunch, Mr. Chef." She leaned in so only I could hear what she said next: "My mom passed away and I live alone, so you might get dessert if you're a good boy." She patted my crotch lightly and let her hand linger on it for a couple seconds—just long enough for me to feel things waking up down there—and she laughed.

She'd never touched me like that before—never showed any such interest whatsoever—took me *completely* by surprise. According to the response from body parts below my belt, I was interested. I probably should have told her I was sorry to hear about her mom, but honestly, there wasn't a whole lotta blood circulating in my brain for cognitive thinking. My blood supply was heading south quickly, destined for that area slightly below my belt.

Now, I don't care who you are. You could be having the worst day of your life. Your dog could have just gotten run over by your own mother, but when a good-looking woman whispers something like that into your ear and puts her hand on your … well, let me tell you. Everything you were thinking about just before that moment flushes out of your head like it was taken away by a tidal wave. The next thing you know, you're tryin' to think about baseball lineups and pizza, hoping you stop yourself from waking up too much down there to the point things become apparent to everyone around you. Know what I'm sayin'?

My heart was beating a little harder and quicker as we started walking back to her house. We talked about people who lived in one part of the neighborhood or the other and she pointed at a couple shops whose owners were talking about closing up and moving after being in business forever. GG reminisced about moments here and there and how it's been so long, blah blah blah.

GG and Johnny
PART 1

We reached her front door, and being an old-school gentleman, I grabbed her keys from her hand and trotted to the door to open it. She barely broke stride as she passed. She grinned slyly, snatched her housekeys back from me in a single, smooth motion and tossed her hair at me in the process. Her thick, wavy hair brushed across my face, and at that moment I was struck by her amazing aroma.

She smelled like Sunday Gravy and meatballs, only twice as delicious. Okay, not literally, but she smelled like home—familiar and welcoming.

Once inside, I regained my composure, closed the door and asked suspiciously, "So what are we *really* doing here?"

She spun around quickly and stopped within inches of me, stood on her tippy-toes (she was REALLY short) gazed up into my eyes and smugly replied, "Why, John, it only took you about fifty years to learn 'lunch' doesn't always mean *lunch.*" With that, her right hand gently cupped and squeezed my groin, while her left hand grabbed the back of my neck and pulled me down to her level for a strong, passionate kiss.

She pulled back from the kiss, looked me in the eyes and said, "This has been a long time comin', my friend."

Lunch was definitely going to be delayed.

Like most Italian men, I like to consider myself to be something of a Don Juan, so I scooped her up in my hands, carried her to the sofa and proceeded to paw at her spastically while we simultaneously tore off one another's clothes.

Perhaps "Don Juan" isn't exactly the image I'm projecting. To be fair, I did say I *like to* consider myself to be Don Juanesque. I would also *like* to say I can dunk a basketball, throw a 95-mph fastball, and break 75 every time I play golf. The truth is, I can't dunk a basketball because I'm actually shorter when I jump than I am when I'm standing. I can barely throw a ball across a room these days because of my old and worn out rotator cuff, and I don't even play golf. Worse yet, instead of passionately molesting each other for hours on the sofa, in less than ten minutes, Geez was looking around on the couch for her bra, and I was wondering why I was still wearing one of my socks.

"No wonder I wasn't getting any traction on the push-off ..." I said in a feeble attempt to excuse any perceived performance issues.

She found her skirt first and held it up for me to see.

"Damnit!" she said, completely ignoring what I just said. "You tore the button off the back of my skirt, you friggin' Neanderthal!" and then she laughed.

I glibly replied "Well, I'd care a little more about that if I was eating that sandwich you had promised me."

She glared back at me and mockingly back-handed me across my chest.

She threw her bra (which she finally found on the floor) and her skirt on the sofa and stomped off into the kitchen wearing only her underwear, to see what there was to eat. In the meantime, I took that opportunity to grumble about not being limber as I tried to pull my pants up from a seated position.

My self-loathing was interrupted by Gina's voice calling from the kitchen. "How hungry are you?"

"Pretty fuckin' hungry, except this time, I'm not speaking euphemistically. I really do want food, and something to drink, if you've got it. I suddenly find myself mildly dehydrated, for some reason."

"Well, shit. That could all be a problem, unless a glass of tap water will satisfy all your needs, including hunger. My fridge is more barren than an eighty-year-old nun."

"… and somehow, with that image, I've lost my appetite. Thanks for the visual. Tell you what, come back in here and put on some clothes, and I'll take you to lunch."

"That's the least you could do," she quipped as she sauntered back into the room.

I stared a little too long at her naked torso and her tussled hair. She stopped a couple feet away, caught my stare, shrugged and said "WHAT?!"

I grabbed her wrist, spun her back onto the sofa, leaned in for a kiss, and gazed into her eyes.

"Oh? Are we doing this again?" she asked playfully.

"Yeah, but this time, I'm takin' things nice and slow."

Four minutes later, we leaned back on the sofa again, gaspin' for air like the geezers we are.

I placed my palm on her thigh, took a deep breath and said "I really don't feel like goin' anywhere for food. I'm a trained professional. Let me take a look in that fridge of yours and make an informed decision whether or not we have options."

I made it over to the kitchen, wearing only pants and that one sock, threw open the refrigerator door, and was boggled by the sheer emptiness of it. I returned to the sofa, plopped down beside her, looked her square in the eyes and said "You're right. You got nothin'. Put on some clothes already so we can eat, you cheap slut. I'm starvin'."

She tried to swat me again, but this time I caught her hand before it hit me and kissed it—always the hitting with this one!

AND FOR DESSERT ...

There comes a time in every sexual marathon where the desire to copulate (*screw* seems so crass) becomes overshadowed by one's craving for food. Sometimes these things can be combined, god knows, but since Gina apparently considers her refrigerator to be a secret passage to Narnia, instead of a place to store food, we were going to have to disregard any kinky food-related thoughts tonight. Instead we started collecting our clothes off the floor and furniture to get dressed and go eat like normal people.

Gina fixed her hair and makeup in the hallway mirror, because no self-respecting Italian girl can leave the house without full war-paint and carefully styled hair. I made sure my shirt wasn't misbuttoned and ran my fingers through my hair. Done, and done.

One of the reasons many urbanites never own cars, one of the MANY reasons, is because between walking and public transportation, everything one's little heart desires is remarkably accessible. Tonight, we decided we needed food, so we stepped out GG's front door, took two steps to the sidewalk and within a block, we were seated in what seemed to be one of about a thousand good Italian restaurants within the confines of the city.

For the record, ethnic East Coast cities tend to be like this. Some family decides to convert its row home into a restaurant and there you have it—a restaurant smack-dab in the middle of a residential street.

Like any of these places, menus were for show and tourists. Every locally owned Italian restaurant offers the same fare.

Some nights I'm in the mood for lasagna; others I'm looking for a spicy Bolognese, clams or mussels in a red or white sauce, or maybe a nice veal parm or saltimboca, but tonight—after an afternoon of debauchery—I was committed to purity: "spag and balls!" That would be spaghetti and meatballs smothered in a nice ragu, for those of you who are not well-versed in the local dialect.

Gina ordered a salad, of course, because like every middle-aged Italian woman, she was on a perpetual starvation diet. I knew the spag and balls would be a huge order, but I also knew damned well, even though Gina was desperately projecting the "dainty flower" image, she was going to end up eating half of whatever was on my plate. I started preemptively planning dessert to avoid leaving the table hungry.

Chicks. They think we don't notice these things.

The food came out quickly, as it should, so we didn't spend much time chatting before the meal. We spent even less time talking once it landed on our table. Never underestimate the appetite an afternoon of fooling around generates.

As anticipated, Gina ate her share of my food, but I almost had to break her hand when she reached for the last piece of garlic bread. Chivalry is one thing, but when you've intentionally left a puddle of gravy on the plate to be swabbed up with whatever sliver of bread is left on the table, you're not about to surrender that husk to anyone under any circumstances.

After dinner, I very reluctantly resisted the urge to unsnap my pants, lean back and belch, even though I really wanted to. GG wasn't much better off than me. We both looked at one another, bulged our eyes out and exhaled heavily like we'd just gone three rounds in a Gold Gloves match against a couple forks and ten pounds of pasta.

We finally got around to talking about why I'd come home, and what was going on with Sonny's, and how pissed off I was. I don't ordinarily talk about myself too much when I'm on a date, but GG was hardly a date. Plus I was so obsessed about my family's circumstances, I couldn't help but pour out my soul.

GG hung in there like a trooper. She sat and took it all in, nodding occasionally when I'd make a particularly demonstrative point. Otherwise she sat there staring at me and blinking occasionally, even though she was probably bored out of her mind and really didn't follow what the hell I was bitching about anyway.

When I finally stopped for a breath after what was probably 10 minutes of monologuing, she interrupted me and told me she had to hit the lady's room and then go home to feed the grandkids. She got up and I settled the tab. I was just putting my wallet back in my pocket when I heard the scream from back beyond the dining room.

It was Gina.

Like I had been blown out of a cannon, I bolted through the place, which was only as deep from front to back as a typical row home since that's what the place was before it was converted into a restaurant. I burst into the alley through the propped-open back door.

Two thugs were back there. Gina was curled up on the ground, shielding herself from the attacker who was kneeling in front of her, wrestling with her hands, grabbing at her clothes and her purse. The other guy was standing back near the door I'd just exited, looking like he'd just thrown Gina across the alley.

It was all happening too fast to take in many details, but both of these guys were Italian, and not from here—at least I didn't recognize them. They were both big, like not quite the size of a side-by-side refrigerator/freezer, but definitely big enough they'd have to turn sideways to get through a standard doorway. I did notice they were both very hairy and smelled like they hadn't bathed since, I don't know, let's say the third grade. Oh, and they had very large hands and feet, because their fists felt like the size of bricks when they hit me, and when they kicked me, it felt they were wearing Frankenstein's monster's boots.

I'm not naive. These guys were muggers (or worse). I was no match for them, but I also knew I was going to hold up better against them than Gina, so I shoved the guy next to the door when I came out, ran and grabbed the other guy up off the ground and spun him into the dumpster and told Gina to get up and run. She bolted back inside the restaurant, past the thug who was getting himself to his feet and she slammed the door behind her.

I turned to run but didn't get far. The guy against the dumpster swung out his arm and caught my foot. It was a lucky flail, but he caught just enough of my foot to send me flying and landing in a heap on the loose alley gravel. I was done.

While the one guy blocked the door back into the restaurant, the other guy who knocked me down was on me before I could turn around. He was punching and kicking every part of me.

Funny thing about getting beaten up (as long as it's just punching and kicking) is after the first couple hits that hurt like motherfuckers and basically shatter the serenity of not being beaten, all the other hits sort of blend together—no single strike really being any more memorable than the last—and certainly not as memorable as the first.

It's like we used to say as teenagers when someone would ask how the school year was going. We'd say "it's like being ass-raped in prison: the first few times are horrible, but then you sorta get used to it."

Laying on the ground, taking punch after punch and kick after kick, I was getting used to it.

All that would change if a sharp weapon or handgun was introduced to the party, but if these guys had one of those, they never got the chance to use it. GG burst back out through the door with the entire kitchen staff. The thug at the door was knocked backward again about a half dozen feet from the impact of the door being blown open in his face by the rampaging crew, and the other guy—at the sight of this sea of pissed off Italians—took off down the alley and disappeared.

A few of the gang who came to my rescue rushed to me with Gina and helped take inventory of the damage I'd incurred. The others focused on the guy who was knocked down by the door and proceeded to give him what his buddy had given to me, and then some.

Gina helped me inside and to a seat at an open table. Some of the others went to the kitchen to grab a few wet towels to help clean me up. The rest of the patrons just sat at their respective tables, slack-jawed, marveling at what they'd heard and seen. Some of them were from the neighborhood and got up to help while the ones from the suburbs silently vowed to never return to the big city again—it's just too violent and they'd be better off eating at that nice Olive Garden near the mall.

Another funny thing about getting the crap beaten out of you is it never hurts completely until you actually *see* the damage. I was in no rush to see my bruises or look at the cuts on my face. I figured it wasn't a pretty sight, judging by the look of horror on Gina's face as she looked at me and dabbed a towel into cuts, pulling back quickly whenever I winced. I really didn't need to look.

I could feel my eyes and lips and nose swelling up, even under the bags of ice being pressed against my skin. The bruised muscles all over my body were beginning to stiffen up. If I could have opened my swollen lips wide enough to push a capsule into my mouth, I would have consumed an entire economy-sized bottle of Ibuprofen if it had been offered. It wouldn't have made a difference, though.

Remember earlier when I said only the first few blows hurt? Well, that's true when it's happening, but later on—when the beating's stopped and your adrenalin is coming back down from orbit—the effects of every single one of the subsequent blows are felt … times ten.

"Do you need to go to the hospital?" one of the out-of-town guests asked.

"Of course not! He'll be just fine. We'll get him cleaned up and I'll get him home to bed. He's *fine*." Gina snapped.

I looked at her and winked, or at least I think I winked. That eye was pretty swollen, so the wink may have only been perceptible inside my own head. Us neighborhood kids may be stupid, but we're tough. That's one piece of our heritage we haven't lost. We still play tackle football in the street, and we still take beatings like cavemen—just get up, brush yourself off, and get back into the fight.

A couple of the cooks helped me to my feet and then supported my weight as I staggered back to GG's place up the block.

All of the kitchen guys in the neighborhood knew each other. It was like a college fraternity … except most of our members possessed virtually no formal education. We'd all see one another at after-hours clubs, where we'd descend after working all night and closing up our respective kitchens. Waitstaff, cooks, dishwashers, and hostesses, we'd all land at some bar and wait for our own bar crews to close up and catch up. More often than not, we'd all spend whatever money we made earlier that night on drinks and food and service at the after-hours place, but that was our lives. Every day we'd wake up, take care of personal crap, go to work, get cash, go out until all hours of the morning, go to sleep and then repeat the process over and over and over.

Gina opened the front door of her house and the crew carried me in, trying to gently place me in a chair—except they lost their grip on me from about a foot above the cushions. I dropped down and landed hard against the bottom frame of the chair. The cushions were apparently there for looks only—they didn't remotely absorb my weight. I must've let out a huge groan when I landed because everyone stepped backward with their hands in the air and a look of shock on their faces.

GG rushed them out of the house, thanking them for trying, and then returned to prop me up on the "chair of cruelty."

"Who can I call?" she asked.

"Do I still have my cell phone?"

"Yeah. It's right here."

"Good. Press the number sign and '1' and hand me the phone."

Gina did as asked and Uncle G answered. "S'up, kid?"

"I got the crap beaten out of me and I'm sitting in Gina Giannetti's living room, bleeding."

"What da FUCK?! I'll be right there. DO NOT MOVE!" and he clicked off.

"Who was that?"

"It's my uncle."

"Oh." She did a horrible job of veiling her disapproval. "What'd *he* say?" Gina asked, transitioning from concerned to pissed off, taking a step back from me and crossing her arms against her chest, looking like she was ready to get into it with me for whatever she thought Guido had to say.

"Calm down, okay? He's coming by to pick me up. I can't stay here. He's going to take me back to Angela's."

"Why *can't* you stay here?! Is there something *wrong* with here?!" she snapped.

"Yeah, there is. First of all, your refrigerator is empty and I have an aversion to sleeping somewhere where there's no food. Secondly, I've monopolized you enough for one day. I need to go home and regroup. Thirdly, your grandkids don't need to see a bleeding, beaten old man on a chair in their living room when they come down in the morning for their oatmeal."

"Fine. Am I going to see you tomorrow?" she asked, as if her feelings were hurt.

"Assuming I don't die tonight from this beating? Yes, but you have to go buy some goddamned groceries."

I had barely gotten the words out of my mouth when the room lit up with headlights from a car screeching to a stop in front of GG's. Guido and two of his guys burst through the door. They reached me and very methodically picked me up and carried me back out to the car.

Guido said something polite to Gina on the way into and out of her place and we drove off.

'Splaining to Do

"Why were you with *her*?"

"Uncle G, would you please relax? I'm really not in the mood for …"

"Don't tell me to relax, kid. Your family is under siege, and we need to be circling wagons. Everybody in the circle has to be family. No outsiders."

"Unc, I've known this woman since we've both been in diapers—50 years. She and I grew up next door to each other until I was halfway through high school. She's the closest thing I have to a sister besides my own sister. She *is* family."

"Just keep your eyes open, kid. There are five people in this world you can trust—me, your mother, your father, your sister, and Joe Acchione—your family. You should always be suspicious of everyone else."

"That seems sorta paranoid, doesn't it? Besides, you and Mr. Acchione aren't my family. By your logic, I can only trust my parents and my sister. I should be wary of you and these guys in the car right now."

"Keep using that wit of yours to take the place of common sense, Johnny, and one of these nights I'll get a call to come pick up your *dead* body instead of just your *beaten* body. Start being careful."

"I'm sorry, Unc. I'm really not that sharp right now. I think I just need to go lay down and start putting pieces back together. Just get me to Angela's and I'll hit the sack."

"We're not going to Angela's. We're going to Acchione's. His nurse is always there. She can check you out and help put you back together."

"She's not family. Are you sure we can trust her?"

"I swear to Christ, kid: If you don't cut this shit out, I'm not even going to slow down or pull over. I'm just going to push you out of this moving car. I might even speed up a little."

I tried to laugh until I realized how much it hurt. Then Uncle Guido laughed at my discomfort. Dick!

"They did a nice job on your face. I can barely recognize you," he said.

Knowing I would regret this, I asked anyway: "Is it an improvement?"

"I'm still trying to decide," he joked as he looked into the rearview mirror to see my reflection between his bodyguards on the backseat.

"Did you get a look at the guys who did this?" He was serious again.

"Only briefly—Italian, big, not from our neighborhood, definitely not guys I recognized."

"I'll ask around and find out who they were and why they went after you."

"They didn't go after me. I went after them."

"You paid the bill and then decided to go out back and mix it up with a couple muggers? What, they were out of tiramisu and you decided a nice ass-kicking would be a good alternative?"

"Not quite. They had grabbed Gina when she went to the lady's room. She screamed and I ran out to help."

"Still not clear why …"

"Unc, can we please just get to Mr. Acchione's in quiet? My head is pounding and I really don't feel like enduring your third-degree interrogation right now. You can pull out the 'rubber hose' and interrogate me in the morning, but right now I desperately need peace and quiet and sleep."

"Okay, but we're not done here."

"Yes, dear …" came rolling out of my mouth condescendingly. The two mesomorphs seated on either side of me looked at me in shock for speaking this way to G. Family can get away with shit like this—even though we're not *really* family.

The ride was only a few minutes across town, but my body nearly completely cramped by the time we reached the old man's house; I almost couldn't move. Unc's two bruisers pretty much had to lift me out of the car and carry me into Mr. Acchione's place. Although his nurse answered and opened the door, Mr. Acchione was there in the foyer waving his arms and panicking.

"Oh, my boy. When I suggested you stay here with me, I didn't mean in a hospital bed. *I'm* supposed to be the invalid here, not you! Quickly you two, carry him upstairs. Marilyn, show them where to set him down and then take care of him. Guido, you and I need to talk. Please join me in the study."

The two old power brokers adjourned into the study where we'd all met this morning. They closed those massive, solid mahogany pocket doors behind them. The room was like a wooden vault, but I could hear them murmuring as I was carried up the steps, following Marilyn, the nurse.

"His room is up here at the top of the steps," she said matter-of-factly.

I was set down on the bed much more gently than I was set into the chair at GG's earlier in the night. The two gorillas stepped back and waited for their next instruction, which Marilyn didn't hesitate to bark out.

"Don't just stand there, take off his clothes while I get my medical bag."

The guys were visibly uncomfortable with that plan. They stammered, looked at one another and then nearly knocked each other over as they bolted down the steps.

I should mention I've known these two since we were in kindergarten together. Trust me—none of us want to see each other naked, and we'd all be especially uncomfortable stripping off one another's clothes.

Marilyn shook her head and muttered something about homophobes, then proceeded to peel off my clothes in a completely emotionless—if not clinical—manner. Some things stuck to me, like the shirt and my underwear, where blood had acted like glue, sealing the fabric to my skin. She was delicate and capable when it came to unsticking those things, even while she kept repeating the word "ugh" and the phrase "tsk tsk tsk tsk" as she got a clearer and clearer view of my impressive bruising.

Regardless, no matter how clinical disrobing is—and no matter how battered my body was—I was singularly focused on the rousing of my groin.

Being a guy really sucks sometimes.

Contrary to popular belief by women, men have absolutely no control over what goes on down there. In fact, during puberty, it was painfully common to get what we would affectionately refer to as "bus woodies."

These were exactly what they sounded like. In the morning, on the way to school, when we're only half awake, the bus ride would be just long enough and would jostle us just enough for us to produce unintentional erections. There, I said it—okay? Erections.

The most frustrating thing about erections is they can't be stopped. We can't will them away. Of nearly equal frustration is the fact they are not always sexually inspired. Sometimes a warm tail bone is all that's necessary. Sometimes just being released from underwear will do it.

Invariably, no matter how much we prayed it would go away, the erection would be at "full throb" just as the bus was pulling into the school driveway. Not a single pubescent boy was in a rush to stand up for fear of inadvertently tapping the kid in the seat in front of us on the shoulder with our peckers. We'd wait as long as possible to get up, and then hold something—lunch bag, backpack, history book, coat, whatever—in front of our laps all the way into school until the goddamned thing would relax. God forbid you tripped off the bus and landed stomach-down on the sidewalk. You'd likely break your dick—a fear of every teenaged boy.

In this case, as Marilyn was slowly, methodically disrobing me, I could feel tingling and arousal. I knew it was just the cool air hitting my junk as it was released from the confines of my underwear, but regardless, the skin was beginning to stretch and my member slowly, almost imperceptibly began separating from being stuck to my thigh. "FUCK!" I thought, and I silently repeated this mantra in my head: "Don't get hard. Don't get hard. Don't get hard."

I started thinking about disgusting images, or stared at pictures on the walls or at the sconces next to the fireplace or at the alarm clock on the table next to my head. I was never able to distract myself sufficiently to stop the erection process, however. In the back of my mind I knew exactly what I was trying to do, so my efforts were moot.

Marilyn was a fine-looking woman and all, if not a little "sturdy," but that had nothing to do with my sudden arousal. The fact a woman was stripping me got my pulse quickening and my blood flowing. It all seemed to be settling into the chambers in my … well, penis.

There—I said "penis," too.

She spoke up as she was peeling off my boxers. "I think the bruising actually looks worse than it is. Don't get me wrong, you're going to hurt for a few days and most of your skin is going to be varying shades of purple. In the long run, though, none of this looks permanent. Nothing's broken and none of the cuts need stitches."

"Well, that's reassuring, I guess." I sighed through my obvious concentration.

She added, "By the way, don't let the erection upset you. Such a reaction is very common as your penis is let out from below your garments and the air hits it. It happens to Mr. Acchione all the time."

And there it was. The thought of Mr. Acchione getting wood was all it took to reverse the trend. The drawbridge was going down and I started to relax.

Wow, THAT was an image.

"… even though his is much bi—"

"Please, GOD don't finish that sentence," I blurted out.

She started laughing and smacked me lightly on one of the non-bruised sections of skin on my thigh. The next thing I knew, she injected me with something. "You have nothing to worry about Mr. Valmonti. You stay right there and I'll be back with some bandages and ointment."

DEBRIEFING

Joe Acchione's drawing room took on a different personality at night. Sunlight didn't stream in through the leaded glass of the large front window like it did in the morning. Colorful shards of light didn't dance across the walls and floor as though the room's occupants were seated within a private kaleidoscope. Instead, the room's nighttime personality was dominated by the absence of light. The dark wood paneling covering the walls from ceiling to floor absorbed the ambient light, making the darkness seem almost deep—like a black hole. At night the room was like a subterranean bunker with fancy woodwork. Only the glow from the low-wattage sconces near the door and the small task lamp on Joe's desk lit the room enough for the men to navigate the floor without bruising shins on a lurking ottoman.

The old friends filed in and sat together on the upholstered furniture near the window—Joe on the velvet sofa, and Guido in the arm chair where he leaned forward, like always, ready to pounce.

It was late. Every day since he began high school, Joe trained himself to be up before dawn and on the river to row. That discipline has lasted him a lifetime. Although he's not getting out on the river anymore, he's still an early riser, getting out of bed no later than 6:00 a.m. Under normal circumstances, to be an "early bird," he would have been asleep for a few hours already. Conversely, Guido's world had always been predominately focused on nocturnal activities. Even though he was a night owl in his younger days—both out of necessity and natural body clock—he rarely made it past midnight these days before falling asleep, usually in an overstuffed chair in front of a television, probably leaning forward, his elbows on his knees, ready to leap out of his chair and go at the slightest provocation.

Both men should have been exhausted by now—especially as busy as they both had been since they awoke this morning—but their adrenaline was pumping overtime, keeping them both *more* than awake. They were sharp and oblivious to the hour as they sat together, assessing the day's activities and plotting their strategy.

"I think we both know who this is, Joe."

"No we don't, Guido. It's the first conclusion you always jump to. You're so sensitive to them, you tend to think they initiate every atrocity on the planet. You'd blame them for global warming, if you could."

"You're saying I'm paranoid?"

"No. I'm saying you're always on alert for them—and for good reason—but not every affront in the world is by their design. I'm here to play devil's advocate—to punch holes in your theory in an effort to keep us objective. You've been singing this same tune for years and years, and not once have your concerns borne fruit. I, of all people, know we should always be on our guard, of course, but we should also be prepared to consider alternative protagonists. If we had some facts to support your assumption, maybe I'd be more likely to agree with you. As it is? I see no basis to lend any credence to it."

"Sometimes I worry your quest for objectivity tilts you off-balance to excuse them from everything and that will leave us ill-prepared and exposed one of these days."

"That's why we are such a good yin and yang for one another, old friend. Together, we make up two halves of one logical strategist."

"And our other two halves make a misguided tactician?"

"Ha ha—too true, I suppose. So argue your case to me. Why now, Guido? After all these years, what's changed? They've been dormant for *decades* here, yet suddenly, our little family has become a bright blip on their radar screen? Why? You've said yourself, they've grown so huge—*international*—that we've become almost imperceptibly insignificant in their world. Why would they surface now? What's changed? If anything, we're all so old we're more likely to die of natural causes than at their hands. I doubt anyone in their organization even remembers us anymore."

"Maybe that's it. Maybe the giant finally woke up and realized it nearly waited too long. If it doesn't act soon, nature would do what they themselves had sworn to do long ago. Maybe this is the last gasp of the old guard. Did you think of that?"

"I think you give the beast too much credit, my friend. But who knows? You may be spot-on. Right now, we have no idea. It's all con-jecture. All we *do* know is someone is targeting our family—John Sr. and Toni, Tom, Angela, John Jr.—and their offenses are becoming more dangerous and more personal. It feels as though we're fast approaching the crescendo of a song we've never heard before, and we don't know who wrote it or who's playing it."

"Then let's turn up the 'house lights,' to continue your analogy. Today may have been a dark day, but it could have been far worse if we hadn't been so lucky. In the end, it worked out okay. Johnny should be fine—badly bruised, sure, but he'll recover. Had those restaurant employee friends of his not run out and rescued him, he could have been beaten to death. He wasn't. That was some amazingly good luck. Angela is hardly any worse for wear, although she'll probably need a new minivan to replace the one that got rumpled. Technology was the stroke of luck that protected her. Tom lost his job—not exactly the end of the world. If our family was a prizefighter, it would be staggering against the ropes, but it would still be up when the bell rung to end the round. Quite the accomplishment after the other fighter took their shots."

"Action by them means there are instigators—actual human beings instead of the faceless corporate ghosts we've been chasing for months. This is great news! *People* are finally making moves—scuttling Tom's career, running Ange off the road, beating Johnny—people can be found. Someone somewhere must have seen something. We just have to find one witness to start the chain of discovery. If we're looking for facts and proof, we merely need to find those who have perpetrated those acts and we know they're in town, somewhere."

"You and I need to divide and conquer here, Joe. My crew has already begun work on finding answers to what happened with Angela and Johnny. Can you navigate your legal network to figure out what happened to Tom? When we come back together with our facts, I'll bet you fifty bucks I'm right and they're behind the whole thing!"

"I don't have the contacts I once did, but I have some," Joe replied. I'll start making calls first thing in the morning and hopefully they'll lead somewhere. You're right. Now that they've come out a bit from beneath their rock, we should have better luck finding them—fortunate, indeed."

"I just hope we find *them* before they *end* us. This family has a lot of faces out there on our perimeter, and I need to dedicate at least some of my resources to protecting them. I have work to do. The night's not getting any younger, so I'd better be on my way, Joseph."

"At this late hour? Guido, you need to rest or you'll be of no use to us. Stay here. Goodness knows, there's plenty of room."

"Too much to do, and too little time to do it. I'll fit in sleep where and when I can. My world is at its most active at night. I need to monitor it. My crew is out there getting answers. I need to be available when they finally get some. See you at 10:00? And don't forget to get fifty bucks out from under your mattress, buddy. I'm winning this bet!"

"I haven't lost such a bet with you since the 1950s. I think my money is still safe. We'll reconvene here at 10:00 a.m. For now, if you'll excuse me, my world is still asleep, and I intend to join it."

A BRAND-NEW DAY

It was a morning like any other, and by that I mean I felt like shit.

I loathed morning. I had been trained at an early age to live like a vampire—stay up all night and wake up after noon. Since the sun was streaming through the window horizontally, I knew it wasn't noon—and the smell of bacon and coffee meant it was probably morning.

Good. I knew what time of day it was. Now if only I knew where the hell I was!

You know how it was when you wake up in a hotel and your first thought is "This is not my bedroom"? You lay there for a second while the squirrel in your brain gets up to speed on his wheel. You gradually piece things together and remember where you are. Well, I guess my squirrel was limping—or hung over or something—because it took that wheel a little longer than usual to get spinning. In the meantime, I was not acclimating to my surroundings. To be fair, this was my third different bed in as many nights—New Orleans, then Ange's and now, as it turns out, Mr. Acchione's.

Combine that bed-hopping with a few shots to the head in an alley last night—and a shot of Marilyn's mind-altering drugs—and I was willing to forgive the squirrel.

Still, once the cobwebs cleared, I realized I'd been asleep for ten hours—possibly my longest uninterrupted session of sleep since I was a kid.

Whatever was in that syringe last night was magical. It knocked me out. I never moved once all night. I'm sure I had some psychedelic dreams, but being a guy, I never remember them once I wake up.

While I'm on the subject, why do women make such a big deal about their dreams? One woman I lived with considered her dreams to be the most fascinating sources of conversation imaginable. She'd always go into great detail telling me about her dreams. She'd get so excited, she'd almost fall off the bed from all the gesturing and exaggerated commentary. Of course, the dreams never made any sense to anyone but her—and would be about completely ridiculous topics—but since I shared her bed, I was stuck listening to these stories, trying to look like I cared.

The worst times were when I did something bad in her dreams and she'd be mad at me all day for it. She'd ignore me, or sneer at me, and when I'd ask her what was wrong, she'd be offended, like I was an insensitive jackass for even asking such an obvious question. When she'd finally tell me why she was angry with me, I'd delicately point out that I never actually *did* what she dreamt I did and therefore shouldn't actually *be* in trouble for it. Bizarrely, she'd agree, and then tell me she was angry anyway but would be better tomorrow after a good night's sleep.

It was times like that that made me wish I'd just become a priest like my mother wanted, so I'd have avoided all this.

Anyway, Marilyn's medicinal cocktail was so great, I had nearly forgotten how sore and incapacitated I was as I spun to the edge of the bed and hopped onto my feet. I crumbled to the floor and yelled "MOTHERFUCKER!" as the pain shot through my body like lightning bolts.

Mr. Acchione's house was mammoth and quiet as a church. As loud as my explosive profanity was, the sound multiplied three-fold as it echoed through the stone and wood interior walls of this fortress. I rarely get embarrassed, especially when I'm cursing, but in this case, I felt like an asshole.

Marilyn, completely unfazed by my outburst, came in with a fresh change of clothes for me. That's when the brain squirrel kicked it up a notch and I realized I was crouched on the floor, naked.

"Here," she said, as she handed me a bundle of clothes. "These are yours. Angela brought them from her house this morning. Do you need help putting them on?"

"NO!" I embarrassingly yelled, but as I made my first effort to get my boxers around my ankles, my entire body froze up. I changed my tune to a far-more civil and humble "Yes, please?"

"Here—give me your hand, and I'll help you onto the bed."

You know the sound a dog makes when you step on its paw? That's the one I made when she practically lifted me off the floor and assisted me to a seated position on the fluffy and obnoxiously high-off-the-ground mattress.

"You forget. I saw you in all your naked glory last night. You haven't changed much since then."

" … still embarrassing."

"For both of us, dear. For both of us. Now try to lift your leg and rear end so I can get you into your underwear and then your jeans. Is there a reason why 'home of the whopper' is printed across the crotch of your underwear?"

"They're joke underwear. A girl I knew bought them for me."

"Obviously, she was being sarcastic," Marilyn said with a smirk.

"Your bedside manner sorta sucks, Marilyn. Anyone ever tell you that?"

"Only people I need to help into their joke underwear …"

After several more minutes of witty exchanges with the house nurse (and my performance of the Quadriplegic Ballet), I was finally fully clothed and Marilyn helped me—this time off the bed—and then gently guided me to the bathroom so I could pee and brush my teeth, in that order. In both cases, blood was visible.

I resurfaced a few minutes later from the bathroom, and she eased me to the hallway and down the steps to the kitchen. Believe me when I tell you, saying that sentence was a LOT quicker than me actually accomplishing the task. Each time my foot settled on a descending stair tread, a shockwave shot through my entire body like a bolt of lightning. By the time I made it to the kitchen table, I was soaked in sweat from the effort.

Angela and Mr. Acchione were already on their second or third cups of coffee by the time I got there. Uncle G joined from the main hall. He'd just returned from the front door with the morning *Philadelphia Inquirer*. He slid the paper out of its plastic bag and onto the table.

"Looks like the front-page headline this morning is all about you, John: 'Dumbass Dego Beaten Bloody Behind Dumpster,'" Uncle G quipped with his back turned to the table as he balled-up the plastic sleeve the newspaper had arrived in and tossed it in the trash can under the sink.

One of Uncle G's bodyguards spoke up from his chair in the corner "Is that really the headline today? Hey, Johnny, you're a celebrity!"

We all simultaneously looked over at him and tilted our heads.

"Gee thanks, Dom. You're lookin' particularly muscular today. You get to the gym already this morning?"

"Nah, John. I been here at the house all night wit all youz. Can someone hand me the sports section?"

Uncle G had lost his patience with this conversation and snapped at Dom "Just sit there quietly, okay?"

"Yes, boss," Dom replied contritely. He put his head down and stared at his coffee cup.

Uncle G looked at me as I crinkled my nose and mouthed "Yes, boss" back at him. He snickered and resumed his routine with the coffee maker.

Angela hadn't stopped staring at me since I entered the room or sat down. "Holy shit. You look awful," she blurted out almost by reflex.

"And you look like a 19-year-old supermodel. Thanks for nothin'," I replied, but I couldn't blame her. The only thing that looks worse than someone right after they've taken a beating is that same person the following day. Van Gogh would have been envious of the colors I'd achieved with my hematomas. "And what's with the extra make-up this morning, Ange? You didn't have time to go home and cleanup after your late night of pole dancing?" I jabbed, taking every opportunity to poke fun at my dear sibling.

Angela started crying.

"Jesus *Christ*, kid. Could you be any more of an oblivious asshole?!" Guido yelled.

"What?! What?!"

"You're an asshole," she barked through her tears. "The same monsters who destroyed Mom and Pop's lives got Tom *fired* yesterday, and possibly *disbarred*—and then they ran my van into a barricade on the Schuylkill and nearly killed me—but thanks for all the concern, dickhead! If the boys had been in the van …"

"Whoa … I had no idea. Are you okay? Is Tom okay? Uncle G, what the fuck?!"

"Just relax and focus on your own bruises, dumbass. And do me a favor. *Think* before you say anything else stupid this morning, okay?"

"I'm not making any promises," I replied, but I was only half-kidding.

"Baby steps, kid. Try to make it past breakfast without saying anything stupid, and then if that works, maybe try to make it all the way to lunch."

Mr. Acchione hadn't said anything at all since I sat down. He just sat there looking concerned and finally tilted his head and weakly pointed toward me. "How are *you* feeling son?"

"I avoided seeing my reflection this morning, Mr. Acchione, but I'll lay cash money—no matter how bad I look—I feel ten times worse."

Unc chimed in: "Today'll be the worst of it, kid. Tomorrow you'll feel a little better. By the weekend, you'll be back out trolling alley dumpsters lookin' for a good beatin'."

"Uncle G, you are more inspirational than Jesus himself."

"Well, I do try," he said with a smile and laid a fresh cup of coffee down in front of me. "I'm all outta loaves and fishes, so here. Have one of these biscottis with your coffee." And he made a papal sign of the cross with the biscotti in front of me.

Coffee is a staple of life for kitchen workers. Cigarettes are too, but I gave up smoking years ago when a girl I was dating gave me the ultimatum: cigarettes or sex, but not both … tough choice. Because my family practically lived in a restaurant, every morning started with pots (plural) of coffee. We all kept pouring cup after cup until we were coherent, or until our bowels couldn't hold out anymore. For the record, I credit coffee with my family's regularity.

And we don't need a damned barista. That fancy shit is fine for what it is, but morning coffee should come from a pot and be ordered either with two simple syllables—"Cof-Fee"—or better yet, a point of a finger at a cup. It sounds cliché, but this is a blue-collar town. We all tend to either drink run-of-the-mill diner-style coffee or Italian espresso. Today, our kitchen's elixir of choice came from the sixty-year-old percolator on the countertop and tasted like someone poured pure liquid energy into my cup.

I leaned over and let the pungent steam from the cup wash across my face, opening every pore in its path. "Ahhhh. It's almost too good to drink."

"I'll make more, kiddo, so go ahead and drink up."

"Thanks, Unc."

Once all the formalities concluded, Angela started in on me.

"So what the hell possessed you to get into a fight with two muggers in an alley?"

"I was bored."

"Seriously?!"

"No, dumbass. You remember Gina, from next door?"

"You mean the girl I lived next door to for decades and have known since I was born? Yeah. I think I can place her ..."

"It's good to see your sarcasm survived the accident. Anyway, she and I bumped into each other by accident on the street yesterday and we ended up going out to dinner. We had just finished eating. She excused herself to the ladies room and the next thing I knew, she was screaming. Long story short, I investigated and got the shit beaten out of me."

"You *saw* Gina?! Jeeeeeesus. I didn't know she was back here. I thought she left to live with that no good husband of hers somewhere."

"Yeah. She did, but they broke up and now she's back here livin' with her daughter and grandkids in her parents' old house."

"Poor thing. To be alone at her age must be awful. Tell her I was asking about her 'next time you see her?"

Almost on cue, the doorbell rang, and Gina burst into the house yelling "Where's my sweet hero? I *have* to see him!" Ten seconds later, GG was standing in the kitchen, holding a box of more biscotti. Angela popped out of her chair and hugged Gina. After all, she was practically a sister to her too, not just to me.

Guido and Mr. Acchione visibly bristled when they saw Gina. She was definitely disrupting our inner sanctum. Conversation was going to go from talking about real shit to being polite and superficial.

I invited her to sit next to me. I asked Mr. Acchione if he'd mind if Gina could stay and keep me company, since I was obviously not going anywhere for at least the day. Always the gentleman, he agreed, and offered us the run of the place.

By that point, Uncle G had gotten past the surprise, stopped glaring at the guard he had specifically put at the door to prevent anyone from coming in, and retrieved a cup of coffee for Gina. He placed it in front of her at the table and asked "cream and sugar?"

"Neither, thanks." She hugged my arm and joked "I like my coffee like I like my men, strong and black!" She laughed a little louder than she had too, but no one else joined her. They just looked at her incredulously, and it wasn't because I'm not black. It was because it was a completely inappropriate thing to say in polite company.

You know that little switch most human beings possess preventing them from saying inappropriate things among mixed company? Gina doesn't have one of those switches. She and Angela and I were tight—always had been—but we really weren't very similar. We can all be crass around friends, but most of us watch our Ps and Qs when necessary. Gina wasn't sophisticated enough to know any differently, and frankly, she probably wasn't bright enough to notice either.

Uncle G just rolled his eyes and asked Marilyn if he could get her anything while he was up. She matched his eye roll, declined his offer, grabbed a biscotti, and left the room to get started on her routine. My presence here today was going to mean more work for her, so she wanted to get a jump on it.

"How are you feeling, Gina?" Angela asked with noticeable concern—but with at least a twinge of a lawyer-curiosity undercurrent.

"A little shaken up, to be honest, but I'd be a whole lot worse off if it wasn't for my Superman here. If he hadn't come running into the alley and taken charge, I don't know what would've happened to me."

Gina's voice was one of those on the higher end of the register, and what came out of her mouth under normal circumstances was more of a screech than words. Today, she was extra screechy. Maybe she was nervous, or maybe it was the tribal drums playing in my head since last night's beating making me more sensitive to it, but this morning, every sound from her mouth made my eye twitch in discomfort and made me wince a little, like when you're listening to an elementary school band concert and the clarinet squeaks and drowns out every other sound in the room.

Before she could continue, Uncle G took advantage of Gina taking a breath to ask his own question. "Forget how you're doin' for a second, and tell us how you found us here, this morning."

"Oh, that's easy. One of your boys on the street told me where Johnny was, and he gave me a ride. We're all old friends."

G glared at Dom, who obviously couldn't have said anything to anyone because he had been here all night, but the poor muscle-head shrugged and looked apologetic anyway.

"Did you recognize either of the guys who attacked you, Gina?" he continued.

"No. I didn't."

"Did you notice anything particular about them—tattoos, scars, names, anything?"

"I'm sorry, no. Honestly, it all happened so quickly, the whole thing was a blur. One minute I'm walking back to the ladies room, and the next, some guy pops in from the open back door, grabs me, and throws me across the alley. I slammed against the dumpster—or wall or something—dropped to the ground and curled up like a ball, fending off the other guy as he started to pull on my clothes and my purse. I screamed and right away, Johnny came dashing out through the door like Batman to save me. He got me loose from that guy on the ground, and I raced back into the restaurant and closed the door behind me. I saw the waitress, and she called all the kitchen guys out from behind the line. We all ran back outside."

"You must've been terrified," Angela said, consoling her and placing her hand on Gina's hands, both of which were bracketed around her coffee mug, which hadn't moved from its place in front of her on the table.

Mr. Acchione quietly and sympathetically spoke up. "It may not be a good idea for you to be walking around alone, Miss Giannetti, at least not for now. I'm not sure how much John has shared with you about what's been going on, but we have reason to believe there's an element of danger out there associated with this family. Your association with John could place you in jeopardy."

"Do you really think so?" Gina blurted out as she stared at me, obviously frightened. "I never thought about it. Do you think those guys were waiting for Johnny last night, and they grabbed me to get to him?"

"We don't know what to think right now," he said. "That could have been an entirely random incident, or it could have been carefully orchestrated. To be safe, we should assume the worst and recognize the inherent danger in any of you being alone."

"I don't know if I should be relieved or panicked. It was frightening to think I was unlucky enough to be in the wrong place at the wrong time last night—so I guess I'd feel better believing this was planned—but then realizing I'm being included in this mess of yours is pretty scary. What about my kids and grandkids? Johnny, maybe we shouldn't be together right now. Maybe this isn't a good idea."

"GG, you gotta do what you think is best for you and yours. If you need to put a little distance between us, I get it. Personally, I don't think this was all part of some big plan, but maybe that's just me. I mean, why would they hang out in the alley if they wanted to get *me*? Anyone with a brain would've waited for us to leave out the front door, like normal people. If they were really waiting for us, they'd have been waiting out front. They may have never seen us at all if they stayed out back. Seriously, it doesn't make any sense to me. You guys are all paranoid."

She lifted one hand from her coffee mug, grabbed one of mine and squeezed. She looked at me with a smile, saying "I'm glad to hear you say that. After all these years, to finally get together only to split up from fear would be tragic. I really want to stick around and see how we play out together, John."

"Good. Let's take Mr. Acchione up on his generosity and stay here today. We'll watch some TV, lounge around, and you can keep me in pills and blankets." I leaned over and kissed her and immediately squeezed my eyes shut and winced with pain, having once again forgotten how bruised and sore my face and lips were!

Angela spoke up. "We checked into the corporate entity used to purchase Mom and Pop's business. It was a single-purpose entity, meaning the only reason it was created was to be the owner of whatever was acquired through that sale. It had no history and frankly, it's not doing much of anything now, either. Basically, if you imagine the buyer purchased a filing cabinet to dump Mom and Pop's asset into, you get what the single-purpose is."

"Well, that's useless," I muttered.

"Not exactly," she continued. "Such an entity requires articles of incorporation, and that identifies who *owns* the entity."

"Well, that's good then, right? Who owns the entity? We'll just go find him or her and get moving on this."

"Yeah, not so fast. These guys have more shells than an oyster farm. This entity is owned by another single-purpose entity, and that one is owned by something similar, and so on. Ultimately, we've traced it to an offshore shell company. At that point, the trail gets even fuzzier because of international law and jurisdiction. We're far from beaten here, but it's very possible this is just a gigantic wormhole. We could keep digging forever and never really get an answer. We'll keep at it, but no promises on timing or results."

"So, we're back to 'sucks.'"

"Well, yes, but not for the reason you thought in the first place."

"Now I know how lawyers make their money. They give you nothing and try to make you feel privileged to get it."

"Hey! There are at least two lawyers in this room and they're both trying to help. Kiss my tiny white ass."

"It's not so tiny anymore. It's actually kinda lumpy … and old" I told her.

GG piped-up and asked Ange, "He talks to you like this, too?"

"Only when I don't have reinforcements. Do me a favor and poke one of his larger black and blue patches would you?"

GG did and I responded in kind "OW!"

The two women cheered one another on and high-fived each other.

"Oh, shit. I should have kept you two separated. I'm suddenly remembering why I needed therapy since the first grade."

Guido interrupted: "Well, not that this flirtatious little stroll down memory lane isn't a swell way to spend my day, but I have things to do. Angela, thank you for what you've shared. Please keep at it. Joe, as always, it's great to see you and I appreciate your assistance with the kid, here."

"It's my pleasure to have him here, Guido."

"Wait. Weren't you going to see if any of your contacts know anything about these guys, Mr. Acchione?" I asked.

Before he could reply, Guido did it for him. "We'll discuss all of that later. I really need to get rolling. Stay off the streets, John. Unlike you, I'm not convinced last night's incident was entirely coincidental. I'm not saying it has anything to do with all of this family business, either. For all we know, it could just as easily be someone associated with Gina's ex, rolling you out of jealousy. Regardless, you're in no shape to exchange blows with a kindergartner right now, let alone some 'back-alley muscle.'"

"No worries, Unc. I'll be snuggled here watching movies and drinking Ovaltine."

"Mmm-hmmm. Sure."

G waited for his entourage to get on their feet and proceeded to exit out the front of Mr. Acchione's home. Ange declined the ride he offered and as soon as he left, Dom, the human mountain who had joined us in the kitchen this morning returned, and sat down.

Remember how I mentioned the commissioner yesterday was about three hundred pounds? Well so is Dom, except unlike the corpulent commish, Dom is about two percent body fat. The rest is all muscle. He looked like Mr. Olympia—only bigger—and was only average compared to the rest of the human billboards Guido uses to surround himself.

Physical development had obviously been a life choice for Domenic, because he had clearly sacrificed intellectual development on its behalf. Look at the nearest inanimate item near you. Go ahead. I'll wait. Picked one out? It has nearly twice the IQ of Dom. Dedicated guy, but dumb as a tree stump.

"Didn't you just leave?" I asked him.

"Guido assigned me to stay with Angela. I go wherever she goes and I stay wherever she stays."

"You are NOT hanging out with me and my family in our home. No way!" Angela protested, but it was in vain. Uncle G was calling the security shots and there would be no way to deter him—no reasoning, no begging, no nothing. He was not about to let what happened yesterday to her, her husband, and her brother happen again. Even she knew, beneath her bravado, she felt a little relief knowing someone would be there to protect her and her family. She was genuinely shaken by yesterday's events.

Another goon was seated in the parlor waiting to see where GG and I ended up. It seemed we had a meat suit of our own to wear, just like Angela.

Speaking of Angela, she took that opportunity so stand up and announce, "I suppose Charles Atlas back here and I should get rolling too. I have some errands to run that include stopping to see Mom and Pop. Any message for them, brother-of-mine?"

"Nothing specific. Tell 'em I said hi."

Mr. Acchione got himself up from the table and was slowly making his way to the sink with his dirty dishes when he offered a few words of advice: "Please don't tell your parents anything of the sort, Angela. John and Toni have no idea your brother is in town, and we certainly don't want them to find out now. They'd only want to see him, and considering his condition, that's not a great idea. If the goal is to keep them on an even keel, showing them their beaten son would achieve the opposite."

None of us had thought of that. We were all so focused on avenging my parents, we had accidentally overlooked them in the process. Once all the dust settled, I was going to need to visit and spend some time with them. For now, I needed to fly low under the radar so they wouldn't find out about my failed street fighting debut.

GG and I made the long climb back up the steps to my room so I could lay down. There was a couch up there and a TV, so it seemed logical for us to spend our day there. Mr. Acchione tried to play it cool, but he still half-glared at me from the corner of his eye as we headed toward the steps. Above all else, I was a guest in his house and I did not intend to disrespect him by using his house for hookups. When we got upstairs, Gina went to close the bedroom door. I asked her to leave it open so no one would assume any impropriety was going on in the room.

"But there *is* going to be *impropriety*, isn't there?" she asked seductively. "I mean, I'm expecting to inspect every square inch of your heroic body and kiss everything to make it better … *everything*."

"And that all sounds great. It does, except my body *hurts* everywhere. I'm not really in a sexy mood, and I'd feel wrong doing those things here, anyway, in Mr. Acchione's guest room. He's being very kind and considerate to extend me his hospitality. I'm not about to disrespect him by banging some chick on the guest bed."

Shit. I immediately regretted those words the instant they passed through my lips.

"Some chick? Really?! Some *chick*! Is that who I am? Is that what we're doing here, John, *hooking up*? You're gonna *bang* me? I'm a fifty-year-old woman. *NO ONE bangs* me. I'm just some convenient lay while you're in town? We've known one another all our lives. I assumed that meant something, but apparently I'm just some anonymous slut you hit on the head with a club at the bar and dragged to your cave by the hair!" With every word she became more and more angry.

"Gina, I'm not calling *you* 'some chick.' I'm saying it would be inappropriate for me to have sex on Mr. Acchione's guest bed with *anyone*."

I tried to diffuse the eruption, but couldn't get another word in. She had built up such a momentum by this point, her anger took over.

Not surprisingly, she continued. "I thought our history meant something and we were going to build on it, together, not just exercise some animal urges. You know what, though? You're right! This was just a hookup, and you know what else you're right about? You're not having sex up here today unless you go *fuck* yourself! I'm *outta* here. Give me a call some time … or don't!"

I sat there calmly and watched GG turn and storm down the steps. Although I didn't see her do it, she continued her storming out the front door, which she banged hard for effect once she went through it.

If that sounded like an over-the-top overreaction to you, then you have no idea what Italian women are like. Frankly, I was surprised my little slip of the tongue didn't end up in a lamp or flowerpot being thrown at me.

Her sudden, angry departure didn't affect me in the slightest. I grew up surrounded by Italian women. Hell, two of them lived with me in my house for decades, and they were borderline psychopaths. GG's rant was like a thousand others I'd witnessed. It was 90% bluster, and

I was pretty sure she'd call later to check in, anyway. Regardless, even if she was serious—which I doubt she was—our little fling was just that. Emotions got the better of us yesterday, and that's that. Don't get me wrong. I liked GG, and always had—probably always will—but I didn't think the feelings went much deeper than that, at least not after one afternoon of passion. That's not to say I won't patch things up if she doesn't call me first. I hate burning bridges—especially when good sex could be at the other end of that bridge—but that's not my priority right now.

I'll give her a little room and call her once I'm up and around—probably tomorrow. For now, I'm going to prop up some pillows, watch whatever I can find on the TV, and make a mental note to *never* refer to a woman as a chick—at least not to her face.

To Nap, or Not to Nap

One thing about old people: At some point, technology stops advancing for them. They stay in step with everyone else until one day they stop evolving and the world sails past them in a whoosh. That appeared to have happened to Mr. Acchione around 1986. All there was in this house were tube-TVs and cable boxes. I think there was even a VCR downstairs. So that meant today, there would be no internet streaming or wifi access. No pay-per-view or even premium channels. There was basic cable and an AM/FM radio. This was going to be a *very* long, boring day.

I was starting to reconsider my decision to chase off GG when Mr. Acchione came in to join me.

"No girl?"

"She wasn't too thrilled with my agenda for today—little too tame for her tastes. It looks like it's just going to be us, sir."

"Please, John. Let's refrain from the 'sir' business, okay? I'm Joe."

"Okay, sounds good to me s … um, Joe?"

"I apologize for the limited accommodations here. I rarely have guests and my own needs are pretty simple. I'm not much of an internet user, I'm afraid. In fact, between my eyes and my arthritis, I'm not much of a computer user at all. That's fine for me, but visitors tend to be disappointed when they ask me what my wifi is called, or what my password is.

"Since you'll be staying with me for a while, if you'd like, I could ask Marilyn to make arrangements to get the internet in here and maybe some better TV programming."

"You know what Mr. A … Joe, I'm really not much of an internet or TV guy either. If I have free time, I tend to go out and do things. I wish I could do that today, but I can't—maybe tomorrow. So here's a thought: Instead of watching fiction on the tube, why don't you tell me some factual stories from your time here in Philly? I suspect you've accumulated quite a portfolio of tales. Let's start with Uncle Guido. As long as I can remember, you guys have been close friends, even though you travel in *very* different circles."

"That's an interesting story actually, but not a short one. I'd better sit down."

The old man shuffled from the bedroom door to the over-stuffed sofa across the room. It was upholstered in dark red velvet and its frame was ornate with dark wood. It looked like it came straight out of an 1800s brothel, but—like everything else in this monster of a house—it was immaculate and looked brand new. Even though he barely weighed 120 pounds these days, I expected a huge puff of dust to blow into the air when he parked his ancient frame on its cushion, but there was no drama. It swallowed him up and he made an "ahhhhh" sound and closed his eyes, as if sitting down had taken thirty years off his odometer. Then he started into his tale.

"Guido and I have a long, long history together. We met somewhat auspiciously, but over time we became friends, colleagues, confidantes, and even business partners of sorts."

"It all began years ago. Your father had been drafted into the army and was being shipped off to a base in Germany for three years. It was quite a few years after the war, so he'd be safe enough. In your father's absence, though, your grandfather was struggling to keep up with the restaurant, and was considering taking on a temporary partner. He'd been referred to me by a client of mine, and he brought Guido with him.

"Guido was a young man—twenty years old or so. He'd only been in this country for a couple weeks when we met, and he had a very limited command of the English language."

"His command still isn't very good," I kidded.

Mr. Acchione smiled, shrugged in agreement, and continued: "Regardless of his limited verbal skill, he had a commanding presence.

"I was a young attorney. I'd only been practicing for a few years, but my firm was growing. People were starting to come to *me* with work, instead of the other way around. Professionally, things were progressing nicely. Every day I was becoming more and more entrenched in Philadelphia society. With the Kellys' assistance, I had gradually connected myself politically and socially with the most affluent and influential people in the city. I was recognized as someone who was hungry and could get things done.

"That's an invaluable trait, by the way. Many people have ideas, but very few can implement them. The 'doers' will always be the ones to succeed. Remember that.

"Anyway, I had this small, two-room office in town. The space itself was hardly impressive, but the address made up for it. I was on Penn Square, across the street from city hall. I could be in the mayor's office in less than a minute or the NFL headquarter offices across Broad Street just as quickly. Every major company, politician, law firm, accountant, real estate developer, broker, or newspaper was located within a couple block radius of city hall, and I was at the center of it all."

"It was a different world back then. There was no internet, cell phones, fax machines, or even email. Everything was done on the phone or in person, preferably the latter. It was important to mingle at lunch or within one's own building. Transactions literally occurred in elevators or over drinks at lunch. And don't kid yourself, even today *with* all the technology, important networks are forged and deals are transacted in relics like The Union League, where I've been a member for decades.

"Back then, one's network was his stock in trade. My ability to get an audience with virtually any politician, attorney, or business executive in the city made me valuable to my clients, who could *never* access those people otherwise. As long as I could provide value to political and business kingpins, I could get my working-class clients in to see them.

"Quid pro quos or horse trades are often more valuable than currency exchanges. They were what helped me get established in this town. Most times, my neighborhood clients couldn't afford to pay for my legal assistance with money. I'd provide them with my services in exchange for them wallpapering an influential man's house, servicing his car, or getting him a deal on a mink coat for his wife or mistress; then that influential man would owe me a favor. I would use that leverage to help some of my wealthy clients get approval for their development project, get some code violations to go away, or erase some family member's petty crime.

"With my reputation as a capable liaison, folks like your grandfather sought my services when they were in need. Unfortunately, many people didn't understand the concept. They believed—when there were no other options—I could get someone who would magically make it all better, like the hand of god coming down and plucking them out of their misery and placing them into fields of clover.

"The problem was, unless there was something in it for the hand of god, that hand wasn't budging.

"Al was different, though. He was savvy and seemed to understand the concept of value propositions. His business was solid, but he was over his head without his son to pick up the slack. Once his son returned, he knew (or at least hoped) he'd come back to the kitchen and all would be fine again. Until then, though, he needed help to bridge that gap. He wasn't prepared to turn over any portion of his ownership in his business, though. He knew partners were the bane of long-term success, and there already wasn't enough profit to support *his* family, let alone enough to entice an investor. He needed different currency to get help."

"Instead of using his restaurant for leverage, he brought along Guido."

"Guido was a young, tough street kid. During his brief tenure in town, he had already begun to organize neighborhoods. That sounds a lot more nefarious than it necessarily was.

"The common perception of neighborhood organizing is the mafia or unions. Those are certainly examples of power being brought together through organization, but they're also rife with criminal activity and violence. Guido was different.

"He brought neighborhoods together to support one another. On a more 'street' level, he was doing exactly the same thing as I was. Where I was brokering deals for services with politicians and businessmen, Guido was brokering deals with neighbors and small business owners. He would get everyone to buy their produce from the neighborhood grocer instead of the big wholesaler at the docks, and then he'd get that grocer to provide neighbors with discounts. He'd get locals to eat at neighborhood restaurants that were using that grocer, and in turn he'd get those local restaurants to employ men and women from the neighborhood. The neighborhood funeral parlor would use the neighborhood florist, and the florist would refer business to the funeral parlor.

"This all sounds commonplace today with the internet, but back then, there was no mechanism for bringing together such cooperation and order.

"Guido was smart, young, energetic, convincing, and confident. He was also strong and tough. If someone from another neighborhood came in and tried to establish their own controls—or extort protection money—he and his ever-growing group of confederates would stop the move in its tracks. Guido's neighborhood became a bubble within the rest of the city—a place where others knew to tread lightly. The neighborhood was cleaner than others. It was fully occupied. Every storefront was open and vibrant. There was also virtually no crime. Everyone was earning a good living and was safe—all thanks to Guido's organizational acumen.

"Al was right that I could use a colleague like Guido, and with my own connections, we could expand his influence from just that neighborhood to entire sections of the city. Of course, every small-time hood dreamt of such power, and when they'd get it, they'd become overzealous, exploit it, and probably wind up dead. I could find guys like that hiding around every corner of the city.

"Guido's greatest value to me was his character.

"He wasn't looking to make a big name for himself. He didn't want to be the king of the city. He had an entirely different motive—one that he kept to himself. He was a young man with integrity and potential and I knew, if we worked together, we could help others and bring order and prosperity to those who desire it.

"I guess you could say, back then, the nation was full of optimism, and we were as naive and optimistic as they came."

"In the end, I helped Al and he was a special client for me until he passed away—at too young an age, I might add. Guido and I accomplished many wonderful things together. Hopefully we still have a little left in us, even though we're both old men—me more than him."

"So how'd he end up falling for my mom?"

"Oh, that's an even longer story and one you should ask *him* to tell. For now, I'm running out of steam and need to take a nap. You should probably do the same."

And with that, the old man rolled to his side and pushed hard against the armrest to get to his feet. He staggered a little as he gained his balance, then shuffled out the door, each step getting more confident as his old bones and muscles gradually warmed and loosened. He lightly tapped my feet through the bedsheets as he walked by and suggested some homemade raviolis and sausage for dinner. I agreed, and he told me he'd start making gravy before he settled in for his nap.

He was a hell of an old man, and I wondered why we'd never really spent time together before. Then I remembered he's the family law-yer—not family. I had no "quid" to offer for his "pro quo," so I guess there was never any reason for him to associate with me before now. The only reason we were working together now was because of my uncle. Funny how odd circumstances can bring people together.

I settled my head back on the pillow and the sunrays streamed in from the side windows, washing across the bedroom with tree limb shadows dancing on the walls. The shadows were almost hypnotic, and I closed my eyes. Before I knew it, I awoke to a dark room and a clock that read 8:00.

The house was silent, and dark—as though everyone had abandoned the place while I was sleeping. I switched on the lamp on the night table, and by the time I got my bearings, Marilyn walked in with a TV tray.

"We were going to wake you for dinner, but you were so sound asleep, we figured it was more important that you stayed that way."

She set the tray on the bureau and asked me if I wanted to go to the bathroom before eating. Since that was probably a great idea, I agreed. She helped me to my feet. I was able to swing my legs around beneath me and stand on my own easily this time. Although the walk to the bathroom wasn't quick, it was much easier than it had been that morning.

I returned to bed, where Marilyn had propped the pillows up for me so I could sit up. She set the tray on my lap and I enjoyed a fabulous, if only lukewarm, dinner of homemade ravioli, sausage, and gravy.

"Did you make this?"

"No. Mr. Acchione makes the sauce. We get the sausage from the butcher who used to supply it to Sonny's, and the ravioli comes from a lady up the block. When she makes extras, she brings them to us. Mr. Acchione had helped her family with something a few years ago. He didn't accept any money from them, so she sends food once or twice a week."

"Quid pro quo," I thought to myself. He'll be a horse trader to his final day.

"Well, everything is delicious. The gravy tastes exactly like what my family makes."

"I think your grandfather taught Mr. Acchione how to make it. You seem to be moving a lot better. How are you feeling?"

"Thousand times better. I have a few aches and pains, but everything is moving and working properly. I think I'll be up and around tomorrow."

"We'll see. For now, finish your dinner and grab a bath. The warm water will help loosen everything. I'll give you something tonight before you go to sleep, and tomorrow you'll probably feel better than you have in weeks … even months."

She slipped back downstairs where I could hear the droning of the TV in the parlor. I imagined Mr. Acchione sitting in a chair with a blanket laying across his lap in a dimly lit room, with only the flashes from the TV to light him.

For the first time I thought about him—how lonely his life is and how sad it must be to outlive one's peers. He's the last of his group. All those political and business big shots who were older than him in his prime have been gone for 40 years, and their successors and *their* successors have all disappeared as well. He's a dinosaur, whiling away in a giant stone house with his nurse, waiting for the moment he can finally let go.

If I didn't know better, my paranoid mind would think *he* was behind this mess with Sonny's just so he could be in the game again, one last time, surrounded by Guido, me, and Angela. I did know better, though. As he said himself, and as Guido has vouched, he's a man of integrity who has spent his life building things. He'd sooner commit suicide than tear down a decades-old family business he'd helped build.

Day with Gina and Mom and Dad

The next morning, the squirrel in the wheel in my mind must've had his shit together, because I quickly recognized my surroundings and climbed out of bed without drama. I was still moving slowly and had some *epic* black-and-blue bruises. Overall, though, I felt pretty damned good, especially because I didn't collapse in a heap on the bedroom floor like I had the morning before.

Don't get me wrong—I was still miserable, but that had more to do with being awake before noon than anything else.

The *lovely* thing about bruises is before they get better, they spread out across the skin and hatch myriad colors. Small indigo spots turn into sprawling yellow, purple, red, and blue blotches that look much worse than they actually are. I looked like I had bad tattoos of the African, Australian, and South American continents all over my body.

The bad news was I looked terrible naked.

The good news was what's visible when I'm dressed is pretty innocuous, and I didn't expect anyone to see me naked today anyway.

The great news is I was feeling like my old self—not sore, not stiff, not impaired.

When I came down for breakfast, Mr. Acchione and Marilyn were the only ones to greet me, except for Rocco, my bodyguard, who was down there too. He hadn't moved from the chair he was seated in since yesterday morning after breakfast. I couldn't say for sure, but he may not have changed clothes, either. I was starting to wonder what protocol was for bodyguards. Would I be out of line to ask Rock to bathe or maybe brush his teeth?

I grabbed a quick slice of toast and a cup of coffee and informed the house I was tip-top. Then Rock and I went out and caught a bus down to the neighborhood. I could have taken my car; it was safely and securely nestled in Mr. Acchione's garage, though, and I was perfectly content leaving it there. Besides, whether I was feeling a little better or not, manually shifting a muscle car through urban streets was probably beyond my physical threshold today. The clutch is heavy, and I'm not sure my legs were up to the workout.

Besides my physical limitations today, there's another reason why I didn't want to drive. It had to do with why city people don't typically have nice cars. It's because those cars get beaten up. If I had driven to the neighborhood, I'd have struggled to find a parking space. Parking spaces are rare commodities in that part of town. If you're lucky enough to find one, there's a good chance your car will either be accidentally damaged, intentionally damaged, or stolen entirely by the time you return.

The bus is great. It takes me right to where I want to be and when I'm ready to return home, it'll be there, ready to go. An added bonus was I got to sit with 40 other people who hadn't showered for at least the past day, as I learned was also true of Rocco. Big guys and bad hygiene are *not* a winning combination. Rocco smelled like he was homeless, with overactive glands. Perhaps stench was his means for guarding my body?

Once the bus reached our stop, we hopped off and started to make our way to GG's. My goal that morning was to check in on her and clear the air. She's a hot-head, but I've known that about her forever. She blows up, and then she comes back down to earth and can be reasonable. I don't need to rekindle our short-lived romance, but she's one of my oldest and dearest friends, and I don't want to forfeit that. I doubt she does either. It would not be a surprise if there was some requisite groveling—because she'll almost definitely play hard to get— but before she lets me leave, I'm sure she'll agree to patch things up.

At least that was my expectation going in. We'll see how it turns out.

I knocked on the door and waited for a response. It could have quite literally been anything from not answering, to answering and slamming the door in my face, to answering and throwing hot coffee on me, to answering and being coy. What I got was unexpected.

Gina opened the door, barely looked at me, handed me a toddler and walked away talking. "Here. The one you're holding needs to be fed. His bowl and dish are on the table next to the box of Cheerios. For god's sake, whatever you do, do not add milk to the Cheerios. Very few of them are actually going to end up inside him anyway, and Cheerios are a lot easier to clean off the floor when they're not wet. I need to bathe this one quickly because that one over there threw up on him. The one who threw up needs a new shirt and pants. When you get the little one started on the Cheerios, help the pukey one into new clothes—there's a pile of clean laundry on the sofa. Pick something *appropriate*. The puke-er and the puke-ee need to be in school in 15 minutes."

"Shouldn't the one who puked stay home from school?"

"Do you want to stay home with him?"

"New clothes it is!"

I got the Cheerios poured into a bowl, which the toddler immediate-ly flipped into the air, sending Cheerios everywhere. I, in turn, placed *him* on the floor to forage for food. There were plenty of Cheerios everywhere for him to eat, and I didn't see a dog or cat anywhere to compete with him. I figured he'd be fine.

Then I turned my attention to the slobbering, crying, puke-soaked eight-year-old sitting in the middle of the living room. I thought Rocco and the bus people stunk, but this kid's odor was like snorting acid while simultaneously throwing it into my eye sockets. I held my breath and tried to peel his shirt off him without getting chunks of vomit in his hair. For the most part, the endeavor was a success. The kid was going to smell a little during his day in a second-grade classroom, but that shouldn't really make him unique among his fellow students. They all stink, too, and odds were good he was going to throw up again at some point in class anyway. So except for a pile of clothes soaking in throw up in the middle of the living room, the morning was going swimmingly. Sorry—bad choice of words.

Between Rocco, the public transit population, and this child, my nose had been cruelly assaulted. I was likely to carry the scars of that treatment for the rest of the day.

GG returned with a sparkly clean first-grader who was complaining strongly because he figured being thrown up on was his ticket to staying home from school. No such luck, kiddo.

The two school-aged boys were shuttled off to school. The toddler continued to search and destroy floor-bound Cheerios, and GG scooped up the defiled clothes pile from the living room floor and took it elsewhere. She'd probably end up cleaning those clothes, but I think they'd be better off tossed into the furnace. There are some smells you just can't get rid of.

Having dispatched the school-aged kids and the heinous laundry, GG was refocused on the toddler, but on her way past me, she ran her hand through my hair and kissed the top of my head. That was it. No drama, no drawn-out discussion about feelings and which words to use and not use. A simple gesture was all it took, and it's done.

"Where's this thing's mother?"

"She and this *thing's* father are at work. My function in life now is to be a caregiving grandmother. Pretty glamorous eh?"

"Well, it obviously agrees with you. You still have a great ass for an old hag."

"Just keep at it, Valmonti. Just keep at it, and next time I'll beat you in the alley myself. Speaking of which, you seem to be moving around better. Is everything working now?"

"Much better, but not perfect. You staying here with this cereal killer today?"

"He's no serial ki ...oh. You meant cereal, like food. Oh, I get it. That's witty. Anyways, that's the plan, but I'll be available later tonight if you're interested in having food ... or something." and she winked.

"I'll have to let you know. For now I'm doing okay, but as the day drags on, I'm not sure how I'll feel. Call you later?"

"Can hardly wait," she said, and then there was that awkward silence where the conversation was done. Nothing more needed to be said, and we both just wanted to no longer be there, staring at each other. Fortunately, as if on cue, my burner phone chirped. It was a frantic Raj.

Before I could even acknowledge the call with a simple "Hello," Raj started blurting out that I had to run to Sonny's fast. His mother saw my mother yelling at the gorillas operating out of there. *His* mom tried to move *my* Mom along, but couldn't, so she's staying there until someone comes to help—namely me.

It wasn't my *favorite* alternative for leaving GG's, but it would work.

"I have to run. My mom is screaming at the guys at Sonny's and there's a big scene."

"Shit! I'll come with you. Just give me a second to put a jacket on the baby and we'll run."

"You don't have to do th..." but it was too late. She was already in full gallop. There would be no deterring her. I had sort of hoped to be solo today, but that was looking pretty unlikely now.

Sonny's was a block away. As I'd mentioned before, Gina's family lived next door to me my entire life. When my parents were married they needed a place to live. They saved up to buy a row house near the restaurant. Them needing someplace to live may sound obvious, but most people assumed my family lived in the apartment above the restaurant all my life. That was a fair assumption because my grandparents lived there until my grandfather passed away in 1974 and my grandmother followed him in 1978. My dad was raised there, but the place was too small for two families. My parents wanted (*needed*) their privacy after they were married (even though they shared the apartment for five years first while they saved up!). My grandparents stayed above the restaurant, and my folks bought a row home a block away, which was about as far as any respectful Italian son would move from his parents back then.

After my grandmother passed, the apartment became our "pied-à-terre"—sort of a small home away from home. Even though our row house was only a block away, Angela and I came to Sonny's every day after school. We'd go upstairs and do our homework, then come down later and help with the restaurant—cleaning up, bussing tables, doing food prep, etc. And then, every night, as a family, we'd lock up the restaurant and apartment and walk home together.

By the mid-eighties, it became my and Angela's apartment, where we could have independence, but only a little. Eventually, Angela moved out and it became my place exclusively. I never had to pay rent and stayed there almost thirty years until Mom and Pop sold the place a few months ago.

It was a pretty sweet gig!

"Should we get your dad?" Gina asked as we locked her front door.

His front door was literally a matter of inches from hers, but I said no rather abruptly. I was trying to insulate my parents from all of this, and even though Mom was engaging the enemy directly, I didn't want Dad to step out of his oblivion. He was *not* good with confrontation—imagine C3PO, only clumsier and far less eloquent.

Gina carried the kid—Cheerios stuck to his face and all—against her chest and we ran to Sonny's. Of course, Gina's hair and makeup were perfect.

Here's something few people realize about Italian women: They wear high heels virtually everywhere, and can do absolutely anything in them. They can run, jump, dance, and possibly swim in them. By middle-age, their bare feet are hideous and contorted from the narrow toe-wells of high heels.That rarely mattered, though, because if an Italian woman wasn't wearing high heels, she'd be wearing over-stuffed, fluffy house slippers. Seeing such a woman's gnarled bare feet was a rare sighting indeed.

Rocco ran with us, but I asked him to stay on the sidelines when we got there, low-keying it. He reluctantly agreed, but told me at the first sign of physical confrontation, he was getting involved. I agreed (and secretly welcomed the backup).

High heels, baby and all, Gina kept up with me all the way to the scene.

When we turned the corner, we spotted Mom and Mrs. Patel in the middle of the street. Mrs. Patel was literally holding Mom back, and Mom was pointing, screaming, and fully immersed in her own froth and fury. I've been on the wrong end of more than one of her tirades in my life, and I can tell you, the best thing that happened to those guys at Sonny's that afternoon was Mrs. Patel stopped by to block Mom's path. 85 years old or not, she's scary.

"MOM!" I yelled, and both women turned to me and simultaneously said "Johnny!" with noticeable relief in their voices. It would have been funny to see both of them responding to me saying "mom" if it wasn't so sad for two eighty-plus-year-old ladies to be standing outside in the chilly air, blocking traffic, and being surrounded by a gathering crowd of onlookers.

I made it over to them and asked my mother what she was doing.

Mrs. Patel's shoulders finally relaxed and she exhaled. "Johnny, thank goodness you're here. I was walking by and saw your mother out here screaming at these animals and I got so scared."

"It's fine now, Mom (in this case "Mom" was Mrs. Patel; I call them both Mom, so try not to get too confused). Here. You remember Gina, right?" and I gestured toward GG. "Why don't you both go over to the curb and wait for us."

Mrs. Patel did, indeed, know Gina, and her disdain for her was written all over her face. GG and Mom's daughter Indi were not friendly (that's polite for "fucking hated each other"). One can only imagine the stories Indi shared over the years with her mom about GG. Fact is, she wouldn't have had to bend the truth too much either. I loved GG; she was always a little trampy and vulgar, though, and she would never hesitate to insult Indi. I'm sure the fact Indi and I were always an exclusive item back then made GG dislike her even more (assuming that level of emotion was even physically possible in GG).

Even though their mutual contempt was palpable, Mrs. Patel and GG moved out of harm's way quickly, leaving me to my mother.

She was hyperventilating and furious by this point. Unlike every other Italian woman dispersed across the face of the planet, she never wore makeup during the day. Today this was a stroke of good fortune, because if she had, her mascara would have run so much and so far, it would have stained her nipples. You're welcome for that visual.

As soon as I reached her, my mother cupped my face with her hands and became instantly maternal and tender. "Johnny, when did you get into town, and what happened to your face?"

"I just got in yesterday (little white lie) and was coming to see you, and don't worry about my face." Then I waved my arms around in a huge gesture as if to show her the entire world and asked "Mom, what the hell, Mom?!"

"Those rat bastards," she started. "They buy our restaurant, our family's legacy, and disgrace it and our neighborhood like this. We still live here. It's like they spit in our faces!" and she spit toward them, never taking her eyes off the guys at the door. This was laughable because the two guys at the door were so big they could eclipse the sun. Compared to them, mom was a Lilliputian and weighed less than one of their thighs. She's a tough old broad, though—which is why we called her John Wayne toilet paper when we were kids. She didn't take shit off anyone!

"I know all this, Mom—and we'll work through it—but coming here yelling at them … is that really the best decision you made today?"

"I was walking home from the grocer and these 'men' (she made little quotation marks in the air) started whistling at me and making lewd suggestions about me going inside and having them show me what real Italian men could do for me."

I bristled. It's disturbing to hear catcalls and disgusting suggestions being tossed at anonymous women, but when the woman in question is your mother, it's all you can do to not go ballistic.

"Mom, they're baiting you. You're giving them exactly what they want right now. They want you to get angry. They want you to scream and rant. The only thing that would make them happier right now would be for you to fall over dead with a heart attack. Don't listen to them. Let's just walk home and put your groceries away."

"They're *laughing* at me," she said, and she started to cry.

I hugged her (blocking the sight of her from the jackasses at Sonny's) and whispered in her ear I understood. She needed to stiffen up, though, so they wouldn't get the satisfaction of seeing her like this, and then they could all go fuck themselves. And yes, I said all that in those exact words.

I took the bag of groceries from her and gently grabbed her arm to lead her away. She pulled her arm away from me abruptly and made the requisite Italian gesture where she made a fist at the end of her outstretched left arm and slapped her open right hand on her left forearm as she stuck out her tongue and made the "raspberries" noise toward the group of laughing jackals at Sonny's—basically, "fuck you" without actually saying it.

It's hardly menacing, but the meaning was not lost on the surrounding crowd. They all howled and cheered their approval.

I turned to the crowd and said loudly "Thanks for catching the matinee folks. We hope you enjoyed the show and you tell your friends all about it. We'll be performing again tonight at 5, 7:30 and again at 10." Then I turned back to mom and rolled my eyes.

She reclaimed her groceries from me, straightened her back, tilted up her chin and stepped away with purpose ... in her high heels.

She is still one tough old broad, even as this entire situation with the buyer of Sonny's balloons out of proportion and control. We still had no idea why they had singled out my family, but they'd gone from gaining control of our livelihood and "stiffing us" on what they owed to verbally attacking my mother. At some point, we were going to have to stop seeking damage control and assert ourselves. Right now—in the middle of the street—with my mother in tow was not that point.

Rocco looked at me for guidance. I made eye contact and shook my head as if to say "don't interrupt her exit." When we got around the corner he and I caught up to Mom and walked together. Gina was quickly in tow, leaving Mrs. Patel. I looked back for her in the crowd and saw her. We made eye contact and I nodded my appreciation for what she did. She shut her eyes and nodded.

This is family.

"Johnny," my mother whined in an affectedly pathetic little old lady tone—as if I was to instantly forget the Mussolini-esque performance she had just delivered a half a block away—"What are you doing in town?"

"Uncle G invited me up to see you and to see what's going on with Sonny's."

"Oh, he should never have done that. We're fine and there's *nothing* going on with Sonny's. We sold it and it's not reopening, apparently—end of story."

Women from this generation have this uncanny knack for never discussing anything important with their children. Maybe it's been like that for generations. Who knows? I wasn't around to witness it. I *was* here to witness the antics of this crazy lady, though. She had cancer a few years ago … and never told us. I answered a phone call at their house one time and it was her oncologist. "Why do you have an oncologist calling you, Mom?"

"Oh, it's nothing. I had a few lumps on my breasts removed, but I'm fine."

And that was the end of that—no further explanation, no discussion.

If someone shot her right in the face, her final words to me would be, "This is nothing. Put the leftovers in the refrigerator before they go bad."

So, hearing her interpretation of what's going on with Sonny's was neither surprising, nor anything to which I would pay any measure of credence.

"And who is this?" she asked, cocking her head toward Rocco.

"This is Rocco …" I didn't get to finish.

Mom interrupted "I know who this is, I just haven't seen him in years because he stopped coming by the restaurant to visit."

"Hello, Mrs. Valmonti," Rocco said, and then bowed his head and in the same breath said, "I'm sorry, Mrs. Valmonti."

"Well, at least I'm seeing you now, and that's what matters. How's your mother?"

"Fine thank you, Mrs. Valmonti," he replied, but never lifted his head and continued to avert his eyes.

Here's an 85-year-old woman who is eye-to-eye with this man's belly button and weighs less than his left arm, and she has reduced him to being a self-conscious, bashful five-year-old all over again. Italian mothers have this power!

"Well, you be sure to say hello to her and your father for me. Promise me you will!"

"Yes, Mrs. Valmonti."

"That's a good boy. Gina how did you end up out with these two characters?"

I replied "Oh, you remember Gina, Mom?"

She stopped dead in her tracks and we all almost ran over each other trying to stop in time. She turned to me, with her hands on her hips and asked "Do I look senile to you?! Of course I remember Gina. She visits us every week to see if we need anything and to keep an eye on us, unlike my own biological son, who doesn't even stop by when he returns to town after a four-month stint on the road. Gina, let me see that baby," and she grabbed the toddler off Gina's chest and put him against her own. "Come on. Your father will want to see you. Why, I have no idea, since you obviously don't want to see either of us."

You know that old adage about the guilt imposed by Jewish mothers? I *wish* I had a Jewish mother!!!

We got to my parents' place, and I opened the door so Mom could go in, carrying Gina's forty-pound toddler. She has a back like an old dried-out twig and will probably be laid up in bed for two weeks after this—complaining and wondering why her back hurts—but god help anyone who tries to snatch that child from her clutches.

Gina followed her in, as did I. Without turning around, Mom said "You too, Rocco. Come in and get yourself something to eat or drink from the kitchen. Be sure you say hello to my husband on your way by."

Rocco looked at me for permission. I gestured him in and shrugged as if to say, "Don't ask me, dude. Just do as the old lady says."

Dad was sitting at his desk on his computer, which is where he always seems to be anymore.

The restaurant used to give him purpose and keep him busy. He was vital every day, keeping things moving, managing the operation, and taking shifts behind the bar. I asked once why he sold Sonny's. He said it was too much money to pass up, but I honestly think he did it—like he does everything—for the rest of us.

Money never mattered to the man. He's a simple guy who has what he wants and doesn't have what he doesn't want.

He'd have been perfectly content "working the restaurant" until we buried him, just as we'd done with his own mom and dad. Angela had moved on, though, and I didn't have a passion for the business; the future was pretty bleak for Sonny's. I was content maneuvering in the kitchen, creating meals and talking smack with my buddies. I had no grand plans of running the place. Dad had Mom to rely on to help run things, but there were no prospects on the horizon for me in that regard. Dad saw the writing on the wall.

These days, the man wiles his life away trying to fix imaginary problems on his computer and complaining about the hundred frivolous emails he receives whenever he "turns the darned thing on," as he says (because my father NEVER curses—ever), but he still insists upon reading every last one of those ridiculous emails.

You know those spam emails you get telling you your computer needs to be updated?—The ones you delete without reading? My pop clicks on those links and downloads whatever they're telling him he needs, and then he wonders why his computer suddenly stops working. His computer is a perpetual shambles, and trying to resurrect it is like Jesus resurrecting Lazarus is his daily mission.

Drives us all freaking nuts.

Ordinarily, it would take an act of god to draw his attention away from his flashing computer screen, but when he heard my voice, he sprung from his chair and came running … "JOHNNY!!!"

I've always adored my father. He's the sweetest, most genuinely good and generous man on the planet. He treats me like I'm the reason the sun decides to shine on Philadelphia (which happens now and then, contrary to popular belief, and usually when the clouds and smog part). We've always been buddies and whenever we see each other, our respective days get a whole lot better.

He was a perpetually happy, childlike person—and I don't mean childish. Dad was as responsible as they came. No, he was childlike—bright-eyed about everything, wanting to tinker with new stuff and hear every single detail about every new technology. He once told me had wanted to live forever, just because he didn't want to miss out on anything.

Physically, my dad was almost completely forgettable. He was larger than average, but not big. His hands were as huge as catcher's mitts—and his feet were big as flippers—but otherwise, he was ordinary. Except for the smile he always wore, his face was unspectacular. There was no chiseled chin, nor strong Roman nose, just a regular, nice-enough face that drew no attention from anyone but my mother.

All my adult life, friends have moved on with their lives through school and marriage, having kids of their own, buying houses and building careers, etc. They'd always ask me why I was still in a go-nowhere job, living in my parents' old apartment above the restaurant. They actually felt sorry for me, but I was the one feeling sorry for them.

I lived a life I controlled. I had no debt, no lingering financial obligations, and no compulsion to own bigger and bigger homes or fancier and newer cars. I lived in a perfectly comfortable apartment for free. My daily commute was down a flight of steps. When I got to work, I got to hang out with my friends and spend hour after hour with my pop. When I'd explain that to my friends, they'd change their tunes, become jealous, and tell me I've got the life.

When I got around to talking about my social life they'd nearly break down in tears—hanging with my buddies all day and night, hanging out in a bar I owned and then dating any girl I want for however long or briefly as I decided.

By far, though, the best part of my job was working side-by-side with my dad. We'd cook together. We'd tend bar together. We'd discuss the menu and the daily specials and get all excited about it. Then when the night was over, we'd talk about the day's events and call it quits until tomorrow.

These days I work wherever I feel like stopping and maintain a simple life. I travel now because we never did as restaurant owners, but all those things that sounded like pipe dreams a couple years ago are now underwhelming. Even if the sale of Sonny's had been legit—all the payments were made and the restaurant was being operated by someone else—I'd be sad because I will never again enjoy those days with my dad. I miss that more than anything and am grateful to have ever done it in the first place.

I hugged dad like a grizzly bear and spent the next hours watching over his shoulder as he systematically and unwittingly desecrated his computer. I kept our glasses full of iced tea and kept changing his vinyl records from Sinatra to Dean Martin to Perry Cuomo to Mel "the Velvet Fog" Torme to Tony Bennett. Every once in a while I'd slip in some Oscar Petersen, Pop would immediately tell me how much Guido loved that and all the other piano jazz players they'd listen to when Sonny's would close at night. Even though we'd had this conversation dozens of times in the past, we still had it, and every time I was happy we did.

Every now and then I have to remind Dad about things. I've asked Mom about it and, of course, she denies anything is going on. He's forgetful these days—everything from passwords to what he just asked five times a few minutes earlier. He's an old man, for god's sake, so I cut him a lot of slack, but still …

Gina, who had gone to the kitchen to help Mom put groceries away because the kitchen is an Italian woman's domain, returned to the living room with a very sleepy little boy draped over her shoulder.

Now, before you get all pissed off at that last comment, hang on. Most outsiders will consider Italian males to be misogynistic because they leave the kitchen to women, but that's not so. Italian women don't *want* men in their kitchens. It's theirs and we are considered interlopers. Very liberated Italian women may permit men to do the dishes or set the table, but anything else? Fuggedaboutit!

Gina carried the sleepy tot to the front door and announced she'd be back in a few minutes once she put him down.

Rocco jumped up from the pink, stuffed and plastic-covered living room chair; the sound of his skin peeling off the slip cover could be heard two blocks away. He probably left some arm hair behind, as if it had been waxed in the process. He winced a little, then took two steps and opened the door for Gina. He offered to get her door for her too, but she waved him off. He'd been seated in that uncomfortable, confining chair for the last couple hours while the rest of us were engaged with my parents, so he was thrilled to have a purpose—*any* purpose when Gina needed the door opened.

He retraced his steps a few minutes later when Gina knocked at the door to come back in.

"You locked the door?! I said I'd be right back, Rock!"

"Can't be too careful, Gina. I have my instructions," and he instinctively shut the door behind her and locked it at the handle, at the dead bolt, and with the chain.

Gina sat down on the plastic-covered sofa and placed a baby-monitor on the coffee table next to the porcelain figure of a woman with an umbrella, walking a pink poodle. She switched the device on and we heard the loud breathing and snoring of her grandson.

"Who needs lunch?" Pop asked.

Mom immediately stood up and said "Sit! I got it. Gina, you wanna help me, hon?"

Gina stood up, grabbed the monitor, and joined Mom in the kitchen. Five minutes later, the table was set for five of us, and a large platter was set down, piled with Sarcone's rolls in the middle and layers of cheeses and lunchmeats displayed around the perimeter. Oil, oregano, salt and pepper were on the table and bowls were set out with sweet peppers, pickles, and onions. Tomatoes and lettuce were on their own plates.

We all converged on the table—especially Rocco, who is a big boy with a big appetite, and whose stomach had been loudly grumbling for the past hour. There, we engaged in a dining ballet as we reached over and around each other, grabbing rolls and olive oil and sandwich contents in varying amounts and in different orders. In the end, we'd all constructed culinary masterpieces, the likes of which would make any hoagie shop in the tri-state area jealous. We ate them with abandon. No one uttered a single word until our dishes were all empty.

Rocco ate two.

My mother kissed him.

When the dust finally settled, the men all leaned back in their chairs as though they had just successfully completed a military conquest, and Mom and Gina got up and cleared the table, put everything away, and came out with coffee and cookies.

I remember one Christmas I brought Indi to dinner. We were seniors in high school, and for the first time (and consequently *only* time) ever, her mother permitted her to join us for the holiday festivities. Culturally, that was a big concession for Mama Patel. She wasn't exactly a big fan of Christmas or other Christian holidays.

Sonny's was closed exactly two days every year—Christmas and

Easter. That's not to say we couldn't have packed the place and made tons of money those days, but they were sacred to my Mom. There was never a discussion about it.

As soon as Indi came in the door, my mother recruited her.

Indi had expected to sit around listening to Christmas songs, opening presents, and otherwise snacking on foods laid out all around the room all evening, just as she'd seen families do on television specials. She was sorely mistaken. Fortunately for her, I had a sister who was used to the routine and was able to help her through it.

I don't think Indi ever worked harder in a kitchen in her entire life, neither before nor since.

Mom handed her an apron and started barking out orders. In Mom's mind, inclusion was the greatest gift she could give Indi, just as my grandmother's inclusion of my mom many years earlier was the greatest gift *she'd* ever received.

Indi wasn't Italian and had *not* been raised this way. I was 18 and oblivious to what was going on as Pop, Uncle Guido, and I sat there eating snacks, drinking, and watching TV. Indi looked back at me like an abductee and I never looked up. She was quiet during dinner, and to her credit never freaked out when my mom told her to get me something to drink or go to the kitchen and get more of this or that. Ange, who was seated next to her, grabbed her forearm a couple times to stop her from jumping over the table and murdering my mother.

After dinner we males all sat back as we did after lunch today, and mom beckoned Ange and Indi to get up and help clear the table and get started on the dishes.

If it was physically possible for laser beams to actually come out of a human being's eyes and bore holes through someone, Indi would have created smoldering holes in my skull as Ange grabbed her to get up.

Again, I was completely oblivious to her plight because this is how it had always been in my life. It was completely ordinary.

As Christmas night drew to a close—and the dessert and eggnog Angela, Indi and Mom had served us was cleared and cleaned—I offered to walk Indi home. She held up her hand and said, "Why stand up on my account now?!" and stormed off. Pop, Guido, and I looked at each other with a "What the hell was *that* all about?" look and shrugged and went back to playing cards.

Indi was so pissed, she didn't talk to me until we went back to school a week-and-a-half later. Even then, she didn't set foot in my house again until summer. That's back when we were dating, and it was one of those examples of the cultural differences between us which were too insurmountable to warrant staying together.

Gina had no problem with any of this. This is how she was raised and it's what she expected. By no means was it perceived to be disrespectful. This was part of her role and she took pride in it. This is why we were actually a really good match for one another, and why I was starting to think again I'd miss her if she wasn't with me. She could happily do everything Mom asked of her—and she could do it in heels, makeup, and a dress.

No sooner had we all settled back into that incredibly uncomfortable and crinkly living room furniture than GG's boy started to wake up and then cry. She packed up the monitor and went home to deal with him, letting us know not to expect her return because the other kids would be coming home from school soon. She needed to get started on their dinner.

Rocco had fallen into such a deep food coma that he actually fell asleep in that corner chair, where no one else had probably fallen asleep in 50 years because it was so freaking uncomfortable. I got the door for Gina, gave her a kiss on the cheek, and whispered I'd try to call her later. She gently touched my cheek, stepped from our front step directly onto hers, and disappeared inside.

I resecured Fort Knox and sat down, making sure to keep the noise to a minimum so as not to awaken Rock, who was now snoring like a buzz saw.

"So, what's going on there?" Mom asked with a smile.

"Honestly, Mom, I have no idea. We just bumped into one another the other day, and we had dinner."

"The other day? I thought you just arrived here yesterday?"

We both left that one hanging in the air and then she continued, "Bumped into one another? Is that what you call that? You barely kept your hands off her."

"I kissed her cheek, for god's sake."

"Mmm-hmm, and stop with using the Lord's name that way. I taught you better."

"Jesus, Mom. Seriously?" I said not ironically. She glared back, unamused, which gave me great joy.

"What's up with *you* and her? She seems like she's inserted herself here quite nicely."

"She's a sweetheart, and I've always loved her like a daughter. He mother, God rest her soul, passed away, and Gina moved in to help her daughter with the kids. She's done very well for herself and takes good care of those kids. Whenever she has leftovers or goes to the market and picks up groceries, she brings a few things over for us. She takes me and your father to doctor appointments when we have something scheduled. She's the attentive child we never had …"

Always with the shot.

"Well I'm glad you have someone who cares, so me and Ange can go about our lives unencumbered."

Pop laughed.

"How's your job down south?" Pop asked.

"Oh, I left. I did what I had to do and came home. Not sure where I'll go next."

"Did you leave because of a girl?"

"No, Pop—not a girl. I just wanted to come back home."

"Will you be here long?" he asked, a little hope in his voice.

"Never know, Dad. I'm having a good time, so maybe I'll stick around for a while."

"Have you heard what's going on with Sonny's?" he asked with his head down. He was sitting on the sofa and leaned forward so his forearms were resting on his thighs and his hands, clasped, dangled down between his knees. He started shaking his head, looking at his feet and continued, "I should *never* have accepted their offer. We were doing fine. Life was good and I had to *blow* it. I just *had* to take their deal. *Idiot!* Now we have nothing. Your mother and I have no money. You kids have no jobs. Our family's legacy is gone. I'm 88 years old. How am I supposed to recover from this???"

And then my father started crying.

My mother just sat back on the sofa with her chin in her chest and her hands clasped in her lap, looking like the victim. Her legs were crossed at her ankles, and she was so short, her little feet dangled several inches above the floor. She didn't look up, but simply muttered, "They're destroying us. They're killing your father. We're just lost."

I knew the answer before I asked it. After all, my mother didn't tell *us* she had *cancer* for god's sake. I'm pretty damned sure she'd never air her dirty laundry to outsiders, but I had to ask nonetheless.

"Have you talked to anyone about helping you, Mom?"

"Of course not! You know better than that. What happens in the family stays here. Not even Gina knows what's going on, although I guess she got an eye-full today with my theatrics in front of Sonny's … but I was so *MAD!*"

"Don't worry about Gina, Mom. She has enough going on in her world with her kids and grandkids. I'm sure she took what she saw today in stride. Like everyone else around here, she knows you guys sold Sonny's."

"But our neighborhood … everywhere we go people ask what's happening there, as if we know. They complain about what a blight it's become on the neighborhood, how other businesses are going to close, too, and everyone's going to move away. The neighborhood will change, and they look at us like it's our fault!"

"Mom, how many times have you told me the opinions of others are their problem, not ours? Hmmm? Anyone with any sense knows you don't control something after you've sold it. Those guys, like it or not, bought the right to do whatever they wanted to do with Sonny's. Now, they haven't paid what they owed and that's a problem, but how they operate is none of your concern. Next time, if someone starts in on you, let them know you don't control Sonny's, or the weather, or the Catholic Church, or the owners of the Eagles or Phillies."

She laughed at that last part and said "You don't know. *You're* not *here*"—yet another shot for abandoning everyone. She was relentless.

Dad spoke up "You're right. I just wish they had paid us what they owed us. At least then we'd have what they promised and we could leave if we wanted. As it is, we can only hold on here at the house maybe two years and then we'll have to sell. A life's work, and in two years we'll be on the street. That's all it's worth."

"You'll never be on the street, Pop. Angela and I will never let that happen. You know that. Regardless, we all know it hurts. We all feel it, and together, we're going to make it right."

"How are we going to do that?"

"I have absolutely no idea, but that doesn't mean we won't figure it out. Hang in there, and in the meantime, let's plan on Sunday dinner here with Angela and the kids. I'll even invite Gina and her gang. It'll be like old times—house full of kids. You and I will pick the menu, Pop—*like old times*—and we'll make it together. Mom, you're getting the day off!"

Pop lifted his head "Really? That would be *great*!"

And Mom piped in that there's a lot to do—cleaning the house, buying groceries, fixing a leaky sink upstairs—and that she had no idea how she'd get all that done by Sunday. Then she shook her head, making that "tsk tsk tsk" noise she does with her tongue against her teeth, like I'd just laid a ton of bricks on her shoulders—heartless bastard that I am.

"Mom, the house is fine and I'll pick up groceries. Just *be* here—k? … enough with the drama already."

Then Mom and Pop started bickering about why she was anywhere near Sonny's when he had specifically told her not to go there, and blah blah blah. That was my cue.

"… aaaand, I'm out. Rock? We've got stuff to do."

Rocco awoke from his food stupor when he heard his name and stood up like his ass was suddenly on fire. "Right. I'll get the door." And he started unlatching the locks. In seconds, we were on the street, heading back toward Sonny's although we really had no destination in mind.

For the first time since returning to town, I was feeling pretty good about things and had a little bounce in my step.

We were all working in tandem. I hadn't realized how much I had missed these people. It was refreshing and wonderful to reconnect, and I also felt optimistic about Sunday dinner. I'd just have to get Ange and Guido on board, but I know they'd be up for it. It might even be nice to invite Mr. Acchione. He's *practically* family, and I'm sure he'd love all the activity. Gina would certainly be happy to join in, and her kids will probably be willing to come and bring their kids too—a full house. We hadn't all been together like that for months. It would be just what my parents needed for a little "pick me up" (as Pop always called it).

Of course, I had no way of knowing at that moment there was no way on God's green Earth the Sunday dinner would happen—or at least not as planned. That would all become very clear soon enough.

Raj and Indi

Rocco and I stepped out of my parents' house and started wandering aimlessly until inspiration hit me. I'd stood Raj up a couple days ago and never called to apologize. Quite a bit had happened since then, and since Rock and I had a few hours on our hands before I was supposed to go to dinner with GG, there was certainly ample time to clear the air with Raj.

"Raj, it's me." Silence. "Dude, I'm sorry. I stood you up, but I had a really great reason. I was busy getting laid."

"Damn you. I wanted to stay mad at you, but it's hard to argue with an excuse like that. Who was the lucky lady?"

He was going to find out soon enough anyway, and since he had a crush on her, I figured I'd better be the one to tell him.

"GG."

"Wait. Are you freaking serious?! I've been trying to get up the nerve to ask her out since she moved home. Fuck! So, are you calling me to brag?"

"Well, we still have this problem with Sonny's, and I hoped you could use your technical wizardry to help me make some useful inroads. At the very least, you should join me and Rocco and drink a lot of beer."

"I'm in. I've been doing some research too! Don't move. I'm comin' to you!"

I didn't even have to tell Raj where to meet me. When I said "drink beer" he knew we'd meet at our favorite corner tap room, which is exactly where Rocco was already two beers "in" when Raj finally came through the door.

"Holy shit! Rocco, is that you?" Raj said, extending his hand, hoping Rocco shook it instead of yanking his entire arm out of its socket and beating him to death with it.

Rocco was one of the kids who terrorized Raj the first day he arrived at school, but by lunch Raj was shrouded beneath our umbrella of protection. Even still, that first impression was a lasting one. Raj was always scared crapless of Rocco, and for good reason. Rock was a scary dude. Even I was scared of him, and he was my bodyguard. He was a huge guy—six-foot-five and two hundred eighty pounds of lean muscle—but it took a surprisingly small amount of alcohol to get him half shit-faced. If he got drunk, I had no idea how we'd control this monster, so I suggested he slow down a little, or Guido might not be happy. Mentioning my uncle's name was all it took. He ordered seltzer from that moment forward. Between that and me drinking diet cola, Raj ended up being the only one drinking alcohol for the rest of the afternoon—not good.

We spent the next couple hours catching up with one another, laughing and reminding one another of stupid shit we'd done in our youth. Then we started talking about Gina.

Raj was completely infatuated with GG. He lusted after her some- thin' awful when we were kids, but no matter how hard I tried back then, I couldn't get her interested in him. Regardless how much *he* wanted *her*, if the feelings weren't at least a little mutual, nothing was ever going to happen. Basically, you need a spark and fuel to get fire. Without one or the other, there's no flame. Raj was all spark and no fuel—poor bastard. He was really missing out on something too.

Raj had a few beers and was clearly getting more and more resentful about my fling with GG. His failure to gain her favor turned him against her as he got more drunk.

"You know what she does for a living, right?" he started.

"Funny how that never came up in conversation, even when we were naked. Go figure!"

"Fuck you. I'll tell you what she does. She works for a driveway sealer company. Oh, it's a legitimate enough business when companies actually apply the proper product to protect your driveway, but her company is a bunch crooks. She works for her family's business. They only accept cash under the table and basically paint driveways with black water. The shit disappears with the first rainstorm, but her company is long gone by then. They're con artists! The company changes its name every couple months to avoid lawsuits. You know why she does sales?"

"Because she has great tits and a nice ass?" I asked.

"Because she has great tits and a nice ass, that's why! Oh, and to close the deal, she usually blows or screws the guy making the decision, depending on how big a deal it is. Apparently, guys won't sue a contractor if their suit would expose them cheating on their wives."

"You mean she'd bang a guy to get him to sealcoat his driveway?"

"No, idiot. She'd flirt with those guys, for sure, but she'd seal the deal with guys getting shopping center lots done, or airport runways and shit!"

"Raj, stop. You have no proof of anything like that."

"Yeah, I do!" and he reached into his backpack and pulled out a stack of Better Business Bureau complaints detailing the whole thing, including her tactics.

"Raj, you can't possibly believe these stories. She's been a homebody watching her grandkids since she moved back home."

He responded "Look, man, you do what you want with whoever you want, but there's something here. I know it. One complaint could be seen as bullshit, but there are *dozens* here. Doz ... ens."

"We'll see. I'll ask her the next time I see her."

"… you're seeing her again?"

"Yeah. Tonight. I'm taking her to dinner, and then we'll see where nature takes us."

"God, I fucking hate you."

"Would bringing back video make you hate me less?"

He glared at me. Then his eyes softened. His mouth turned upward into a smirk and he replied, "… well, obviously," and we both laughed.

We finished drinking and started heading home. Rocco was completely sober by this point, and although Raj was probably pretty much "in the bag," I was obviously fine, if a little gassy from all those sodas. I honestly don't drink—part of life as a bartender, I suppose. I ordered one beer which just sat there and got warm, and then ordered Cokes. Since Raj was pretty drunk and would probably never survive walking home alone in his condition, Rocco and I agreed to escort him to ensure his safe arrival.

The three of us together must've been quite a sight too. Rocco was gargantuan; I was a little more ordinary, and then there was Raj. The guy looked like someone just threw a skin suit on a skeleton. Saying Raj was 5 foot 2 was being generous, and he weighed about 100 pounds soaking wet. He was always getting pushed around when we were kids, which I guess is how we ended up together. Even now, when he said "Fuck you," he sounded like a twelve-year-old trying to sound tough—not even remotely worrisome.

Most guys just laughed it off when he said it. Some laughed and hit him in the chest with an open palm, sort of a cross between a kidding "Get outta here," and a serious "Back off, clown." Regardless how it was intended, Raj's eyes would always get big and he'd cough from having the wind knocked out of him. He's a great guy who would fight to the end for me, but I had to be careful 'cause it would take very little to end him.

Raj broke the silence. "You know my sister would cut off your balls if she knew you were banging Gina. They HATE each other!"

Raj was right. Indi and I tried dating when we were kids, but it didn't take long before we realized that was never going to go anywhere. Today we're good friends—such good friends we occasionally have sex—but that would end abruptly if she thought I had touched Gina.

Our arrangement always worked out well for both of us too. Whenever we were horny, or we needed a plus-one for something, or we wanted to go out to dinner or a movie—but not on a date—we had one another. As friends, we had more sex with one another than most people did in relationships, but we always knew how to compartmentalize it.

For me, I didn't have to waste my time slogging through a parade of waitresses and bartenders, and for her, she could focus on school and her career without the distraction of maintaining a relationship. That lasted for a long time, but ultimately, she finished college, got a job, and started mixing with a different crowd. She'd still visit the old neighborhood now and then and would stop in to see me at Sonny's when she did—which usually led to spending the night together—but even that trailed off over time.

By the time she hit 30, she was engaged. By 31 she was married and living in the suburbs. By forty, she'd had two kids—a boy and a girl spaced apart exactly like her and Raj. By her late-forties, she was divorced and living with her parents and Raj again in South Philly.

Raj had never moved out in the first place.

Sorta funny to sum up 20 years of her life like that, but that's really how it happened. She and her ex, some Irish kid from Delco (that's Delaware County, just west of Philly), did okay for a while, but they couldn't make it long term. "'Til death us do part" was a lot easier back when life expectancy was around thirty. It's a whole 'nother thing when you can expect to live to be eighty or more. That's a long freakin' time to be with one person. And just as she and I noticed decades earlier, there's a cultural imbalance to get through too. A Hindu girl from India doesn't have a whole lot in common with an Irish Catholic dude from a middle-class suburb where everyone was whiter than mayonnaise. She and her ex were doomed from the start.

Even though she got divorced, she kept her married name, to keep it the same as her kids. So now she's an Indian girl from Italian South Philly with an Irish last name. She's like the UN with feet!

"Delco Richie" is actually a decent guy and a good dad. He got remarried too, only this time to Jewish girl. I guess marriage between a Hindu and Catholic wasn't complicated enough. He never learns. He even had more kids. He's a nice guy, but damn. At every turn he exhibits the common sense of a bag of hammers.

LESS RAJ, MORE INDI

We reached Raj's house and I told Rock I was going to go in. He wasn't comfortable going in because he didn't know anyone, so I told him to either wait outside—which would suck—or go home and bathe, for Christ's sake, and be generous with the toothpaste.

I promised him I'd call him if I went anywhere.

The door swung open and while Raj jiggled the key ring to extricate his key from the lock, I strode in like I owned the place and waved goodbye to Rocco, at least for now.

"S'up, Paesan?"—Indi's standard greeting, this time asked as she walked past me with her arms full of laundry, stopping only long enough to give me a kiss on the cheek. The fact she hadn't seen me for a year until that exact moment didn't seem to have phased her in the least. If it did, she downplayed it beautifully.

Paesan always sounds funny coming out of her mouth. Her Indian accent is even more faint than Raj's—which is pretty damned faint in its own right—but both of them still have a little South Philly accent mixed in. Indi's accent softened when she went to college. Mingling with the blue bloods, she adopted some of their speech patterns. Raj went to a tech school. It wasn't fancy, so his accent is true-blue—or at least as true blue as a Hindi/South Philly accent can be.

She started calling me Paesan in response to me calling her Indi. Her real name is Swati. That always sounded so ethnic to me as a kid, so I just started calling her "Indi," which is short for "Indian chick." I know that sounds disrespectful, but Indi and I are fine with our nicknames for one another. Why should you care?

I will occasionally opt for the long version when we're kidding around with one another: "Hey Indian Chick, grab me a drink already!" to which she usually cynically flips me "the Bird," after which *I* get up and grab us *both* a drink.

I've been calling her that for so long, even her mom will call her Indi now and then. She doesn't know it stands for "Indian Chick," of course. She just thinks it's an affectionate term between us, and she wants to be in on the joke.

Indi's parents have always liked me. I was the one who had Raj's back, way back when, and they knew it. I've never been a parent, but I'm sure if I was, I'd be relieved to know someone was sticking up for my kid when he really wasn't fit to stick up for himself—no matter how lionhearted he might have been. I was a local kid whose family had been intertwined with the neighborhood for generations. I never realized it as a kid, but that gave me credibility. If Raj was okay by me, he should be okay by everyone. I never really had to do or say anything to that effect, it was just inferred by everyone. The day I befriended Raj was the day the bullying stopped. Period.

Indi walked into her bedroom with her arms full of laundry, still dressed for work, but she'd kicked off her heels as soon as she had gotten home in favor of her light blue fuzzy slippers. They looked positively absurd against her black stockings and below her black pencil skirt and white, buttoned-down blouse.

After saying hi to everyone, I made my exit and joined Indi in her room, where she was folding clothes. I laid on the bed and she sat on the floor with her legs folded under her. She methodically made her way through the crumpled mess of fresh, clean laundry, occasionally holding pieces up to her face and closing her eyes to appreciate the warmth, coziness and fresh smell.

I always figured acts like folding warm, fresh laundry and cooking had a lot in common—heat, savory aromas, peace, comfort—it was all very sensory.

Without her noticing, I watched her as we spoke. She was still beautiful. Even at the end of the day, disheveled and kneeling in her wrinkled work clothes, folding laundry, she kick-started my pulse. Of course, she snapped me right out of that trance with her mechanical sarcasm: "You gonna just sit there and stare at my boobs, or are you going to help me fold some of this shit?" She threw a few pairs of her dad's old boxer shorts up on the bed for me to work on, because she thought me folding his shorts would be funny.

For the record, she had small-ish boobs—perky, but small. There wasn't much to see, but what was there was very nice. So, yeah—I was staring.

She may have sounded Ivy League at work among all the other college-educated professionals in her white-washed office, but when she got home and was among her people, her speech returned to its roots. She sounded like the girl I grew up with here in the neighborhood.

"So Raj tells me you're back in town because your mom and dad were conned out of Sonny's."

"Pretty much," I said, as I kept my head down and continued to fold her dad's underwear. Part of me looked down to focus on what I was doing, but part of me also didn't want to risk catching her gaze—as if just seeing my eyes would mean she could read my intent to rip off her clothes.

"What are you going to do?"

I tried to deflect. "You mean right now? Probably try to forget I've been putting my hands in your dad's 'poopy underpants,' for starters."

"No, dumbass." I didn't have to see her to know she was smiling when she said it. "What are you going to do about those fuckers who ruined Sonny's?" Even though the words weren't saying it, she was flirting a little bit. Her spark was lit, too—at least that's what I wanted to believe.

"Only so much I can do, and even then, I'm not sure what that is."

"Have you talked to attorneys yet?"

"Attorneys, really? Wow. FUCK! That's a great idea. I wish my brother-in-law and Mr. Acchione, *our attorneys* had thought of that. Great suggestion."

"Sarcasm, really? I'm trying to be helpful. Can we have a big-boy-and-girl conversation here?"

"… I'll give you a big-boy-or-girl something."

"Stop.

"Look: I get it that you're not excited about legal process, but what else are you going to do, take Raj and Rocco down there and beat 'em up?"

"Yeah. I'm thinking that's exactly what we should do. Raj can go down and kick some serious Neanderthal ass, and I can go back into the kitchen and start making gravy so it's ready in time for the dinner rush. Whattaya think, good idea?"

"Keep it up with the sarcasm, Johnny, and the only underpants you'll be touching tonight are my father's."

"Why don't you give me some of your mom's bras to fold now? It'll really help get me in the mood." I jumped down from the bed, dropped the folded boxers on the pile, and walked past her to the bedroom door to close and lock it.

That combined sound was our telltale sign, the most pathetic form of foreplay imaginable.

"What do you think you're doing?" she said in a sing-song tone, still looking away from me and down at the laundry she continued to fold.

I kneeled down behind her, eased my hands around her waist, gently kissed her neck, and jokingly said, "Oh, nothin.' I'm just gonna tear off your clothes and bang the shit out of you."

She laughed, complimented me on my foreplay, pulled her shirt off over her head and started undoing my pants. Not once did she ask about my bruises—even when I clenched my eyes shut or winced in agony when some of them would get touched.

Man's Gotta Eat

After our little interlude, we returned to the living room, where everyone was watching TV.

"So? What was for dinner tonight?" I asked as I walked into the kitchen, held the fridge door open and leaned into the box.

Mom spoke up: "Indian food. You'd hate it."

I responded quickly: "You know me so well, Mom," as I walked over and kissed her cheek. "Anybody else here hungry for something other than Indian food?"

Raj was sound asleep on the sofa, the result of having too many beers earlier in the day and too few pounds to absorb them. Indi's kids both had to get to bed for school the next day. Pops was sleeping with his head on Raj's shoulder, and after the day she'd had with my mother, Mom was ready to call it quits.

So it was just the two of us—me and Indi.

"Well, I'm not sure," she said. "I was thinking about making it an early night tonight. I have to work in the morning."

"That's fine. I sorta told GG I'd take *her* out tonight anyway, so ..."

She just glared at me, and blinked two or three times for effect. "Where are you taking me?" she asked, almost accusatorily through her gritted teeth.

Mom looked at me and smiled. She knew it was a low-down dirty, manipulative thing to say to Indi, but it worked.

Indi and Gina really, *really* hated each other.

I called Rocco and told him where we were heading, and he asked me not to leave until he got here. Considering all the weird shit going on the last couple days, I was happy to oblige.

I actually felt like eating a large slab of red meat, so Indi and I went to a chophouse and settled into a table. Rocco dined at the bar. Three hours later, we were still sitting there, nursing about our hundredth cup of coffee. We'd had a great meal and dessert. She and I had gone to the restroom about three times (*way* too many coffee refills), but we kept coming back and sitting down. We simply didn't want the evening to end.

We hadn't seen one another for almost a year—or been out alone together for months before that. This was nice. Sometimes being absent from one another provides an objective view of how great someone is.

We talked about anything and everything, and never once about Sonny's or my family. We never had lulls in our conversation, and every now and then, she'd put her hand on mine—or vice versa—and we'd leave them there like that.

I'd forgotten how special she was, and how much we clicked. As much fun as I'd had messing around with Gina, that's exactly what I was doing—messing around. The difference between Indi and Gina was like the difference between a Ferrari and an Oldsmobile. One is a good, functional and occasionally reliable car, and the other one is a Ferrari, for Christ's sake. Ironically, the Italian girl in this analogy was not the Italian car.

That night out with Indi proved what I knew all along as a kid. She's the one, whether we ever figured out how to make it work or even tried was irrelevant. She was the one for me. Gina wasn't.

It's amazing how in a matter of a couple days, I went from everything being simple—living and working in New Orleans—to being back home and being surround by every sort of conflict imaginable. A very large part of me wanted to run ten blocks back to Mr. Acchione's, get in my car, and leave this place in a cloud of blue smoke.

Of course, in order to do that, I'd have to evade poor Rocco, who had spent the entire evening sitting at the bar watching an horrendous basketball game on the TV with one eye watching us in the bar mirror. The poor guy needed sleep. I finally conceded to my better judgment, stood up, helped Indi out of her chair, and rescued my bodyguard from more exposure to the Seventy-Sixers.

We walked Indi home. I gently kissed her good night, and asked her to give my best to her family. I promised to call the next day, and then Rocco and I headed back to the bus to head home.

The bus ride back to Mr. Acchione's was actually more sad and "aromatic" than the one this morning. The thing was half-full with ripe, inebriated, or simply exhausted zombies. Even the bus driver looked like he'd been lobotomized.

We got dropped at Mr. Acchione's and I reached for my key. As I fumbled at the lock, Rocco sat down on the front step.

"What are you doin', Rock?"

"I'll stay out here tonight so I can be ready for you in the morning."

"That's fucked up. This house has something like 137 bedrooms. I think we can find more suitable accommodations for you in here than out on the front step. Besides, in this neighborhood, I don't think the cops will let you sleep on the front step."

Rock got up, followed me, and thanked me profusely for being so decent. I never realized what a tight ship Uncle G ran. Even guys who can bench-press a small house fear him.

We went upstairs. Rocco found a room and I fell onto the bed in mine.

I am an Idiot

I read somewhere once we only use 10% of our brains. I also read that was entirely untrue, but for the sake of argument, let's assume it's not. Apparently, we also only use about 10% of that 10% for cognitive thinking. The other 90% is used for awareness—maintaining balance, not bumping into stuff, hearing things, seeing things—sensory shit.

Back in the mid-1950s, isolation tanks were created to test people on the effects of sensory deprivation. Subjects would climb in and lay in skin-temperature salt water. Once the tank was closed, there would be a total absence of light and sound. The goal was to have a human subject floating in silent, dark stasis, unburdening the mind of its situational awareness duties so it can engage in nothing but cognitive thought.

The theory was subjects could lay in that environment for a brief period and experience the benefits of several hours of sleep, and at that same time solve the world's problems with their super-computer brains that would be unencumbered by the distractions of physical senses. It's called a "theta state". This same phenomenon is said to occur immediately before or after sleep and is believed to be a catalyst for creativity and problem-solving.

This had the potential to be man's greatest discovery. Unfortunately, sixty years later, this concept struggles for credibility. Most of these tanks tend to be relegated to the back rooms of spas where incense is burned and people wear socks with sandals.

Even if you've never laid in such a contraption, you've probably experienced this "theta brain wave" feeling in your own life, as you drift in and out of sleep.

You know those mornings when you know you're awake—but only sort of—and you have about ten minutes before the alarm goes off? Those times when you can't dare fall back to sleep because you know if you do you'll be deep in REM when the alarm finally *does* go off, and that will suck?

You're not dreaming anymore, at least not really, but you might have the presence of mind to conjure up conclusions for the dream you were just having—like a director putting finishing touches on a movie. Sometimes, as your body lays still and the room is dark and quiet, you might find yourself scrolling through your mental calendar, preparing yourself for what the day has in store for you.

Regardless, with so little other stimuli to distract you, you have great clarity of mind and can get an unfiltered look at your life, putting what you've been doing into context.

Well, if you've never experienced that, you're missing out on one of life's greatest pleasures. If you have experienced it, you'll know exactly what state I was in the moment I remembered I was supposed to have gone out with GG the night before, and not only didn't do that, but also forgot to call her and *tell* her I wasn't going to do that.

After a lovely evening with Indi—and a magnificently restful sleep in a mattress that may be more comfortable than the clouds in heaven—I bolted upright and blurted "fuck me!" Because I knew Gina was going to go completely nuts when she got me in her sites.

When I went to Gina's yesterday, I fully expected to grovel for forgiveness for things I had said a couple nights before, but she surprisingly let me off the hook as soon as she saw me. Now I was going to have to go back *again* and explain why I stood her up. This was not going to be good.

The big difference between these two occasions was *last* time I was prepared to be completely honest and fall on the sword of stupidity for speaking out of turn. This time I absolutely, positively *could not* be honest. She'd freaking murder me. Seriously, that was no exaggeration. She's hot-headed enough I could absolutely see her burying a kitchen knife several inches into my chest if I told her I had stood her up in favor of having sex and dinner with Indi. Of course, that assumes GG actually has a knife in that barren wasteland she calls her kitchen.

She'd blow up like Hiroshima after that confession. The mushroom cloud she'd create would be visible from Jupiter!

It's not like I need to get her to forgive me so we could resume a romantic relationship with her—because I realized last night I don't want that—but I also don't want to ruin a fifty-year friendship. Plus I need her to help keep an eye on my folks and keep them on an even keel in my absence. Basically, I needed her to keep doing all the things she'd been doing since Sonny's sold. I really just wanted things to go back to how they were a few days ago, before we bumped into one another on the street—and then repeatedly bumped into one another naked on her couch.

This was going to take some doing. I was going to have to withhold information from her (not lie *exactly*), and figure out some plausible excuse for me being a no-show.

To add a little more difficulty to an already impossible situation, I'm the world's worst liar. I'm so bad at lying, *Helen Keller* would have seen through me.

Gina is going to rip me apart. Ugh.

After a quick shower and some attention to my oral hygiene, I walked downstairs and joined Rocco and Mr. Acchione, who were already at the table drinking coffee, eating a light breakfast, and not acknowledging one another. As I stepped into the room, Marilyn offered me a cup of coffee and asked me how I was feeling. I accepted the cup like a starving man accepts a morsel of bread and let her know, physically speaking, I was "tip-top." This was actually entirely accurate. I really did feel good. Except for the colored blotches on my body, I'd have a hard time being convinced I had the snot beaten out of me only a few nights earlier.

Mr. Acchione and Rock both greeted me and I did likewise.

"What's the plan for today, young Volmanti?" asked Mr. Acchione.

"Well, I need to start with a trip to Gina's with my tail between my legs."

"Uh-oh. What'd you *do?*" he asked somewhat urgently, showing a little more interest in my personal exploits than I expected.

I told him about the night before (specifically leaving out the part about me molesting Indi), and how I was supposed to be with GG. He groaned, but there was a slightly perceptible difference in how he did it versus how most other guys would. Most guys would groan empathetically, as if to say "Dude, you're so screwed," but his groan was a little more like I was upsetting the apple cart.

"Is there a problem, Joe?" I asked.

"Not a problem, exactly, but we need you to be particularly cautious. It's times like these when we really need to ensure everyone on the team is pulling the oars in the same direction. If there's any dissention among the team, the ship's likely to capsize and sink. Do you follow me here?"

"Yeah, but it's just Gina ..."

"Nonsense. Guido and I agree her involvement is integral to our ability to proceed. We actually need her. Son, you really need to make this right and get her back on board with everyone else."

I had enough self-imposed pressure on me already to take care of this. I didn't need him adding to it. I sniped back "I get it. It's important and I fucked up. I get it. Okay?"

He looked at me. His eyes betrayed his anger, but only briefly. He quickly got past that and returned to being conciliatory. "John, I'm not trying to put more pressure on you. I'm just focused on the larger matter at hand, and I am concerned Gina could derail us. Please let me know if I can be of any assistance with this."

Now I felt like shit. Here's this generous, smart, accommodating 95-year-old man who's trying to help me and I'm barking at him like an entitled 15 year old. I couldn't apologize quickly enough. "Joe, I'm sorry. This situation is entirely of my doing and has jeopardized what we're trying to accomplish. Unfortunately, to get out of it, I have to lie—or at least withhold critical facts—and that goes against every fiber of my being. I'm a little short-tempered. I'm sorry."

"Why can't you tell the truth?"

"Because if Gina learns I was out with Indi, whom she hates more than anyone else on the planet and has done so since about the fourth grade, she will never forgive me. That will definitely end her involvement with us. It'll end a fifty-year friendship, and it will also end up depriving my parents of a next-door neighbor who looks in on them—and *after* them—nearly every day."

"If you're saying you were intimate with Indi, I understand your dilemma," he said, and then he looked me straight in the eyes, and in a very polished, lawyerly manner, with a steel look and a calm, level delivery, continued, "but you absolutely have to do what is necessary to ensure our mission is not jeopardized. That is your single imperative, above everything else. Your family is more important than your friend. That may seem cold, but it's a fact. When all of this is over, you can be honest with her and risk losing her, but for now you simply cannot. Frankly, as is always the case with any lie—white or otherwise—you will be found out. She'll learn of your infidelity and of your intentions toward the other young lady, but by then, this should all be finished."

Crap.

In a single comment, he brought total clarity to what I needed to do.

I thanked him for his insight and then I turned to Rocco and told him we have some ground to cover. We walked out the front door and made our way to the bus, as we'd done the day before, only this time we *both* smelled decent.

"Thanks for showering today, Rock."

"Gee, thanks for giving me a place to sleep and bathe, Johnny," he said sarcastically, and then playfully shoved me. Of course, when normal-sized people playfully shove, you get knocked for a step. When Rocco does it, you almost fly into traffic, but that's okay. His heart was in the right place, even if his brain always seems to have a hard time keeping up.

We boarded the bus and Rocco confessed, "I'm sorry you're going through this, John, but I also can't wait to see how you get out of it. Gina's one scary chick!"

"Well, Rock, you know, as my bodyguard, you'll be expected to deliver the message for me. That way, if she loses her shit, she'll lose it on you and I'll be safe."

Rocco sat there quietly for a few seconds, ruminating on the bomb I'd just dropped on him, and then looked up at me "Really? Is that what Guido told you?"

"It's not so much what he told me, Rock. It's what he *expects* of you, but you do what you think is right."

I kept torturing Rocco like that until we reached our stop, at which point he stood up—resigned to his fate—and told me to stay on the bus where it's safe while he went and dealt with Gina. I couldn't take it any longer, so I told him I was just messing with him and that he didn't need to protect me from a five-foot tall grandmother of ten. The worst thing she'd do is yell at me and possibly punch or slap me. Not only did I think I could endure such treatment, I also secretly thought I deserved it.

All he could say—besides "Phew!"—was "No offense, but she has a great ass for a grandmother of ten."

We walked up to Gina's just as she was stepping out of my parents' house.

"Hey, you!" I said, a little taken off guard. I was expecting to knock on her door and wait to see her.

"Oh. You finally found your way back here. Wait. Let me get my purse and my time machine and we'll go to dinner last night," she said, her words dripping with sarcasm.

"Yeah, about that. Sorry? Rock and I left here yesterday afternoon, had time to burn and called Raj. We met at the corner tap room. We were there a very, very long time."

Gina looked right past me, and in a classic "mom" tone asked Rocco "Is that true, Rocco?"

Rock just looked at her like a deer in headlights and nodded his head affirmatively. Gina frowned and looked back at me. "How *is* Raj?"

"He's good. He's trying to help us with this Sonny's thing, so we discussed that and then talked about the neighborhood. We talked about you, too," I added, hoping to flatter her a little. "He always had a crush on you."

"Oh boy," she said dismissively. "Did you see Swati?"

Gina never referred to Indi as Indi, only by her given name, Swati (and she scrunched up her nose when she over-enunciated the "ah" part), because nicknames are terms of affection, and there was absolutely none of that between GG and Indi. That thought bounced around in my head while I tried to think of the best way to answer whether or not I had seen Indi. It was crunch time, so I decided to be *mostly* honest.

"Yeah. We saw her when we got back to the Patel's. Her mom was there too. She said it was good of you to help with my mom yesterday."

"Mm-hmm. I'm sure she did. The old lady's a regular fan of mine too. How's her daughter?"

"Oh, she's fine. She was doing laundry when we got there, no big deal. Why don't we go inside and talk?"

"I don't think so. I'm not too thrilled with you right now, John, and I'm afraid if I'm alone in a room with you, I'll say things I'll regret. I'm going to be in here by myself, continuing to calm down. Maybe we'll talk later."

She went inside her place and slammed the door behind her, right in my face.

I was right there on my parents' front stoop, so it would be natural to go in and visit, but I really wasn't up for it.

"C'mon Rock. Let's head back to Mr. Acchione's and check in with him and G."

"You're the boss, John."

I pulled out my "burner" and called Guido.

"Kid?"

"Yeah, Unc. I think we're going to have trouble with Gina. She's pretty pissed."

"Joe told me. We're already figuring it out. Head back to his house and we'll meet you. I think your buddy Raj could be useful too. Can you get him to meet us at Joe's?"

"Is there anything else I can bring? Bagels? Some fancy coffee from the mermaid place?"

"Goodbye, kid."

Rock and I climbed back on the bus and settled into our seats, deflated. He didn't get the show he was hoping for and I didn't fix what I'd broken.

Getting the Band Back Together

We strolled up the front steps to Mr. Acchione's front door. Before I could pull out my key, we were greeted by my gloating sister.

"Well, look who's here. Mr. Screw the Pooch and his faithful sidekick!"

"I'm not so sure Gina or Indi will appreciate being referred to as a pooch, Ange."

"You just couldn't control yourself, could you? Our family's under fire by who knows who and all you can think of is having sex with the neighbor girls. Nice. Way to put yourself first, as *usual*. You're a typical middle-aged bachelor—a man-child who doesn't give a *shit* about anyone else."

"What the fuck's that supposed to mean?! I'm up here, aren't I? I didn't have to come back to Philly. I was doing just fine on my own, far the fuck away from here and *you*. I came up here for *you* people, to help *you* out! Tell me again how that's selfish."

"Because when you got here, it's been all about you, what *you're* going to do, how *you're* going to do it, whom *you're* going to *fuck*. Did I leave anything out?"

"First of all, it's good to see you're still grammatically responsible when you're angry. Good use of 'whom' there." That did not diffuse anything, nor did it elicit the smirk I was gunning for. I hunkered down for a fight. "Listen, Angela. I'm *trying* to do what I can to *help*. I had no intention of having sex with Gina. *She* seduced *me*!"

"Have you ever heard of the word '*no,*' John? It's a magical word meaning 'I don't want to have sex with you, Gina.'"

"Screw you, Angela!" I yelled.

She screamed back, "No, thanks. I know where your dick has been and I don't want it anywhere near me!"

Uncle G suddenly appeared on the front step from inside the house and started applauding. "That was a lovely performance. I'm sure Joe appreciates you putting on such an exhibition and embarrassing him in front of his entire neighborhood. Bravo. Would you like to come in, or is there an Act 2 to this high school performance?"

"Hey, I wasn't expecting to be ambushed when I got here." I said, and Ange replied with the cogently planned and eloquently delivered response: "Fuck you," complete with *both* middle fingers being fully extended and shoved in my face.

G placed his hand between Angela's shoulder blades, grabbed a handful of shirt, and steered her inside. He motioned to Rocco to do the same to me.

We all sat in the parlor. Angela's body language spoke volumes, with her arms and legs crossed in front of her, her chin pressed firmly in her chest, and her eyes staring at me from just below her eyebrows.

I sat on the other side of the room, acting like I was ignoring her, even though I was seething.

"John, did you reach your friend Raj? Will he be coming?" asked Mr. Acchione.

"I did, and he'll be here. Give him about a half hour."

"Angela," Mr. Acchione continued, "can you please call Miss Gianetti and ask her to join us? She'll be reluctant, but we need her here, and there's no one else from whom I believe she'll consider such a request."

"I don't know why she'd consider …" Angela started, but G stopped her in her tracks.

"Angela, stop it. You and Gina are close friends. Just make the call and be convincing. Her involvement is extremely important. *Please*, make the goddamned phone call."

"Fine. I'll call from the kitchen."

"Jesus Christ," I muttered.

Uncle G sternly added in my direction, "And you're *really* not helping."

Rocco looked at me and rolled his eyes. I smirked.

She returned to the parlor a few moments later. "She'll be here within the hour."

Joe spoke up: "Excellent work."

G nodded his approval.

"How'd you accomplish *that*?" I asked, because—apparently—I can't leave well enough alone either.

"*Understandably,* she was reluctant because she knows you're here, but I convinced her it was for the greater good."

"Thanks," I said.

"And then I told her when we're done, she could kill you," she added.

There were periods of uncomfortable silence and forced conversation while we all loitered in the parlor waiting for Raj and Gina. Raj arrived first, followed by Gina a few minutes later. The dynamics were pretty predictable. Gina and Angela sat together on a velvet sofa near the window. G stood along the room's perimeter by the double doors leading to the foyer. Joe sat at his desk along the wall directly across from Guido, and Rocco, Raj, and I sat or stood near the double doors leading to the kitchen as far across the room from GG and Ange as physically possible.

Mr. Acchione started the conversation. It lit the fuse for what would change all of our lives.

THE PLAN

Rarely, in an Italian home, do guests convene and not get offered food or drink. It's not just a matter of hospitality, it's protocol.

Mr. Acchione has always been very conscious of decorum and has always politely offered everyone beverages or snacks before starting a meeting. Then he usually engages in a little light banter in an effort to loosen the room up and get everyone talking. Then, after setting the stage, he starts in.

Today, he hastily rung for Marilyn, who arrived at the kitchen door.

"We're not to be disturbed," he said to her, and then nodded for her to shut the pocket doors separating the kitchen from the parlor. Guido turned around and closed the doors behind him, enveloping us all in an inner sanctum.

Mr. Acchione wasted no time.

"Let's get started. As we all know, several months ago, a deceitful and anonymous crew swindled John and Toni Volmanti out of their family restaurant. They agreed to pay, and John and Toni agreed to accept, a little more than two million dollars for the privilege—three hundred thousand up front and one hundred fifty thousand per month for a year. Contracts were drafted, negotiated, and executed and the three-hundred-thousand-dollar down payment was received. The first installment due date came and went without payment. Neither that payment, nor any subsequent payment ever arrived.

"We pursued legal process and tried to serve notice upon the legal entity who was listed as the buyer, but we learned it had subsequently sold the restaurant and assets to another entity. That one sold to another entity, etc., ten times over. None of the entities had any discoverable members, nor history. It became increasingly apparent John and Toni had been the target of a complex confidence game intended to separate them from their livelihood, their legacy and their assets.

"In the meantime, miscreants have been ransacking the restaurant, removing furniture, fixtures and equipment of all sorts, but not for resale—for disposal. Little if any of the contents of Sonny's exist either on site or elsewhere anymore. It has all been taken to the landfill and lost forever.

"Our greatest quandary through all of this has been why?

"Theft is one thing, but why demolish what's been stolen?

"Why commit three hundred thousand dollars and untold labor hours to a venture producing no revenue?

"Why Sonny's?

"Why now?

"No matter how hard nor how deeply we dug, we could never seem to find those answers. Somewhere there is a connection to tie all of this together, but like finding the Rosetta stone, until we discover that connection—that link—we'll be unable to solve this mystery. Regardless, even if we can't solve it, we can attempt to rectify it.

"To this point, we have been unable to find a valid, legal entity to sue, either for performance or for recovery. We either desire payment in full, as contractually agreed, or we want the contract to be voided and for the property and its remaining contents to be returned to the Volmantis. If the contract is voided, we will then sue the 'Buyer' for all damages inflicted on the premises, as well as business damages imposed on the restaurant's reputation, as well as pain and suffering imposed on John and Toni.

"Of course, monetary judgments are often uncollectible, but gaining control of the facility and being able to resurrect the business may be victory enough.

"This brings us to strategy.

"Because the entities who have bought and sold the business over the past several months are hollow shells with no visible legal validity, we are trying to go back to the original buyer. The agent who represented the buyer has disappeared. His identity was artificial anyway, and we'd never met his clients. However, with the aid of Guido's information-gathering efforts, we're a couple steps closer.

"John, will you please hand these photographs around?" He held up eight-by-ten photos of a middle-aged man in a suit that I handed to everyone in the room.

"Guido? The floor is yours, my friend."

"Thank you, Joe," Guido replied, and he turned to the double doors behind him, opened one of them and gestured for someone to come in. Two of Guido's goons—who were so big they made Rocco look like Raj—stepped into the room, carrying a man with his hands zip-tied behind his back.

The man's pants and shirt were torn and filthy. His knees were scuffed and bloody, and his face was bruised and bleeding here and there. For the most part, though, he was no worse for wear. One of Guido's men told the captive in a very deep voice to sit down on the floor. The zip-tied man defiantly stayed on his feet, and the other Guido goon kicked the back of the guy's knee, probably dislocating it, and said, "SIT!" The captive quickly and landed on the floor with a thud and a whimper.

"Recognize this guy, kid?" asked Uncle G.

"Should I?" I asked, puzzled.

"You're right. Sometimes it's difficult to recognize someone out of context," G continued. Meanwhile, the man scanned the room in panic. Guido acted like the guy wasn't there. "The other day, for instance, I was walking down the street and a beautiful young woman came up to me and said hello. Now, she was really beautiful, and probably not even thirty years old, so when someone like that comes up to an old man like me and says hello and acts like I should know her, I should definitely have some inkling who she is. I didn't, though—no idea at all. She kept talking to me. I kept responding politely as I urgently rifled through mental file cabinet after mental file cabinet of every young woman I have come in contact with. I couldn't put a name to this girl. We spoke for probably five minutes, and when we stopped and went our separate ways, I still had no better idea then of who she was than when she first approached me. I racked my brain trying to place that girl, to no avail.

"The next morning I went to the dentist, and as soon as I walked in the door, I said 'Hello Caroline,' because there behind the counter, in her dental hygienist scrubs, was the girl I'd met on the street the day before. See what I mean? Context is everything, so let me help you out here."

Guido went behind Joe's desk, "'scuse me, old friend," he said, and leaned down and picked up the trash can, walked over to the guy who was still whimpering on the floor and poured the contents over his head. "How 'bout now, John?"

I shook my head.

"Really? Try this: Imagine there's a dumpster right behind him and Gina just ran into the back door of a little Italian restaurant."

"Holy sh—" I said and stopped. "How'd … who … that's the guy who beat me in the alley that night, the guy who was mauling Gina!" I looked at her and pointed to the floor. "It's the guy, isn't it?" I asked.

Gina looked half-sick, probably because she was suddenly forced to revisit that night in the alley.

I answered my own question. "I'm positive. That's him! How'd you find him?"

"You'd be surprised, my boy," said Guido. "You'd be surprised."

He continued, "So we have been 'interviewing' this sorry sack of humanity for most of yesterday, and it turns out your little meeting in the alley the other night wasn't a coincidence after all. As we initially suspected, he'd been sent there to grab Gina with the intent to lure you out and beat you to death. I hope you don't mind, John, but we thought it only fair that we returned the favor to some degree. Okay with you?" he said lifting his eyebrows and smiling.

"Sure, who am I to question your methods of hospitality?"

Guido kneeled on the floor and started picking up the trash he'd dumped on the guy, putting it all back into the waste basket. Mr. Acchione raised his hand and told G not to worry about it, but Guido said that was nonsense. He didn't want to mess up Joe's lovely parlor.

Angela interrupted: "So, what does all of this have to do with this photograph?"

Guido held up a finger and turned to Ange. "No fair jumping ahead there, young lady. We'll get to that man in due time. Patience ... *patience.*"

"Right. So where were we? Ah, yes, we interviewed this piece of garbage and he was kind enough to tell us who told him to do this and why. Turns out, it's this big, hairy-knuckled guy right here who works inside Sonny's coordinating the desecration in there." And Guido stopped, grimaced, rolled his eyes, and went back to the double doors and cleared his throat.

"Sorry, I got ahead of myself." Two more gigantic human beings carried another man into the parlor and dropped him next to the other guy. This guy was more than dirty and lightly bruised. He was one of the huge guys who was laughing at my mom the other day in front of Sonny's. Guys like that don't usually cooperate peacefully when they're abducted, so it wasn't too surprising to see he'd been pummeled into submission.

G's guys always offer options. The first guy didn't take much persuasion to avoid the worse of the two options. The second guy wasn't as practical.

"I meant to have him brought in first before I said that last piece," and he stopped for a moment as if he was regrouping. Guido was having the time of his life.

"As I said, 'this big, hairy-knuckled guy'" and he pointed to the bleeding hulk on the floor, "hired this other piece of shit to beat you. Well, of course, the further up the chain you go, the more questions you want to ask, so this time we not only asked who sent him and why, but what the heck they're doing inside Sonny's? As it turns out, this guy is the lowest level of management possible. He does what he's told because he's told to do it and never asks questions like 'why?' Instead, he dutifully performs whatever is asked, like a monkey attached by a chain to an organ."

Guido made a sweeping motion to his audience and said "He was told to have someone beat Johnny to death, so he did. Didn't matter why. His answer to the other question of what they're doing in Sonny's was sort of interesting, though. He and his crew were told to remove every single personal item they could find and destroy it—pictures, utensils, pots, pans, dishes, knick-knacks, everything. As I said, though, he never thought to ask why. All he gave us was the what … and the *who*."

"That's quite a slab of beef," uttered Raj, almost unconsciously as he pointed to the motionless, hairy-knuckled guy on the floor.

Guido stopped and smiled a little, looked at Raj out of the corner of his eye. Without turning his head, he said "Raj, I'm pretty sure this guy's shits are bigger than you, but you know what? There's always someone who shits bigger," and he pointed to his own two goons.

And then he continued. He was really on a roll.

"That picture you're holding, the one you asked about, Angela? *That* man is the one who instructed *this* man (he pointed to Mr. Hairy

Knuckles) to hire *that* man (he pointed to the guy next to Mr. Hairy Knuckles) to beat up my nephew, whom I love like my own son." He looked at me, batted his eyelashes, clutched both hands to his heart and said sarcastically "I luva you with alla my heart, Giovanni."

And he started laughing. He was really enjoying himself.

"Now, if I may continue, Joe" he said, as he looked to Mr. Acchione, who, in turn, bowed his head once and waved Guido on with a swipe of his ancient hand. "I would hazard a guess the man in that picture is somehow connected to the assholes behind this whole scheme. In fact, I might even go so far as to suggest he is personally invested in this scheme, but herein concludes my chain of facts."

Angela spoke up. Unlike Gina, who looked like she was going to throw up the minute the first guy was brought into the room, Angela never so much as blinked quickly during any part of the show. She just sat there and processed everything as if she was replaying it in a courtroom in her mind, deciding what would stick and what would bounce.

"We can't very well go to court with this and hope to get an injunction. We can't stop them from dismantling Sonny's, and we certainly can't compel them to return the assets to Mom and Pop. We can't get a monetary judgment with this, either. Yes, *someone* has defaulted on the sales contract, but we have no way of connecting the guy in this photo to that purchasing entity. Certainly, Mr. Acchione, you don't see this otherwise."

"Actually, dear," Mr. Acchione replied, "I am in full agreement with you, but let's wait until Guido is finished before we render final opinions. Guido? Once again, the floor is yours."

"And once again, I thank you, sir," Guido said, tipping an imaginary hat in Joe's direction.

"In order for us to make the connections you've noted, Angela—and good for you for recognizing the gaps in our situation—we're going to need to get him to tell us what he did, with whom he did it, and how it was done. With that confession, we will be able to go through proper legal channels and produce precisely the legal results you seek."

I spoke up "Oh, that's all?! We just need to draw this unknown guy out of the shadows—from *where* we have *no* idea—and then he'll confess everything to us, just like that? Well, why didn't we think of that in the first place?"

"Always with the sarcasm, kid."

"But he's right," offered Gina.

"Are you, of all people, defending my nephew, Gina?" asked Guido.

She kept going. "Look, everything else aside, Johnny is absolutely correct. We didn't even know the guy in this photograph existed before now. There are two million people within the city limits alone. Finding a middle-aged Italian guy isn't exactly narrowing your search very much. How do you propose we find him, and moreover, how do you propose we get him to confess?"

Guido wagged his finger and walked over to her. "The key, child, is to possess something he wants, and force *him* to come to *you*." And then he finished his statement and just stood there in front of her, looking at her, never breaking his gaze. "What if I told you," he continued, "I have his late-sister's great grandchildren?"

Guido handed Gina another photograph, except instead of a well-dressed, middle-aged man staring back at her, three children peered back. An eight-year-old with a sensitive tummy, his one-year-younger sibling, and a toddler who loved eating Cheerios off the kitchen floor.

Gina's face dropped, as if someone had just torn out her soul.

"Gina, my dear, I know you. I've known you since you were born. I knew your mother. I knew your father. I knew why your family was here, and I know who your extended family is, and I definitely recognized your uncle. I didn't know he was in town until 'knuckles' over there told us about him. With a little patience and a little luck, our surveillance of Sonny's paid off and your uncle appeared. When I saw him, all the pieces came together and we knew what was going on. So here's what's going to happen."

"WAIT! WHAT?!" I blurted. "He's Gina's mom's brother? Gina and him are related? That can't be. Gina, how did you not know about this?"

Guido tilted his head, looked at me and then walked over to me and Raj.

"Are you really that naive, kid? Johnny, she's *in* on it. She's *part* of it. Hell, for all we know, she's the mastermind behind the whole thing! How else do you think these two assholes on the floor knew where you would be? She lured you into the alley, like a lamb being led to the slaughter."

Gina had composed herself by then and started to slowly clap. "Well, congratu-fucking-lations, old man. If you knew why my family was here for so many decades, why did it take you so long to figure out we were doing this? Everybody up the chain, including my uncle and grandfather, warned me about you, but they clearly overestimated you. You're a joke. Let my grandchildren go. Forget about Sonny's and maybe—*maybe*—we'll let *some* of you live."

She sat back smugly, arms crossed across her chest and smirked, like Guido was going to be angry—or threatened or something. Instead, he ignored her and returned his attention to me and Raj. That wiped the smile off her face.

Guido continued. "Boys, this is where you need to get involved. John, I'm going to send you into Sonny's to speak with Gina's uncle. Before you go in, call Raj on your cell phone and make sure he answers. Everything you discuss in Sonny's will come through Raj's phone and we'll record it. Take this contract," Joe produced a document from his desk and handed it to Guido, who in turn handed it to me, "and have the man sign it. It's a termination agreement forfeiting all contractual rights to the premises and the business as well as the three hundred grand he'd paid thus far. Once he signs, he and his crew should leave and never look back. It's that simple. No admission of guilt, just a business transaction. All the necessary legal protection is in here. He won't have to worry about us coming after him. We simply want him and his people out of our lives, and we want Sonny's returned to its rightful owner."

"Why would he do that—just get up and walk away?" I asked.

"Because if he doesn't, he won't get Gina's *grand*children back. But of course, we still need him to show up on schedule, and that's your job, Gina. As much as I'd like to detain you—or worse—I'm releasing you. Since we have your grandkids, I don't really need to keep tabs on you. I'm quite sure their absence appropriately motivates you to go find your uncle and convince him to show up at Sonny's, let's say tomorrow at noon. That's when they used to open for lunch. Perhaps it will be a trend for them to open again at that time in the future, eh?"

The room was silent. None of us could believe what we had heard. Gina just sat on the sofa, looking pathetic. Angela got up from the same sofa, leaned over, and spit on Gina. Gina glared at her, but never moved.

The huge, heavy pocket doors to the entry hall opened again, and Mom and Pop appeared. Mom was livid. She didn't run into the room and go crazy or anything. She was in complete control of herself, but you could almost see the fury in her eyes. Pop remained in the doorway as Mom walked in past the two detainees on the floor. She looked at me and Raj, nodded to Mr. Acchione and then walked over to Ange. She gestured for Angela to go to the door next to Pop. Mom looked at Gina, who looked up and returned her gaze but sneered at her, like she was telling my mom nonverbally to go fuck her condescending self. Mom slapped Gina so hard she probably almost broke her ancient hand. Then she spit on her, turned, and walked away.

Gina clenched her eyes shut in a wince of pain. When she opened them, she caught my father looking back at her. He just looked at her with a combined looked of contempt and disappointment. He silently shrugged, mouthed "Why?" and then took Mom and Angela out of the room. By this point, Rocco was on his feet and closed the pocket doors behind my folks.

Guido looked at me and shrugged, as if to ask if I wanted a shot too, but I just shrugged and waved him off.

"I have nothing to say to her"—which is not to say I didn't actually have a *thousand* things to say to her—but I knew I couldn't trust myself once I got started. Better not to start at all.

Guido turned his attention back to Gina. "Here's how this is going to work. You're going to return to your uncle and you're going to tell him to meet my nephew at Sonny's tomorrow at noon. If anything happens to any of these people—John, Toni, Angela, Johnny, Joe, me, the Patels—anyone—these three children are going to be burned alive. Then each of your children and their *other* children will be found and burned alive. These instructions have been extended to very reliable, very deadly people, and they're not waiting for my instructions to act. They're scheduled to act unless I tell them to stop—big difference. Is that clear?"

She quietly replied, "Yes," but you could almost taste the contempt in her response.

"Good. Tell your uncle we'll see him at Sonny's tomorrow at noon. Now get out of my sight!"

Guido turned his back to her. One of his goons went to her side of the sofa and stood there, as if to imply he would throw her out if she didn't walk out. She stood quietly, raised her head, and walked defiantly out of the parlor and out of the house.

Once she was gone, and the doors were closed, I blurted out "Jesus! What the HELL, Guido? We can't do that to *children*. Who the hell are we, anyway?!"

"Relax kid. We're not monsters. Her kids are fine, and they'll *be* fine. They don't even know they've been abducted. They're just leverage, having a sleepover at their friend's house down the street. It just so happens those friends are *my* people. I told Gina that other stuff to provide a little gravitas. I know her uncle and grandfather better than she does. I kicked her grandfather's ass a couple times back in the old country. There should be no question in his mind about the lengths I'll go to to protect what's mine. He was smart to warn that little bitch of a granddaughter about me. Her uncle was still in diapers when I came here, but if he listened to any of his family stories, he'll know better than to question me or my motives. We'll be fine. Family is the only thing they truly care about, and those three children are that family's future. They won't risk them."

Idle Hands, and All That ...

After such a dramatic event, one expects there to be something equally impactful to follow, but sometimes that's it. Everyone sort of looked at one another, shrugged, and wondered what to do. There's a word for that: *anticlimax*.

This was a great example.

Gina had exited quickly, as expected. I'm sure she was relieved to get outside, after she saw the mugger and underboss she'd recruited bleeding in the middle of the room.

Guido and his boys collected their prisoners, ostensibly to put them on ice until this whole thing was over. Mom, Pop, and Angela went back to my parents' house.

Mr. Acchione was already home, so Raj, Rocco, and I were sort of left behind to occupy ourselves.

Just as quickly as everything wrapped up, there was no trace of the event. It was sort of like the houselights coming up and the screen going dark after a movie. I had a strange urge to ask the guys if they wanted to grab ice cream on the way home.

None of us had anything urgent on the docket, so we thought practically. Raj had to get home. It was dusk out, and considering what had just transpired here, sending him off on his own to go across town was probably not the best plan to ensure his safety. The three of us decided to go back to his place together.

Of course, I had the ulterior motive of going over to play with Indi some more, but even without that incentive, escorting our weakest link home seemed like the right thing to do. We stepped out of the house, made it to the corner, and grabbed a bus to Raj's. Then we walked the half a block to his door and Raj let us in. I greeted the Patel clan. Rocco still didn't feel comfortable coming in, so he stayed on the sidewalk, freezing.

As was the case the night before, Indi walked by me again with yet another basket of laundry, kissed me on the cheek and said, "S'up Paesan?"

This time, though, instead of going in and mingling with her family, I followed her into her bedroom and closed and locked the door.

She dropped the basket on the floor and turned to me.

This time she was wearing dress slacks with a buttoned-down blouse. No slippers, though—she was wearing low-heeled, zip-up black boots.

I approached her and she held out her hand to stop me.

"John, what are you doing?"

"Well, tearing your clothes off and banging you went so well last night …"

"Yeah, no."

And I stopped, but she sat down on the bed and continued.

"Sit down with me, John," and she patted a spot next to her on the comforter.

I nervously started talking as I made my way to her bed. "Indi … *Swati* … before you go on, I have something to say,"

"John, look …"

I stopped her and continued.

"We have a big history together, and last night, after being apart for a year, I came to realize you're the most important person in my life. We have a connection that's deeper than any I've ever felt with another woman—or human being for that matter. Being back here this week, after being away for months, brought it all to the forefront for me. I'm *home*, and *you're* my *family*. *You're* my home. When all this crap with Sonny's is done, I want us to be together. I'm not sure how that looks yet, but we can figure it out, together. I love you. I guess I've always loved you ever since we were in the fourth grade. Even though dating didn't work when we were kids, I think we can make it *all* work *now*. That cultural stuff we couldn't get past back then was just noise. We're adults now. We've had our knocks and bruises, and we aren't idealists anymore. What we are is in love, and that's what should matter. I can help take care of you and the kids. I *want* to take care of you and the kids."

She looked at me and a gentle smile crossed her face.

"Oh, John," she said as she took my hand. "Are you out of your *fucking* mind?!"

My eyes popped wider than they did earlier in the day when Guido outed Gina.

She went on: "We've been friends for a long time, but unlike my brother, I don't *need* you. I've never *needed* you. You rescued him from bullies—and I suppose you being my friend insulated me too—but I had things handled. Those girls back then couldn't get through to me because I wouldn't let them. I don't need you for strength. I have my own. We only dated for a brief time. When we broke up, I told you it was because of the cultural differences between us, but I only said that to preserve your feelings. I knew you'd take the truth to heart and hate me, and I didn't want to lose you as a friend. The real reason we broke up was I didn't want to date you anymore. You weren't right for me then, and honestly, you're still not right for me now."

"Then why did we keep having sex together all these years?"

"Because I like having sex with you now and then. It's not

complicated. Look. I'm a divorced mother of two with a full-time job and I live with my elderly parents. Do you know how many potential suitors I meet these days? Make a fist and count the fingers. The only thing worse than having no social life at all, though, is possibly pursuing one with someone who becomes clingy—dating services, setups by friends, connections with colleagues—every single option is fraught with unwanted baggage. I'm busy, really busy—*always* busy. Being a mom is *not* a part-time job, and even though Jimmy and I are divorced, we still have to maintain a relationship with one another. Even *that* is a lot of work, and he's a great guy.

"My parents? Holy shit. They're old and virtually incapable of taking care of themselves. Mom tries. She'll cook now and then, but that just leaves dishes and cleanup for me. She *watches* the kids, but that's it. She literally sits there and stares at them. When I get home I have to get them started on homework and then find out what they need for school tomorrow, or next week, or next month. I have to make their lunches and get them bathed and then find out what's going on in their worlds. All the while I'm running around doing laundry, and trying to balance my father's *endless* medical issues. And you'd think Raj would be helpful, right? Not so much. He comes and goes as he pleases and never lifts a finger around here. He actually expects me to pack him a lunch every day. I'm doing it for the kids and Pop anyway, so I might as well do it for him too, *right?*

"Why do I have sex with you when I see you? Because it's the one thing that satisfies a need and requires no effort from me. You come over, strip off my clothes, throw me onto the bed, which for you suffices as foreplay, do what you have to do and then get up and leave."

"That's not fair. If you want me to take my time and be romantic and all that, let me know. I didn't get the impression …"

"No. No. No. You're missing the point. I don't *want* you to be romantic. I don't *want* foreplay. I don't *want* to snuggle. I want you to come in, hopefully satisfy some part of my needs, and get out. That's all I'm looking for and it comes with absolutely no baggage. You're the perfect partner because you do your thing and leave. In fact, leaving quickly is usually a plus because if I'm still in the mood, I can usually get myself to where I wanna be with a little help from my battery-powered pal in the night table."

"*…nice.*"

"Oh, sorry. Did I offend your ego? Get over it. You got what you wanted. Don't begrudge me getting what I want too.

"John, you're the absolute last person on this Earth I would ever want as a significant other. You're a boy in a middle-aged man's suit. You're eternally immature, and that's fine. It works for you."

"What the fuck is that supposed to mean?!"

"Seriously? Your job requires no future planning and I'm sure you've put no thought whatsoever into what you're going to do when this thing with Sonny's is over. And beyond any *immediate* plan, do you have any sort of *retirement* plan?"

"Why do I have to retire? I like what I do."

"Of course you do. Because it's *perfect* for you. That's my point. Every day is a fresh start. You can come and go as you please. If you had a bad night at work the night before, it doesn't matter. The slate is completely wiped clean the next day, like it never happened. In the real world, when you screw up, you have to fix it—not you, not in your world. The person who had the bad meal may never come back, but they'll be replaced by a sea of others, so who cares? If your mistake the night before is so bad your job is jeopardized, so what? You can just run away to another restaurant, or another town. Your entire *life* is like that. Bad night out with friends? Go home. Bad time at a bar or club? Go to another one. Bad night with a girl? Pack up your trash bag and clear out before she knows what hit her. Your existence is the epitome of transience."

"But I'm ready to settle down, with you."

"God forbid! I'll give you the benefit of the doubt, sweetie. You may actually believe that, but you have absolutely no clue what it means."

She didn't wait for me to defend myself.

"You have never known what it is like to not be the most important person in your life. You were placed on a pedestal at birth by your parents and grandparents and there you stayed.

"Your father is probably the single best role model for a dad I've ever seen. In fact, I used *him* as the yardstick against which I measured every potential future father for my children. There's an old saying that there's a big difference between a father and a dad. A father is the biological donor to a child, but a dad is the one who helps raise it. Your Pop? He's a dad, and more than anything, it's his selflessness that defines him.

"He has always worshipped your mother. When he married her, he put her needs above his to the point where only her needs were important to him. Has your dad owned a car since you were born?"

"… no."

"Why do you think that is?"

"I guess he never really needed one. You know that. We live in the city. We use public transit."

"Mm-hmm. What happened every time Guido got a new car and brought it by the restaurant?"

"Pop and I would always run out and check it out."

"Right, except your Pop knew *everything* about whatever Guido drove. He used to be the one to show Guido around his own car. He practically swallowed car magazines whole every month. He knew everything there was to know, because they were his passion. Every year he'd take you to the car show at the Convention Center, right? Why would a guy who didn't have a car do that? Because he *loved* them. Did he ever tell you about the last car he owned?"

".. no."

"It was a '51 Mercury hot rod with 'glass pipes' and custom paint."

"How do you …"

"Because your mom used to tell me the story of that car. It was your dad's pride and joy. He sold it to buy an engagement ring for your mother, because he decided she was a greater source of pride and joy than his car."

"I never heard that story."

"Of course not. Your Pop was embarrassed by it, and your mother knew you'd never understand the trade. You'll love why she told *me* that story."

"I'm afraid to ask."

"She was always hell-bent on keeping us apart. We both knew that. She made it so apparent, she practically took out ads in the Sunday *Inquirer*. Sometimes she would pull me aside and try to act like a girlfriend, helping me out, but really she was trying to be slick and convince me not to date her son. Anyway, in this case she was right. She told me the story to show the huge difference between you and your dad. Your own *mother* told me you were too selfish to ever sell your '51 Mercury for a girl. And you know what? She was *right*."

"Look. If you want me to sell my car to get you a ring …"

"No, you moron. I don't want you to sell your car, and I especially don't want a ring. My point was your father not only had the capacity to put others before himself, he did so as second nature, without prompting. He never got another car because that money could be used for your mom, or for you, or for your sister, or for Sonny's. When he married your mom, your Pop became the second most important person in his own life. When you were born, he moved into third position; when Angela was born, he moved into fourth. If you ever had a dog, your dad would have been fifth.

"The sale of Sonny's is a perfect example of his selflessness. He loved that place. It was *named* after him by his own Pop. He sold it for you and for Angela. He sold it for you," and she shrugged and shook her head like she was apologizing for me being so oblivious.

I just sat there listening to her, because I had no idea what to say.

"John, you're a perpetual bachelor. The only difference between you and a college frat-boy is you're old. You come and go as you please. When you were younger you dated waitresses and bus girls. When you got a little older you dated bartenders. All the while you dated customers. At some point you'll get too old for any of the restaurant employees, and you'll end up hooking up with the old ladies who come into the bar late at night, desperate for a companion. Shit. For all I know, that might be me one of these days."

She was on a roll, so she kept going. "Restaurants are like one big, seething hormone. Everyone's horny all the time and you *love* that."

"That's not true. Everyone dates people from work, not just restaurant people. Even the accountants and lawyers you and Angela work with fish in the company pond."

"Okay. Let's not label the industry. Let's look at you, specifically. How many women have you had sex with this week?"

I thought for a second about what day it was and reluctantly answered "four."

"*FOUR*?! Jesus *Christ*! I was sort of expecting to hear *two*—me and Gina, but *four*?! I haven't slept with four people *in my life!!!*" She leaned back, folded her arms across her chest, exhaled heavily and said, "Please elaborate."

"Well, before I came back here, I was living with this nurse …"

"Really, John?" she interrupted. "You were involved with a woman, living with her, and that relationship meant so little to you that you not only left, but got laid pretty much the next day?"

"It was a casual th …"

She held her palm up to about an inch from my nose. "Never mind. That makes three. Who was the fourth?"

"… it happened at work an hour or so before Guido called me to come home. I was downstairs in the walk-in refrigerator where we kept the produce, and the owner's wife—who also worked as the hostess—came in to get the flowers for the tables. She looked like Ertha Kit—*very sexy woman.* She had a thing for me and locked the door from the inside and started pulling off my clothes, and …"

"In a walk-in refrigerator? Isn't that a little *chilly?*"

"Surprisingly, it's not really that bad. It's sort of refreshing, actually, when you're getting all heated up."

Not the answer she was looking for. She sorta stared at me.

"On the produce??? That sounds less than sanitary," and she crinkled her nose dismissively.

"Yeah, I was going to let the waitstaff know to try to steer guests away from ordering anything with bib lettuce that night. That's where she was facedown and her sweaty torso was pressed into flats of it in the walk-in. I left the restaurant to come back here before I had the chance, though."

"That's gross."

"To be fair, the lettuce would get washed before it would get served anyway, so … you're mad at me. Indi, that was them. You're different. I'll *be* different. I'll be *better.*"

"I'd be offended by such a ridiculous come-on if I didn't believe you actually meant it. Sweetie, be honest with yourself. You can't be that person. You're *not* that person. Asking you to change is like asking a zebra to become a giraffe. It's a physical impossibility!"

She didn't stop there.

"Can you imagine yourself coming home to me and my kids every day? Trust me, there won't be any 'little Johnnys' toddling around. My baby-making days are over. You'd stroll in at three in the morning. I'd already be asleep because I'd have to be up in less than three hours to get myself and the kids off to school and work. You'd climb into bed and try to fall asleep. By the time you woke up the next day, I'd be at work and the kids would be at school. By the time we came home, you'd already be gone preparing the restaurant for the dinner rush. We would *never* see each other, and that's no way to sustain a relationship. Even the best marriage would collapse under that strain. After a while, someone at the restaurant would start paying special attention to you—possibly in the walk-in refrigerator, for example—and you'd justify the fling because you aren't getting anything at home and you deserve it, and blah blah blah. How long do you think that would take? Would you even make it through the first week?"

"Somehow my parents made it work," I replied in a very serious, flat tone.

"You're right. Would you like to know how? Your parents worked those hours *together*. They were with each other all day every day. Their schedules were completely in sync. I'm not about to stop my career and come work the hostess stand at whatever restaurant has you as its cook. I don't *want* to be a hostess. I don't *want* to live the restaurant life. I want to *eat* at restaurants, not *live* in them, but after that produce story of yours, I'm rethinking the 'eating at restaurants' part now too."

And she went on: "Aside from the *how*, would you like to know the reason *why* your parents made it work and you can't? Because you're not your Pop. … You're your Mom."

That hit me like a shell fired out of a bazooka. "What the f—"

"You heard me. You're manipulative, self-absorbed, and controlling. Tell me I'm wrong."

I hated hearing that. I always imagined I was like my Pop. He was my hero. I adored him. I only ever wanted to *be* him. Now, to find out others see me as *my mother*?

"You wonder why you two never got along? It's because you're both exactly alike. A relationship between two people can never work if they're both selfish and controlling. Someone needs to be self*less* and *passive.* That works for your parents. It never worked for you and your Mom, and it would never work with me either, pal. I love you as one of my oldest and dearest friends. You're as close to family as anyone can be to me who isn't actually related, but I would *never* be in a romantic partnership with you again. I realized that as a teenager at Christmas dinner at your house. It was true then, and it's even more true now."

I sat there dumbfounded and started to get up.

"What are you doing?" She asked.

"Leaving, I guess," I muttered dejectedly.

"Did you not hear me? You're not through here yet," and she pulled her blouse off over her head and stuck her leg out for me to unzip her boot. "I didn't say I wanted to stop what was working. I just said I wasn't willing to have more of a relationship with you. I'm going to make one change, though," and she leaned over and pulled her little buddy out of the nightstand. "This time around, we're *starting* with this."

Who was I to say no?

THE WALK OF SHAME
ON THE BUS

We finished what we were doing and I must say, I never enjoyed being lectured about my own inadequacies more in my life. If every teacher I ever had finished lectures with sex, I'd have been a much better student. I'd have also made it a point to only have female teachers.

Indi got up matter-of-factly, put on comfortable clothes and went down the hall to the bathroom. Most of these old row homes had only one bathroom, which is absolutely amazing, because many of the *very* Catholic families who occupied them had eight, ten, maybe a dozen kids. One can only assume some of those kids never peed, pooped, or bathed in their own homes during the entire span of their childhoods. Even here, the Patels were overloading this room with six people, so Indi was lucky this time when she got there and it was vacant.

I tapped on the door while she was still in there and told her I'd call her when all the shenanigans were over tomorrow. She acknowledged me through the door, and then added something about her deciding to get her bath now and to let her parents know before I left.

Does it get more romantic than that???

I walked into the living room and everyone's eyes turned to me. I guess I didn't realize how long we had been in there alone, and although I guess their assumptions of what went on in there were well-founded, they had no idea of the totality of what transpired.

I announced Indi's intent to shower tonight, as if I was delivering some big important news like she had just given birth to a baby boy or she had just discovered the cure for cancer, but it's all I had to go with, so I used it.

I bid everyone a good night. Raj came to the door to say goodbye and to let me know he'd be waiting for my call tomorrow so he could record Gina's uncle's confession over my phone. I left to get Rocco, who had found refuge from the wind, across the street at end of the block where he could avoid freezing to death and still keep an eye on the Patel's door. Raj grabbed my arm as I turned to go and told me to be careful tomorrow and to be sure not to die. I agreed to do my best with that, winked at him, and laughed.

The first few steps of the walk to the bus were peaceful and intro-spective, if not a bit chilly, but then the frigid wind kicked up. When those gusts arrived one after the other, we dipped our heads down and looked at the sidewalk, pressed our chins into our chests, and shoved our hands deeper into our pants pockets.

Without pulling our hands from our pockets or picking up our heads, we ran with the grace of a pair of Frankensteins across the street and a half block to the corner where the bus had pulled up. The driver barely acknowledged us as we stepped in and paid the fare, but the occupants of the first couple seats in the toasty warm bus complained "SHUT THE FUCKING DOOR!" about a second after we climbed aboard. Philadelphia bus passengers are known for their tact and decorum.

We sat down and Rocco asked, "Everything go okay between you and Indi? You seemed uncomfortable when you came outside."

Rock was one of our group of friends from childhood, so it was perfectly normal for him to call her Indi.

"Rock, you and I've been friends forever. Why would I mind you asking?" Then I messed with him and said, "You can ask me anything. It doesn't mean I'm going to tell you anything though, you nosey fuck!"

And we both laughed.

"It went fine. I told her I loved her. She told me I'm an idiot and she didn't want a relationship with me."

"Shit. I'm sorry, John."

"Don't be. I still got laid."

"You lucky asshole," he said and laughed as he shook his head. Then we just sat silently for the rest of the ride, while the other six people on the bus stared at us like we were Martians.

We got off the bus when we reached our stop and hunkered down for the gusting chill until we returned to Mr. Acchione's. We ran up the steps, never lifting our heads. I asked Rock with a half-yell so he'd hear me over the wind, "You wanna sleep out here tonight?"

"Would you please stop fucking around and unlock the door already?" he responded.

We stepped inside the warm foyer and relaxed our necks and shoulders.

"You want a cup of coffee or something before you turn in?"

"Yeah," he replied. "I might pour it over my head to warm up."

When we got into the kitchen Mr. Acchione was sitting there. It was late—well after midnight—and we were both surprised to see the old man sitting there all alone.

"You okay, Joe?" I asked.

Our sudden arrival hadn't startled him in the least. "I'm fine. I'm just going over the plan for tomorrow in my head for the thousandth time. I've had this routine since my earliest days as an attorney. I have a script and a plan of attack and I repeat it so many times to myself, it becomes rote."

"Yeah, but this is a little different, Joe. You're going to be behind the scenes for this one. If anyone should be practicing, it should be me. I'll be on the front line."

"I know, and that's why I'm more anxious than usual. I've never been good at sending someone out to execute my plan. I've always liked to be the one with the ball, if you know what I mean. Being 'behind the scenes,' as you said, isn't a comfortable role for me."

"I get that. I'll do my best to do it like you tomorrow, Joe."

"I have every confidence in you, my boy. Every confidence."

"Could I get you a cup of coffee or tea, Joe?"

"That would just keep me up. I'll tell you what I could go for, though. In my desk, bottom left hand drawer, is a bottle of very old, very good single-malt scotch. I usually save it for celebrations, but in this case, I don't see a problem with a little pre-celebration nip, but I'll only do it with company."

"I don't really drink, Joe," I said.

Rocco added, "If John doesn't drink, I can't either, Mr. Acchione. Sorry."

Joe looked down at the table, a little dejected and I piped up, "You know what? What the hell?! Rock, go get that bottle. I'll get the tumblers from the tray in the parlor. You want it 'neat,' Joe, or with a little ice?"

Joe perked up. "A real aficionado adds a drop of water," he said, as Rocco leaped up to get the bottle, because he really wanted this and had declined only as a courtesy.

I brought the glasses back in. I went to add a drop of water and Joe piped up, "What are you doing?"

"I'm adding a drop of water, like you suggested."

"Why? Do we look like aficionados to you, John" and we all blurted out a laugh. "Pull up a chair and sit down boys. We're draining this bottle before we hit the sack."

It was an excellent way to relax before bed, and it was the perfect cap to what turned out to be a pretty amazing day. An hour later, the bottle was empty and laying on its side. Rocco and I each had one of Mr. Acchione's arms around our shoulders, and our hands were locked behind his back as we helped him upstairs to his room. Unintentionally, we made enough noise that Marilyn came out to the hall from her room, visibly agitated because we not only woke her up, but got Joe pretty drunk. She dismissed Rock and me and then took control of Joe and guided him to bed.

Rock and I quietly waved one another off in the hall and turned and went to our respective rooms. I fell face-first into the bed and it was glorious.

Always Be Prepared

It's never a good idea to take a knife to a gun fight—unless the gun you bring doesn't work, then the knife turns out to be a decent choice. The moral of that story is, before heading to the gun fight, check the gun and make sure it works. Take it apart. Inspect every part. Lubricate it. Reassemble it with care. Check the munitions to make sure they're in good shape, and then test the gun to be sure it works. Then do it all again.

Guido and Joe had a plan, and like any good plan, it had as few moving parts as possible. Knowing Guido, he'd probably prefer a knife fight over a gun fight any day of the week because a knife would never jam or misfire. He was a big fan of simplicity.

By the way, in this scenario, I am the gun, and Joe and Guido were going to go over this plan with me relentlessly until they were convinced I knew it backward and forward.

Everyone except Raj had been instructed to reconvene at Joe's by nine in the morning. That was an ungodly hour to me, even though I only had to roll down stairs. Everyone else started filing in dutifully, one after the other on or ahead of schedule. Raj had been spared because he was to go to work as usual. He had been instructed earlier to merely accept my call and record it. If he had any problems, he was to call

Guido and let him know. Otherwise, he was to stay as far behind the scenes as humanly possible. With his Lollipop Guild stature and his underwhelming physical acumen, he was anything but a front-line asset, and everyone—including Raj—knew it.

9:00 AM

At nine o'clock, Guido was banging on my bedroom door telling me to get up and get my ass downstairs immediately. He woke me from a deep stupor and continued to bang until I acknowledged him and was clearly up. Somehow, the one with the shortest commute was the last to arrive. Go figure.

I visited the bathroom, took care of typical morning business, showered quickly, changed clothes, and was at the kitchen table drinking coffee fifteen minutes later.

9:15 AM

"Nine o'clock means nine o'clock, kid, not 9:15 or 9:30," Guido said, half-joking and half-serious.

"This feels like 3AM to me, Unc, so forgive me if I'm a few minutes late."

I looked at Joe, who sat at the end of the table, bright as a newly minted dime—bathed, dressed, hair combed and alert. I squinted down at him and wondered how in God's name that man, who was nearly twice my age, could look so damned refreshed after drinking at least as much scotch as me and Rocco just a scant few hours earlier.

Speaking of Rock, he was in a wooden chair against the wall and looked like death with feet. For a very big guy, he had a very low tolerance for alcohol.

Angela was seated on one side of the table. Mom and Pop were seated next to her, and Guido sat opposite them.

Two of Guido's guys stood in the kitchen, another stood outside the kitchen door facing the rear yard, and two more were standing at the front door—one on the inside and one outside. Guido glared at

Rocco more than once, clearly displeased with his condition and lack of discipline the night before.

Marilyn poured coffee, was dismissed by Joe, and disappeared upstairs.

The plan was simple, but merited review to ensure everyone was on the same page. I would call Raj from my phone and wait for him to answer. I would go into Sonny's and meet with the boss (AKA Gina's uncle), get him to admit he's the actual buyer, and then get him to sign the termination agreement. It sounded so simple.

That was the front-line offensive. Behind the lines, preparation and precautions were necessary.

To succeed, everyone involved had to be protected. My protection would be the most difficult to ensure, but everyone else's could be manageable. Guido took control of the meeting and outlined the plan.

"As soon as we adjourn from here, Joe, you, John, Toni, and Angela will be escorted back to the Valmonti home. You'll all stay there until the deed is done. My men will be with you the entire time, securing the perimeter and interior. I can't guarantee your safety, but I'll guarantee no one is going to get to you without getting through my men first."

"What about Tom? What about my boys?" Angela asked.

"Tom is welcome to join you, Angela, but it's my understanding he feels safer at home with Dom and the boys. I'm not going to argue with a grown man. Frankly, I don't think these guys care about Tom, except to use him to get to you. He's not your blood. The boys are another story. They are your blood, but I think being in their grandparents' house with armed men would frighten them unnecessarily. This is not a situation you should have to explain to little boys. Let them go to school. I've assigned men to surveil them until Tom brings them home. They should be safe."

"Anyone else?" he asked.

I spoke up. "Why don't we use Mr. Acchione's home? It's a veritable stone fortress. Mom and Pop's little row home seems to be a softer target."

Guido explained Joe's was too large and had too many exposures. My parents' row home was secure on the sides because it shared those exterior walls with other homes on either side and had narrow front and rear facades. Made sense when I thought about it, even though Gina was one of those on the other side of the wall.

"Kid, you and Rocco will be on your own. You need to get yourselves there on time and you need to perform exactly as instructed. Are you comfortable doing this? If not, now is the time to speak up."

Before I could utter a word, my father *stood* up and *spoke* up. "Guido, up to now, I've sat back and let you run the show, but I can't sit back anymore. I can't condone using my son for this. It's not worth it. So what if they took the restaurant? What's done is done. So what if they threw everything away? We still have our memories. They can't take those, and even if we get the place back, that won't bring those things back. Let this go. Let Gina have those children back and let's move on with our lives. Let them choke on that building. We've lost enough. I can't take losing any more. I think we're letting our pride blind us. Let it go. Please."

"John," Guido replied, "You've known me for over sixty years. I knew your father. I knew your mother. I was there when your boy was born, and I was there when your girl was born. I ate every dinner for decades in Sonny's, right there next to your wife. You are my family, and I would never, ever let anything blind me to your safety. *Your* son is *my* own son. I love him and Angela, Toni and you more than I could ever love anyone else. I agree. Losing Sonny's, though devastating, is not the end of the world. Losing the property is a setback, but to be honest, I can afford to make you whole and take care of you forever out of my own pocket. That's not it either. There's more at play here. More than you can imagine. Those people inside Sonny's don't care about your business. This is personal. They are trying to destroy you, all of you, and if we don't act now, we'll have no other choice than to wait as they pick you off one at a time. We need to take this step. This is our best option."

Guido continued, but now in a more subdued, almost embarrassed tone: "I know these people, John. You're *like* my family. You are the family I *chose.* The people at Sonny's are the family into which I was born. They're the reason I came to America in the first place. I was sent here to protect your family from them. They're out to destroy your family, John. To kill you all and wipe the planet of your genes. They don't care about Sonny's, old friend. There's more to this than you know, and today, I'll be forced to do things I hoped I'd never have to do."

Dad was unfazed. "Then use me. Take my son home and use me. It's my business. It's my family. They want to hurt us? Let them come at me. I won't stand behind my children for protection. I won't do it. Give me a gun and send me in. I was in the army. I know what to do."

Indi's little analysis of me hit home as I listened to my father. Even in his eighties, my *dad* put himself in last position again.

Guido took in a breath before responding and I interrupted.

"Pop. You've had your neck on the line for this family for sixty years, since you married Mom. You always put everyone else, *everyone* else ahead of you. It's time to let us repay that. I don't need you to protect me anymore, Pop. Guido has this covered and I trust him. Look around the room. Look around this house. He has an army prepared to keep us all safe. I would as soon permit you to walk into that lion's den alone as I would put a bullet into my own head. It's not happening. I'm not a little boy anymore, Pop. I'm a man, a middle-aged one at that, and I have this. What I really need from you is to keep Mom and Ange safe. If I know you're there with them, I'll be able to do my job with a clear head. Can I count on you to do as Guido is asking? Please???"

Pop quietly nodded and sat back down next to Mom. She grabbed his hand and squeezed it, but he kept his head down. He was crying. I could only imagine how terrible and helpless he felt imagining his son stepping into harm's way for him and his family. For the first time in his life, I think he understood the stories of his own father sobbing the day Pop was drafted into the army. No parent should ever have to see their child sentenced to such risk.

I spoke up again. "Not to poke the elephant in the room, Unc, but what about Gina's three grandkids? Will they be at the house with you? We haven't really discussed them."

"And I plan to keep it that way, kid. The less you all know about them, the better. No one can coerce information you don't have out of you. They're safe. Okay? Probably safer than they ever would have been with that psychopath you were screwing."

My mother looked at me in shock, and I glared at Guido. "*Thanks,* Unc!"

He looked back at me with an "Oh, shit, I fucked up" look on his face.

"Well, I can't put *that* cat back in the bag. Sorry you had to hear that, Toni," and he shrugged, smirked, and rolled his eyes at me.

The room was quiet again. Guido motioned to his men to gather everyone together. As they did so, he called up to Marilyn to come back down and then asked her to get a bag together for Joe. Although he was surprisingly healthy for an old man, he was still an old man and there were precautions to take. His medication was handed to Guido along with instructions. Guido invited Marilyn to join them, but she declined. She was going to take the day as an opportunity to rattle around the old house by herself and take it easy.

9:45 AM

We all went to Mom and Pop's together. It would be an easier point of departure for me and Rocco later, and until then, having us all in one place made it easier for Guido to protect us. When we arrived,

Guido made sure everyone was in place, that his men knew their roles and the expectations he had of them, and then he left.

He told us he had to tend to a few more things before noon. I asked him if that was wise, leaving everyone behind like that, and he asked me to trust him. Then Guido grabbed my arm, looked me in the eye, kissed my forehead and hugged me like he never planned to let me go. His eyes welled up and he told me very clearly to go with the flow in there and that no matter how bad it might get, he would *never* let them do anything permanent to me. He made sure I understood that and that I believed him, and I did. For the first and only time in my life, he called me "son," not "kid."

I hugged him back and told him I wanted to hear this whole story about him and the old country, and he assured me he'd tell me everything tomorrow. It was his way of telling me there was going to *be* a tomorrow. And then he was gone.

11:45 AM

Two hours after the day's events began, Rock and I were saying our farewells. I hugged everyone in my family—hopefully not for the last time—and we started walking to Sonny's.

I had been making this same trip practically since I could walk and must have done it up or back more than ten thousand times. I was nearly overwhelmed by the reality this could be the last time I'd ever do it. Suddenly this one trip over all the others had meaning and significance.

I wasn't trying to be melodramatic, but this was a journey into the unknown. We all expected Gina and her crew to cooperate, considering we possessed her grandchildren as leverage, but who knew? They may feel like their backs are against the wall and may come at us. All we wanted them to do was sign this agreement and send me on my way so we could legally reverse the title and resume possession of Sonny's—no battle, no injuries, no deaths—but there's no way to accurately predict the behavior of an animal backed into a corner. Regardless Guido's assurances, it was very possible I would enter Sonny's for the last time, and never exit.

With every step, that possibility felt like more and more of a probability. My fears were bubbling to the surface and any confidence I had in the plan and all those executing it was gone.

Sonny's was in sight. Rocco told me he was instructed to leave me once we were visible to the restaurant so they wouldn't know he was with me. He stopped and stepped behind a parked car. He also told me he would come running if he heard me yell for help. I thanked him, not just for that, but for everything the last few days, and for being my friend for forty years. We shared a man hug—the kind where you put your chests together but make sure your laps never make contact with one another, pat each other on the back twice and then pull away—and then I set off by myself.

Here we go.

ANTICIPATION

A few scant months earlier, Sonny's had been a thriving enterprise, a neighborhood icon. Now it was dark. Faded rectangular shadows on old wood-paneled walls were all that remained of the framed photos that hung there for most of a century—photos of my grandfather's home in Italy, of his wedding to my grandmother, of my father's childhood, of Pop in his army uniform, of his and mom's wedding, and my and Angela's lives. The tables and chairs were all gone, and the white and blue mosaic tiles in the floor that were obsessively polished every night for seventy-five years were dull, scuffed—and in some places—cracked or even missing. Only a few bar stools and some of the built-in booths remained, and the cretins who swindled their way into the place not so long ago loitered there, waiting for the next assignment in the continued, methodical dismantling of my family's legacy.

CRESCENDO

Our plan was reasonably simple. I was to get them to talk. My cell phone would transmit the conversation to Raj and he'd record it at the other end. I'd get their guy to sign this contract termination agreement and we'd usher them all out. Gina's grandkids would be released to her somewhere and my family would get the building and the business back. No one would get hurt. No one would get killed. We'd handle everything mostly legally (there *was* the small matter of kidnapping three small children) and we'd let the system do all the heavy lifting for us to get Sonny's back into our name. Easy peasy.

There were only a couple of obstacles to overcome. We'd need someone on their end who's responsible for this mess to sign our transfer document. We'd need them to verbally say *they're* the actual buyers of Sonny's—not some nameless, faceless legal entity behind which they can continue to hide. We weren't looking for anything else. We didn't want blood. We didn't want anyone sent to prison. We didn't want anything extraordinary. We were willing to sweep all the damages and the beatings and running people off the road under the rug, but we did want them to renounce everything in that file against Tom. That was bullshit and they had to fix that. I'd have to be the one to get all of it to happen. I had no experience doing it, but that was my role. Whether I embraced it or not, it was going to *remain* my role.

I was going to have to walk alone into this nest, this snake pit, accuse these bastards of what we all know they did, and then hope they monologue like movie villains, boasting about their plan and how they pulled it off so Raj could record it for safekeeping in case these guys don't follow instructions. Then as soon as that document is signed, I have to hope I get an opportunity to turn around and walk (*RUN*) out unharmed. Uncle G assured me my safety was guaranteed as long as we held their kids, but the closer I got to the door, the more I questioned that logic.

I'm no bookie, but if I was laying odds on me, I'd bet the other way, no matter how many points they gave me to bet otherwise. Regardless, this is the best plan we have, and at least it was me stepping in there instead of Pop. For once, *I* was looking after *him*. Indi would be proud—assuming I didn't die in the process.

If I didn't survive, she was going to have to find herself a new fuck-buddy, and with every step, that felt more and more likely.

The forty-foot walk across the street seemed like a mile. I was so distracted by all the variables and risks at hand, I was halfway across the road before I remembered to call Raj. I turned my back to Sonny's door and dialed and made sure Raj answered before I turned around to continue onward. He answered and told me to stay strong, then he told me Indi never liked me and secretly always wanted Rocco.

It's always good to have friends to keep you grounded.

Now, I'm no Oompa Loompa. At 6'2", 220 pounds, not too many people fuck with me. I'm a big guy with big hands. I can easily palm a basketball and I can reach 11 notes on a piano keyboard. I mention this because for the first time in a long time, when I walked up to Sonny's front door and knocked, the gorilla who opened the door made me feel like Raj. When he put his hand on my shoulder to pull me in, I felt like I'd just been grabbed by a bear wearing a baseball mitt. My hands were like Barbie hands compared to his.

When this had all been outlined for me, my expectations were pretty conservative. I didn't expect to be greeted like a long-lost brother or anything—smothered with hugs or handed a glass of wine. I expected to be greeted monosyllabically, ushered in and frisked or checked for a wire, then led to a wooden chair at one of the tables for two in the middle of the dining room where I'd enter a quasi negotiation with the boss or some agent of his.

So imagine my surprise when, before I knew what was happening, I was yanked in through the door and hurled abusively through the former lobby of Sonny's. My flight was interrupted by the old hostess podium where my mother had been stationed for sixty years. The thing splintered into a gazillion pieces upon impact and I landed sprawled out on top of its remnants.

I only lay there for a couple of seconds, though—barely long enough to realize what was happening—when the same two hands grabbed my shoulders, lifted me straight up in the air to the point where my feet dangled above the white and blue mosaic floor tiles, and threw me five feet toward the wall and the open booth where Uncle G used to dine every night for decades. I sailed over his reserved table and crashed shoulder first, head second into the back of the next wooden booth. Unlike the hostess podium that appeared to have been made of balsa wood, this booth was made of solid oak—or mahogany or something equally solid, like granite—because I didn't even dent it. Instead, *I* was the one to crumble to the ground with a whimper. Before I could gain my wits, I was picked up again and thrown across the room in the opposite direction, toward the bar. I bounced across the filthy floor, spinning and sliding uncontrollably and landed in a heap against the brass footrail which had been worn shiny by thousands of shoes over seven-plus decades.

Strangest thing. I was getting tossed around like a sack of birdseed and for the briefest of moments, I actually had the presence of mind to glance at the brass next to me and think how unsanitary it was for my face to be pressed against a bar where people used to rest the filthy soles of their shoes … then I was brought back to reality as the Neanderthal kicked me squarely in the ribs like he was attempting to send me over some imaginary uprights forty yards away. He was clearly having far too much fun beating me to death, even though he wasn't even breathing heavily from the effort.

The breath blew out of me when he kicked me, though, and I made an involuntary groan upon impact. My ribs may have been cracked from that shot, but between that and the impacts I'd sustained in the last fifteen seconds on my shoulder, head, neck, arms, back, and everywhere else, I couldn't discern one piercing pain from the next.

I was getting my ass kicked and was completely disoriented and all I did to instigate any of this abuse was knock on the *fucking* door. I got picked up again and this time I cowered and covered my face. The goon spun me and pinned me against the bar and held me there with one hand while he turned out all of my pockets with the other.

My cell phone fell on the ground and was summarily crushed under Godzilla's heavy heel. There went any hope of this conversation getting recorded. Then he grabbed the contract from my pocket.

He lifted me higher in the air, except this time instead of throwing me, he slammed my ass into a bar stool—literally, so I was sitting upright. Before I could tip over forward and land on the floor, he grabbed the back of my shirt, which was now ripped and covered in grime from the floor and blood from my many fresh contusions, and held me in place on the stool so I could speak with my host, who calmly and patiently sat on a chair a few feet in front of me. He held up and methodically proceeded to tear the contract they'd just pulled from my pocket into narrow strips so I could watch.

My head was lolling around, like my neck was a noodle trying to hold up a watermelon. At my best, I was groggy, and at my worst, I was broken, concussed and only barely conscious.

In another odd moment of clarity, I suddenly realized the bottom of my feet had not yet touched ground since I'd come through the front door. Oh, sure—the *tops* and *sides* of my feet had touched the ground multiple times when I was laying facedown on the ground at various points during my aerial tour of what-used-to-be-Sonny's—but the bottoms? Not so much.

Clearly, things were *not* going as planned. What I thought had been a pretty conservative assessment of what this experience was going to be like turned out to be *wildly* optimistic. I was also starting to question what Uncle Guido had meant by "having my back." I hadn't experienced any intervention from him yet, and pretty much the only person in this room who had my back was the gigantic mesomorph who'd been beating on it.

A guy I recognized, the one who was at the door in the alley when Gina was getting fake-mugged, stepped toward me out of the shadows and clubbed me across the face with his fist. "This is my way of saying thanks for the beating I took from your kitchen buddies in the alley the other night."

"Well, you're welcome, I guess?" I quipped and was greeted with another fist across my face. What was that Uncle G was telling me about being cautious instead of trying to live by my wits? I seem to remember it was something about me keeping my mouth shut, or he'd be getting called to collect my dead body.

I hate it when he's right.

The restaurant was dark except for the light peeking through the drawn horizontal blinds on the front windows and a small table lamp lit next to the seated boss. Everything else was shadows.

It wasn't pitch-black, though. I could see shapes everywhere, just no faces, and there were a LOT of shapes—big ones. He must've had twenty guys the same size as the doorman stationed around the room. I don't know what *he* was expecting from *me*, but from the looks of things, *I* was now expecting another severe beating from *him*.

Thirty seconds in the room, and it was glaringly apparent I was the fluffy toy poodle being thrown into a room full of starving pit bulls, and I was probably going to fare about as well.

After sitting unmolested long enough to try to take a deep breath ("try" being the operative word), I was able to bring order to some of the cobwebs in my head and started taking physical inventory of myself. There were very few parts of my body that weren't battered or cut open. My face was definitely bleeding—no deep cuts, but facial wounds bleed … a *lot*. I didn't think anything was broken, but my arms, back, legs, face, jaw, head, ears, hands—pretty much everything—hurt. As I sat there trying to reassemble my scrambled mind, the man in the chair spoke.

He was the man from the photo we had seen in Mr. Acchione's drawing room—mid-sixties, handsome, trim, meticulously combed hair with an equally meticulously tailored suit. His tie was tied perfectly and was tight to his throat. Even in this dark room, his expensive watched twinkled, as did the gem in the ring on his right hand. His knees were elegantly crossed, exposing expensive shoes, shined so bright they didn't have a visual scuff on them. It was as though the man had been gently placed in his upholstered chair and he was calmly, casually ordering drinks at a beachside table instead of sitting in a dark, grimy former restaurant watching me take a beating.

Aesthetically speaking, he and I were currently at polar opposite ends of the same continuum.

"I assume I have your attention?" he asked, wryly. "You wanted to talk? Let's talk. You wanted me to confess? I'll confess. You wanted to record me and use that against me? Well, sorry, but I can't give you *everything*, now, can I?"

"What about signing the document? We could probably tape it back together if you wanted to. I think I saw a roll of tape in the hostess stand when I flew through it." The Neanderthal from the front door who was still holding me upright hit me across the back of the head with his right hand, in a nonverbal effort to tell me to shut up unless I was asked a question. Message received. My vision blurred for a dozen seconds, and gradually realigned.

The seated man maintained eye contact with me as he extended his left hand to his side like he was inviting a partner to dance, and Gina appeared from the shadows.

"You, of course, recognize my niece and accomplice?"

"Think about your grandkids, GG. This doesn't have to go this way!" I said desperately.

She smirked and went over to the man in the chair. He took her hand and patted it. "As expected, Gina here told us all about your little plan from last night. Actually, she's been telling us everything since you returned to town. Thank you for that, by the way … coming to town. It saved us a lot of time having to find you and bring you back or go to wherever you were to kill you. Of course, you wouldn't even *be* in town if not for Gina, but more on that in a moment.

"After yesterday's little club house meeting at the lawyer's house, you realize my niece is working with me, but you have no idea how deeply involved she really is. Allow me to elaborate. Years ago, she was a young mother of four with an abusive husband. We had him removed. As you'll find out, we frown on men disrespecting our family's women.

"Gina needed financial support, so we offered her an opportunity to return to the area and join the family's business, where she thrived. She not only became one of our strongest earners, she also became one of our strongest organizers. She was a natural, and had a great future. We started involving her more and more in family discussions—those to which she had never been privy before—and one day she learned why her family lived in Philadelphia in the first place, and why we were so focused on your family.

"If it wasn't for her involvement, we may not be here at all. Imagine that. If her abusive husband had been loving and attentive, she would still be with him, and your family would still be operating this shit-hole of a restaurant. Fortunately for us, since he was who he was, she became who she is—the mastermind behind this endeavor. She realized it was just a matter of time before someone in a position of authority would listen to her and she could set this plan in motion.

"The day you stood out on the sidewalk across the street from here, staring at the building, willing us to do … *something* … was the culmination of her dream. We called her and she came and took you away. Her opportunity to finally bring this all to closure had arrived in the form of an idiot cook. You were much easier prey than we expected—quite the sucker."

I looked at them both and asked Gina, "Be honest, GG. You did all of this to see if you could get a man to have sex with you without having to sell him aluminum siding or parking lot sealer, didn't you?"

She exploded: "Let me hurt him, uncle!"

Another Neanderthal grabbed GG, told her to shut her mouth and pushed her down into a booth like a sack of sugar.

The well-dressed man in the chair held up his open hand to the thug like he was Diana Ross about to sing "Stop in the name of Love," and said "Please. We do not hurt women, especially not women who have been as resourceful and helpful as Gina. You'll be taking direction from her soon enough, so heed my advice, and watch yourself."

The muscle-bound three-hundred-fifty-pound oaf hung his head, apologized to Gina, and then took two steps backward into the shadows.

The natty boss turned his attention back to me and pointed at my head. "We do not extend that same courtesy to family members who *hurt* our women physically or through insults. Such betrayals are handled quite differently. Hurt *them*, and *we* hurt you back," and then he went from pointing his finger at me to making a closed fist (like a signal). The monster holding me up slammed my face against the bar and brought me back up to an upright seated position. I swung around in his grasp like a drunk. "And we're all family here, John Valmonti, or shall I say Mantelli?"

I blinked a few times, like I was trying to clear the cobwebs from my mind. "Wait. What? Who the fuck? Are you sure you're beating up the right guy, old man?" I said through a mouthful of blood, with about a dozen imaginary bluebirds chirping and flying around my head.

And with that, the gorilla behind me boxed my right ear, *hard*. Now the little bluebirds were flying around a halo of bright gold stars, and bells were ringing in my head. Loud ones. I felt like I was a character in a Tom and Jerry cartoon.

Gina's uncle was in his mid-sixties. He was solid, and very tidy—everything in place, necktie knotted high on his starched shirt collar, jacket buttoned, handkerchief folded and placed in his pocket, hair trimmed and combed neatly. He looked important and polished, like an Italian banker. His voice never raised to more than a conversational tone. He spoke in a very controlled, metered manner—in very proper English and with no detectable accent—just as he had in the commissioner's office earlier in the week when he was submarining Tom's livelihood.

He was not a banker, though. He was a cold-blooded villain—not that bankers aren't cold-blooded villains, but they perform their particular brand of villainy for the benefit of their banking business. Villainy *is* this man's business. *Big* difference.

"Gina tells us you want to know why we're doing this. Why did we take your parents' business and destroy it? Why didn't we operate it? Why didn't we just sell it? Why did we target you? Why is it all happening now? Why? Why? Why??? ... Your branch of our family sounds like a pack of pathetic three-year-olds.

"Have you figured it out yet? It's because your family is an abomination. You are all repugnant. Every breath you or any of your family members take brings us pain. The longer your family exists, the longer we are reminded of your *disease*. Destroying you *rodents* has been the singular focus of certain members of my family for more than a century! But we were prohibited from acting out by my great-grandmother who—for some unfathomable reason—wanted us to extend you mercy, even though *she* was the one who had been *harmed*.

"One of my uncles had taken it upon himself to try to wipe out your bloodline back in the 1920s, attempting to kill your grandfather, but my uncle failed and merely killed your grandfather's wife. My uncle was dismissed from the family for violating the wishes of my great-grandmother. She wanted our branch of the family to leave your branch alone. Once she was gone, though, well, let's say strategies changed and my uncle's plan was restored."

I should have kept my mouth shut (something that should probably be inscribed on my tombstone), but I couldn't help myself (something to be inscribed on my casket). "What are you talking about? I have no idea who you are, or what you're going on about, and is it the mental blur from the obvious concussion I'm suffering through right now, or did you just say you killed my grandmother? I swear to God, I think you got the wrong family here, buddy. I really do," and I started laughing.

He ignored me and continued: "My father gained control of the family after my great-grandmother passed. He placed my older sister, Gina's mother, here to keep an eye on your family. My sister and her family have been reporting to my father since my own youth. Father's plan was for all of us to wait for him to decide what to do. So we waited, and we waited. We waited for *DECADES!* Well, we've waited long enough. Like my uncle before me, I've grown impatient. After all, I was raised to run this family, and that can't happen until my father is out of the way. Why wait? Today is my coronation, the day all old business is closed, and I ascend to assume my rightful place at the helm of our family's business as my reward."

He continued, clearly quite impressed with himself. "Gina convinced me if we continued to wait, opportunity would pass us by. My father is an old man. Perhaps he's lost his will. At the very least, his focus is slipping. Someone needs to step up and protect this family's interest before it's too late. Someone needs to step up and prove he's the one true leader. Gina was the one to convince me to take action. She was the one who convinced me now was the time. This was all Gina's idea—*all* of it, and I couldn't be more proud of her. She concocted this whole scheme to buy your parents' restaurant, renege on the payments, and dismantle it right in front of them.

"She knew you all, all of her life. She knew what was most import-ant to you, and she knew destroying the business your grandfather built—destroying the building and that *ridiculous* sign—would unravel you all. She was correct down to the last detail. It was an inspired plan. You were all so focused on the business, thinking it was somehow precious, you never realized it was of absolutely no importance to us. It was a means to an end. It brought you all together and blinded you to our true agenda. All my life I had been led to expect so much more from your family. To be honest, I'm disappointed in your mundanity. It's frankly embarrassing."

Gina chimed in. "All we wanted was to hurt you … and then exterminate you."

"Shut your mouth, cun-" I said, dismissively, but I was punched in the face again before I could finish saying it. Another lesson learned that Guido tried to teach me, but I was too blind to learn. She's not family, so she can't be trusted. Goddamnit, Uncle Guido! Right again!

She arrogantly smirked back at me, proud of her work as a home-wrecker, and gloating over the beating I was taking at the hands of her uncle's henchmen.

"Gina's reward will be assuming a new leadership role, guiding these men and our entire local operation. She's earned it, wouldn't you say?"

The old man continued: "She played you well, John. She seduced you, and arranged for you to be beaten to death in that alley. Unfortunately, your kitchen-worker buddies intervened and rescued you, so she adapted and arranged for you to be her hero instead. She got you to take her everywhere with you as her protector, and all the while, she was listening to your little schemes and was reporting every step back to me. It couldn't have worked out better for us. Too bad you won't all be enjoying that dinner you planned together at your parents' house this Sunday. I'm sure it would have been a great source for more information on you hapless fools, if we actually needed it. Perhaps Gina can attend your funeral luncheon instead. Once you're gone, she'll destroy your parents, your sister, your uncle, even that ancient lawyer. You'll all die one … by … one. And Gina will be the architect of the entire show.

"What really matters to us, you see, is the systematic destruction of your family and all the members of it. Of course, it would have been easier to just kill all of you, but that's too quick and really doesn't accomplish what we've set out to do. You don't need to merely die. You need to suffer. We also need to be sure your name dies with you. Although it sickens us knowing your sister has reproduced, it's almost tolerable knowing her progeny don't have your surname—*almost* tolerable. They have their father's name, which is the only thing keeping them alive to this point, but that's not going to continue. Fortunately, you haven't reproduced, or we'd have eliminated those children already. The name needs to stop. Your gene pool needs to be drained and filled in with cement."

He kept droning on, pontificating, as if even he needed convincing that he was as wonderful as he believed himself to be. "Once I finish with you, I'll turn my attention to your sister. That little bump on the highway was only intended to scare her, but don't worry. She and her family won't survive the weekend. She'll live just long enough to see you buried and endure all that grief. Then your parents will get to bury her and their grandchildren. If John and Toni can survive the horror of burying both of their children and their grandchildren all in the same week, they will be permitted to live—even though they'll wish they were dead. Actually, we'll be hoping they live. Our greatest desire is for them to live until natural causes take them, and every day they'll be reminded of the loss of their children, their business, their identities and future. Their existence will be misery. And that's a fate far worse than death, wouldn't you say?"

And he smiled. He fucking smiled.

"You motherfu-" SMACK! Once again, I couldn't get the word out of my mouth before the goon hit the back of my head, this time even harder than before. I turned and look over my shoulder, "Keep at it, monkey-boy. You'll get yours."

He must have been nearly seven feet tall and about four feet wide at the shoulders. He smirked and hit me again.

I looked at the man in the chair. "You'd better kill me now, because if you don't, I'll kill *you*, and I won't do it this slowly."

"This isn't a movie. There is no elaborate plan to kill you that will buy you enough time to be saved. No hand of God is going to swing down from the sky and snatch you out of harm's way. The only ones who know you're here are back at your parents' place, waiting for your call. They have no idea what's going on right now. As far as they know, your little Indian buddy is recording this entire conversation so I and everyone else here will go to prison, and you'll return with the contract so they can all go back to the lives they had just a few months ago. No one's coming for you, John, because they don't think you need any help. We're going to take you out back into the alley, put you in the trunk of a car, take you to a quiet empty building a couple miles from here along the Delaware River, beat and torture you for hours and then, when your body can't take it anymore, we're going to dump you into the river and hold you below the water's surface until you drown. Then we'll cast your corpse adrift in the tide to be found by someone or some*thing* downstream."

"Well at least it's not an elaborate plan," I said sarcastically.

"You want simple?! I'll give you simple!" He screamed.

Finally! I was turning the tide. I broke through his over-affected persona, and through his bullshit calm demeanor. His eyes lit up, and there was genuine anger there. He wasn't used to being disrespected. I figured if I'm going out anyway, I might as well make the experience as uncomfortable for him as possible.

He leaned forward to ensure I was looking him squarely in the eyes and said, "You'll die today. Is that simple enough for you? You're not going to have the chance for the revenge you're desperately craving, or to stop us from killing your sister and her family. That will all be happening while we're beating the living *shit* out of you this evening, you piece of garbage. You and your entire family are an abomination. *We* are the ones who have been wronged, and *we* are the ones exacting justice and revenge today. You see, you have the roles reversed in your feeble, short-order cook's mind. We're not the aggressors. We're the victims!"

I spit out some blood that had pooled in my mouth at him. It missed by a couple feet, but the gesture was pretty clear. I told him I had no *fucking* idea what he was talking about, and that the boredom he was inflicting upon me was far worse than the physical beating his apes had handed me since I arrived. I had reached the point where hope was gone and I just wanted the whole damned thing to end. I wasn't asking him for mercy. I was asking him to hurry the hell up!

Gina responded, "Uncle, he's telling the truth. They really have no *fucking* idea what we're talking about." And she started laughing. The old man's eyes widened with clarity and he started laughing too.

Smiling, he turned his gaze to Gina. "Oh, that's better than I could have ever hoped. The only thing better than him dying is him dying unaware of why. Gina, my dear, you've made my day. Now go wait in the car. The boys will take you home on their way to the river."

Gina spoke: "No. NO! Why can't I watch what they do to him? I've come this far. I want to see this through to the end. Don't shut me out now, uncle. I want to watch what you do to this piece of shit."

He shrugged. "As you wish, my dear. Go wait just the same."

Gina got up to leave and the dapper man in the chair gestured to the monster behind me to follow her out, with me in tow. "We're finished here," he said as he turned away from me, laughing and brushing his hand from side to side across his face like he was waving off a fly.

"Wait. WAIT!" I yelled. "What about those three children? What about your grandkids, Gina? If anything happens to me, they'll die, and not just die—they'll be burned to death!"

She looked at me with icy coolness, shrugged and replied, "Casualties of war."

My jaw dropped as I was propelled out of the room quickly, like a toddler who had just said *fuck* in front of the monsignor. My feet still barely touched the floor as I flew through the kitchen where I'd worked thousands of nights, where my father and I had cooked together, where my grandfather taught me to shave and sauté garlic.

I guessed this is what it was like to see my life passing before my eyes before I died.

In a single motion, I was expelled out the back door into the rear fender of an old sedan waiting in the alley, which I hit with a boom. Before I could stand up on my own, I was picked up by my shirt collar.

The trunk popped open, but before I was tossed in, I was punched in the stomach with what felt like a jackhammer. I dropped to me knees, crumpled again, only this time my head dipped low in my chest and

I threw up the entire contents of my stomach. My eyes watered and bile flowed from my nostrils.

Then the head of one of the giants landed with a splash into my pool of puke, his lifeless eyes looked up at me, but there was no one home behind them. What the …?

Deus Ex Machina, Mother F …

It wasn't a scuffle, only the muffled sounds of gunfire—not exactly silenced like in the movies with a "phsh phsh," but muted to be less deafening. Large, heavy bodies landed all around me. Thud, thud, thud.

A hand gently patted me between my shoulder blades and a familiar voice said, "Let it out, kid," and then I was helped to my feet and given a seat on the bumper of the sedan.

"Catch your breath and relax, John. When you're ready we can talk. By the way, you really look like hell."

I just looked at Uncle G's face and worked a smile of relief across mine. Men rushed into the back door of the kitchen from the alley. All hell was already breaking loose inside.

"They'll go out the front door," I blurted, almost inaudibly because I still had to wait to get my wind back.

He was cool and calm, like he knew how everything was going to end because it was already over. "It'll be the last desperate thing they do. They won't get two steps out the door before they're gunned down. They're trapped. Fish in a barrel. It's over.

"This has been my neighborhood for 65 years, kid. Everyone who lives here acts as my eyes and ears. Why do you think it's so safe here? Everyone tells me what's going on and my crew takes care of it. These jerks came in here thinking they could work under my nose, but everyone in this neighborhood has been watching them since they set up shop.

"I've known who Gina is, and who her family is, for decades—since they moved in after you were born. When you first told me you were at her place and had been beaten up, I knew she and her family were somehow the cause. We finally understood who was behind the purchase of Sonny's. Just the mention of her name and her coincidental meeting with you helped all the pieces fall into place. We included her in our discussions at Joe's house so she could think we were naive and she was slick. Fact is, Joe and I were performing for her benefit. We fed her exactly what we wanted her to know, and nothing of what we'd discovered. I knew what Gina would do after we released her last night. I knew her next actions before *she* did. Unfortunately, I couldn't tell you what was going on today, or you might have blown it, so I had to let it play out. I had to make sure her uncle was physically here, and he felt like he was in control. Sorry, kid. I had to use you to make this work, but don't worry—I had your back the whole way. The guy behind the bar is mine. If things for you ever approached fatal, he'd have ended everyone in there.

"These grifters live by the double-cross. It's their strength and weakness. They're good at it, but they can't do anything else. It's in their blood. They're liars and cheats. They're pathological. They don't even realize when they're doing it to themselves.

"They caught your parents, Mr. Acchione, and me flat-footed when they started this. We didn't see it coming. We know their game now, though, and we learned. This time, we *counted* on them double-crossing us—that would put them right in the middle of our mouse trap. We told Gina we wanted them to sign a release—so she'd believe we were trusting her to do that—and that we only wanted the business and the building back. What she never figured was we knew she was going to double-cross us, so we double-crossed her instead. We needed to cut the head off the snake, and that's what we're doing. We needed her to get everyone here under one roof so we could completely clean house. We didn't need a signed transfer, or an audio confession. Dead people aren't going to complain about us reopening Sonny's, and they're not going to be much good to anyone in jail, either."

Gunshots continued going off inside Sonny's as Uncle Guido calmly, quietly spoke—as if it wasn't really going on. It was like he was listening to someone flicking off light switches inside before coming outside to leave. He just waited and continued to talk.

"We sat back and let them play us, because we were actually conning them right back. Only this time, no one was going to be able to use their new knowledge for future strategies. There's not going to be a next time."

"What about the kids, Unc? She called them casualties of war. Are they okay?"

"Relax, John. Like I told you, unlike her, we're not monsters. Everybody in this neighborhood is my accomplice. Some of their parents and grandparents have been keeping eyes open for me since the fifties. The kids are safe with good people and will be delivered back to their parents. When we're done here, everyone will work together to pick up the pieces and clean up. No one outside this block will know what happened. These guys will never be missed. For your own sake, though, don't buy any sausage or ground beef around here for a week or so," and he laughed.

"What about her?" I asked, nudging my head toward the back of the sedan where they were going to put me ... in the trunk. Gina was sitting on that backseat, looking at us through the rear window, watching all the death happen around her—screaming at first and then just watching everything unfurl. I couldn't see low enough in the car, but I was pretty sure her seat was saturated with urine—and possibly diarrhea by now. Suddenly, she had aged twenty years. The color had completely left her face and she looked every bit the grandmother of ten.

It's funny how fearing for one's life can erode the facade created by makeup. She was panicked and seemed convinced the moment everyone's attention turned to her would be pretty close to her last moment of life.

"What would you like us to do to her?" Guido asked me.

She looked at me, pleading with her eyes—asking me to ignore her betrayal and to show mercy—but why should I? She had as much as sentenced me to death a few minutes earlier, and orchestrated the betrayal of my family and my friends and signed all of our death warrants. She had her reasons for giving me up, for playing me, for using me to her own means. Were those reasons any better than mine now?

"Make her go away, Uncle G." Then I continued. "Don't hurt her. She's just a bully—harmless without her gang's muscle to back her up. Just make sure none of us ever see her again. Make sure she knows if any of us *do* see her again, it's the last time she'll be seen alive. She needs to know this is her one and only chance at leniency. There won't be a second one."

Everything inside Sonny's was quiet now. The deed was done.

Uncle G calmly made eye contact with one of his soldiers and tilted his head toward the front seat of the car as if to say, "You heard him. Get her out of here." And that's what G's man did, quietly stepping over to the other crew's car that held Gina, reaching into the front seat to pull out the corpse who was supposed to drive, taking the key from his pocket, dropping the body on the ground next to the car, climbing behind the wheel, firing up the motor, and driving off.

Gina's eyes pleadingly watched me until the car was out of sight. She'd heard the conversation, but as far as either of us knew, Uncle G's man had prior instructions to do something more permanent. G'd let me believe the path of mercy was the one taken—to preserve my innocence—but he'd do whatever he thought was right. Frankly, I was good either way.

There's nothing I hate more than liars. That bitch lied to me on every possible level, and she was good at it. This wasn't new for her, and like Uncle G said, she was behind this whole thing from the beginning.

He put his hand on my shoulder and looked at me with a smile. "You ready to go, kid?"

"No. Not yet. I want to go in and see the motherfucker who gave the order to kill me. I want to be sure he's dead and my sister and her family are safe."

He helped me inside, and I saw large bodies strewn everywhere—very dead. Most had a few dozen holes in them. Blood was splattered everywhere—on the bar, the walls, the furniture, the floor. There was even blood on the ceiling. It wasn't a bloodbath. It was a blood *shower*.

The man in the chair was still seated there. He hadn't moved and hadn't been harmed. He looked at me and his eyes grew huge. He didn't expect to see me, of all people. At the very least, he figured his crew would have wasted me before any of this shit went down.

He wasn't calm anymore. He wasn't cool anymore. It was *his* turn to be shitting his pants.

G's man from behind the bar spoke: "As you requested, he hasn't been touched. He's waiting for you. Everything's finished."

For the first time, I got the sense of how surgical Uncle Guido's operation is, how he'd maintained order and peace in the neighborhood for all those years, and how fortunate we have been to have him as our benefactor.

"What do you want to do, kid?"

"Well, *he* wanted to torture and kill me."

" … and?"

"But I told him I wouldn't waste any time on him. I'd kill him quickly, turn his coronation into his execution, and I'd like to believe I'm good for my word."

Uncle G nodded, shrugged, and handed me a gun. "It's loaded and the safety is off. Just point it and squeeze the trigger."

The gun had materialized in his hand without me knowing, and then it was in my hand just as quickly.

According to Hollywood, when cowboys had duels in the wild west, such things as the position of the sun—either behind or in front of duelers—the quickness of the draw, and the weight, accuracy, and mechanical reliability of the weapon itself were all considered critical factors affecting the success or failure of the participants. As John Wayne, the Duke himself, said in his last movie, however, none of those things matter as much as a shooter's willingness to pull the trigger. Hesitation, conscience, and second thoughts were what lost duels. What won was decisiveness, and not everyone possessed the intestinal fortitude to inflict death on someone else without so much as the blink of an eye.

Turns out, I possess such fortitude. I instantly pointed the barrel at the man in the chair and shot him in the stomach because I wanted him to hurt. As he leaned forward, blood soaked through his crispy laundered dress shirt and his perfectly tailored suit jacket. I shot his upper torso, opposite his heart. As momentum pushed him back in his chair, I fired a third and final shot into the middle of his motherfucking face. There would be no "open casket" at this asshole's funeral.

No hesitation, no question, no indecision and after the fact, absolutely no regret. My hand didn't shake before, during, or afterward, and when the job was complete—and Uncle G extended his hand out for me to return the weapon—I handed it to him safely and slowly. "Thank you, Uncle Guido, for everything. He had to be destroyed. He was going to kill Ange and the kids and make Mom and Pop suffer for years. I couldn't let him live."

"Sure, kid. Now let's get you out of here."

Family

It was easier to protect everyone if they were all in one place, so Guido made sure—while I was in Sonny's—everyone else was at Mom and Pop's, protected by an army—armed men upstairs, downstairs, on the main floor, and even on the roof. There was nothing left to chance, not with this precious cargo.

As soon as everything at Sonny's was done, Guido called the house to deliver the good news and put everyone at ease. They were all able to relax, at least a little, but Guido instructed his men to stay there and stay sharp, just in case there was an unforeseen backlash or a different plot had been hatched that neither he nor any of his legion of spies had detected.

Of course, there were to be no surprises. As always, he and his crew had been thorough and we were all safe.

Angela, Mom, Pop, and Mr. Acchione hadn't left since arriving earlier in the morning. Tom was waiting for Angela's call confirming everything was okay before coming downtown, but before he left, he needed to get a sitter for the boys. Ordinarily, they'd stay overnight with Mom and Pop, but there was too much going on here with armed men everywhere. It was better for them to stay in their own beds tonight.

Raj would arrive from work and he'd bring Indi. Her kids were with their dad in Delco tonight, so she was free to join us.

Guido, Rocco, and I returned, but only after we went back to Joe's for Marilyn to patch me up again. This was becoming an unwanted habit.

Except for more new bruises and a few cuts, I wasn't that much worse off than I'd been after the beating in the alley earlier in the week. To be honest, if I didn't have to get punched anymore, that would have been great.

Marilyn worked her magic and I bathed and changed again. Rock, G, and I left immediately thereafter and returned to Mom and Pop's.

For the first time in months, *everyone's* spirits were high. Pop kept bugging everyone to take him to Sonny's so he could get started on tomorrow's menu, but everyone kept telling him the place needed to be cleaned first. Of course, as we had all come to expect, Dad forgot answers to questions immediately after he heard them—and also forgot ever asking the questions in the first place—so he just kept at it for the rest of the night. None of us minded one bit, and in fact we were all a little relieved to realize he had no memory of anything this week, or that someone had purchased Sonny's at all. He had really slipped since I moved away a few months ago.

Mom pulled me aside and asked if I was okay. She touched my bruises and winced every time she noticed another one. "What did they do to my baby?" she kept repeating. "Why did they do this to me?" she asked.

Typical narcissist to believe they beat me up to get to her.

I just hugged her and held onto her, realizing how much we really are alike, whether I liked it or not. She had always been able to get on my last nerve, and for the first time, particularly since last night with Indi, I understand that I may have been the one to get on *her* last nerve too. We drove one another nuts, but it was good to know there's one person in the world who would set herself on fire for me. As it turns out, I'd do the same for her.

Angela joined us for the hug, but was also on the phone the whole time monitoring Tom and her boys. In many ways, she was a prisoner under protection and just wanted to escape and tend to her family.

Mr. Acchione sat quietly in a plastic-covered chair, out of the way, surveying the room and smiling. He looked content. There was a photo of my grandfather on the table next to him. He grabbed it and stared at it for a moment. Guido went to him as soon as we arrived. Joe grabbed Guido's forearm and pulled him down to eye level. "Al wasn't here to do this himself, so we did it for him, Guido. We did it."

Guido grabbed Joe's shoulder firmly, smiled and nodded. Theirs had been the longest con ever recorded—sixty-five years—and they won.

Mr. Acchione got up with the assistance of Guido and asked Mom if it was okay if he went upstairs to one of the bedrooms to take a nap. She waved him off and nodded. I decided that was a hell of a good idea. I escorted him up and took one of the other rooms for myself. I asked Angela to let me know when Raj, Indi, and Tom arrived because I wanted to go out and celebrate with them tonight. She assured me she would.

For the first time since I arrived in South Philly this week, I lay down, closed my eyes, and didn't have any worries. I hurt like hell to the point even the bed pillow irritated my battered face, but I felt good knowing the barbarians were no longer waiting to storm our gates. We had prevailed, and I had held up my end in the process.

A Dish Served Cold

I'd been asleep for a couple hours before Angela came to wake me. I didn't exactly spring to my feet when she came in, but at least my adrenaline rush from earlier in the day had leveled off and I'd rested a little.

I came downstairs to find all the soldiers had gone and the house resembled Mom and Pop's place again. Mr. Acchione was still asleep upstairs, and Guido was gone. Mom and Pop were sitting on the living sofa together, sleeping, and Raj, Tom, and Indi were waiting for me so we could all go out and eat.

A celebration was certainly in order. Although I couldn't imagine wanting to do so with anyone other than these four idiots, I felt a little odd around Indi. This was the first time we were together since our moment of total honesty the night before, and no matter how unintended it may have been, the result of that conversation was a permanent change in our relationship. For decades, we'd been "friends with benefits," but the prospect, at least in my mind, had always been there for us to be more if I was interested. As it turns out, that had never been an option, but I only found out yesterday. Even though it turned out to be ancient history, it was still news to me. Going forward, things would be the same in Indi's mind. We'd remain "friends with benefits," but for me, the whole thing was a little less captivating.

When I came down the steps and reached them, *Raj* was the only one to rush over and hug me. Indi smirked and walked out the door, and Tom and Ange followed suit.

We considered a number of options—someplace loud and festive (that option was immediately and universally declined by everyone), someplace crowded, or someplace quiet. We opted for quiet so we could talk, relax, and not worry about interruptions.

There was no time to obsess about my relationship dynamics with Indi. As soon as we stepped out the door, we started talking to one another about everything all at once. We joked around, playfully insulted each other, and ultimately started telling stories and reminiscing about our multitude of shared experiences over the past half-century, and especially the past week. That continued from the time we left Mom and Pop's, all the way through dinner and right up to the time we were ordering our third round of espresso after dessert.

We settled back as the clock was closing in on 2AM. The kitchen had closed long ago. We'd settled the check and opened a new one with the bar. Now even that one needed to be closed out.

The place was virtually abandoned. It seemed as though only the bartender and we remained in the joint, as an old man quietly approached us. He was in his eighties for sure, but he was trim. His clothes were well-tailored and immaculate, but clearly not new. His plaid, wool blazer was thick and heavy with a handkerchief folded into a triangle and exposed from the breast pocket. His dress shirt was blue and the tie was silk and complementary, if not subdued.

He looked like a man of means who appreciated quality and took care of it. He didn't move quickly, but not because he was feeble—he clearly wasn't. He just wasn't in a rush. He moved *deliberately*.

No one noticed him at first, but as he came within a couple feet of the table, everyone stopped to look up at him pensively. He wasn't physically imposing—or even threatening—but after everything we'd been through recently, especially today, we shared a certain, warranted degree of paranoia.

He looked like an Italian banker.

"Good evening," he said respectfully and rather formally. "We've never met, but you were acquainted with my son and my granddaughter. I believe you know her as Gina. You never knew my son's name, but that didn't stop you from murdering him in cold blood this afternoon."

The table went silent, and we all began to squirm and survey the room, convinced we were about to die in a hail of bullets. There was no reason in the world why Guido would be here, but I suddenly felt the desperate need for one of his "hand of God" rescues.

I stood up and said "Hey, look! This is ..." But the man held up his hand to stop me from speaking and then calmly continued.

"Now is not the time for discussions, and I certainly wouldn't want my own mourning to dampen your celebration. My purpose is to merely step out from behind the curtain and introduce myself, and then leave you to your evening. Please excuse the interruption."

The old man bowed his head as if to say "good night," took two steps backward without lifting his head, and then pivoted to walk away. As he did so, Indi's cell phone "blinged." She received a text—a photo of her two kids in the backseat of an unfamiliar car, looking very scared.

Without specifically acknowledging the text, the old man turned slightly and stared at Angela as he did so. Without looking over at Indi, he said, "You have two beautiful children, Swati. You too, Angela. Who's watching them all for you tonight? Surely, not the same people who were watching my great-great-grandchildren last night and who had threatened to burn them alive." He held Angela's stare long enough to see the look of horror wash across her face and then he walked away, still deliberately. Then he stopped and turned completely to face us again.

"Oh, by the way, I'd nearly forgotten. While you were here celebrating, we visited the old attorney at his home. Before you ask, let me set your minds at ease. Yes, we killed him. We'd let him live all these years out of deference to my mother, but after you killed my son, I considered the old man's protection canceled. You probably weren't aware, but 'Acchione' was his mother's maiden name. His father's name was Mantelli—Fredo Mantelli. You knew Fredo as in Alfredo Valmonti, your grandfather. My brother killed Fredo's first wife when the old attorney was just a baby. Al survived and sent the child away to live with his maternal grandmother, and take her surname to throw us off the trail. It didn't work, obviously. Anyway, enjoy the rest of your celebration and don't worry—you'll hear from us soon enough, once we decide if we'll be murdering *your* children, the way you threatened to burn ours."

Angela turned to Tom and screamed "Call home, NOW!" He was already fumbling with his phone, trying to unlock the front screen and access the phone function. He looked like his entire *body* had been slathered with butter as the phone slipped from his trembling hands and landed on the table where he tried twice, unsuccessfully, to pick it back up.

Indi turned to me with a combination of rage and panic in her eyes. I froze and stared at the old man walking away toward the restaurant's front door. I felt like I'd just been punched in the gut for about the thousandth time this week, and my eyes were again as big as saucers. I had foolishly thought this was over. It'll never be over.

Indi's body quivered as she exclaimed in a hushed, controlled, almost maniacal tone, "John Valmonti, you get my children back." She struggled to maintain her composure, and as she continued, she spoke more and more quickly. "I don't care what you have to do, but you have to get them back right now. Do you understand me?" And then composure was gone. "YOU FIGURE IT OUT. I DON'T CARE WHAT IT

TAKES OR WHAT YOU HAVE TO DO, OR WHO ELSE YOU HAVE TO KILL *TONIGHT*, BUT YOU NEED TO DO IT NOW. *NOW!*" Her volume continued to escalate right along with her own panic. She stood up and shut her eyes and started slamming her fists on the table, screaming "GET UP! GET UP GOD DAMN YOU AND GET MY CHILDREN NOW! NOW!!! GO!!! *GO!!!*"

I barely heard her. It felt like my brain had short-circuited. Joe was dead—murdered—and he was my step-uncle all along. No wonder my grandfather took me to the river to watch his favorite rower. His favorite rower was Joe, his son. What the fuck had these people done to my family? Why did they continue to attack us, and what of this bullshit about *them* being the victims?

The old man casually picked a mint out of the bowl at the hostess station and smiled broadly as he tossed it in his mouth and exited into the dark night.

Outside, a long, black, elegant limousine sat idling by the curb, awaiting his return. The driver opened the rear door for the old man, who rested his hand on the roof and leaned down to get in. He hesitated there long enough to address his riding companion, "Thank you again for giving me advanced notice of what was happening here."

He blamed himself for not stopping his son in time, and only wished he had arrived a day earlier. Perhaps, if he had, he could have dissuaded his son from his fool's errand and prevented his death.

Once he heard about his son's subterfuge, he planned to peacefully remove him from power, and replace him with this confidante who had earned this reward and his own loyalty. The role will still be filled as planned, but his son was not removed from his post as planned or even hoped.

He settled into the plush rear seat, his driver closed the door, and the old man sadly continued, "There was a reason why that family was to be left alone, but that reason no longer matters. My son's blood is now on that entire family's hands, and there will be a price paid for taking him before his time. We have only just started."

For Romani, family is everything—their strength, their purpose. He could no more overlook this attack on his family than turn his back on his entire heritage. No. He had no choice. After more than one hundred years of restraint, the entire weight of their gypsy clan was finally about to be brought down on the Valmontis.

"She would be proud of you, you know? My grandmother? You remind me of her. The resemblances are strong in character, loyalty, and decisiveness. You even look like her. I think one day you'll run this family as she did."

Gina looked at her grandfather, nodded her understanding, and uttered a single word as the car slowly pulled away from the curb: *"Justice."*

About the Author

MICHAEL ATTIANI is a second generation Italian-American. Three of his grandparents were born in Italy, and one was born to recent Italian immigrants in the coal mining region of western Pennsylvania. If he tried, Michael could probably trace his Italian lineage back to Romulus and Remus, and possibly to Adam and Eve because Italians believe the Garden of Eden had to be somewhere in Italy because Italy is Heaven on Earth.

Somehow his grandparents all ended up in the southeast corner of Pennsylvania, settled in Philadelphia, and stayed there for the remainder of their days. Michael was born and raised in this city of brotherly love. After starting out attending local public schools, he ended up where most Italians do: Catholic school. He endured that unique form of purgatory from 8th grade through college graduation, shrewdly compacting an entire lifetime of Catholic obligation into the first twenty years of his life.

Once he was paroled from academia, he spent three decades pursuing a career in commercial real estate and continues to do so today. There is a lot of money to be made in commercial real estate, but Michael has deftly avoided doing so thus far.

Michael somehow convinced a beautiful woman to marry him and produce two sons. Then they added four dogs because two boys didn't produce enough mayhem and mess on their own. In addition to his family and career, Michael enjoys spending as much time as possible with his friends, writing, drawing, skiing, traveling and doing pretty much anything with cars. As an enthusiastic member of the automotive community, he enjoys driving on racetracks, slaloming between orange cones in otherwise empty parking lots, and attending car events around the globe.

Although most of his family stayed rooted in Philadelphia, Michael extricated his family from those familiar confines and settled a couple thousand miles west, in Idaho. They lingered there for nearly a dozen years until returning to Philadelphia, because there's no place like home, and truly, there is *nowhere* like Philadelphia.

It's a land of infuriating sports teams, over-enunciated vowels, spectacular restaurants (especially Italian ones), too many pedestrians dressed like Ben Franklin, too many arguments about who makes a better sandwich, and an infinite supply of sarcasm and cynicism.

If you live in or around Philly, you are luckier than you will ever admit, and if you've never visited, you are missing out on one hell of a fun town stocked with surprisingly friendly helpful people. They know how to boo with gusto, and how to hurl snowballs at Santa when the Eagles blow their chance to draft a generational talent, and that's a true story. Most of all, growing up in Philadelphia heavily influenced Michael's formative years and made him what he is today ... whatever that is.

Learn more about Michael and his writing at www.sonnysvendetta.com.